AUTHOR'S NOTE

Wicked Games is a dark high school bully romance book. It contains certain elements that some may find offensive or disturbing and is recommended for readers over eighteen.

WICKED GAMES

Sinners of Babylon Prep

KRISTIN BUONI

PROLOGUE

Anonymous

"I've lived among them all my life. You can't believe a word they say. You know that. I mean, they're born liars." – ***Juror #10, 12 Angry Men***

Have you ever considered the significance of the number twelve?

It's not just a numerical quirk. It's a thread woven through the tapestry of time, a rare consensus across myriad cultural boundaries—the practical, mythological, and magical symbolism of that number, representing perfection and order.

Twelve principal gods ruled in the Greek pantheon, preceded by the twelve Titans. We have twelve people on a jury, twelve months in a year, twelve astrological signs in various zodiacs. It's also important in timekeeping, music, religion, and a multitude of other subjects.

Like I said, twelve is a big deal. I could go on about it all day. But enough of the banter. Why am I telling you this?

I'm telling you because there are twelve of us here tonight, trapped inside this grand old mansion. Twelve souls with twelve haunted pasts, unwitting participants in twelve meticulously planned games. I seriously doubt we'll make it through all of them.

Why? Well, you see, I'm sitting on a secret so big, so well-guarded, that none of the others can even fathom its existence.

Can I tell you that secret?

I am the architect of this gathering. I brought everyone here for these games, and they weren't designed for survival. Not at all. They were crafted specifically to force every one of these nasty little liars to confess their sins and secrets before the reckoning they damn well deserve.

As the echoes of all this deception resound through the dark corridors, one truth remains certain: by the end of the week, only one of us is going to make it out of here alive.

CAREY

"Take the deal, Carey. Trust me."

I chewed on my bottom lip, glumly staring at the opposite wall. The air hung heavy with the weight of my predicament, and the faded faux-wood-paneled walls seemed to be closing in on me, squeezing the air from my lungs. I couldn't show my fear, though. Where I came from, you never showed weakness. Not unless you wanted to get totally fucked by life.

"Carey?" The public defender—a graying man named Mr. Tellier—leaned forward. "Did you hear me?"

I frowned. "I'm not taking the deal. It isn't right."

He sighed wearily and drummed the end of his pen against the table. "What are you talking about?"

"There's something off about it. I mean, *way* off," I replied. "It's just too good to be true. Don't you think?"

Tellier leaned back again. "I'll admit it's a bit odd, and it really came out of left field, but it's completely legitimate. I've checked all the details and contacted everyone involved to confirm everything," he said. "To be honest, it's the opportunity of a lifetime. I'm surprised you haven't jumped right on it."

I pursed my lips and went silent again. Clearly, he wasn't

seeing what I was seeing when I looked at the so-called 'deal' that had miraculously landed in my lap earlier this evening. The best boarding school on the West Coast—actually, probably the best school in the entire country—wouldn't just offer a scholarship to a random wayward teen from a shitty backwoods town for no damn reason. Especially not when that teen was facing multiple charges that could sully the school's pristine reputation.

Tellier's eyes narrowed slightly. "Carey, you know why the prosecution is dragging your case out like this, right?"

"Yes."

"Your eighteenth birthday is in two weeks," he went on, ostensibly deciding that I didn't actually know why the other side was dragging out my case with delay after delay. "Right now, it's up to the discretion of the judge whether you're tried in the juvenile court or moved up to be tried as an adult. If we keep letting them drag all of this out, you'll become a legal adult, and then there'll no longer be any doubt about it. You'll be tried as an adult."

"Would that really be so bad?"

Tellier arched a brow. "Depends. Do you think a prison sentence is bad?"

"Point taken." I sighed and rubbed my temple. "But I still can't take the deal."

"Why not?"

"Because part of taking it involves me admitting guilt so I can accept the rehabilitation terms. And I'm not guilty. I can't admit to something I didn't do."

"Perhaps I didn't explain the terms clearly enough," Tellier said, tapping on the paperwork. "If you sign the deal, you won't have an official criminal record. It will be expunged the second you turn eighteen. Gone without a trace. It'll be like none of this ever happened."

"Except for the fact that it *did* happen," I said flatly. "And I still have to admit to being at fault for everything, when really, it's that fucking asshole's fault. Not mine."

"Don't let your pride get in the way, Carey." A warning tone entered his voice. "If this all goes to trial, how do you think it's going to go? Who do you think they're going to believe? You or him?"

I swallowed thickly. "Me, hopefully. Everything I've said is true. I'm innocent."

"It doesn't matter if you're innocent, and hope isn't going to get you very far. What really matters is perception. You're a teenager with a rather sketchy background. Through no fault of your own, of course. But when the jury looks at you, most of them will think you fit the profile perfectly."

"Fit the profile?" I snickered and shook my head. "You're making this sound like an episode of Criminal Minds or something."

Tellier didn't smile. "Carey, you *are* a criminal. At least you are in most people's eyes right now. You're in very serious trouble and you're being offered a lifeline. I suggest you take it."

I cast my eyes down at the pockmarked old table. I knew he didn't believe me when I said I didn't take anything on the night of Jamie Miller's party. No one did. And how could I blame them for that, given the results of my blood test after I was arrested? They showed that I was clearly intoxicated when I took that car and crashed it into the other one.

To any outsider, I was obviously guilty as sin. They just didn't understand the extenuating circumstances. They had no idea what led me to that desperate act. If they actually heard my story during a court trial, perhaps they'd feel sympathetic and let me off with a slap on the wrist.

Or perhaps Tellier was right on the money with the profiling comment. Maybe they'd take one look at me and my shitty background and automatically slide me into a box in their minds. The sort of box that contained offenders who were *definitely* guilty.

I looked back up at Tellier. "Could I see the brochure again?"

The hard look on his face faded, and he cracked a sliver of a smile. "Sure."

He reached into his briefcase and pulled out a glossy pamphlet. The cover featured a stunning panoramic view of Babylon Preparatory Academy, perched on the rugged cliffs of the northern California coast. The Gothic architecture of the main building was highlighted against the backdrop of crashing waves and misty coastal crags, and the school crest was subtly embossed in silver at the bottom.

I flicked to the first page.

Welcome to Babylon Preparatory Academy

Nestled amongst the untamed beauty of California's stunning North Coast, Babylon stands as an architectural masterpiece amidst nature's grandeur. Our historic institution is a beacon of excellence, providing an unparalleled educational experience that will enrich your child's mind and prepare them for a future of leadership and success.

I rolled my eyes and flipped to the next page.

Discover the extraordinary at Babylon!

Our school provides a nurturing environment where students form lifelong friendships and networks. Our distinguished faculty is committed to cultivating critical thinking skills and a passion for knowledge, and our curriculum is filled with challenging courses, ensuring that all students are well-prepared for the world's finest universities.

- *Extracurricular activities: We have a multitude of offerings, designed to create and foster a harmony between mind, body, and spirit.*
- *Social scene: Fun events and spirited academic competitions foster a sense of pride and unity.*
- *Arts: We boast a vibrant arts community with students delving into creative pursuits inspired by the beautiful scenery surrounding our campus.*
- *Community: Students engage in beach clean-ups and marine biology studies, fostering a deep appreciation for the environment whilst helping the community beyond the gates.*
- *Luxury accommodation: Picturesque dormitories perch on the cliffs, offering breathtaking views of the Pacific Ocean. Each room is designed for comfort and inspiration.*

Embark on your journey with Babylon Preparatory Academy today! For admission enquiries and application procedures, please visit our website or contact our admissions office.

God, what a load of bullshit.

These places always made it so easy to read between the lines. 'Historic' referred to long-standing generational wealth and the nepotism that came with it, giving the rich kids every possible opportunity while shutting out most regular Americans. 'Pride and unity' and 'lifelong friendships' were similarly-coded—it all referred to the impenetrable clubs that people from these elite schools formed within their ranks. Rich people helping each other stay rich, essentially.

So why were they suddenly offering to help *me*?

"It really doesn't make any sense." I looked back up at the public defender. "Why would they offer me a scholarship? And why would they help with all my legal stuff? I'm a total nobody to them."

Tellier smiled patiently. "We've already been through this, Carey."

"Tell me again. Because it honestly made no sense to me the first time." I slowly shook my head. "I'm not sure if it'll ever make sense."

"Several members of the alumni committee are heavily involved in justice projects, and they've recently decided to start one of their own with a bit of a twist. They had their lawyers bring them recent cases involving juvenile offenders, and they ended up picking you. They have enough power and influence to make your charges go away forever. In return, you accept the scholarship and attend Babylon for your final year of high school. Keep your head down and your grades up. Get a full-ride college offer. Go to—"

I cut him off. "I have to prove that I can actually be rehabilitated from my trashy criminal background, you mean. To make the alumni committee look good and feel good. Am I right?"

Tellier's lips thinned. "I suppose that's one way of putting it. But really, they're trying to help, and this is a once-in-a lifetime offer. You're very, *very* fortunate to have received it." He paused and raised a brow again. "As I said before, I suggest you take it, given the alternative."

I still had a feeling something was very off about this deal, because it seemed highly suspicious for a group of rich folks to hand a literal Get Out Of Jail Free card to a random stranger on the off chance they might become rehabilitated. It was simply too good to be true, and every single person on the planet knew how things like that tended to turn out.

At the same time, I didn't have much of a choice, did I?

If I was forced to choose between maintaining my innocence and risking prison or admitting my culpability and getting a free ride to the best private school in the country... well, the choice was glaringly obvious. As much as it begrudged me to admit it, this was an offer I simply couldn't refuse.

"You could have a real future in this place, Carey," Tellier added, nodding toward the brochure. "It's an incredible school. The best of the best. It could be helpful to build connections in the town, too."

I nodded slowly. Everyone knew about Babylon and the sort of connections you could build there, if you were ever invited into the fold. It was the richest coastal city for miles in this part of the state. Only fifteen miles from Oakfield but worlds away in terms of lifestyle.

"I guess so," I murmured, hands knitting in my lap.

"So… what's it going to be? Yes or no?" Tellier lifted his pen, letting it hover right over the signature box on the paperwork.

I took a deep breath and nodded slowly. "Yes," I said. "I'll take it."

CAREY

"So this is actually happening," I mumbled to myself as I smoothed the fabric of my new tartan skirt, a mix of anticipation and fear coiling in the pit of my stomach.

The private driver that the Babylon Foundation had hired to transport me to the school had just maneuvered the car onto a winding coastal road, and the landscape of Babylon Prep was rapidly unfolding before me in a blur of rugged cliffs and crashing waves, each turn revealing glimpses of soaring pillars, imposing gray stone buildings, and spiked towers.

It looked nice in the brochure, but in person, Babylon Prep looked more like a Transylvanian vampire's castle than a school for the well-heeled.

The driver glanced at me in the rearview mirror. "Did you say something, Ms. Saracen?"

"Um... no. Just clearing my throat." I swallowed hard and looked out the window again, taking in my new surroundings with wide eyes.

We passed an ornate sign that was partly obscured by creeping vines. BABYLON PREPARATORY ACADEMY. Beyond that, the open road narrowed into a private cobblestone drive flanked by towering trees, hedges, and manicured lawns leading up to the main building. As we drew closer, I spotted row after row of leering gargoyles staring down at me from the roof.

"Yup. Gotta be vampires living here," I said under my breath as the driver pulled to a stop.

He grabbed my suitcase and bag from the back and escorted me to the administration office, where I was greeted by a friendly receptionist.

"Good morning," she said, flashing me a cheerful smile. "How can I help you?"

"Morning." I returned her smile. "I'm a new student here. I was told to come here before anything else."

"Wonderful. Let me just check a few things..." She trailed off and bit her bottom lip as her fingertips clattered across the keyboard in front of her. She frowned at the screen briefly, then glanced back at me with another smile. "Sorry, I'm also quite new here," she said. "It's a bit of an adjustment, figuring out where to find everything on this computer system. By the way, what's your name? I completely forgot to ask."

"Carey Saracen. Sorry, I should have said that earlier."

"Ah, yes, here we are." She clicked on her mouse a couple of times, and a printer started whirring behind her. She turned to gather the documents, slid them into a folder, and handed them to me. "Here's your class schedule, a campus map, and a welcome package that should answer any questions you might have. A school-issued laptop will be delivered to your dorm later today. Speaking of which..." She returned her attention to her computer. "I've put you in Dressler Hall, room 4. Your key should already be in the welcome package. If I remember correctly, Dressler is all the way over on the other side of campus, so it may take you a while to get there. I've made a note on the system that will allow you to miss homeroom this morning. That way you won't receive any penalties for being absent."

"Great. Thanks."

"It might also give you a bit of extra time to settle into your dorm and unpack a few things. Do you need help finding your way?"

I shook my head. "No, thanks. I should be fine with the map."

"I'll take her," the driver piped up. "I have her bags already, so I might as well."

I turned to him with a grateful expression. "Thank you."

So far, every Babylon-related staff member that I'd encountered had been unfailingly polite and helpful. I just hoped the students were the same.

"Thanks so much for this," I said to the driver when we finally arrived at my dorm. "I wasn't looking forward to lugging all this stuff on my own."

"No problem." He dipped his chin toward the lock. "Did you manage to find the key?"

"Yup." I held it up and slid it in. "I can take it from here if you need to leave now."

He glanced at his watch. "Yep, I should probably head off," he said. "Anyway, good luck in this place, kid. I mean it."

He left without another word, and I stared after him with wide eyes. What did he mean by that comment? Was he just aware of how poor scholarship kids were often treated at elite schools? Or did he know something else about this place? Something that might require a lot of luck to deal with?

I shook my head and brushed off the comment. The guy was just being nice and wishing me luck. My nerves were making me paranoid.

I lugged my case inside before returning to the threshold for the rest of my things. Then I took a proper look around my new room, scanning every inch of the place with wide eyes. God, it was huge. Bigger than the crummy old apartment I shared with my mom and occasionally my dad when he was around.

As well as being spacious, the dorm was beautiful to look at, with elegant furnishings and décor which exuded opulence and comfort. Two king-sized beds with lavish headboards sat on opposite walls, ends pointing toward the center of the room, which featured a carpet runner so soft that my shoes seemed to melt into it. Farther along sat chests of drawers, closets, and large desks with top-of-the-range leather computer chairs.

I was obviously sharing with another student, but I didn't mind one bit. The room was enormous, and my dormmate seemed neat.

Scratch that. A pair of scrunched-up panties lay on the floor near the bed on the left side, so she wasn't so neat after all. I didn't care if she was a bit messy, though. My own life was such a damn mess that it would be hypocritical of me to care about a bit of dirty clothing dropped on the floor.

I checked out the shared bathroom—gorgeous, with a rain shower and premium toiletries—and then headed back into the main space to unpack a couple of things. Then I returned to the bathroom for a quick nervous pee. While I was washing my hands, I looked in the mirror and mentally psyched myself up.

I could do this. I *had* to do this.

With a deep breath, I grabbed my bag and found my way to the main building, where my English class was due to start in ten minutes. As I arrived in the first hall, the bell went off, signaling the end of homeroom. I was just in time, as long as I managed to find my classroom quickly enough.

Students poured out of the doors on either side of the hall, some milling around with friends while others rushed away. No one seemed to notice my unfamiliar face, which I saw as a good thing, because being gawked at like a zoo animal totally sucked.

I turned a corner and promptly shrank backward, my heart beating like a hummingbird's wings. *He* was here, standing by a drinking fountain with some friends. Hudson Calloway—the asshole who was responsible for my legal woes and threats of prison time.

God, of course. He was from one of the wealthiest families on the West Coast. It made sense that his family would send him here.

Nausea bubbled up in my system, and I whirled around, legs feeling wobbly. In my haste to get away before the rich prick spotted me, I accidentally bumped right into another person's chest.

"Shit, sorry," I muttered, lifting a palm as I pulled back. My timetable and map had fallen to the polished floor during the collision, so I knelt to pick them up.

"No worries. Let me help." The other student knelt beside me and picked up half of my paperwork. "Here you go."

"Thanks. I—" My words dried up as I caught a proper look at him. Dark, floppy hair framed a handsome face with gorgeous green eyes that held a certain intensity, filling my stomach with butterflies. A playful smile tugged at his lips as he waited for me to finish speaking. "I... uh... thanks for the help," I stupidly repeated.

I rose to my feet, wishing my whole body wasn't trembling. The hot guy rose to his full height too, towering over me by at least ten inches. The air around us seemed to crackle with an unspoken promise of excitement, and my earlier terror from around the corner was all but forgotten.

"Are you new here?" Hot Guy asked, tilting his head. "I haven't seen you before."

"Yeah, brand new. Just arrived half an hour ago." I forced a nervous smile and stuck out my free hand. "I'm Carey Saracen."

The twinkle in his eyes immediately vanished, and his face settled into a cold, stony expression. His smile was gone too, replaced with a furious twist to the lips. Without another word, he stalked away, radiating fury all the way down the hall.

"What the hell?" I muttered to myself. I'd never met the guy before, so as far as I knew, he had no reason to respond so negatively to my name.

Perhaps he was a total snob and he'd heard a new scholarship kid named Carey was due to arrive at school soon. I doubted the school made announcements about new kids, though, so that theory didn't seem likely to be true.

Whatever.

I lifted my chin and stepped back around the corner. The guys from earlier were gone, thankfully, so I strode down the hall until I reached the doorway to Room 12.

The classroom was only half full when I arrived. A bespectacled man in his forties sat at the front, looking down at a notebook. When he heard me step inside, he looked up at me and offered me a pleasant smile. "You're Carey, aren't you?"

I nodded. "Yes. How did you know?"

"I recognize all my students, but I didn't recognize you, so I put two and two together. I'm Professor Garrick."

"Nice to meet you."

He smiled again and gestured to the array of desks in the room. "Sit anywhere you like."

I scanned the room to assess my options. Some students looked up at me, but from the dirty looks they shot me, I could tell that I wasn't welcome to take the empty seats beside them. A couple of guys raised their brows, signaling that I could sit with them, but the smarmy looks in their eyes gave them major douchebag vibes.

At the back, a blonde girl lifted her hand and waved at me. *Sit here,* she mouthed. I nodded and headed over to her, grateful for the friendly face and the offer of a place to sit without feeling like an intruder.

The girl smiled as I sat down. "Hey," she said. "You looked a little lost, so I figured I'd invite you over here."

"Thanks. I'm Carey. I'm new here, in case that wasn't completely obvious," I said with a wry grin.

"It's totally obvious. Sorry." She grinned back at me. "I'm April Garrick."

"Any relation to the teacher?" I asked, glancing at the front of the classroom.

"Yup. He's my dad. That's why no one ever wants to sit with me in here. They think I'll act like a snitch or something."

"I thought it would be the opposite," I remarked. "I'd assume your desk-mate might get the occasional special attention because of their close association with you."

April nodded. "That's exactly what I think! But nope. Always alone in English class," she said. "You're new here and didn't know any better, so I successfully lured you into my trap."

I laughed. "Well, it's like shooting fish in a barrel for you, because I'll take all the help I can get around here." I paused and looked back at Professor Garrick. "You must get discounted tuition as the child of a faculty member, right?"

An oddly confused expression crossed April's pale face. "Um... well, it's true that faculty members can get cheaper tuition for their kids if they want."

"Don't worry, I'm here on a scholarship. No judgement from me for not being one of the Richie Riches."

April still looked confused. Then she laughed. "You really don't know who I am, do you?"

It was my turn to be confused. "Uh... what?"

"Sorry, that made me sound like such a dick." She shook her head and went on. "I just meant that people usually recognize my surname immediately."

I whipped out my phone. "Guess I should Google it?"

"Go ahead. But I can explain too. My family owns Garrick-Graystone. As in the aerospace and defense conglomerate."

"Oh, right. I've heard of that before. I just didn't make the connection," I said, glancing down at the search results on my phone. The Garrick family's net worth was in the billions.

"My dad teaches here because he loves literature and didn't want to go into the usual family business. But anyway, we don't take the staff discount because we don't need it. It feels... unfair."

"That makes sense." I could feel my cheeks flushing with heat, and I knew they were probably bright pink. "Sorry, I hope I didn't offend you with my Richie Rich comment."

"Of course not. It's totally fine."

"I guess I should've known that almost everyone at this school is the child of millionaires or billionaires."

An amused expression flickered in April's eyes, and I was immediately certain that I'd just said something stupid again. "Want to know a secret?" she asked.

"Sure."

"I guess it's not actually a secret. But I'm always surprised that hardly anyone seems to have heard about this." She leaned closer, voice dropping to a conspiratorial whisper. "Okay, so... quite a few of the so-called billionaires in this world aren't actually billionaires at all. Especially those who send their kids to places like this."

My forehead wrinkled. "They're just pretending to have tons of money?"

"Nope. The opposite. But they pay to have their names kept off the rich lists."

"Because they don't want to brag?"

April shook her head. "It's for protection."

"Oh, that makes sense. People might go after them if they knew just how much money they have. Ransom their kids, or whatever. Right?"

"Exactly." April's brows rose. "So, there are quite a few families around here with a net worth in the *trillions* because they own and control so much stuff. Not just millions or billions."

"Wow. That's crazy."

I felt like I was in way over my head now. Some of the kids at this school had access to so much money and power that I couldn't even wrap my head around it. I couldn't even remember how many zeroes a trillion had.

"But don't worry," April said. "There are quite a lot of scholarship kids here too." She paused and pointed to a girl with auburn hair in the second row. "See her? Total math genius. Free tuition in return for repping Babylon at mathlete events."

"Cool."

"So what's your talent?" April asked, tilting her head slightly.

I gnawed on the inside of my cheek, wondering exactly how honest I should be at a time like this. Should I say my talent was grand theft auto? Or being in the wrong place at the wrong time which miraculously turned into the right place at the right place?

I settled on a half-truth. "I got decent grades at my old school, and I'm also really good at coding."

April's face brightened. "Oh, awesome! You mean like, building apps and other stuff like that, right?"

"Sort of, yeah. Programming in general. I got into it because my old school had computers that anyone could use during school hours, and there's tons of free courses online. Plus, it turned out I was pretty good at it."

"That's so cool. Do you have Snap or Insta?"

"Yup. I have practically every social media thing. I just don't use them much," I said.

"I'll follow you. What's your handle?"

I told her, and she grabbed her phone and tapped at the screen a few times. "There. Request sent."

I accepted the Instagram request and followed her back before briefly scrolling through her top photos. "Cute dog," I said, looking at a photo of a panting black labrador.

"His name is Fido. It's a running joke in my family that we always give our pets the most clichéd names ever," April said with a grin. "He was even cuter as a puppy. Scroll down further. There's some older pics of him on there, so you can see."

I scrolled all the way down and finally spotted a puppy pic from a couple of years ago. "Aww, he's adorable!" I said, smiling at the screen. My eyes were quickly drawn to the photo on the left, featuring April with another blonde girl who looked very similar to her. "Is this your sister?"

"Yeah, that's Abby."

"She's so pretty. Is she older or younger than you?"

"She was a year younger than me."

My gaze shot up to meet April's. "Did you say... was?"

"Yeah." She looked down, lips tightening. "She died."

"Oh my god. I'm so sorry," I said, heart lurching.

She waved a hand. "No need to apologize. You had no way of knowing."

"I know, but still, I'm really sorry you went through that. It must've been so hard," I said.

I didn't ask her what happened, but there must've been a question flickering in my eyes, because April swallowed hard and supplied the answer. "She was a real party girl from a young age. Got into some bad stuff. She overdosed last year."

"God, that's terrible. I'm so sorry. And... I'm sorry for even bringing her up."

"You don't need to keep apologizing. It's okay. I like talking about her. It helps me feel better when I'm really missing her." April paused and smiled. "She would've liked you."

"What makes you say that?" I asked, brows lifting.

"Your whole coding skills thing."

"Oh, was she good at that too?"

"No. Not at all. But she and her friends were obsessed with that Gossip Girl show. Remember it?"

I nodded. "Uh-huh."

"They wanted to start a Babylon version of GG with an app. But none of them knew how to do that. So I bet Abby totally would've roped you into building the app for her," April said. She laughed softly and shook her head. "An app like that would never have worked at a place like this, though."

"How come?" I asked.

"Gossip spreads here like wildfire. No app necessary. You

could drop a pen on the fourth floor and everyone on the first floor would probably know about it within five minutes."

"Oh, wow." I swallowed hard. "So, um... speaking of the social scene here, what's it like apart from the gossip? Is it hard to make friends?"

April grimaced slightly. "You should be fine. But some advice—be careful about who you trust. Like, really, *really* careful. People will pretend to be nice to your face and then totally stab you in the back as soon as it suits them."

"Should I be wary of you, then?" I said in a joking tone.

April grinned and pretended to swipe at me like a cat. "Yeah, totally," she said. Her smile suddenly faded. "Seriously, though, be careful. Some people here will act like your friend, and then you'll find out that they secretly hate you and just want to mess with you. Or they're just trying to use you for something. See her over there in the third row? Brown ponytail."

I nodded. "Yeah."

"That's Regina Barnett. We used to be friends. Or so I thought." She grimaced again. "One day I accidentally saw a text on her phone to one of her other friends. It said, '*Did you convince April to get it yet?*'"

"Get what?" I asked, raising a brow.

April sighed glumly. "Turns out she was only hanging out with me and having sleepovers at my house so she could try to sneak into Dad's study and steal English exams. That way she and her real friends could cheat."

"That's horrible."

"Yup."

I wrinkled my forehead. "Why would anyone here even want to cheat at tests? Can't rich kids just buy their way into most colleges?"

"Yeah, you're right, but it's a status thing, I guess. Attending an elite school like Babylon is one thing, but being able to say that you were the top student at Babylon is another thing entirely."

"Ah. That makes sense." I smiled wryly. "At least that's one good thing about not coming from money. Who would ever try to use me for anything?"

April laughed. I laughed softly alongside her until a flash of movement caught my eye. Instinctively, I turned my head slightly to the right to glance at the door and spotted a newcomer to the class. My heart instantly sank.

It was the angry asshole from earlier, and he was looking right at me with the same scowl on his face; a face that I had now decided wasn't just handsome but *annoyingly* handsome.

April noticed the sour look on his face and frowned. "Um... do you know him?" she asked. "He's totally glaring at you."

I shrugged. "Not really. I sort of bumped into him earlier in the hall, and I guess he has a problem with me now."

"Weird."

"Who is he?"

"Maverick Reinhart."

My eyes widened. "His name is *Maverick*?"

"Yeah, why?"

"I've never heard a name like that in real life. Just in movies. It's a bit like an AO3 name."

April's brows rose. "AO3?"

"Like... fanfic."

April started giggling. "Oh my *god*. I would literally pay you to say that right to his face. It would be so funny." Her laughter promptly ceased, and a more serious expression appeared on her face. "Actually, no. He's not someone you want to mess with too much."

"Why?"

She rolled her eyes. "He's one of the most popular guys here. No one messes with him. You know the type, right?"

"Yeah. I think there are guys like him at every school."

"Totally." April lowered her voice. "It's weird that he keeps glaring at you. Are you sure you haven't met him before?"

I considered it for a second, chewing on my bottom lip. "Wait... did you say his last name is Reinhart?"

"Uh-huh."

With an internal groan, I realized why Maverick knew my name. He was the guy whose car I crashed into last year. He wasn't in the vehicle at the time—he was standing at a nearby lookout with some girl, apparently—but I'd completely fucked it up to the point where it needed to be written off.

I'd never actually met Maverick in person after the incident, because his parents were the ones who dealt with all the legal stuff, but he must've heard my name from them.

April looked at me expectantly. "So do you know him or what?"

I hesitated again. There was no way I could tell her everything about that night. She wouldn't believe me. No one ever did.

I decided to give her a brief account of the story instead, leaving out ninety percent of the details. "I was on my way home a while ago and accidentally crashed into his car. I totally ruined it."

April's eyes widened. "Was he in it?"

"No. Parked."

"So why would he care so much? He's rich enough to get a new car easily. Besides, insurance exists."

I swallowed thickly. "Well... there's a bit more to it than that." I took a deep breath and filled her in on the scholarship. "I was going to get in a ton of trouble, but instead I ended up here. The Reinhart family actually helped to sponsor the scholarship, among others. They were *very* forgiving."

April nodded. "Ah. So Maverick is probably pissed as hell because not only did you wreck his car, you're now benefiting from the accident in a financial sense."

"Yeah, I guess so," I murmured. My face was burning with embarrassment now.

"Thanks for telling me about it. It's rare for people to be so honest at a place like this," she said. "But you should know something."

"What?"

"If Mav recognizes you, then the whole school will know what you did by lunchtime."

I sighed. "So even if I didn't tell you, you would've found out anyway."

April nodded. "Yes. But now I know you're a decent person, because you admitted it to me *before* any of that gossipy shit started going around. Seriously, that's super rare here. Takes guts." She paused and gave me a small smile. "Other people will eventually notice that about you too. So I think you'll be fine here."

"I hope so," I said, stomach twisting.

"If anyone is nasty to you, let me know. I'm the child of a faculty member, so I could possibly arrange for them to wind up with a few detentions. Or perhaps thrown off one of those nearby cliffs," she said with a playful smirk.

I laughed, already feeling a little calmer. "Thanks."

The bell finally rang, and our class started. The lesson ended up being fine for me, because we were at the very beginning of the school year, which meant everyone else in the room was in the exact same boat as me—unsure and a little lost, but ready to jump in and figure things out.

The bell rang, and April offered to show me where my next class was. I walked past Maverick's desk with my eyes stalwartly forward, because I was afraid he might say something if he saw me looking at him. I could feel his gaze on me as I passed, practically burning a hole in my new blazer with the fury held within them, but thankfully he stayed silent.

I stepped out into the hall and didn't look back, but when April decided to open her phone camera and take a selfie to commemorate the end of the first class on the first day back, I spotted Maverick on the screen, standing a few feet behind us.

Watching me.

CAREY

April was right about this school's predilection for gossip. She was also right about Maverick's probable campaign against me—by lunchtime, everyone in the school knew my name and the fact that I was here on a scholarship that I seemingly received for breaking the law. Thankfully, the details around my case were still hazy at best to everyone on campus, and I had no intention of sharing them. Not anytime soon, anyway.

The rest of the school day absolutely sucked. People glared at me in the halls and classrooms, whispered to each other while staring at me, or straight-up hurled insults at me as I walked past. They were stupid, uncreative insults like 'whore' and 'trailer trash', but it still stung to hear those words thrown at me.

The most annoying nickname that my fellow students had come up with was 'crim', short for 'criminal'. Multiple people had addressed me with it over the last few hours, and I was currently staring at it spray-painted in bright red on the locker that had been assigned to me to store my books between classes.

I thought this school was for smart kids, but if 'crim' was really the best insult these fuckers could come up with, then I figured I probably had a decent shot at a top spot in one or more of my classes. Silver linings and all.

Feeling more than a little deflated at the way the day had gone, but hardly surprised, I returned to my dorm and trudged inside. My dormmate was still yet to reveal herself, so I knew nothing about her, apart from the fact that her aim wasn't great when it came to tossing things in the washing basket.

Part of me was pointlessly clinging to the hope that it was April, but I already knew that she lived with her parents in one of the staff houses during school terms, so it couldn't be her. I also knew it wasn't Brooke—April's best friend that she'd kindly introduced me to during lunch, along with their other friend Zach— because she'd spent several minutes at lunch complaining to us about her roommate Leah, who was apparently extremely messy.

With a sigh, I dumped my bag on the end of my bed and started properly unpacking my suitcase. After a while, I took a break and headed over to the window to check out the view. The sky was overcast and spitting rain, but it was still nice to look outside and take in the ocean and cliffs. Certainly a lot better than the view from my apartment back home, which was a direct look into a rundown auto repairs shop.

I leaned forward and squinted, spotting something in the distance. A small island, perhaps, or maybe a huge container ship. It was too far to tell. I grabbed my phone and used the camera app to zoom in, confirming that I had in fact spotted an island that lay right off the coast. When I zoomed in further, I was able to make out the vaguest outline of a building. It was made of gray stone and looked a lot like a castle. That was crazy, though. A castle in Northern California? It made no sense.

I texted April. **Hey, this sounds kinda nuts, but when I zoom in with my camera, I can see what looks like a castle on an island from my dorm window. Any idea what it is?**

She texted back a few minutes later. *Yup, that's Icarus Hall. It used to be part of the school.*

Me: ***Really? So far from the rest?***

April: *Yeah. Back in the day, like almost 100 years ago, it was the girls' section. Parents didn't want their daughters anywhere near the boys at school, so they thought having all that water between their dorms and classrooms would be enough to protect their little darlings. But that fell out of favor in the 60s, and they made this place properly co-ed. Apart from the dorms, obviously, because there's still separate accommodation halls for boys and girls.*

Me: ***How did they get over there back then? Boat?***

April: *Yeah, there's no bridge because the island is too many miles out to build something like that. I think that was part of the reason they wanted to stop using it. It was too annoying to keep taking boats back and forth to transport all the people and stuff like food and equipment. Anyway, now the building is heritage-listed. But no one goes there. No point, really. It's just an old building that's basically the same as every building right here on campus. And the island is pretty much a giant rock with nothing else on it.*

I was still musing over this piece of information about Babylon's history when I heard the door open behind me. Before I could turn around to check out my dormmate, a familiar voice carried across the room.

"What the fuck?"

MAVERICK

Un-fucking-believable.

Carey Saracen was in my dorm. Her shit was all over the place, too—bags, half-unpacked suitcase, textbooks, notebooks. For a second, I thought I had to be hallucinating, but when I blinked, she was still standing there looking at me like a deer in headlights.

My fists curled at my sides as I stared back at her from the entryway. I still couldn't believe she had the audacity to take that fucking scholarship and show up at my school after the crazy shit she pulled in June. But this? Invading my room with all her crap? That was a whole new level of fuckery.

"What the hell are you doing in here?" I asked, eyes narrowing.

She nervously licked her lips—plump pink lips that looked kissable as fuck, much to my chagrin—and stepped forward. "This is my room. What are *you* doing here?"

I folded my arms over my chest. "It's *my* room."

"That's not possible." Carey shook her head, thick brown hair swishing around her narrow shoulders. "The girls and boys are separated in the dorms here."

"Thanks for explaining how my own school works," I said,

voice dripping with condescension. "This is Dressler Hall. The senior *boys'* hall. So I'll ask you again. What the fuck are you doing here?"

"This is the dorm they assigned to me," she replied, nostrils flaring with indignation. "Why else would I be here?"

I took a deep breath and raked a hand through my hair as I considered this fucked-up turn of events. "It must be your name," I finally said. "It's unisex. Whoever was overseeing the room assignments probably thought you were a guy, saw the empty spot in my dorm, and placed you here."

Carey nodded slowly. "The woman at the office *did* say she was pretty new to the job and still getting used to stuff. I guess she could've made the mistake."

I gestured around the room. "How the hell did you not notice earlier? Didn't you see any of my stuff?"

She scoffed and planted her hands on her hips. "Everything you have out in the open is generic-looking. Like the stuff on your desk. It could belong to anyone, male or female. And it's not like I rifled through your closet and drawers when I arrived. I'm not a total psycho."

Aren't you? I wanted to say, upper lip curling. It was seriously pissing me off to look at her right now. Not only because I hated her after what she did, but also because she was irritatingly hot. Nah, not even hot. That word didn't do her justice.

She was fucking beautiful. Long, shiny hair, big chocolate-brown eyes that seemed to sparkle even when she looked confused or pissed, delicate button nose, and pouty lips.

Before now, all I knew was her name, so I had no idea what she looked like. No idea that she was essentially the perfect girl in terms of looks. But I guess she had to have something going for her, given her major shortcomings in every other department.

"Oh, wait. There was *one* exception which made me think you were a girl," Carey went on, arching a brow. She turned her head, looking pointedly at a pair of panties that lay on the carpet near my bed. "Nice underwear."

I rolled my eyes. "Obviously they aren't mine," I said. I grabbed a tissue and used it to pick up the panties so I could toss them in the wastebasket.

"Really?" Carey flashed a sardonic smile at me. "I think they'd look cute on you."

I glared at her, wishing my eyes could shoot laser beams that would melt her right into the fucking carpet.

Her mocking smile faltered, and she looked down at her feet. "Jeez, I was just making a joke," she muttered.

"Pack your shit and come with me," I said icily. "You're getting reassigned."

"I'm not packing anything until I know exactly what's going on," she retorted, crossing her arms.

"Fine. Let's get this shit sorted right now."

I turned and marched out of the room, jaw clenched so tightly that it felt like my teeth might shatter. Carey dashed ahead of me in the hallway, leaving a fragrant trail of cinnamon and vanilla-scented perfume that lingered in my nostrils as I followed her.

I hated it. I hated *her*.

After a heated discussion at the main admin office, we were informed that the issue had snowballed from a simple room assignment mistake to a total clusterfuck. Apparently, all the available spots in the girls' hall were taken, so there was nowhere to send Carey.

"How the fuck is that possible?" I asked the principal, who'd gotten involved after he heard me shouting at the reception staff. "Do you have any idea what my parents are going to say when they hear about this bullshit?"

"I'm very sorry, Maverick. Very sorry to you too, Carey," he replied, dipping his head contritely toward Carey. "I'm really not sure how an error of this magnitude has occurred, but let me assure you that we are going to do everything we possibly can to fix it."

He stepped into his office with two of his staff members to confer with them. Five minutes later, they returned. All of them had harried expressions on their faces.

"We checked the staff housing to see if there are any empty rooms for Carey to stay in, but unfortunately there's nothing available there either," Principal Saunders said, wringing his hands.

"Are you serious? How the fuck did this happen?" I asked in an acid tone.

"We looked into the problem, and it seems that our new receptionist was responsible for the room assignment once Carey's scholarship was, er... created," he replied in a delicate tone, glancing at her. "She thought Carey was a boy, so when she saw the empty spot in Dressler Hall, she placed her there. If she knew she was a girl, she would have alerted us to the lack of space in Sundance Hall much earlier."

"What about the other girls' hall? The one for freshmen and sophomores?"

He shook his head. "It's completely full too, as we've had four new transfers this semester."

"So what's going to happen, then?"

"One of our female students is leaving us partway through the semester to return to her home country. Carey can have her spot then."

"When will that be?" Carey asked, tilting her head.

Saunders rubbed his chin. "In seven weeks."

I stared at him, aghast. "What do we do until then?"

"We've come up with a temporary solution. We'll have the maintenance staff install a divider curtain in your dorm. That should be easy, seeing as your beds and desks are on opposite sides. The room is also big enough to ensure that you both have plenty of space despite the curtain. You'll have to share the bathroom, but I'm sure you can come up with a schedule between the two of you."

My jaw dropped. "You can't be fucking serious."

"We have to keep sharing?" Carey squawked at the exact same time. "For nearly two months?"

"My deepest apologies, sincerely," Saunders replied, lifting his palms. "Something like this has never happened at Babylon before. Rest assured, the person responsible will be terminated from their employment immedi—"

Carey interrupted him. "No, don't fire her," she said hurriedly. "It was an easy mistake to make, and uhh… it's fine. I don't mind sharing. It's only seven weeks."

I stared at her, surprised at her sudden change of heart. "Are you fucking serious?" I muttered.

"I don't want to be responsible for someone losing their income," she whispered to me.

I was about to snap back at her and insist that the receptionist deserved to lose her job for causing so much havoc when something suddenly occurred to me.

I could drive Carey out of Babylon a hell of a lot faster if we were sharing a dorm, because I'd always be right there in her space, messing with her head until she was ready to have a full-on nervous breakdown.

"Carey's right." I smiled pleasantly at Saunders. "It was an easy mistake to make, given the unisex name situation. We can share for a few weeks, and there's really no need for me to call my parents and tell them about the screw-up."

Saunders' shoulders sagged with relief. "Thank you. That's a very level-headed response, Maverick," he said. Translation: *I'm so glad the school won't be losing the massive donation we get from the Reinhart family every year.* "And thank you to you too, Carey. I'm sure you were expecting better when you arrived at Babylon."

"It's fine," she murmured.

We turned and headed back to Dressler, footsteps echoing

loudly through the halls. Carey didn't say a word, and neither did I. Not until we stepped back inside the dorm.

"Have you ever seen the movie Watchmen?" I asked, casually lounging on my bed.

Carey shrugged. "I think so. Ages ago."

"Remember the part where that guy's in prison and he says something like, '*I'm not stuck in here with you. You're stuck in here with me.*'?"

"Uh-huh." She stared at me, lips pursing, and cocked her head. "Let me guess. You're saying that to me now? As some sort of threat?"

"Pretty much."

"If you actually expect that to scare me, you're completely delusional," she said, rolling her eyes. "Pathetic, too. Truly."

I smiled thinly and stood. "You might not be scared now, Saracen," I said, rising to my full height. "But you will be."

CAREY

"Hey, Crim! Hungry?"

I automatically looked up at the sound of my nickname just in time to see an entire poached egg sliding off the end of a fork from the overpass above me. I dodged it, but not quickly enough to avoid part of the egg white splattering on my hair.

Jasmine Briarwood smiled sweetly down at me from the overpass. "Oops!"

Over the past two weeks, I'd learned through multiple encounters that she was the reigning Queen Bee at Babylon Prep. In fact, I knew it the first time I ever saw her, with her impossibly pretty face, perfectly styled blonde hair cascading over her shoulders, piercing blue eyes that surveyed every space like a royal perusing their kingdom, and long manicured nails that looked like they could slit someone's throat. On top of all that, she simply radiated an aura of entitlement and superiority.

"Seriously?" I glared up at her, nostrils flaring. "You're throwing food now? Are you in fucking kindergarten?"

I was pretty sure this was exactly why she'd decided to hate me so much since my arrival on campus. Even though she was supposedly the ruling girl at this school, sending other girls skittering away from her in the halls like terrified deer, I was completely unafraid of her. If she made a nasty comment to me, I talked shit right back to her. If I saw her acting like a bitch to some poor innocent freshman, I called her out on it.

What was the worst she could do? Make up some awful rumor about me?

That didn't matter at all, because every possible nasty rumor about me had already gone around the school three times, thanks to Maverick and his minions. Jasmine would only be adding to the already-gargantuan pile of shit if she tried.

She sneered down at me. "I just thought you might be hungry, that's all," she said. "I heard people can't really afford food in Oakfield, and I guess it must be true, because your body is so malnourished it forgot to grow a pair of tits."

Her minions giggled around her, as if she'd said the funniest thing in the world. I was about to snap back at her when Zach Roberts-Smith spoke up beside me. "Grow the fuck up, Jasmine," he said, glowering at her. Like me, he was unafraid of her and her cronies. "Oh, and we all know *your* tits are fake, by the way. Your surgeon has pretty loose lips."

Jasmine scoffed. "If I knew your name, I might actually care about your opinion. But I don't, so..." She trailed off, flipped her hair dismissively, and flounced away.

I grinned at Zach. "Thanks."

"No worries. I'm so fucking sick of her. She was horrible to Abby, too," he said, lips thinning. "Someone really needs to teach her a lesson. I just wish I knew how. If I did, I'd totally do it."

Zach was one of April's best friends, and he'd quickly become my friend too. He and April had grown close after her sister's death—he was Abigail's long-term boyfriend before it happened—and now they ran a drug awareness program together, mostly aimed at the freshman and sophomore kids.

"She'll move on to another target soon," Brooke chimed in,

gently pulling a stringy piece of egg white off the left side of my head. "She's just going after you because you're the new girl."

Brooke was April's other best friend. Chemistry whiz, bookworm, and also my lab partner in bio. She was just as sweet and kind as April, although she was a little shyer and quieter.

Zach rolled his eyes. "That's exactly what I mean about her needing someone to teach her a fucking lesson. She's always got a target. It's totally fucked up."

"I know. But what can we do?" Brooke asked, wiping off her eggy hand with a napkin. "It's not like anyone would ever listen to nobodies like us. We might as well be invisible."

"Hey, I'm actually *glad* we aren't super popular," April chimed in. "I like blending into the background. That way no one ever notices me and goes after me." She paused and cringed. "Sorry, Carey."

I gave her a small smile. "It's cool. It's not your fault things have been so shitty for me here."

"Fucking Maverick." She shook her head and took a small bite of the ham and cheese croissant in her right hand. Through her mouthful, she added, "He's such a dick for starting all this shit."

"Language, missy," a familiar voice called out.

We turned to see Professor Garrick looking at us from the hedge-lined pathway that ran behind our spot.

"Ugh, *Dad!* Stop interrupting us at lunch!" April said. "This is the third time this week!"

"Your lunch spot is on the way to my office. You know that, sweetie, and you still choose to sit here every day." He flashed her a good-natured grin and took a few steps closer. Then he turned his gaze to me. "By the way, Carey, I was going to wait until our next class to give this to you, but seeing as we're both here now..."

He trailed off and riffled through his messenger bag. Then he smiled again and handed some papers over to me. "Your essay on the Count of Monte Cristo," he said. "Congratulations. You got an A+."

My eyes widened as I looked down at the cover page. True to his word, a big 'A+' was scrawled at the top in purple pen. "Oh, wow. Thanks!"

"You have some interesting thoughts on revenge. I'd love to read a few paragraphs to the rest of the class, if you're okay with that."

"Sure." I held the essay out to him. "I guess you'll need it back, then."

He waved a hand. "It's okay. Just bring it on Friday," he said. He looked at April. "Don't worry, sweetie, I'll get out of your hair now."

He continued on his way down the path, and Brooke gently elbowed me. "That's one good thing for you, right?" she said. "You're doing great here. Academically, I mean."

"Yeah, I guess I'm doing pretty well, huh?" I said softly. Perhaps the people who created my scholarship were correct after all—if someone on a wayward path was simply given the right opportunities in life, they could really excel.

Then again, grades were never my problem. Getting involved with the wrong people... *that* was my problem. Babylon was a fresh start for me, though, and judging by my new group of friends, I was already making much better decisions about who I chose to hang out with.

The rest of the day drifted by in what had quickly become a familiar haze—abuse shouted at me in the hallways, whispers all around me in my classes, and nasty notes slid inside my locker, all followed by leering gazes on the staircase as I headed for my dorm in the boys hall after a long study session in the library.

With a heavy sigh, I unlocked my door and glanced over at Maverick's side of the room. The school maintenance staff had hung two curtains in the end—one surrounding my space and one surrounding Maverick's, leaving a narrow open pathway between the entryway and the other side of the dorm, which led to our shared bathroom.

Maverick's curtain was currently open, so I could see him reclining on his bed, reading something on his phone. He didn't look up when he heard me enter the room, which I viewed as a small mercy. It was always better when people ignored me at this place. Especially people like *him*.

I opened my own curtain and promptly screamed bloody murder. Dangling from the light fixture above my bed was a crude effigy of me, dripping red all over the duvet from the throat area as it swung in slow circles.

"Shit!" I placed a hand on my chest, surprised my heart hadn't jumped right out of my ribcage from the shock. "God, Maverick, you're such a fucking asshole!"

He appeared next to me. "Huh? What the—" He stared at the effigy, eyes wide. "Oh, nice. That looks cool as fuck."

"Cool? I almost had a heart attack!" I snapped, narrowing my eyes at him. "Although I guess that's what you wanted, right?"

"I didn't do this."

I scoffed. "Are you seriously going to pretend it wasn't you?"

Over the past couple of weeks, Maverick had made my life at Babylon hell. He'd spread a ton of nasty rumors about me, destroyed my already-tenuous reputation, and made numerous threats about reporting me to the school administration for plagiarism and cheating—which he couldn't prove, because it wasn't true—but this was the first time he'd taken things this far, with what essentially amounted to a death threat hanging over my bed.

"It wasn't." He folded his arms. "It was probably your friends."

"Huh?"

"Your friends," he repeated. "They were here earlier."

"Bullshit. April, Brooke, and Zach were all with me in the library until five minutes ago."

Maverick sneered. "Not *them*. Hudson and some other guys. Can't remember their names."

My heart froze. "Hudson Calloway?"

"Yeah."

"He was here?"

"That's what I said." Maverick rolled his eyes. "He knocked earlier and said you guys were supposed to hang out, so I let him in. He and his buddies hung out in your section for a while, and then they said they had to go. I figured they were going to find you."

"You didn't hear them doing anything while they were in here?"

He scratched his jaw. "Uh... I heard them laughing."

"And that didn't tip you off that they might be doing something like this?"

"No." He lifted a brow and cocked his head. "Most people laugh with each other when they hang out. Maybe you'd know that if you didn't have a stick up your ass all the time."

I gritted my teeth. "Listen. Hudson Calloway is *not* my friend. Don't ever let him in here again. Okay?"

I assumed Maverick would smirk and make some comment about being allowed to do whatever he wanted in his dorm. Instead, he casually shrugged, face settling into a neutral expression. "Okay," he said before turning away and heading back to his side of the room.

I wasn't sure I trusted that '*okay*,' but I figured it was better than the alternative.

Before I could formulate another thought on the matter, someone rapped on the door. I headed over and tentatively opened it a crack, worried that Hudson and his cronies were back for more. Instead, I saw Jasmine, tapping one foot impatiently on the floor as she waited.

"Uhh... are you here to apologize to me?" I asked.

She looked genuinely surprised by my question. "Apologize for what?"

"Never mind. Stupid question," I muttered. "What are you doing here?"

"I'm here to study with Mav, *obviously*." She pushed past me and stomped over to Maverick's bed. "You know, I can't believe that dirty little bitch is still here," she went on loudly enough for me to hear as she pulled the curtain around their section of the dorm. "My parents complained to the school about her criminal history, but they don't seem to care."

I couldn't make out Maverick's muttered response, but I didn't care. I closed the door, strode back over to my side, and began the arduous process of cutting down the horrible effigy of me from the chandelier. After that, I scrubbed as much of the 'blood' off my duvet as I could—it smelled sickly-sweet, so I guessed it was actually corn syrup—and then I whipped my curtain back around my section and settled at my desk to get started on some research for a history essay.

I put some headphones on so I could listen to music while I browsed journal articles and web results, but that didn't stop the occasional noises from drifting over to me from Maverick's section. For the first fifteen minutes or so, it was mostly just Jasmine's annoying voice cutting through, but eventually I heard loud moans and grunts through my tunes.

I rolled my eyes and turned my music up, but the moans grew louder and louder, peppered with the occasional gasp or scream. It all sounded unbelievably performative. Clearly, Jasmine and Maverick had decided to have extremely loud sex just to bother me.

I kept turning my music up in a futile attempt to drown out the noises, but then I couldn't concentrate on my work. Finally, after a particularly loud, drawn-out shriek, I snapped and shouted toward Maverick's section. "Can you fucking *stop?*"

The noises abruptly ceased, and Maverick called back to me. "What?"

I ripped off my headphones, stomped over to his section, and yanked the curtains back. Jasmine was hiding most of her body under the blankets, and her hair was mussed. "Um, can we help you?" she said in a snide tone.

"Yeah, you actually *can* help me, by shutting the hell up. It's obvious you're totally faking it anyway."

"What are you talking about?"

I sighed and pinched the bridge of my nose. "Listen, Jasmine... you might like bouncing on Maverick's dick, but everyone else in the building is sick of hearing it. Especially me. So please, *shut the fuck up.*"

She batted her long eyelashes at me. "We weren't having sex. We're just studying."

"Sure." I snorted. "That's why you're hiding under the blankets."

She pushed the duvet off herself, revealing that she was fully clothed. "I only got under here because I'm cold, and I know Mav isn't a total creep who'll try to touch me," she said. "You really have a dirty mind, Crim."

"So what the hell was that noise, then?" I asked, eyes narrowing. "I know what I heard."

"Oh my god, who cares? It wasn't *that* loud."

"Yes, it was," I snapped. "I had noise-canceling headphones on at my desk, and it still sounded like I was working at a porn shoot."

Jasmine sighed. "It's a horror movie, okay? We're watching it for our film studies class. See?" She paused and grabbed a laptop from the end of the bed. Then she turned it to face me and hit the space bar on the keyboard.

She wasn't lying. Onscreen, a crying girl was crawling through the mud, letting out the occasional moans and screams as a killer slowly stalked her, dragging an axe by his side.

"Right," I muttered, feeling stupid. "Whatever."

She batted her long eyelashes. "So... you want us to turn it down?"

"Yes!" I threw up my hands. "That's literally *all* I want right now. Some damn peace and quiet."

"You got it." She smiled sweetly at me and lowered the volume. Next to her, Maverick stared at me, lips turned upward in a smirk.

I turned away, and Jasmine called out to me. "It's totally obvious, by the way."

I looked over my shoulder. "What?"

"Your crush on Mav," she said in a taunting tone. "It's so obvious. Why else would you be making up these crazy jealous scenarios about him fucking other girls right next to you?"

"Oh, sure," I said, voice dripping with sarcasm. "You caught me! I totally have a thing for annoying, entitled assholes!"

With that, I strode back over to my side and whipped my curtains back around my section so hard that they almost came off the temporary rail. My face felt hot, and my legs were trembling.

As much as I hated to admit it, Jasmine was partially right. Obviously, I didn't have a crush on Maverick, because he was a total prick, but I *was* attracted to him. Only in the most private way, of course. I would never admit to him or anyone else that he was the sexiest guy I'd ever seen. I would never act on the attraction, either. His shitty personality rendered him utterly undatable and unfuckable.

The evening finally rolled around, and I went to the dining hall to meet up with my friends for dinner. When I returned, Maverick wasn't in our dorm, and his curtain was open all the way. He didn't return while I watched TV and TikTok for the rest of the evening, and by the time I went to bed at eleven, his side of the room was still unoccupied.

I woke up several times throughout the night to pee—I drank way too much water during dinner thanks to the spicy Madras curry I'd enjoyed—and each time, I noticed Maverick still hadn't come back yet. For once, I was sleeping alone in our shared space.

That was fine by me. With him out of the dorm, there was no chance of him harassing or annoying me.

At three-thirty in the morning, I settled back into bed after my fifth bathroom trip and lay my head on the pillow, letting out a deep sigh of relief. My alarm wasn't due to go off until seven-thirty, and my bladder finally seemed to be empty, so I could enjoy another four hours of uninterrupted sleep.

Unfortunately, that didn't happen. Just after six, my phone started going off. Groaning, I picked it up to silence it, sleepily thinking that I must've set the alarm wrong. I spotted a flurry of notifications instead. Someone had tagged me in something on Instagram, and people were commenting on it like crazy despite the early hour.

I blinked slowly, wondering what the hell was going on. A second later, a text from April came through. ***Don't look!***

CAREY

I was wide awake now, adrenaline coursing through my veins and goosebumps peppering my arms. April's plea had the opposite effect than she intended—by telling me not to look, I instantly *had* to look just to see what was so terrible.

Another message came through from her just before I could click on Insta. ***I know you're probably looking anyway, but seriously, ignore it! These dumbasses literally have nothing better to do with their lives. Why else would they all be up at six commenting on this bullshit?***

Now I was even more curious. I clicked on the first notification, which took me to Kiara Swift's account.

Kiara was the only person I already knew of before I started at Babylon, due to her social media fame. She boasted over five million followers on TikTok and Instagram, and she also had multiple brand deals and sponsorships. It all began when she posted some dancing videos a couple of years ago. After they went viral, she spun the newfound renown into a full-on influencing career.

She was also Jasmine Briarwood's best friend.

Upon closer inspection, I realized I wasn't looking at her main account, but a second private one she'd made just for friends, otherwise known as a finsta. I could tell because she only had four hundred followers on this one... including me. I couldn't remember following it, but somehow, I was on the list anyway.

Maverick.

He must've taken my phone one night while I was sleeping and followed the account for me. It wouldn't be hard for him. I usually slept like a log—last night was an outlier—and my phone had biometric ID set up, so he could've used my thumbprint to open it.

With a sigh, I clicked play on the video post I'd been tagged in. The thumbnail image for the video was just a black screen, so I had no idea what was coming.

The plain black image persisted for a couple of seconds. Then some puke emojis appeared, followed by laughing emojis and bold white text saying, '*EWWWWWW, no surprise though, right guys?????*'.

This was followed by a voice recording of me, clearly made yesterday afternoon during my angry rant at Jasmine and Maverick. However, they'd edited the recording by adding new things to it in their own voices and moving my statements around to make it seem like I was saying something completely different than what I'd actually said.

Maverick: *So, Carey, what do you think you'll be doing in five years?*

Me: *Working at a porn shoot.*

Jasmine: *Oh my god, really? You want to do porn?*

Me: *Sure.*

Jasmine: **Giggling* Wow, that's really sex-positive of you. You obviously love sex.*

Me: *Yeah. You caught me!*

Jasmine: **More giggling* What's your favorite thing about it? I mean, what would you most like to be doing right now, bedroom-wise?*

Me: *Bouncing on Maverick's dick.*

Maverick: *You want me that bad, huh?*

Me: *Yes. That's literally all I want right now.*

Those childish fucking pricks.

Fuming, I opened the comments section, predicting that it was going to be filled with even more childish pricks. I was right, for the most part. It seemed like half the school had commented, and only a few people were coming to my defense.

Biancababy: *Omg she just said that out loud? What a dumb whore*
Johann_atwood: *Hahahaha OMG is this real?*
Louvera2004 *That's def her! I sit behind her in bio so I know her voice!*
BrookeSanford04: *This is pathetic. Obviously fake. Take it down, Kiara. I thought you would know better than most people how horrible it is to have people shit-talking you and trolling you online.*
Louvera2004: *It isn't fake! It's literally her voice, idiot*
Jayjay77: *Sluuuuuuuuttttttttt*
Bare.minimum.33: *How drunk was she to admit this shit out loud lmao even the KGB couldn't waterboard this info out of me*
Tater69: *Of course she's a ho lol she's from one of those inland towns, they're all the same out there*
AprilG: *So someone who doesn't live near a beach is automatically a ho? What??? That doesn't make any sense!!!*
AprilG: *Seriously guys this is so pathetic and fucked up. I know Carey and she didn't say any of this shit. It's so fake and immature, even by Babylon standards. Take it down now!*
Tater69: *Lol go cry to your teacher daddy about it April*

I stopped scrolling and threw my phone down, stomach churning as fury and hurt spiraled through me. I'd never been a doormat who refused to speak up when trod on, but I still felt every footprint, and right now, I felt like I was being crushed under the weight of the vitriol aimed at me by all these Babylon bastards.

My chest tightened as I thought about the worst one of all. *Maverick*. He was the architect of this entire situation—my bad reputation, the bullying, the rumors, the pathetic herd of sheep constantly following along to trash my name in order to gain some popularity points for themselves.

My anger toward him only grew over the next couple of hours as I prepared for the day. By eight o'clock, I was incandescent with rage. I wanted to punch Maverick straight in the face. Or kick him in the balls. But of course, I couldn't actually do either of those things.

Could I?

I felt like I was in one of those cartoons where the main character had an angel sitting on one shoulder and a devil on the other. My angel was telling me to stay calm and ignore Maverick. If I punched or kicked him as I so dearly wanted to, I'd probably get expelled from Babylon. Even if I didn't, I'd definitely lose my scholarship, and there was no way I could afford this place and the opportunities it offered me without it.

On the other shoulder, the devil was whispering to me, telling me how good it would feel to march right up to Maverick and jab him right in the face. Not just good... amazing. So unbelievably cathartic.

Fuck it.

The last of my composure crumbled, and I stormed out of my dorm and headed for the main senior building, where I proceeded to stalk the halls until I found Maverick. He was standing at his locker, shoving some books inside it.

"Asshole," I muttered under my breath, nostrils flaring.

As desperate as I was to hit him, I'd decided on the way over here that I wasn't going to give him the satisfaction of watching me get kicked out of school, which he so clearly wanted.

However, I *was* going to give him a good tongue-lashing in front of everyone. That would have to be enough.

Sorry, Shoulder Devil.

"Hey!" I shouted, marching into the middle of the cross-hall that intersected the locker hallway.

Maverick turned and looked right at me, brows rising.

Before I could take another step toward him, Hudson Calloway stepped out from the left side of the cross-hall.

"Hey, Carey," he said, lips twisting in a smirk. "I've been meaning to talk to you."

MAVERICK

"Hey!"

I whipped my head to the left at the sound of Carey's voice ringing down the hall. She was storming toward me, hands bunched in fists at her side. Her face was twisted with rage, and I could almost feel the angry heat radiating off her sexy body.

My lips curled into a smirk. She must've seen the audio prank I conjured up with Jasmine. Fucking classic shit. It was unbelievably easy to bait her into it, too.

All Jasmine and I needed to do was loudly play pornos on her laptop—with a horror movie in a different tab on the browser to gaslight Carey with later—and then increase the volume until Carey inevitably stomped over to complain. Jasmine recorded the ensuing conversation on her phone, which went even better than expected, considering the 'dick bouncing' comment Carey furiously spat out.

Once we were done, we took Jasmine's phone to one of our tech-oriented friends, who spliced parts of the original recording into a new one that was carefully crafted to seem like a real conversation. Then Jasmine sent that final recording to her best friend Kiara, who had the biggest finsta at Babylon.

Result: schoolwide humiliation for Carey.

Hopefully, she wouldn't last much longer in these halls. After all, there was only so much shame one person could take, and judging by the expression on her face right now, it looked like she'd already reached her limit.

She drew closer, eyes practically spitting angry sparks of electricity in my direction. My smirk curved into a grin. She looked like she was going to punch me as hard as she possibly could, and I honestly wouldn't mind if she did. Firstly, she'd get expelled, so she'd no longer be a problem for me. Secondly, it would be hot as hell.

Fuck… now I *really* wanted her to do it. I was actually getting hard at the mental image.

Mere seconds before she reached me, Hudson Calloway intercepted her. I'd known the dude since middle school, but we'd never been friends. He and his baseball team buddies were all colossal douchebags, and coming from a guy like *me,* that was really saying something.

I turned my attention back to Carey and clocked her expression and body language as Hudson leaned down to talk to her. She seemed to have shrunk several inches, and the pure rage from a moment ago had morphed into a look that was a combination of sickness and terror. I'd seen that look on enough girls' faces when they were around certain guys to know what it meant.

Shit.

I strode over and planted my body in front of Carey, blocking Hudson's access to her. "Fuck off, Calloway."

He lifted his palms, eyes crinkling with amusement as his mouth stretched into a lazy grin. "Jesus, Mav, calm down. I'm just chatting to my friend," he said in a smarmy tone that made me want to break his fucking jaw. "She your girlfriend or something?"

"It's Maverick to you. Leave her alone."

His shit-eating grin faded. "What the hell is your problem, man? I can talk to whoever I want."

"She's not your friend and she doesn't want to talk to you. Now fuck off."

Hudson scowled. "You don't own this place. You can't dictate who—"

My hand shot out to grab his striped black and red tie, yanking it backward to cut off his airway. His eyes bulged, and he put his hands up again. "Fuck, man, *stop*," he choked out. "I was... I was just kidding. I'll go."

I knew he'd cave instantly when I grabbed him. I had three inches and at least twenty-five pounds on him. Weak little bitch.

I dropped his tie and shoved him in the chest. "Do what I fucking say next time," I snarled. "And stay the hell away from Carey."

"Yeah, whatever," he muttered, rubbing his throat. With that, he stepped away. I was pleased to note that he didn't look in Carey's direction again. Not even a brief sideways glance.

I turned to face her. "What did he do to you?" I asked in a low voice. My hands itched to rub the side of her arms, but I knew it wouldn't be appropriate. Besides, it wasn't my job to comfort her. We weren't friends. We were nothing.

She swallowed audibly. "Nothing. He was just talking to me," she replied. She wouldn't meet my eyes, but I could still see the emotions swirling inside hers. Fear, despondency, defeat.

"I don't mean *now*. I mean in the past. What did he do?" I demanded. "Did he hurt you?"

Carey finally looked up at me. "Not exactly," she said, voice barely above a whisper. "But... I think he might be planning something."

"What do you mean?"

She opened her mouth to respond. Then she suddenly seemed to realize who she was speaking to, and she straightened her shoulders and set her jaw. "It doesn't matter. I have to go."

She took a step away, and I tapped her on the back. "Wait. Don't you have something to say to me?"

She looked at me over her shoulder. "Why would I have anything to say to you?"

"Because you were storming over to me a minute ago with a pretty clear look of intent on your face. So what is it?" I said, crossing my arms over my chest. "What were you going to say?"

Carey hesitated. Then her shoulders sagged all over again. "Nothing," she murmured. "Don't worry about it."

With that, she darted away, shoulders still hunched over and head facing downward.

I watched her go with a frown, endlessly curious about what had happened between her and Hudson. She said he didn't hurt her, which was my original assumption, but whatever it was, it was bad enough to distract her from her fury toward me over the humiliating Insta prank I'd pulled on her.

Did she and Hudson date and have a bad breakup? Did he use her for sex?

Did they even *know* each other before she came to Babylon? They were from two totally different worlds. What were the odds that they'd run into each other if they weren't attending the same school?

I frowned, mulling it over. Then it occurred to me. Of course they could've met before Carey started attending this school. Hudson had lived all his life in Babylon, just like me, and Carey was from Oakfield, which was only a twenty-minute drive inland. They could've met at an event somewhere. Had a fling. Maybe even a full-on relationship that ended badly.

Nah, that's not it.

The look on her face when she saw him wasn't sadness caused by a shitty breakup. It was fear. Either Hudson had done something to her, or he had something on her. Something really fucked up.

An idea popped into my head as I pondered the possibilities. Revenge porn could fit the profile in this scenario. The two of them could've dated for a while, and now Hudson was threatening to leak explicit pics and videos of Carey. That would explain why she said she thought he was planning something.

A knot formed in my stomach as I thought about the two of them dating and fucking. At the same time, a wave of confusion hit me. Usually, all I felt toward Carey was anger, but now... now there was something else in my head. A new emotion; one I'd never really felt until this moment.

Jealousy.

CAREY

Panic and fear gripped my churning stomach like frozen hands as I raced down the hall. I didn't even know where I was going. Didn't care. I just needed to breathe air that was anywhere else, anywhere away from Hudson.

I'd tried my best to avoid him over the last couple of weeks, ever since I discovered his presence on campus, but I knew we were bound to run into each other eventually. Even though we didn't share any classes, we were in the same grade and walked the same halls every day, so an encounter like today was only a matter of time. I'd been dreading it for days, planning what to say and mentally psyching myself up for it.

And yet, nothing could've prepared me for it. No amount of planning could've compared to the real-life thing, where I instantly froze with no idea what to say or do.

Stupid, stupid, stupid, my inner voice chided me as I hurried down the hall. Why did I let him affect me like this? I did nothing to him. *He* was the problem. He was the bad guy. I should just suck it up, ignore him, and walk away. So why didn't I do it? Why did I just stand there motionless with my jaw hanging open and my eyes bulging like a stupid Halloween mask?

Stupid question, really. I already knew the answer. Hudson Calloway had scared the shit out of me ever since I met him, and he had so much power over me that I'd almost ended up in prison because of him. In fact, if it weren't for the benevolence of the group who started the Babylon Foundation, I'd probably be getting sentenced in court right now.

His words flashed back into my mind. *Hey, Carey. I've been meaning to talk to you. I thought you might be planning on spreading more of your bullshit around this place, so I wanted to tell you that it would really be in your best interest to keep that pretty mouth shut as long as you're here. Or... I guess you can open it for me if you want. But no talking allowed. You know what I mean, babe. Finish what we started, huh?*

That was when Maverick showed up to rescue me. God, what the hell was *that* about? He hated me. But I guess he hated Hudson more.

"Carey!"

I stopped and turned at the sound of my name. It wasn't Hudson or Maverick this time. It was a friendly voice and a friendly face. *Thank God.*

April caught up with me a second later, followed by Brooke and Zach. "Hey!" she said. "We've been looking for you everywhere! We tried your dorm, and then the library. Where have you been?"

I choked back my tears as I replied. "Left... earlier than usual."

God, I could barely speak.

"I'm so sorry," Brooke said, squeezing my arm. "We saw what Kiara posted, and... ugh..."

She trailed off, head shaking with disgust. Zach jumped in. "I can't believe she posted that shit. It's so obviously fake."

A tear slipped out, and April wrapped her arms around me. "It'll be okay," she murmured, stroking my back. "It'll blow over."

"It's not that," I choked out over the flood of emotion clogging my throat. "I don't even care about that stupid tape right now."

April pulled back, confusion knitting her delicate features. "What?"

"I just... I..."

That was all I could get out before the tears flooded my face.

April tugged on my hand. "Come on," she said softly. "Let's go to our spot. We still have twenty minutes before the bell."

I let her lead me down the hall toward the closest exit, tears still streaming down my face. Zach and Brooke trailed behind us, throwing dirty looks at anyone who sneered or laughed at me as I passed.

We arrived at our spot under the overpass a moment later. I sat in the center of the stone bench, and the others huddled around me. "What's going on with you?" Zach asked in a low voice. "Did someone do something to you? Something else, I mean."

I wiped my face and took a deep breath. "I need to tell you something."

"You can tell us anything." April patted my arm. "No judgment."

"Promise," Zach added. Brooke nodded alongside him.

I took another deep breath and began. "I wasn't exactly honest with you guys about how I ended up here," I said softly. "At this school, I mean."

April's brows rose. "You told us you got a scholarship through the Babylon Foundation. Is that not true?"

"It's true." I nodded bleakly. "But I was kind of vague on the details. I told you I got into trouble because I crashed into Maverick Reinhart's car. That's only part of the real story. A very small part."

"Okay, well... spill," Zach said. "Like I said, no judgment from me. There's obviously a reason you kept it from us."

I nodded again. "It's just... I was so ashamed. And scared. I was facing a real prison sentence. And I didn't want you guys to look at me differently. People here already call me a criminal, and all they know about is the accident."

"You were really going to go to *prison*?" Brooke's eyes widened. "Just for a car accident?"

I swallowed hard. "Probably, yeah. You'll understand when I tell you the whole story. But it's super long."

April glanced at her watch. "We have ages. It's fine."

I looked down at my feet. "Well... I'll start at the very beginning, even though it's not going to sound relevant to anything. My best friend at my old school was this girl called Mikayla. She was super sweet and pretty. Unfortunately, she was always a bit delusional too."

"How so?" April asked.

"You know the town I'm from, right? Oakfield? It's a real shithole. No point dancing around that fact," I said. I paused to wipe my cheek again. "It's nothing like Babylon. Might as well be two different planets."

"Yeah, I know. People from that place have... um... a certain reputation around here, as awful as that sounds." Zach's thick brows knitted. "But what does that have to do with this Mikayla chick?"

"Like I said, she's really pretty. She knows it, too. So she's always had this idea in her head that she could use her looks to get out of our shitty town and away from her shitty family, if she just found a guy to rescue her. A rich, connected guy, I mean. Someone who could fall for her and save her."

"Ah. The classic fairytale scenario," Brooke said softly. "Deluding girls and women since the dawn of time."

"That's exactly what I always thought," I said, nodding fervently. "I mean, it's a nice idea. Suddenly having money, security, and real power over your life. Never needing to worry about anything again. But it's a fairytale, like you said."

"No shit." Zach snorted. "Life isn't a movie."

"That's what I tried to warn Mikayla about. But she didn't

listen. She'd still go to all these crazy Babylon parties that she managed to get invited to, and she'd always drag me along for moral support. Then I'd have to watch her get used over and over again," I said bitterly. "Every time she met a new guy at one of these things, they'd be sweet to her and say all the right things. But it was just to convince her to open her legs for them for the night. They barely see girls like us as human. Just sentient dolls to fuck and toss away when they're done."

"Sentient dolls," Brooke echoed in a low voice. "Ugh, that's awful."

"I know." I sniffed back more tears. "That's why I kept trying to convince her to stop going to these parties with all these toxic assholes. I knew some rich guy wasn't going to swoop in and make her his girlfriend, let alone his future wife. It was pure fantasy. But at the same time, I kept going with her because I wanted to make sure nothing really bad happened to her."

"Did something happen to her anyway?" April asked in a tentative tone.

I shook my head. "No. It happened to me," I replied. My voice was starting to sound choked-up again. "It was all because of Hudson Calloway. I met him at the last party I went to."

Brooke's eyes widened. "Oh my god. Did he..."

I raised a palm and shook my head. "No. He didn't. But he sure as hell tried."

"That fucking asshole." April's face twisted with fury. "What happened?"

"Mikayla dragged me along to yet another shitty party at some mansion on the outskirts of Babylon. It was a birthday thing for some guy named Jamie Miller."

"Oh, I know him," Brooke cut in. "He's friends with my older brother. Total douche."

"Right." I briefly nodded. "Anyway, I usually don't mind having a drink or two at parties. But that night, I couldn't drink anything at all because my stomach had been feeling bad all day. So I was one-hundred percent sober. All I had was a glass of lemonade that I poured from a brand-new bottle that I opened myself. It *definitely* had nothing in it."

"Until you met Hudson, I'm guessing," April said. Her face was red with anger now.

I nodded and paused to clear my clogged throat. "Yeah. After a while, I started to feel weird. Really, really weird. Then several minutes of my life just disappeared. I have no idea what happened in those minutes. But when I opened my eyes, I was lying in a bed, and Hudson was on top of me. He was trying to take my jeans off, and he had this look in his eyes. A cold, dead look. Like a shark."

"What a piece of shit," Zach muttered.

"Even though I'd obviously been drugged with something, I guess he didn't give me enough, because I was still able to think and move. Enough to realize what was happening and defend myself."

"Please tell me you punched him right in the dick," April said, nostrils flaring.

"Close. I kneed him in the balls to get him off me. Really hard. While he was rolling around crying in pain, I got out of the bedroom and went back into the main party room. Then I grabbed the first set of keys I could find and ran outside. I clicked the key fob until a car unlocked... and I took it. I know it's not okay to steal a car, but I wasn't thinking straight."

"Of course you weren't," Brooke said. "You must've been terrified."

"Yeah. I was. I was also totally off my face on whatever the hell Hudson slipped into my lemonade. Whenever I think about it, it seems like it was a dream, because that's what it felt like when it was all happening."

"Sounds more like a nightmare than a dream."

"That's true." I clenched my jaw. "Anyway, because I was so messed up on the drugs Hudson spiked me with, I couldn't drive properly. I went off the road a few miles away and crashed right into a parked car."

"Maverick's car?"

"Yes. But he wasn't in it. No one was. That was lucky, because I T-boned it and totally fucked it up. If someone was inside it, they'd probably be dead now."

"That means you're lucky to be alive too," Brooke said softly, squeezing my hand.

"Yeah, I guess so." I sniffed and wiped my face again. "Anyway, everything was a shit-show after that. I was charged with a whole bunch of crap, which was no surprise. I mean, I was on drugs and stole a car. I could've killed someone in that crash."

"But it wasn't your fault!" April said. "None of it was!"

I shrugged. "I tried to tell them that. I gave them Hudson's name. Told them he drugged me and tried to attack me. But no one believed me."

"Seriously?"

I nodded. "The cops questioned him, but only because they had to after they heard my accusation. It was a waste of time. He said he never met me. Said he didn't even *see* me at the party. His friends all backed him up when they were questioned too, and they all said they'd seen me snorting stuff at the party. It was my word against all of theirs. And let's face it—cops in places like Babylon hardly ever believe people like me anyway. They believe and support the rich kids who circle the wagons to protect each other."

"I believe you, Carey," April said firmly. "I want you to know that right now. I totally believe you. A hundred percent."

"Me too," Brooke chimed in.

"I believe you too," Zach said. "Hudson is a fucking prick. Also, I know I'm rich, which probably makes me an asshole in a million different ways, but I'm at least self-aware enough to see how differently people like me get treated. I see the corruption and the cronyism. All the time."

"Thanks. It really means a lot that you guys believe me," I murmured. I cleared my throat again and went on. "But you know, my own parents didn't believe me. My mom told me that I'm just like my dad, because he's been in and out of lockup for decades, and my dad just laughed and told me I'm a chip off the old block. Mikayla didn't believe me either. So we aren't friends anymore. To be honest, when I arrived here, I didn't have a single friend in the whole world."

Brooke's eyes filled with sympathy. "That really sucks."

"Yeah." I pressed my lips into a thin line and slowly shook my head as the memories poured back in. "Anyway... Hudson lawyered up, thanks to his family, and I was probably going to get some serious jail-time when the case finally went to trial. But then the Babylon Foundation took pity on me and decided I deserved a chance at rehabilitation."

"Even though you did nothing wrong," April said, rolling her eyes. "Apart from trying to escape a piece of shit who was attacking you."

"Well, I guess they didn't know all those details. They were looking up active criminal cases for their new justice project, saw a wayward teen, and decided to offer a lifeline. I can't be mad about that, can I?"

"Guess not." Zach sighed. Then he cocked his head. "So what exactly happened this morning? Why were you so upset?"

"I ran into Hudson, and he..." I trailed off and twisted my lips. "Well, he threatened me. Not directly, but it was implied. He basically told me to keep my mouth shut."

"Or else he'd shut it for you?"

"He didn't say that, but it was implied," I said. "Even though no one believed me when all the shit went down, I think he's worried that people are eventually going to start believing me. Because it wasn't just the threat today."

I quickly filled my friends in on the bloodied effigy I found hanging over my bed yesterday afternoon. All three pairs of eyes filled with horror as I spoke.

"Oh my god," April said. "What the fuck?"

"I'm really scared," I admitted in a ragged whisper. "I think he might be planning something to hurt me. Get rid of me. All so his reputation isn't smeared or destroyed when I tell people the truth about him."

"We won't let that happen," Zach said in a firm voice, squaring his shoulders.

"But what if he goes after you guys too?" I said, heart thudding with anxiety. "Just for being on my side?"

"I don't give a fuck." Zach narrowed his eyes. "Hudson Calloway might be a piece of shit, but he's also a fucking idiot. The only reason he gets away with anything is because of his family. Not because he's smart enough to do it all himself. So as long as we stick together and protect each other, we should all be fine."

April nodded. "We won't let him get away with hurting you, Carey."

"I just wish you'd told us everything sooner," Brooke added, gently squeezing my arm again. "We could've helped you. Or at least comforted you. You didn't have to go through this alone."

I bit my lip and looked down at the ground. "I'm sorry. I was just so embarrassed. And scared, too," I murmured. "I was also worried you wouldn't believe me, just like everyone else."

"I get it," April said. "But don't worry. We believe you, and Hudson isn't going to get away with this shit."

"Thanks." My throat tightened with another rush of emotion. "Really. Thank you so much."

"That's what friends are for."

"I'm sorry, I totally hate to ruin this moment, but we should really get to our homeroom," Zach said, looking at his phone. "The bell is about to ring."

"We'll talk about this more at lunch, okay?" Brooke said, giving me a small smile.

"Sure. Thanks, guys."

She and Zach headed off down the hedge-lined path that ran alongside the stone bench, and April and I went in the opposite direction. We had our shared homeroom first thing, followed by our English class. I was extremely grateful for that because it meant I had a friend to sit with for a while, unlike so many of my other classes where I had to sit alone and endure all the nasty words and cold stares thrown at me.

During the first few minutes of our English class, Professor Garrick went around the room handing out the results of a pop quiz we took a few days ago. "Good job, Carey," he remarked, giving me a faint smile as he placed mine down.

I looked down at the paper to see that I'd once again received a good mark. I was totally killing it in this class. That was one bright light on the dark horizon of my life right now.

Professor Garrick handed April's test back to her and headed over to the desk next to us. Then he doubled back and placed two black envelopes on our desks. "I forgot to give you these," he said. "They were on my desk this morning."

"What are they?" April asked, brows knitting with puzzlement.

"I'm not sure. Birthday party invitations, I presume," her father replied. He cleared his throat and raised his voice. "Which reminds me," he went on, addressing the whole class now. "I'm not your personal assistant, okay? If you want to hand out party invites, please do it yourself from now on."

April and I stared at each other with wide eyes. "What do you think it is?" she asked in a hushed tone, staring at her envelope as if it contained the government's nuclear launch codes.

"I'm guessing it's a party invitation, like your dad said," I replied, lightly shrugging.

"No one else in here got one," she said, eyes flickering with doubt. "At least not that I can see."

"Maybe it's a very exclusive party. You know, because we're so popular," I joked.

"Yeah. Maybe." She bit her bottom lip and slit the side of her envelope.

I did the same with mine and carefully pulled out the contents. As I did so, April unfolded hers on her desk. She gasped as she read the words on the paper, and my breath hitched in my chest as I scanned mine.

"What the hell?"

CAREY

"So we all got one?"

I peered around the group as we huddled over our lunch trays. Zach, Brooke, and April nodded and replied in unison. "Yup."

"It has to be a prank, right?" I said, unfolding the letter again. "It looks so over-the-top."

An emblem featuring a singular eye filled with printed Latin words and enigmatic symbols took up the top third of the page. Below was the so-called party invitation.

Dear Carey,

It is with great pleasure that the Galileo Society extends to you an invitation to an exclusive gathering at our esteemed headquarters. We are always keeping a watchful eye on potential members, and we believe you possess the qualities required to join our society.

Please arrive at 4 Sutherland Drive at 8:15 on the 28th of September. Ensure your discretion in this matter, as we value secrecy above all else. During your stay, our top-ranking members will conduct an interview to gauge if you are indeed a true candidate. If it is determined that you are *destined to be one of us, we will provide you with insights into our society's goals and principles. A formal initiation ceremony will then be held. Should you accept our invitation and successfully pass the initiation, you will join a lineage of individuals dedicated to the pursuit of wisdom and the protection of ancient truths.*

The dress code for the evening is casual, as we are far more interested in your mind than your appearance. All personal belongings, including electronic devices, shall be surrendered upon arrival, and they will be returned to you at the end of the night.

If you accept our invitation, kindly confirm your attendance by the 24th of September via this email address: galileomaster@galileosociety.com.

We eagerly anticipate your response.

Yours in secrecy,
The Galileo Society

"Definitely a prank," April said, nodding emphatically. "I've never heard of a secret society at Babylon."

"I have," Brooke said. She raised her brows and leaned forward, lowering her voice. "My mom was a student here back in the early 90s. She said there was a secret society that ended up getting banned by the administration. Apparently they were doing all sorts of crazy shit."

"Seriously?"

"Yup."

"But you said it's gone, right?"

Zach lifted a hand. "If it's a *secret* society, how can the school really ban it? They can say it's not allowed, but realistically, they can't stop it. Not if all the members are good secret-keepers."

April nodded slowly. "Fair point."

"Also," Zach went on. "If it's a prank, what's the point of it? I don't get it."

"Maybe it's Maverick. Or Hudson," I said, stomach flipping. "Trying to lure us all somewhere to mess with us."

"I don't think so, because we aren't the only people who received these invitations," Brooke said.

I frowned. "You saw other people get them?"

"Yes. I got mine in first period math, and I saw Courteney Phang get one at the same time. I'm pretty sure Evan Holt got one too, but it was hard to tell because there was so much shit on his desk."

"Hudson wouldn't have any reason to mess with Courteney or Evan," Zach said, brows furrowing. "I don't think Maverick would either. So I really don't think it's a prank designed to fuck with us."

"Okay, but if it's real, why did *we* get invited?" I asked, forehead wrinkling. "Out of anyone in the school, why us? And why Courteney and Evan?"

"Well, it sounds like they're looking for smart people, given that line about being interested in our minds over our appearances," Brooke replied. "And not to brag, but I'm number one in chem. Also, I remember something about Courteney being good at geography. Or maybe it was geology. Something like that."

April sat up straight, face brightening. "That must be it!" she said. "I'm top of the class in trig. And Carey, you're really good at coding and robotics. You're probably at the top of that class, right?"

"Er, honestly... I didn't know we could check class rankings," I admitted.

"I bet you're number one. That would explain it. The society wants the smartest students."

Zach sighed and looked at the ground. "I'm not number one in anything."

"But you're so good at history. You always get the best marks there."

"I'm only number two in the class." He paused and scratched his chin. "Actually, I think I totally bombed last week's test, so I might have slipped to three. I've been too afraid to check, to be honest."

"Two or three is still really good, so I think Brooke is right," April replied. "The Galileo Society probably invites the top three students in every subject. That way they get a large selection of smart kids as potential members."

"Are you guys going to go?" Brooke asked, looking at each of us in turn with wide eyes.

"I'll go," Zach said with a light shrug. "Might as well see what it's about."

April's lips thinned. "I don't know if I will. My interview time is 7:30, and I'm pretty sure I have a family dinner that night. It's my cousin's birthday."

"Just make an excuse to get out of it!" Brooke said. "Mine is 9:45, and that means I'll have to sneak out of the dorms and risk getting in trouble. But I'm totally going to do it, and so should you! I mean, aren't you even a *little* curious about this stuff?"

April twisted her lips in contemplation. "I guess so. I can probably come up with an excuse." She turned to me. "Carey, what about you? Are you thinking of going?"

I hesitated. Part of me still wondered if this invitation was a prank orchestrated by Hudson or Maverick to mess with me and my friends.

The thought of Hudson being behind it troubled me the most. As I said to my friends earlier, I was worried he was planning something to destroy me, and I knew a nasty guy like him wouldn't hesitate to include the three of them in that destruction.

Then again, Zach had informed me earlier that Hudson was an asshole but also a total idiot. Coming up with a fake secret society was probably a bit beyond his planning capabilities. Also, there was the matter of other students being invited. Courteney Phang and Evan Holt had nothing to do with me. I'd never even met either of them. There could be other students invited, too.

The more I thought about it, the more I realized it probably *wasn't* a prank or trick of any kind. It seemed far too elaborate, even for Babylon bully standards.

Another aspect I needed to consider was the potential benefit for my life if the Galileo Society was real. I'd read a lot of books about real-life secret societies, and the common thread amongst them was the way they aided their members with opportunities and connections. My future was already looking brighter with the help of the Babylon Foundation's scholarship, but an elite secret society membership could make all the difference between a good future and a seriously great future.

That thought alone sealed it for me.

I took a deep breath and nodded. "I'm going."

CAREY

I anxiously glanced at my phone to check the time. 8:09.

Shit. I was probably going to be late. Not a good look for a person attempting to join an enigmatic secret society which presumably valued punctuality.

I leaned forward to speak to the Uber driver I'd booked to take me to 4 Sutherland Drive. "Hey, sorry, are we almost there?"

"Yeah. Couple more minutes," he said, tilting his head to glance at the GPS mounted on the dash. "One more turn and we're there."

Breathing a quiet sigh of relief, I sat back again. I was going to make it after all.

I turned my gaze to the window, nervous energy churning in my stomach as I watched the car's headlights slice through the night. With a jolt, we lurched around a sharp bend in the hilly coastal road. A huge set of wrought iron gates appeared on the right, guarded by grotesque gargoyles sitting atop towering stone pillars on either side.

As the car slowed, the gates swung open with an ominous creak, revealing a long driveway flanked by overgrown hedges. At the end loomed a colossal Gothic mansion, its spiky silhouette menacing against the moonlit sky.

"You sure this is the right address?" the Uber driver asked, glancing back at me as we headed down the driveway. "Doesn't look like anyone's home. No lights on or anything."

"Um... yeah. I'm going to a murder mystery party," I replied. "It's meant to look a bit creepy."

"Ah, that makes sense." He nodded briskly. "Have a nice night. And don't forget to rate me."

"No problem." I pulled my phone out of my pocket and hit the five-star button on the screen as I stepped out of the car. "Thanks!"

Tires loudly crunched over gravel as the car maneuvered to head back up the driveway. With a deep breath, I approached the imposing wooden doors at the front of the mansion. A large, ugly wrought iron knocker adorned one of the doors, mirroring the hideous figures perched atop the gate pillars. Just as I reached for it, I noticed the left-hand door was slightly ajar.

I tentatively pushed the door open and stepped into the foyer. The faint glow of candlelight danced across the space, casting eerie shadows that made the place seem alive despite the lack of people.

I glanced at my phone again. 8:14. Just in time.

"Um... hello?" I called out, peering around. On my left was a closed door. Directly ahead lay a soaring double staircase, winding up to unseen levels. On the right was an open doorway, but it was too dark to see anything beyond it.

"Good evening, Miss Saracen."

I almost jumped out of my skin at the sound of the voice behind me. It wasn't human—it was one of those robotic modulated voices that could only be achieved with the aid of a device.

Heart racing, I whirled around to face the person. I had no idea where they'd appeared from, and their appearance was even more confounding. They were dressed in a black hooded robe that hid any physical features that could determine their sex, and a black mask with magenta neon lights covered their face. The lights formed crosses over the eyes and a pattern over the mouth which gave it the appearance of lips that had been stitched shut.

"My apologies for startling you, Miss Saracen," the person said. The robotic voice was devoid of emotion. "You're right on time. May I have your phone, please?"

I handed over my cell, and they dipped their head in a polite nod. "Thank you. Please follow me."

I swallowed hard as I trailed behind them, heading through a narrow passage that ran beyond the stairway. I hadn't noticed it when I looked around earlier because it was so dim in this place.

We arrived in a lounge with a bar on the left side. The space was lit by a roaring fire in a hearth on the other side. In the center lay a low coffee table surrounded by two ornate chaise sofas with deep purple velvet covers and golden accents.

The creepy masked guy—I'd decided the person was probably male based on their towering height—beckoned me toward the bar area. I followed him, and he stooped behind it to pick up a silver tray. Two cocktail glasses sat on it. They were filled with dark purple liquid and decorated with gold flecks and maraschino cherries.

"My employers are still conducting their interview with the previous candidate, and they send their sincere apologies for their tardiness," he said. "Please accept one of the society's traditional welcome libations to enjoy while you wait. It's a cherry-liqueur-based cocktail. The left one is a non-alcoholic version, if you prefer that."

"Um..." I bit my lip. "I'd like to try the non-alcoholic drink, but would it be okay if I got a fresh one? Sorry to be a pain. I just don't like accepting drinks when I—"

The masked man lifted a hand to cut me off. "Of course. I understand completely," he said. "You feel more comfortable seeing the drink made in front of you."

"Yes. I, uhh... I've had bad experiences in the past."

"No need to explain." He turned to a minifridge behind him and pulled out three bottles. Lemonade, cherry liqueur, and cherry juice. Then he grabbed a bottle of flavored sugar syrup from a high shelf above him. "All new bottles," he went on, breaking the seal on each one to show me they were indeed unopened before now. "Your drink will be ready in no time."

"Thanks."

After a moment of stirring and shaking, the neon-masked man placed a brand-new cocktail in front of me. "One virgin drink for you, Miss Saracen, courtesy of the Galileo Society."

"Thank you." I lifted the glass to take a sip of the sweet concoction. "Mmm. Very nice."

The masked man motioned toward the lounge chairs. "Please have a seat. I'll check with my employers to see how much longer you'll need to wait."

With that, he stepped out from behind the bar and disappeared into the darkness of the hall, thick robes loudly swishing around him.

I headed over to one of the chairs and sat down, drink in hand. As I took another sip, a wave of tiredness washed over me. Today had been a very long day. Hopefully I could still pull off the interview followed by a successful initiation.

God, what on Earth was even going to happen during this initiation? All week, movie-style images of flaming torches, stone altars, and sacrificial daggers had played nonstop in my head, but at the end of the day, I still had no idea what to expect.

First things first, I reminded myself. I wouldn't have to worry about the initiation ceremony if I failed the interview segment. I needed to stay calm and collected. Give all the right answers. Prove I was a good candidate for membership.

Sipping at my drink, I mulled over potential questions, but I struggled to focus, overwhelmed with nerves. I sat up straight and took a deep breath, telling myself to get my shit together. I couldn't let anxiety get to me now. Not when I'd already made it so far.

Despite my best efforts to center myself, the nerves intensified, twisting my stomach into knots. Each breath felt shallower, each heartbeat louder, like a drumbeat of impending danger. A sudden wave of dizziness hit me, and panic surged, a cold knot tightening in my chest.

"Oh, no," I gasped, the realization hitting me like a sledgehammer. This wasn't regular nerves. I recognized this feeling, a sinister echo from a past encounter.

The drink… it was spiked.

Fear gripped me as the pieces fell into place with chilling clarity. My initial suspicion about the invitation was correct after all. There was no secret society. This was a trap. A carefully orchestrated scheme to ensnare me in a web of danger. My friends, too.

The implication sent shivers down my spine. The effort it had taken someone to lure us here tonight, one by one, marked the extent of the trouble we were in. Clearly, whatever awaited us in this dark mansion was far more sinister than I could ever imagine. Why else would they go to so much trouble?

I set the cocktail glass down on the table with a clatter, mind racing. April's interview time was 7:30, meaning she'd probably already fallen prey to the same trick as me. But I could still warn Brooke and Zach. *Don't come here.*

I reached into my pocket for my phone, only to recall with a sinking feeling that I'd handed it over upon my arrival as per the masked man's request.

"Shit!"

I stood abruptly to make a run for it before he returned, but my muscles betrayed me, growing heavy and unresponsive as the room spun around me.

I took a wobbly step and immediately crumpled to my knees, letting out a pained grunt. Feeling too weak to get up again, I sank all the way to the floor, sucking down shallow, shaky breaths.

With each passing second, consciousness slipped further from my grasp. The last coherent thought I had was about the drink. How did the man spike it? It didn't seem possible.

As if summoned by my thoughts, he materialized before me, neon mask aglow, casting a disorienting kaleidoscope of light across my blurred vision. "Sorry, Miss Saracen," the robotic voice said crisply. "You were so careful, unlike the others, but it was already in the glass. You couldn't have known."

"Wh-why are you doing this?" I slurred, barely able to keep my eyelids open. "What... what others?"

"You'll see," came the response.

In a final effort to fight the encroaching darkness, I reached out to grab the bottom of his robe, hoping the act of forcing myself to cling to them would keep me awake. My grasping hands found only empty air. The man was gone.

Then, with another wave of dizziness, I was gone too.

CAREY

As I slowly stirred awake, my eyelids fluttered open to reveal an unfamiliar ceiling above me. Confusion crept in as I realized I was lying in a strange bed, covered in a thick plush blanket. The only light in the room came from a dim bulb overhead, but it was enough to clearly show the room around me—large with a stacked bookshelf, desk, closet, paintings adorning the walls, and a door on the opposite wall that presumably led into a bathroom.

With a groan, I attempted to piece together the events of the previous night, but my mind was muddled, memories slipping through my grasp like oil. My mouth was dry, and a faint ache throbbed at the base of my skull, silently indicating a severe hangover. This was no hangover, though. Something was different here. *Off.* I could sense it deep inside me, even though my memories were still shrouded in fog.

With hesitant movements, I pushed myself up to rest on my elbows, slowly blinking the sleep out of my eyes. The sense of unease in my gut grew as I slid out of bed and walked over to the window to orient myself. When I yanked the curtains open, a gasp escaped my mouth, and I took a faltering step backward, heart pounding.

There was nothing to see but a closed steel storm shutter which blocked off the view from the window entirely. Even a sliver of light couldn't slip through.

Whirling around, I spotted a large white envelope on the bedside table, along with... *oh my god.* My phone!

I hurried over and grabbed it, rapidly tapping on the screen to activate it. With a sinking feeling, I realized it wasn't my phone at all. It looked the same, but it was empty apart from one blue app that simply said 'Messages'. There was no cell reception or internet connection.

"Oh, shit," I whispered, panic surging. "Shit, shit, *shit*."

Memories were pouring in now, fueled by the adrenaline racing through my veins. I recalled the mansion, the masked man, the spiked drink, the feeling of sheer terror twisting in my guts... then nothing.

I snatched up the envelope and tore it open. With shaky hands, I unfolded the letter within and scanned the neatly printed words.

Dear Carey,

Welcome to the games!

I trust you slept well after the nightcap. You will find clean clothes in the closet and toiletries in the bathroom. Please shower and dress, and then make your way to the drawing room for breakfast at 9am.

You will find a phone on your bedside table. There is no cell service or internet connectivity, so you will be unable to contact anyone on the outside. However, it is connected to a house-wide intranet that will allow me to contact you via the messaging app on the home screen. You can also use the app to message me or the other participants, if need be.

Thank you for coming to play!

Yours truly,
The Game Master

I re-read the letter over and over, head spinning like I'd just stepped off a rollercoaster. What the hell was going on here? Who was the Game Master? Why did they thank me for 'coming to play'? Play *what*, exactly? And who were the other players?

It suddenly occurred to me that I hadn't tried the bedroom door yet. I'd seen the sealed window a moment ago and assumed I was locked in this room, but the letter made it sound like I was free to leave it whenever I wanted.

Springing to my feet, I hurried over and twisted the doorknob. It was unlocked. I turned it all the way and hesitated as I felt the door open a crack. Something was stopping me from opening it properly. Nothing physical; just a mental block. I was afraid of what I might find outside. Afraid that this room might be my only safe space in the mansion.

I quietly closed the door and followed the letter's request for me to take a shower, figuring it might help to calm me down and prepare me for whatever lay in the hall beyond. It didn't work. By the time I was done, I was still trembling with a mix of fear and confusion, wondering if this was all a nightmare that I couldn't wake up from.

I glanced at the top right corner of the phone. It was 7:43. Still plenty of time before I had to find the drawing room.

I padded over to the closet and opened it to see a row of identical gray sweaters hanging over a shelf containing at least twenty pairs of neatly folded black sweatpants. Black sneakers in my size had also been provided in a drawer beside the shelf, surrounded by countless rolled-up pairs of black socks and underwear.

"I wonder what I should wear today?" I muttered to myself, hoping the vague attempt at humor might help somewhat with the dread churning in the pit of my stomach.

It didn't, of course. Nothing in the world could prepare me to step out of this room. I just had to suck it up and get it over and done with.

With a deep breath, I opened the door and stepped out into the hallway. It was empty. When I looked to the left and right, I could see that my room was one of many in this hall. I was in the fourth one along from the staircase landing on the far right, and there were two more doors before the hall ended on the other side. There were also six rooms on the opposite side of the hall.

If every room was occupied, then that meant there were twelve 'players' in this terrifying situation.

A faint scuffing sound on the carpet snapped my attention toward the staircase landing.

"Oh my god!" I said, eyes widening as I spotted the person at the top of the stairs. "Brooke!"

I broke into a run a second later, and she did the same. "Carey! Thank God! I've been so worried," she said in a choked tone, throwing her arms around me. "Have you seen the others?"

"April and Zach? No." I pulled back from the hug, voice thickening with emotion. "I'm so sorry. I wanted to warn you, but they—"

"They took your phone. I know," Brooke said hurriedly. "They did the same to me. By the time I realized I was drugged, it was too late. I couldn't warn Zach not to come."

"Do you remember much about what happened?" I asked.

She swallowed audibly before replying. "I had a weird feeling the second I got here. It just seemed... empty," she said. "Apart from the guy in the weird mask. Did you see him too? Or was it someone else for you?"

"Was it a black mask with purple lights?"

Brooke nodded. "Same guy, then. When did you wake up?"

"About twenty minutes ago. I only just worked up the courage to leave my room a few seconds ago."

"I don't blame you," she replied. "I woke up at five, and I was too scared to leave until seven."

My brows rose. "So you've been exploring?"

"Sort of. There's not much to explore. You'll see why when you go down the stairs. But..." She trailed off, averting her eyes. "I bumped into some people. They were lured here and drugged, just like us."

"Who?"

Brooke still wouldn't meet my eyes. "Hudson and Maverick. Oh, and Rhys Whitmer was with them. You don't know him, but he's Hudson's best friend."

"I knew it!" Fury surged in my chest, and I clenched my hands into fists. "I knew at least one of those assholes was behind this shit! I—"

Brooke interrupted me again. "Carey, wait. This is exactly why I was so reluctant to tell you," she said, grabbing my arm. "I knew you'd think that, and I totally thought the same thing when I first ran into them. But they really, *really* don't seem to have any idea what's going on."

I took a deep breath and unclenched my hands. "Are you sure?"

"Yes. Very sure. They're just as confused and freaked out as us."

I pursed my lips, unsure if I believed that. Brooke seemed certain, though, and I didn't want to argue with her. "What did you find downstairs?" I asked, glancing to the right.

"Not much. There are hallways and doors in every direction, but they're all sealed off with the same sort of steel shutters that are on our windows." Brooke sighed and shook her head. "Except one. It's the drawing room."

"You went in?"

"Not yet. We only found it a minute ago. The guys wanted to go in and check it out, but I decided to come back up here to see if anyone else was awake yet. That's when I saw you." She paused and looked over my shoulder. "Maybe everyone else is already in the drawing room. Or maybe they're still sleeping. I don't know. I don't even know how many people are here."

"I guess we should go to the drawing room and wait. The others will show up eventually, right? Because of the letter."

Brooke nodded. "Yeah, you're right. We should—"

Her words abruptly dried up as the door directly to our left opened a crack. I stared at it, eyes wide, and watched as it swung farther open to reveal a pretty face with red-rimmed eyes.

"What the hell are *you* doing here?" Jasmine Briarwood snapped, glaring down at me.

My lips tightened. "Nice to see you too," I said in a withering tone, crossing my arms.

"What the fuck is going on here? Did you two losers plan this bullshit to get back at me or something?" she asked, drawing herself up to her full height as her gaze flicked between me and Brooke. She was clearly trying to seem fearless and imperious, but the slight crack in her voice betrayed her underlying distress.

"No." Brooke shook her head. "We woke up here, just like you."

"What about last night? Were you invited here? With the weird black letter about the Galileo Society?"

"Yes."

"I should've known it wasn't a real secret society. Not if they were inviting people like *you*," Jasmine said, nostrils flaring with disdain as she looked at me again.

"And that's my cue. Always a pleasure, Jasmine," I said. With that, I turned around and marched down the hall, Brooke at my side.

"Wait!" Jasmine hurried after us. "Let me come with you!"

"Are you sure you want to hang out with losers like us?" Brooke asked, looking over her shoulder.

Jasmine's face had gone pale, and her hands were shaking. "Look, I just... I don't want to be alone, okay?" she said in a small voice. "I have no idea what's going on."

"Fine. Come with us," I said flatly. "But one more bitchy comment and you're on your own again."

She nodded and remained silent until we reached the staircase. "Is the drawing room down there?" she asked, peering over the baluster.

I nodded. "We haven't gone in yet. We're going now to see if the others are there."

"Wait!" A familiar voice called out behind us, and we whirled around to see April and Zach hurrying down the hallway, faces etched with a mix of panic and relief.

Brooke and I dashed back up the hall and threw our arms around them, clinging to them both for what felt like an eternity. Jasmine awkwardly hung back during the reunion, arms folded and lips pursed.

"Are you okay?" April asked, voice muffled against my shoulder.

"Not really," I said softly. "I'm scared. I don't know what's going on."

"Me neither. This shit is crazy." She finally broke away from the hug and tilted her head. "Do you remember anything about last night?"

"Yes. I was drugged."

Her eyes widened. "By a person in a mask?"

"Yup."

"Us too," April said, motioning to Zach.

"I woke up in that room down there," he added in a tremulous tone, pointing to the second-last door on the right. "The first thing I saw was this creepy letter telling me to find the drawing room. April's room is near mine, so we ran into each other when we left."

"We're heading to the drawing room now," I said. "Oh, and by the way... apparently Hudson Calloway, Maverick Reinhart, and Rhys Whitmer are here too."

April's eyes widened. "You're kidding. Those fucking ass—"

Brooke held up a palm. "They aren't behind this," she said hurriedly. "They were brought here and drugged the same way we were."

"Right." April looked at me with raised brows, and I could see that her bullshit radar was going off the same way mine did when I first heard the news. "Well... let's go and see, I guess."

We headed back to the staircase and descended, one by one. As Brooke described earlier, almost every doorway and window on the ground floor level was blocked off by thick steel barriers, leaving only one hall open on the far right of the foyer. A door at the end stood slightly ajar. Voices drifted out from the room beyond.

Zach entered first. The rest of us followed him, taking in the drawing room with wide-eyed wonder. It was a large and elegant space filled with ornate furnishings, oil paintings, and statues, all warmly lit by a bronze and crystal chandelier that hung from the center of the wood-paneled ceiling. An enormous wooden table sat in the middle, laden with silver trays of food, coffee and tea pots on warmers, and glass juice jugs. Chairs with carved features and purple velvet cushions surrounded the table. There were twelve altogether, and four of them were occupied.

Maverick sat at the head of the table, with Hudson to his right. A lanky blond guy was on his left; presumably Rhys Whitmer. A beautiful girl with smooth brown skin and catlike green eyes sat next to him. I recognized her as Kiara Swift, famous influencer and owner of the finsta account that posted all the nasty stuff about me a few weeks ago. She was also Jasmine's best friend.

"Oh my god, babe!" She sprang up and hugged Jasmine as soon as she spotted her. "I've been waiting for you!"

While the two of them embraced, the rest of us looked over at Maverick, Hudson, and Rhys.

"Did you guys find anything?" I asked.

"And when did Kiara get here?" Brooke added.

"She was in here when we came to check it out," Maverick said. "Apparently, she woke up at six and came straight down here. She said she figured she'd wait for the others to show up."

"Fair enough."

"There's also this." Maverick pointed to an embossed card in front of him. "Name cards."

I squinted at each card in turn until I found mine at the opposite end. April went around the table carefully examining each card. Then she went to her assigned spot and pulled out the chair. "There's twelve of us, if these cards are accurate," she said. "Nine of us are already here, and there's also Courteney Phang, Tate Salinas, and Evan Holt."

"Yeah, I know. I read them earlier." Maverick leaned forward. "Did you see the other three anywhere?"

"No." April shook her head. "They must be in their rooms."

"I guess so. Oh, and there's one more thing," Maverick gestured behind us, and we all turned to look.

A huge flatscreen TV hung on the wall. It was off, but a tiny red light at the bottom let us know it was plugged in somewhere and presumably working.

"Did you find a remote anywhere?" April asked, scanning the room again.

"No. We looked everywhere," Rhys said. "There's nothing in here. Not counting the furniture and the food."

Hudson still hadn't said a word. He'd been glowering at me from his spot at the table since the second I walked in, but I kept pretending not to notice. Fuck him.

April opened her mouth to speak again, but she was interrupted by the arrival of the final three—Tate, Evan, and Courteney. It was obvious who Courteney was, because she was the only girl in the trio, but I wasn't sure who was who when it came to the guys. Both were tall with pale skin. One had prematurely receded brown hair, and the other had curly ginger hair.

"Oh, thank fucking *God*, there's food!" one of them said,

making a beeline for the table. He snatched up a croissant from a tray and lifted it to his mouth.

Rhys stood and knocked it out of his hand before he could take a bite. "Don't be such a dumbass, Tate!" he said. "This shit could be poisoned!"

So that was Tate, meaning the redhead was Evan.

Maverick stood, jaw set like granite. "We're all here now," he said. "Let's try to figure out what the fuck is going on."

Everyone started talking at once, so Maverick briskly clapped his hands to attract everyone's attention back to him. "One at a time!" he said. "Let's go around the table and say how we got here. We might have different stories. Rhys, you first."

The twelve of us shared the same story. We were all given letters in black envelopes inviting us to the so-called Galileo Society, and each of us had shown up at the mansion on 4 Sutherland Drive for the interview, only to find ourselves drugged by the welcome cocktail.

"We all had different times written in our letters, right?" April asked, looking around the group. "So they could take us one by one."

"I think so." Maverick nodded curtly. "Let's go around the table again and say what time we were given."

April was right. Every single one of us had received a different time in our invitations, fifteen minutes apart.

"Who was the first to arrive?" April asked, cocking her head. "Hudson, right?"

Hudson simply grunted, and Maverick nodded. "Yeah, at 7:00. That was the earliest time anyone said."

"Who gives a fuck?" Rhys said, eyes narrowing. "The time doesn't matter."

"We don't know that for sure," Brooke replied in an acid tone. "I'd say the first person to arrive is the most suspicious."

"Exactly," April said. "That's why I asked."

Hudson finally spoke up. "Look, I had nothing to do with this shit, okay?" he said. "I have no fucking clue what's going on in this place. All I want to do is get the fuck out of here, but every single door, hallway, and window is blocked off. We're sealed in."

"Speaking of this place..." Courteney tentatively piped up from her spot between Zach and Brooke. "I don't really know how to explain it, but it seems really familiar."

Rhys snorted. "No shit. We were all here last night, genius."

A pink blush rapidly bloomed on Courteney's cheeks. "That's not what I meant," she said softly, lowering her eyes to the empty plate in front of her. "Something about it feels familiar, and it's not because of last night. I feel like I've been here before, even though I know I haven't."

"I get it," Zach said in a sympathetic tone. His hand was close to hers, and he gave her a brief, reassuring pat. "I was actually thinking the same thing. Déjà vu."

Courteney looked up at him with a small, grateful smile. If we weren't all trapped in such a petrifying situation, I'd think it was a cute moment between the two of them.

"So you guys have looked around?" Evan asked, raising his brows. "Everything is definitely blocked off?"

"Yup." Maverick nodded. "It's obvious that this is a big place, but almost every doorway is sealed, so we can't explore most of it."

"This is so fucking weird." Tate started pacing around the room. "What the fuck is going on? Why *us*?"

"No idea. That's what we're trying to figure out," Maverick said, signaling for him to sit down again. "Did we all see the same person when we got here?"

"Good question," April said. "I assumed it was the same person for all of us, but who knows? For me, it was a tall person with a black cloak and mask with magenta lights on it."

"Me too," I said. "I got the impression it was a man, but I can't be sure because of that weird voice-changer thing they were using."

"Why did you think it was a man?" Jasmine asked, looking over at me with an expression that suggested she'd just witnessed me crawling out of a dumpster.

"Because they were really tall."

"I'm six-two in my favorite heels," she said, rolling her eyes. "It could totally have been a woman."

My lips tightened. "I don't think so. It really seemed more like a guy."

"Smells like internalized misogyny to me," Kiara said. "I guess all women are meant to be small and weak and totally—"

"Shut up, Kiara," Maverick cut in. "Carey wasn't saying that. She was just saying that the person was very tall, and on average, men are taller, so it's statistically likely that this person was male. Right?"

"Yeah, exactly," I said, eyes widening with surprise. This was the second time Maverick had jumped to my defense even though he absolutely despised me. "They looked around six feet three or four to me, so I assumed it was a guy. But I guess it could've been a woman. I don't know for sure. I was just saying what I thought at the time, that's all."

Maverick dropped his gaze from me. "Did we all see the same person? Very tall with the black cloak and mask that April described a minute ago?" he asked. Everyone nodded, and he went on. "Great. That means we probably all saw the same person."

"Which means we might only be dealing with one person here," Evan said, scratching his chin. "But who? And why?"

"Did anyone notice anything about the guy at all?" Maverick asked. "Anything that could be used to identify him?"

Everyone shook their heads except Brooke. "When he was pouring my drink, one of his gloves moved a little. I saw a flash of his wrist. There wasn't much to see. Like, no tattoos or hair that I noticed. But the person is white. I saw that much."

Maverick steepled his hands on the table. "Is everyone willing to concede that this person is probably a man?" he asked, giving

Kiara a pointed look. She rolled her eyes, but she still nodded along with everyone else. "Okay. Now we also know he's white. So can anyone think of a tall white guy who might want to pull some crazy shit like this with the twelve of us?"

"Who would ever want to do this with *any* of us?" Courteney asked, eyes wide.

"I have no idea." Rhys shook his head. "Someone who hates rich people, maybe? We could've been taken for ransom."

"Not all of us have rich parents. Carey, for example," Hudson said, staring at me. His superior tone shot disgust through my veins like poison, and I lifted my chin and glared right back at him, unable to mask my hatred.

"I don't think it's a ransom scheme," April said. "This is too elaborate for something like that. Right?"

"I don't know. People are willing to do all sorts of crazy shit for money," Evan said with a shrug.

A lightbulb seemed to go off in my head. I sat up straight. "It doesn't really matter who it is in the end."

"Well, of course *you* don't think it matters that we're being held captive in some creepy old mansion," Kiara said with another exaggerated eyeroll. "You criminals all have to stick together, right?"

I could feel a warm flush creeping over my chest and neck, but I kept my composure. "That's not what I'm saying," I replied. "I was just saying it doesn't matter because they won't get away with it for long. I mean, we all sneaked off campus last night, didn't we?"

Understanding dawned on multiple faces around the table, but Tate, Jasmine, and Hudson continued to look confused.

"So what?" Tate asked.

"So the school will eventually realize that we've all disappeared. Actually, they probably already have."

"How does that help us? It's not like they know where we went."

"Jesus, man, how slow are you?" Rhys said, upper lip curling. "Think about it. Twelve students from an elite boarding school have gone missing. The cops will see it as their number one priority."

"Exactly. And I don't know about you guys, but I got an Uber to the mansion," I said. "That means anyone who's looking for me can just check my Uber account, if that's possible, and get my last known drop-off address. Or maybe they can trace my phone's GPS signal. I'm not sure. But you see my point, right?"

April nodded. "I got an Uber too. So once the school alerts the police about the missing students, they'll eventually realize that all twelve of us went to 4 Sutherland Drive last night."

"They're probably already looking for us," Maverick said. "Like Rhys just said, twelve Babylon students going missing is a big fucking deal. So it's only a matter of time until they track us here and knock the door down."

"Thank god," Kiara said, inspecting a fingernail. "I can't wait for this bullshit to be over."

"I have a feeling it hasn't even started yet," Courteney murmured.

The screen on the wall suddenly lit up, revealing a crystal-clear image of the same masked person who drugged each of us the previous night. He was sitting in a dim room on an ornately carved chair that resembled a wooden throne.

"That's him!" Jasmine said, pointing a shaky finger at the screen.

"No shit, genius," Zach muttered.

"Hello, everyone." The familiar robotic voice filled the room as the masked man tilted his head onscreen. "I hope you're all enjoying your breakfast. Don't worry—nothing on the table is laced, so if that's been a concern for you up until now, feel free to dig in. You'll need your energy for the next few days."

He paused and lifted a hand onscreen, gesturing to the spread on the table. Tate tentatively leaned forward and grabbed the same croissant Rhys had knocked out of his hand earlier. "Fuck it," he muttered. "I'm starving."

He took a bite and chewed rapidly. Then he gagged and started clutching at his throat before letting out a loud guffaw. "It's fine," he said, voice garbled by the mouthful of food. "No poison."

"Do you really think you're funny?" Kiara said in a snide tone. "Because you're actually a stupid, childish asshole, and this type of bullshit is exactly why no one invites you to anything unless you say you'll bring—"

The masked man started talking again, interrupting Kiara's rant. "You're no doubt wondering who I am and why you're here," he said. "You can call me the Game Master. I have carefully selected each of you to participate in a series of challenges. Each challenge scenario has been designed in the form of a game. If you play well and manage to survive until the final round, you will be awarded with the ultimate prize—your freedom. However, if you die during one of the games, you're out. For good."

He paused again for dramatic effect, and a collective gasp resounded through the room.

"If we *die?*" Jasmine shrieked, leaping to her feet. She looked around the table with a wild-eyed expression. "This is a fucking joke, right?"

"Of course it is. It has to be," April said. Despite her firm words, her wide eyes and pale face made it clear she wasn't sure.

"You may be tempted to assume this is some sort of prank," the Game Master went on. "Let me assure you, for your own safety, that this is no joke. If you fail a challenge, you *will* die. I cannot be any clearer about that."

Maverick stared at the screen, stony-faced. "Who the fuck are you?"

The Game Master paused again. Then he leaned forward, masked face ominously close to the camera. "Oh, and one more thing," he said. "This is a pre-recorded message. I couldn't address you live, because I'm actually in the room with you right now."

Jasmine whirled around, eyes practically on stalks. "Where the fuck is he?" she screamed. "Come out, asshole!"

"I don't think that's what he meant," I muttered, heart aching with fear.

The Game Master leaned back in his chair. "That's right, everyone," he said, cocking his head. "The Game Master is one of you."

CAREY

Everyone started talking or shouting at the same time.

"What the fuck?"

"This isn't real. No way."

"No fucking way."

"This has to be a joke."

I couldn't even figure out who was saying what. I just sat back and stared fearfully at each person in turn, trying to figure out the most likely suspect. I wanted to believe Hudson was behind everything, but I wasn't sure how he'd be able to pull it off, given his supposed lack of intelligence.

Then again, if he had help...

"It's obvious who this so-called Game Master is," Evan said, snapping his fingers to draw everyone's gazes to him. His own eyes came to rest on my face. "Carey."

"What?" I sat up straight, eyes bulging. "*Me?*"

Evan sneered. "Yeah, *you*. Don't act all innocent. I know it's you."

"How can it be her?" April asked, glaring over at him. "Does she look like a tall man to you?"

"Use your brain, April."

"I could say the same to you," she replied hotly. "If you're going to throw accusations around, you need to back them up with some sort of evidence."

"Fine." Evan rolled his eyes. "Think about it. We've all been at school together for twelve years, not counting her, and we've never had any issues like this. Then *she* shows up, and within a month we all end up trapped in a fucking murder mansion."

"That doesn't make any sense," April said. "In fact, your reasoning for why it has to be Carey is actually a reason why it *can't* be her. She barely knows anyone. So why would she arrange something like this? And how? She doesn't come from money."

"I don't know about the money part, but it's pretty clear why she'd want to do something like this," Jasmine said, arching a brow. "Everyone has hated her and treated her like shit since she started at Babylon, and rightfully so, because she's a dirty little criminal. So obviously, she wants revenge."

"Speak for yourself," Zach said. "I'm friends with Carey, and I've never treated her badly. Same with April and Brooke."

"Me too," Courteney said, timidly raising a hand like we were in a classroom. "I mean... I'm not friends with Carey, because I don't know her, but we aren't enemies either. I've never done anything to her and vice versa. She has no reason to want revenge on me."

Evan narrowed his eyes and turned his focus back to April. "Okay, so maybe it's the four friends in on it together," he said. "You, Zach, and Brooke teamed up with Carey to help her get revenge on the rest of us. And I guess Courteney was brought here because Zach has an obvious crush on her, so it's an easy way for him to get close to her while the rest of us are getting destroyed."

"Oh my god." April rolled her eyes. "That's so ridiculous."

"Is it?" Kiara leaned forward. "Your family are literally military contractors. You totally could've built something like this."

April snorted. "Oh, sure," she said, throwing her hands up. "I just called my parents, along with the US Army and the Pentagon, and asked if they'd help me set something up to deal with some kids at school who are being mean to my friend. That all sounds totally reasonable and realistic."

"Okay, fine," Evan replied. "Maybe *you* aren't involved, April. But I'm telling you, Carey definitely has something to do with this. She's the odd one out here. The one we know the least about. How do we know her scholarship story is actually true? How do we even know if Carey is her real name?"

"Maybe *you're* involved, and you're making all these wild claims to divert suspicion away from you," Maverick said, looking at Evan through narrowed eyes.

"Or maybe it's *you*, Mav," Evan retorted. "We all know you hate her and want her gone from Babylon. So maybe this is all a setup to get rid of her. Scare her out of town, or whatever."

Tate piped up. "Nah, my money's on Kiara."

"What?" Kiara screeched. "Are you serious?"

"Yeah. Think about it, guys. She could've set up this shit to build her influencer career even more," Tate said, putting the word 'career' in air quotes. "I bet none of the death threat stuff is even real. We'll all get out of here alive in the end, and she'll have a big story to tell her followers to get even more attention."

"I already have five million followers, asshole!" Kiara snapped.

He raised a brow. "Is that even good?"

"Yes!" she shouted, slamming a hand on the table. "I can't believe you'd actually accuse me, you fucking prick! You're lucky I'm not slapping the shit out of you right now!"

"Go ahead and slap him," Jasmine said, eyes flashing. "He's only accusing you because you said that stuff to him earlier about how no one wants him around unless he brings party favors. Pathetic man-child can't handle the truth."

I flashed a puzzled look at April, and she leaned in and whispered to me. "Tate's the school dealer. At least that's what everyone says."

"Fuck you, Jasmine," Tate said. "And fuck you too, Kiara. I'm standing by what I said. You're the one behind all this shit. All I have to do to prove it is wait, and then you'll all—"

He was cut off by Maverick bringing his fist down on the table. "Everyone needs to calm the fuck down, right now," he snapped. "This is obviously what the Game Master wants. For us to fight and fall apart."

"I agree," Brooke said, nodding fervently. "And you know what? I think he's lying. He's not one of us. He just said that to sow discord among us. And it's totally working!"

"Oh my god." Courteney sat up straight, eyes widening. "You're right. That's the easiest way to fuck with our heads in here—make us hate and distrust each other."

"Yup. I really don't think he's one of us at all."

The room was still filled with tension, but it wasn't so thick now. Everyone looked relieved... except Maverick.

"Guys, if that's true, then it isn't a good thing," he said, slowly shaking his head.

"Why?" April asked, frowning.

"Because if it's one of us, we'd be able to discuss it—or argue about it, as we've been doing—and eventually we'd be able to figure out which one of us has the biggest motive to do this," he said. "But if it's an outsider, it could be literally *anyone*. And we have no way of knowing who."

A somber silence settled over the room. Maverick was right, and we all knew it.

A moment later, the silence was broken by a series of pings and vibrations. Everyone around me pulled their phones out of their pockets. I did the same and glanced down at the screen with wide eyes and a pounding heart.

Better eat and drink up now, players, the text read. **The first game is about to begin.**

CAREY

Tate slowly clapped his hands. "Okay, Kiara. Nicely done with the scheduled texts. It's all very convincing," he said. "But can we end this charade now? I really don't feel like playing a game."

"It's not me!" Kiara jumped up and slammed a fist on the table. "I told you, I have nothing to do with this shit!"

Evan piped up. "Sorry, but I have to agree with Tate. You're the most obvious suspect apart from Carey."

"You can't be fucking serious!"

"I am." Evan raised a brow. "Everyone else agrees, but they're all pussies, so they can't admit it."

"That's bullshit," Maverick cut in. "I don't think it's Kiara."

"Oh, yeah? Then who arranged this shit? Carey?" Evan asked, shooting me a dark look. I rolled my eyes in response before looking away.

"We already discussed this," Maverick replied. "Brooke's theory has to be right. The Game Master is someone outside of this room. Outside of the twelve."

"Guys, can we not have the same fucking conversation over and over?" April said hotly. "You saw the message. The game could be starting any minute now. We need to eat and drink, or else we're going to be exhausted and dehydrated all day."

"Go ahead and pour yourself a coffee, then," Kiara said in a saccharine tone. "Have fun getting poisoned."

"The video said nothing on the table is laced, and Tate is still fine after eating that croissant," I pointed out, lifting a brow.

Kiara turned her sneering gaze to me. "You know, it's *much* easier to slip poison into liquids than solids. Just because the croissants are fine doesn't mean the coffee and juice are fine too."

Damn. She had a point. I still thought everything on the table was probably fine, but I wasn't willing to risk my life for 'probably'.

When I remained silent, Kiara smiled victoriously and waved a hand at the coffee pot. "So... who's brave enough to try?" she asked. "Carey's just proved she isn't. April, how about you? You were just saying how much you need a drink, right?"

April gnawed on the inside of her cheek, eyes wavering between me and the coffee pot closest to her. "You really think it's okay?" she whispered.

"Oh, for fuck's sake," Maverick snapped. He stood and grabbed one of the coffee pots and one of the juice jugs. He poured himself a cup of each and gulped both down. "There," he said, wiping his chin. "If I drop dead in the next couple of minutes, you'll know Kiara is right."

We waited with bated breath for a few minutes. Nothing happened. Maverick was totally fine.

With that, we all dug in, filling ourselves with delicious pastries, fruits, bacon, eggs, and coffee. I could tell everyone was still a bit worried about potential poison or drugs in the food, but April was right—if we were really going to be forced into some crazy challenge scenario in the next few minutes, we'd need our strength and energy.

"I'll give these psycho kidnappers one thing," Tate said through a mouthful of food. "They're excellent caterers. These are the best damn croissants I've ever had. The bacon is top tier too."

"Yeah, thanks for the grub, Kiara," Evan said, smiling smugly at her before turning his attention to me. "Or should I be thanking you, Carey?"

"Oh my god, shut the fuck up!" I snapped, eyes narrowing. I was so done with these preppy assholes judging me when I'd never done anything to any of them, apart from Maverick. "I don't know what the hell your problem is, but you really need t—"

I was cut off mid-tirade by a shrill beeping sound, followed by an automated voice. "Please proceed to the gaming room in five minutes."

Zach stood abruptly. "Where the hell is the gaming room?" he asked, eyes flashing with fear. "And where's that voice coming from?"

Rhys stood too, narrowing his eyes as he moved around the left side of the drawing room. "I'm pretty sure all the statues and paintings in here are bugged," he said as he leaned in to examine a large marble bust on a plinth. He stood up straight again and shook a finger. "Yeah, see? The eyes. There's a small red light in one of them."

"You think it's a camera?" Brooke asked, forehead wrinkling.

"Of course it is. Looks like there's a tiny microphone in the mouth, too." Rhys looked back at the table. "I bet this whole house is filled with cameras and speakers so the Game Master can watch us and communicate with us. The phones are just an added touch."

Maverick strode over to the other side of the drawing room and started examining the bronze sconces lining the damask wallpaper. "Rhys is right. And it's not just the artwork. It's the light fixtures too. There are surveillance cameras fucking *everywhere*," he finally said. "I can't believe we missed this earlier."

"Well, we weren't expecting to be forced into some weird

hybrid of Big Brother and Squid Game," April said. "So I don't blame you for not noticing until now. None of us did."

"So, my other question," Zach chimed in. "The gaming room. Where the hell is it?"

I shook my head. "No idea. I guess we have to go and find it."

"Let's go." Maverick snapped his fingers. "We can search the place for the rest of the cameras and mics later."

Everyone murmured their agreement and stood. When we stepped out of the drawing room, a resounding gasp filled the hall. "It's open," Jasmine said breathlessly.

She was referring to one of the previously sealed hallways that ran out of the spacious foyer. The steel shutter had rolled upward, revealing a long hall lined with doors. Every door was sealed except for the first one on the right, which had a sign on it. *Gaming Room 1.*

"Well, there it is," April muttered. "Who's game to go in first?"

"Are you seriously making game-related puns right now?" Kiara said, rolling her eyes.

"No, I didn't even realize," April said, voice laced with anxiety. "I just meant... who wants to go in first? Because I sure as hell don't."

"I'll go," Maverick said. He headed into the hall, opened the door, and stepped into the room. "Huh," he said. "This is weird as fuck. Come and look, guys."

We all marched into the room after him, eyes wide as we took in our new surroundings. The walls were painted black, and strange metal fixtures hung from the ceiling along with a series of gears and pulleys that were embedded in the ceiling itself. Each fixture hung directly above one of twelve large gray squares on the floor, arranged in a three-by-four grid. The squares had our names embossed in the center, and each was surrounded by four smaller squares—red above, blue to the right, yellow below, and green to the left.

"What the fuck is this shit?" Rhys said, heading over to the square with his name. "Anyone?"

"No idea," Courteney murmured, heading over to her own square. She knelt to examine it. "I don't see anything here, except the name."

"I guess we'll find out," Zach said, flashing a worried look at me, April, and Brooke. Our squares were all in different places. Mine was at the bottom right corner, April was in the middle of the second row, Brooke was on the left of the third row, and Zach was in the top left corner.

The door suddenly slammed shut behind us, and the thudding sound was followed by a loud click.

"We're locked in now," Brooke said. Her olive complexion had turned white.

A crisp robotic voice addressed us from a speaker on the front wall. "Welcome to Simon Says Survive," it said. "All players must proceed to their squares now."

Kiara snorted. "Simon Says Survive? What the fuck is that?"

"Ah, pretending you don't know. Classic deflection technique so no one will suspect you," Tate said. Evan nodded and snickered alongside him.

"What if we don't do it?" I asked, frowning over at my square. "Like, what if we straight up refuse to play any of the games?"

The speaker crackled to life again a few seconds later. "Those who fail to participate in the games will be eliminated."

Rhys whirled around. "He's listening to us," he said, voice edged with panic. "He heard what Carey just said."

"Or maybe it's an automated script playing," Kiara said. "I was just wondering the exact same thing as Carey, and I bet the rest of us were too."

"Ah. A script your employees wrote and programmed, right?" Evan asked, tilting his head. "Do you have a little button in your pocket that you can press to control things around here? Or are your employees working behind the scenes for you?"

"For fuck's sake, I'm not the Game Master, and I don't have anyone working for me in this shithole!" Kiara shouted. "How many fucking times do I have to tell you?"

The robotic voice piped up again. "Here are the instructions and rules for Simon Says Survive. They will be read out twice to ensure you can all grasp them," it said. "The challenge is loosely based on the game Simon Says. For those who've never played it before, it's a classic children's game that involves listening, memory, and following instructions."

"A children's game?" Maverick muttered from the square to my left. "This is so fucked up."

The monotonous voice continued blaring from the speakers. "There are twenty levels in the game. All must be passed to ensure your survival. In the first level, one of the smaller colored squares around your square will briefly light up. When you hear a beep, you must tap your foot on the square that lit up. In the second level, two squares will light up, one after the other. The first will be the same one from level one, and the second will be a new one. At the beep, you must tap your foot on both squares in the correct order. Each subsequent level will introduce a new colored square in the sequence, and you must recall the exact sequence from previous levels while also memorizing the newest addition. If you step on an incorrect square, you will be eliminated. If you make it to the final round without any mistakes, you will survive."

"They weren't kidding about this being a dumb kid's game," Rhys said. "I literally played this at an arcade on my seventh birthday. It's easy as fuck."

"Was there any risk of you dying in that arcade if you lost the game?" Brooke snapped.

"C'mon, guys, we aren't going to die," Evan said. "I'm telling you, Tate is a hundred percent right. Kiara set this shit up for more followers."

"I thought you said it was Carey," Jasmine shot back, folding her arms. "Now suddenly you're totally certain it's Kiara? Make up your mind, dumbass."

"Oh, I *have* made it up. Carey is out, Kiara is in," Evan said. "This is all some stupid influencer bullshit to get views and likes. Pathetic, if you ask me."

"Funny. I don't remember *anyone* asking for your shitty opinion," April said.

Evan opened his mouth to reply, but he was cut off by the robotic voice running through the instructions for a second time.

"The game begins in one minute. I hope you're all ready. Have fun, players!" the voice concluded. There was a faint whirring sound from above, and I looked up to see several of the metal gears on the ceiling spinning in slow circles.

"What the hell is all that stuff?" I asked, pointing upward.

"No idea," Zach replied, lifting his gaze too. "The hanging things look like pipes, but I don't know what they're for."

He was right. When I craned my neck and squinted hard, I could see a hollow running through the center of the thick metal cylinder above my head.

"Could it be for some sort of gas?" Brooke said, lifting a brow. "If we fail the game, maybe we get knocked out with that."

"Or acid could drop on our faces," April said with a shudder. "Anyone else want to hazard a guess?"

"Why don't we just focus on playing the game and hope we never have to find out what the pipes are for?" Maverick said. "Speculating like this isn't going to do shit except scare everyone."

"True," Brooke murmured, lowering her eyes to the floor.

Our squares suddenly lit up around the edges, and a robotic voice reverberated throughout the room. "Level one."

The blue square to my right lit up. I waited for the beep, and then I tapped my foot on it. Everyone else did the same.

"Level two," said the voice.

The right blue square lit up, followed by the yellow square

below. I waited for the beep and tapped my foot again. Blue right, yellow down.

"We all got the same squares, right?" Zach called out to the group. "Blue and yellow?"

There was a resounding chorus of 'yes', and my shoulders sagged with relief. At least we all had the same sequence to follow. The game would be much more confusing if we didn't.

"Level three."

This time, the new addition to the sequence was green left. Everyone passed easily, but the tension in the room had thickened. We were all worried about the upper levels, where we'd have to remember many more squares in the pattern.

"This is such bullshit," Evan said. "Seriously, guys, nothing will happen if we step on the wrong square."

Okay, I was wrong. We weren't *all* worried about the game.

"Do it, then," Hudson muttered. "See what happens."

"I will," Evan said as the robotic voice announced level four. "You'll see in a few seconds. Nothing will happen to me, and Kiara will have to admit she arranged all this shit for views and followers."

The new addition to the sequence was another blue square. After the following beep, I carefully tapped my foot in the correct order—blue, yellow, green, blue. At the same time, I watched Evan's feet out of the corner of my eye. He chose to tap on the red square first, followed by blue, yellow, and red again.

A loud beep resounded through the gaming room, and the robotic voice spoke again. "Player six is out. Remaining players, please stand by."

Evan grinned. "See? Nothing's happening to me," he said, lifting his palms. "Tate was right. This is all Kiar—"

His smug speech was abruptly cut off by a sudden mechanical hiss. A metal rod shot out of the pipe above his head, shaft slicing through the air with lethal precision. In an instant, it found its mark, impaling Evan through the skull with a sickening crunch.

Time seemed to slow down as the horror unfolded. Evan's eyes widened in shock as the steel brutally drove through bone and tissue, and a spray of crimson erupted, splattering the squares surrounding him. He let out a strangled gurgle as the rod retracted with a metallic clang, and his body convulsed in a futile struggle before falling limp on the square below.

I stared at the grisly spectacle with bulging eyes, reeling with a mix of shock and disbelief. Adrenaline surged through my veins, pushing me to run, but that urge was paralyzed by the sheer terror of the moment, leaving me frozen in place and unable to tear my gaze from Evan's body.

The stunned silence in the room was broken by a wailing scream. Jasmine's spot was next to Evan's, so she had the worst view of all, and some of his blood was seeping into her square. She fell to her knees and covered her eyes, strangled shrieks escaping her lips between gasped words. "I... I can't. Can't do this. Can't..."

Her cries blended with a cacophony of shrieks and gasps from the others in the room as the crushing reality finally sank in.

That *really* happened. Evan was *really* dead.

"Oh god. Ohgodohgodohgod," I said in a ragged whisper, whole body racked with tremors.

The bone-chilling screams around me made my stomach lurch, and I fell to my knees on my square, suddenly too weak to remain upright. The realization that we were all minutes away from meeting the same fate as Evan if we failed a single step was constricting my chest in a suffocating grip, leaving me unable to breathe properly.

"Get up," April said, voice thick with emotion. "Carey, Jasmine... get up. You have to. Please."

I couldn't reply. Still couldn't breathe.

Someone hauled me to my feet and held my left arm in a firm grip until I stopped wobbling. It was only when he stepped away that I realized it was Maverick. "Get it together, Saracen," he muttered.

"Level five," the robot voice announced.

I could feel Maverick's eyes lingering on me as the next level proceeded in a blur of colored lights. "Blue, yellow, green, blue, red," he called out to everyone. "Come on, guys. We can do it."

I followed his instructions, not even knowing if they were right. It felt like my head had been scraped clean from the shock of what I'd just witnessed, and it was almost impossible to formulate a single thought. Thankfully, I passed, along with the ten other remaining players, and a collective sigh of relief went through the room.

"I can't believe it," Jasmine choked out. She was still on the floor, but she'd used her hands to tap the squares around her. "He's really dead."

"I know." April reached over and laid a hand on her shoulder. "You should get up. Just in case. C'mon, I'll help you."

Zach joined April in helping Jasmine to her feet. At the same time, Kiara started shrieking all over again. "Do you fuckers believe me now?" she shouted, whirling around to look at Tate through bloodshot eyes. "Can you see it's all fucking real?"

Tate's face had gone stark white, and his gaze was fixed on Evan's lifeless body. "I... I'm sorry," he muttered.

"Sorry?" Rhys said sharply, hands clenching at his sides. "Your theory got Evan killed. You think sorry is enough to—"

He was cut off by the robotic voice announcing the beginning of the sixth level. Zach and April quickly returned to their squares, and Maverick guided us all through the sequence again, loudly calling out the colors.

"We're going to get through this, okay?" he called out once we'd cleared the level. "I know you all want to cry and scream and freak out, but you have to save it for later. For now, it's all about survival. Got it?"

Everyone nodded numbly. Maverick's calm voice guided us through level after level, and after what felt like an eternity, the game was finally over.

"Congratulations, players," the robot voice said. "You all passed, with the exception of player six. You may leave the gaming room now."

There was a mechanical hissing sound followed by a loud click in the door. It swung open, revealing the hallway outside.

"Uh... let's go, I guess," Rhys muttered, looking around at everyone. He didn't move, though. It seemed as if he was rooted to the spot in fear and confusion, just like me.

I looked upward, terrified that this was all some sort of cruel trick where the metal rod would shoot down to impale me as soon as I attempted to leave my square. Several of the others seemed to have the same concern, eyes fixed on the pipes above.

"Carey."

My eyes snapped to the left at the sound of my name. Maverick was standing next to me with his right hand extended. He'd stepped off his own square in order to reach me, and he was totally fine. "Come on," he muttered. "Time to go."

I took his hand and let him lead me off the gaming floor. I was grateful for the warmth and support in this cold, terrifying place, and for those moments, our nasty history and mutual dislike was forgotten.

When we reached the doorway, I lifted my chin and met his eyes. His expression was unreadable. "Thanks," I murmured. "I really thought I was going to—"

"I know." He kept my hand in his and squeezed it. "I get it."

His touch sent a jolt of electricity through me, and I shivered involuntarily. We were standing so close that our faces were nearly touching. Suddenly I felt a surge of desire; a heat spreading through me that had nothing to do with fear.

I quickly brushed it aside, chalking it up to the intensity of the game. We were survivors, loaded with adrenaline and clinging to whatever support we could get in the face of unimaginable danger. That was all. I wasn't actually aroused by Maverick right now. No way.

I took a deep breath and pulled my hand away. "Thanks again," I said.

"No problem." He was staring down at me now, eyes flickering with indecipherable emotion. I had a feeling I knew what he was thinking, though. He was probably wondering if he did the right thing in helping me, given our bad blood along with the earlier suspicion aimed at me.

Then again, he seemed to be fairly convinced that the Game Master was an outsider, meaning he shouldn't suspect me at all, even if many of the others did.

As my mind raced through the possibilities, I inhaled sharply and took a sudden faltering step back. It had just occurred to me that Maverick's calmness and steady hand could be a sign of his own culpability in this situation. Perhaps he was able to remain so cool and collected because he knew he couldn't lose. Knew he was always in control.

"What's wrong?" he asked, frowning as he registered the sudden shift in my energy. "I mean, apart from the obvious."

I swallowed thickly and averted my eyes. "Just the obvious stuff, like you said," I said. "This whole situation. The games. The cameras everywhere. Evan."

"Right." He dipped his chin in a curt nod. "I'll try to help out with the games. Help everyone, I mean."

"Thanks," I murmured.

"I know most of us aren't friends here, so that might be a little hard to believe," he went on, still staring at me with that penetrating gaze. "But you can trust me. I swear."

That wasn't true. I still had no idea what was happening in this mansion or why I'd been selected as a player, but I did know one thing for sure.

I couldn't trust anyone.

CAREY

A series of pings echoed through the hall, and everyone pulled out their phones. I grabbed mine and quickly scanned the new message from the Game Master.

Congratulations on passing the first game!

Right now, you probably all feel the need to relax and recuperate, so there are no more games until tonight. You have free rein of your quarters and can do whatever you want until dinner, which will be served in the drawing room at 5pm.

Lunch would usually be served at 12:30, but I think I can safely assume that none of you have much of an appetite after the shock of losing a player today.

If you need water, there are glass jugs and cups available in the cupboards in your rooms, and the tap water in the bathroom is perfectly safe to drink.

Thanks for playing!

"Well, at least we get some time off," Rhys muttered, rubbing his jaw.

"Are we seriously not getting lunch?" Hudson said, upper lip curling. "That's fucked up."

Kiara glared at him. "You really want to eat right now? After what just happened in there?"

"It was fucked up, sure, but a man's gotta eat," he replied. "Besides, Evan wasn't my friend. I barely knew the dude."

"You're disgusting," Kiara hissed. With that, she stormed up the hall with Jasmine by her side.

The rest of us followed at a slower pace, not quite knowing what to do. There were books in our rooms, so we could spend the next few hours reading if we wanted, but I had a feeling most of us didn't want to be alone right now. Not after the horror we'd just witnessed.

"Guys, I really don't want to be alone right now," Courteney said, echoing my thoughts. "Does anyone mind if I hang out with them?"

"Of course not," Zach said, brushing a hand over her shoulder. "I don't think any of us want to be alone right now."

"Let's go and hang out in the drawing room," Maverick said, glancing at us over his shoulder. "We can talk about everything. Try to figure out what's going on."

"You guys can feel free to do that," Rhys replied. "But I'm going back to my room to take a leak, and then I'm gonna explore again. There's gotta be more stuff we missed earlier. I want to know exactly where all the cameras are, too."

With that, he strode up the stairs, clearly not caring for any company. Maverick muttered something under his breath and reached for the drawing room door handle. "Fuck," he said with a grimace, rattling the bronze fixture. "It's locked now."

"I guess it'll open at five for dinner, like the text said," I replied. "The locks in this place must be set up on an automated schedule."

"Yeah, maybe," April said, lifting a brow. "Or maybe the Game Master is actively controlling them from wherever he's hiding."

"Wherever it is, we'll never find it," Hudson said. "Not with all the fucking doors sealed off."

"Where should we go for now?" Courteney asked, tilting her head.

Maverick nodded toward the staircase. "My room. It's the closest."

We all trudged up the stairs and headed into Maverick's room, which was directly left of the landing.

Almost immediately, the group split into three smaller groups. Kiara and Jasmine huddled on the top right corner of the bed, and Maverick stood next to them, arms crossed over his chest as the three of them spoke in hushed tones. Hudson and Tate went to stand by the window, and I hung back near the desk with April, Brooke, Courteney, and Zach.

"So," Zach said, leaning against the desk. "I won't bother asking you guys if you're okay, because I think I already know the answer."

"No shit," I murmured.

"Do any of you know what's going on yet?" he asked.

April shook her head. "I've barely had time to think about it. I'm still in shock over..." She trailed off and shook her head before starting again. "I didn't say this earlier, because there was already enough drama, but part of me honestly thought Tate and Evan could be right about this whole thing being a joke. At least... that's what I hoped for."

"Me too," Brooke said, hugging her arms around herself. "But now we know it's real. We can actually die here."

"Yup." Zach's lips tightened. "It's fucked up."

"Beyond fucked up," I said, shaking my head. "I just don't get it. Why us? What did we do to deserve this?"

"Nothing," April said. "We were just unlucky enough to get picked out of a crowd by a total psychopath."

"I'm not so sure about that," Courteney said.

Zach's forehead wrinkled. "Why?"

"Well, I've been thinking about it, and there's a few things. Firstly, we're all Babylon students, which makes me think the Game Master must be a fellow student. Or at least he's being helped by a Babylon student. That makes me think we weren't picked at random. This student selected the twelve of us for a reason. I just don't know what it is." Courteney paused and looked down at the floor. "Also, most of us seem to be in friend groups. There's the four of you. Jasmine, Kiara, and Maverick are friends, and Hudson, Rhys, and Tate are friends with each other too. Then there's me. I'm the odd one out, and I worry that makes me look suspicious. But I swear, I'm not the Game Master, and I'm not helping him either." She swallowed thickly and looked back up at us. "I know I can't prove it, but... I promise, it's not me."

April shook her head. "You're not the odd one out. You and Zach are friends from... what is it? History class?"

"Yeah, exactly," Zach chimed in. "Just because we don't hang out every day doesn't mean we aren't friends."

"Also," Brooke said, raising a brow. "Tate isn't actually friends with Hudson and Rhys. From what I've heard, he isn't friends with anyone. His relationships are more... well, let's just say they're more transactional than others."

"Like what Kiara was saying earlier?" I asked, tipping my head. "About the party favors?"

"Yup. People only hang out with him if he gives them stuff in return. So he doesn't have any friends here. Also, Evan wasn't really friends with anyone here either. So you're not the odd one out at all, Courteney."

Courteney breathed an audible sigh of relief. "Thanks," she murmured. She took a deep breath and spoke up again. "There's something else I've been thinking about. About the Game Master."

"Yeah?"

"I know most of us ended up agreeing with Brooke's theory about him being an outsider. But you know how I said I think he's either a Babylon student or at least getting help from a Babylon student?"

Zach nodded. "Uh-huh."

"If that's true, I think it would make sense to have an insider in the group to report back to him. Like, stuff the mics and cameras might not pick up."

"You could be right," April said, nodding slowly. "One of us could be involved even if he or she isn't the official Game Master."

"I think so too," I said, looking over at the window. Hudson was leaning close to Tate, eyes narrowed and head occasionally nodding. The two of them appeared to be deep in discussion, and when I looked at the group on the bed, I could see they were doing the same. I was willing to bet we were all discussing the exact same subject. After all, what else could anyone possibly want to talk about right now?

April leaned forward and lowered her voice. "Now that I'm really thinking about it, I might know who it could be," she said. "The insider, I mean."

"Really?"

She lifted a palm. "I don't want to be a total bitch and point fingers like the others were doing earlier, but... well, it's just something a little suspicious you guys should know about."

"What is it?" I asked, leaning closer.

She sighed and scrubbed a hand over her face. "God, you're all going to judge me so hard for the way I found out about this."

"We won't," Brooke said. "Just say it. I hate being kept in suspense."

"Okay, well, you know how Rhys has always acted like he's one of us? Like, mega-rich?" April said. She glanced at me and gave me a sympathetic half-smile. "Sorry, Carey. I just mean—"

I lifted a palm. "No need to apologize. I get it."

April went on. "He's been lying to everyone for years. I don't know if that necessarily means he's helping the Game Master, or that he's the Game Master himself, but it *does* show that he's capable of deception. He's also damn good at it."

"Wait, he's been lying about being rich?" I asked, cocking my head.

"Yup. He's not."

"How do you know?"

April sighed and looked at her feet. "Here's the part where you judge me," she said. She gnawed at the inside of her cheek for a few seconds before continuing. "A couple of years ago, when I was a sophomore and Abby was a freshman, we both started to worry about our grades in English. We thought Dad might be going harder on us because we're his kids, and we were especially worried about some papers we'd recently handed in. So we decided to steal his office key and check our grades. It was stupid, I know. But we just wanted to see. That's all. We weren't cheating, or anything like that."

"No judgement from me," Zach said. "If my dad was a teacher at our school, you can bet your ass he'd mark me harder than the others. It would freak me out too."

"Well, it turned out that he keeps all the essays stored in a locked filing cabinet, and we didn't have the key for that, so we couldn't even look at our grades," April said. "But Abby noticed something on his desk."

"Regarding Rhys, I presume," I said, raising my brows.

"Yeah. It was a folder with a form on top about financial aid for a scholarship student. Every teacher who has one of these students in their class needs to sign off on them every semester to confirm that they're keeping their grades up," April said. "This particular form had Rhys's name on it. As soon as I saw what it was, I put it down, because it made me feel weird to look at something that obviously isn't any of my business. But Abby was always a major gossip hound. You guys remember, right?"

Brooke smiled faintly. "Yeah."

"Well, anyway, she read the whole form, along with everything else in the folder, and she told me all about it after we left. Rhys is attending Babylon on a full scholarship. His parents' occupations were written on the form. His mom is a librarian and his dad is in advertising. There's nothing wrong with those jobs, obviously, but—"

"They don't pay anywhere near enough to afford Babylon's fees," Zach finished for her.

"Exactly."

"I don't get it." Courteney shook her head. "He's always acted like he was super wealthy. Like, remember his birthday party last year?"

"I wasn't invited, so no," Brooke said, rolling her eyes.

"It was in an absolutely *massive* mansion. Like, twice as big as my place," Courteney said. "He told everyone it was just his family's beach house. The party was fully catered, too. I never would've expected something like that from a scholarship kid."

Zach shrugged. "He probably saved up his allowance and rented an Airbnb for the night," he said. "Just to keep up appearances."

"But how can he hide it from his friends?" Courteney asked, shaking her head. "I can't imagine Hudson hanging out with anyone he deems lesser than him. But they're best friends."

"Well, Babylon's a boarding school," April said. "Rhys probably lies and says his family lives really far away. Different state, maybe. So they can't drive there to hang out on weekends."

"Also, Hudson is really fucking stupid," Zach added. "It's probably not hard to trick him."

"But he's tricked *everyone*," I said. "April's right. It shows how capable he is of lying."

Brooke frowned. "What was the scholarship for?" she asked.

"That's the other suspicious thing," April replied. "The scholarship is for physics, and Abby said there was a personal statement in the folder, written by Rhys when he first applied for it. Apparently, he really wants to study engineering when he goes to college."

"So he's a genius with a passion for engineering. Does that sound like someone we might know?" Zach said. "A certain Game Master, perhaps?"

"Like I said, I don't want to point fingers, because I could be barking up the wrong tree," April said hurriedly. "I'm not saying he's the Game Master. I'm just saying, if anyone here is likely to be helping the Game Master... well, Rhys is looking really good for it right now."

"Agreed." I wrapped my arms around myself as an involuntary shiver wracked my body. "But I also get what you mean about not wanting to accuse anyone too fast. So maybe we should keep this to ourselves for now."

"I was thinking the exact same thing," Brooke said. "If we say anything to the others, one of them could run off and tell Rhys, and then he'd probably make sure he hides things even better. If he's guilty, that is."

"Yup." Zach's lips tightened. "So we all agree? Keep this information a secret for now?"

The five of us nodded in unison. We all understood the reality of the situation—the Game Master wouldn't want their identity revealed so early in the games, given that ten against one wouldn't work in their favor during a fight. So, if Rhys was actually the Game Master, and he discovered that we had information that could jeopardize his position, he might do something to eliminate us just to keep himself safe.

None of us wanted to risk literal death over a theory, so all we could do for now was keep a close eye on him and see how things played out.

Another shiver ran through me, and a tingling sensation crept up my spine. Slowly, I turned my head and found myself locking eyes with Maverick from across the room. Heat instantly rushed to my cheeks, and I tore my gaze away.

"Oh my god." Brooke straightened her shoulders and looked at each of us in turn with wide eyes. "I just thought of something. Carey, remember how you said you were worried about Hudson? That he might be planning something really bad to get back at you?"

"Yes." My gaze flicked over to Hudson at the window, and my skin crawled with revulsion. "Why?"

"Hold on... what are you guys talking about?" Courteney asked, frowning.

Zach nudged her. "I'll tell you later."

"Here's my new theory," Brooke said. "Hudson is an idiot, as we all know, but he's rich as fuck and also a total psychopath. His best friend Rhys is a total genius who has no money. Put them together, and you get—"

"A team capable of setting up this shit," April finished for her in a grim tone, gesturing at our surroundings.

"Got it in one."

I frowned. "So this could all be happening because of *me*?"

"I'm not blaming you," Brooke said hurriedly. "It's just a theory."

"It's okay, I didn't think you were blaming me," I said. "I just meant... I don't get it. If Hudson wants to get back at me, it makes sense that he'd bring me here, along with my friends. But why would he bring the others? Like Evan, Tate, Kiara, and so on."

Brooke twisted her lips in contemplation. "Hm. Good point."

"Like she said, it's just a theory," April said. "It might not be right, but I think it's the best idea any of us have had so far. So we should at least keep it in mind and be wary of Hudson and Rhys."

"Don't worry, I was always going to be wary of them," I said with a wry half-smile.

"Hey, Carey!" Kiara waved at me from the bed. "Get over here!"

I looked at her with raised brows. Then I turned back to my friends. "Um... any idea why she's calling me over?"

"Nope." April shrugged. "But we might as well go and see."

The five of us headed over to the bed.

"What's up, Kiara?" I asked flatly, folding my arms.

She leaned back against the velvet bedhead. "A little birdie told me you're some sort of coding whiz."

"So what?" April snapped. "You think she can write a program to magically get us out of here?"

Kiara rolled her eyes. "No, obviously." She returned her attention to me and sat up straight. "I was just wondering if you could do anything with the phones. Like get online, maybe?"

"I had a quick look earlier, and all the signals seem to be blocked," I said. "But I can have a closer look now."

I pulled my phone out and went through it, trying various new techniques and ideas as they occurred to me. Finally, after a last-ditch effort, I reluctantly shook my head and slipped my phone back in my pocket. "It's not possible," I said. "Whoever set these phones up has managed to block everything. The only thing that actually works is the intranet in this place."

Kiara narrowed her eyes. "What's that? Is that how they're texting us?"

"Yeah, it's like a local network thing."

"Damn." She sighed and leaned back. "Oh, well. It was worth a shot."

Maverick's eyes were on me again. "Did you guys figure out anything while you were chatting over there?" he asked, rubbing his jaw.

"No." Zach shook his head. "We still have no clue why we're here or who set it all up. You?"

"In the same boat. No fucking idea."

Rhys burst into the room, snapping everyone's attention to the doorway. "Guys!" he said. "I found something! Come and see."

He turned and sprinted back out, and we all followed him to the far end of the hall. He was standing by the sealed-off window there.

"Something's changed," he said. "I looked at it earlier this morning, and it was totally sealed. But look at it now."

I took a step closer, squinting. Rhys was right. The thick steel shutter was no longer covering the entire window. There was a gap at the bottom, which was allowing a crack of light to stream through.

"You think the Game Master did this while we were in the first game?" Zach asked.

Rhys shrugged. "I don't know. But if we can find something small enough to slip in this crack, we might be able to pry the whole thing off."

"I can't think of anything that would work," Maverick said, brows dipping in a slight frown. "But I guess we can look around. See if anything jumps out."

"Um, guys? I might have something," Jasmine said in a sheepish tone. She reached into the right pocket of her sweatpants and pulled out a butter knife. "I stole this from the table at breakfast earlier. I thought I might need to defend myself if one of you turned out to be the Game Master."

"You were going to try to kill someone with a butter knife?" April said scornfully.

Jasmine rolled her eyes. "I said *defend,* not kill, and a butter knife is better than literally nothing, right?"

"I guess so," April muttered. She looked at Maverick. "Can you use it?"

He nodded slowly. "I think so. There's no way I can use it to pry off the entire steel shutter, but I can probably use it to make the crack bigger. Then we can use something else to pry the whole thing open. Something bigger and sturdier. Like a chair leg, maybe. Or maybe the metal rod from one of the towel racks in our bathrooms."

"I'll help," Zach said.

Rhys and Tate also volunteered. With determined expressions etched on their faces, the four of them huddled around the narrow gap in the shutter, taking turns wedging the butter knife into the opening. I stood close by, heart racing with a mix of hope and anxiety as I watched their progress.

With each carefully calculated twist and push, the gap widened ever so slightly, allowing just a little more light to filter into the dim hall. Finally, after what felt like an eternity, Maverick let out a triumphant grunt as the gap widened enough to fit the blade of the knife all the way in.

With renewed determination, the guys continued their painstaking work, inching closer to the goal of widening the gap enough to fit the towel rod from Zach's bathroom. When it was finally big enough, Maverick wedged the thick metal rod inside and pressed on.

A few minutes later, the shutter gave way with a loud clang. Light flooded into the hall, illuminating the weary faces of the group.

"You did it!" I said, relief washing over me in waves.

The rest of the group clamored around the window, patting the four guys on the back and congratulating them on their effort.

"What can you see?" April asked, craning her neck. She was too short to see past Zach's shoulders.

"There's a balcony out here," he said. "Wait... this could actually be a way out!"

"What do you mean?"

"It's not just a balcony. There's a spiral staircase leading off the far side of it. I can't see where it goes, but we have to check it out."

"Even if it just goes up to the roof, that's fine," Kiara said. "We can stand up there and wave sheets from our beds until a passerby notices us."

"Exactly." Zach turned to Maverick. "Can you help me open this thing?"

Maverick nodded and picked up the butter knife again. He used it to break the lock, and then he wrenched the window open, grimacing as cold air rushed in. "Jesus," he muttered. "It's freezing out there."

"Yeah, the weather's been horrible lately," I replied, peering out the window as he stepped back. I was greeted by a somber gray sky, whipped by gusts of wind that churned the dark waters of the nearby ocean into countless whitecaps.

"Who wants to go first?" Zach asked, raising his brows.

Maverick stepped forward again. "I'll do it. Unless you want to."

"All good." Zach gave him a tight smile. "I'll follow you."

After the two guys made it out, they gestured for the rest of us to follow. We climbed out, one by one, and huddled together on the balcony, vigorously rubbing our arms to keep warm.

"Those steps look pretty dangerous," Brooke said, warily eyeing the spiral staircase that led off the left side of the balcony.

"It should be fine as long as we're careful," Maverick said, peering upwards. "It looks like they lead to some sort of watchtower on the roof."

April nodded. "That makes sense. The mansion has tons of towers and spires," she said. "I remember thinking it looked like a total Gothic nightmare when I arrived."

"That's exactly what I thought," Kiara said. "It's so fucking creepy."

Zach set his jaw with grim determination. "Well... let's go and see what we can find."

We slowly made our way up the winding stairs. The stone steps were old and narrow, and they were also slick with droplets of seawater flung up by the wind, so we had to take them as slowly as possible.

Maverick made it to the top first, closely followed by Zach. "Oh, fuck," he said. His deep voice almost disappeared in the roaring wind, but I could just make it out from my position as fifth in line. "No fucking way!"

"This can't be happening!" Zach shouted at the same time.

With my heart pounding, I finally made it to the top of the staircase and stepped into a small watchtower, revealing a panorama that stretched as far as the eye could see. All around us, the dark waters of the ocean churned restlessly, smashing against jagged rocks and dirt along the crooked shoreline that surrounded the mansion we stood atop.

"We're not at 4 Sutherland Drive," April said breathlessly, grabbing my arm. Her face had gone completely white. "We're on an island."

MAVERICK

"Oh my god..." Jasmine inhaled sharply as she stared out at the seemingly endless ocean. "How is this possible?"

Brooke slowly shook her head, following Jasmine's gaze. "I don't know. I don't get it," she muttered. Her skin had turned pallid, aside from the purple half-moons beneath her eyes. She looked exactly how I felt—exhausted, confused, defeated.

This was what the Game Master wanted. He wanted us to feel hopeless and scared. Wanted to toy with us mentally, emotionally, and physically before bringing the hammer down. The twisted children's games were just one part of the overall scheme to destroy us.

I couldn't do it. Couldn't let him win. I had to stay strong. If not for my sake, for everyone else's.

"It's okay," I said, lifting my chin. "We can figure this out."

"How?" Kiara screeched, throwing her hands up. "Seriously, how the *fuck* are we going to figure out any of this shit? We're trapped on a fucking island!"

I kept my voice and expression neutral as I replied. "Let's try to approach this like we already know there's a solution. That'll help us stay calm, and that's really important right now."

"How the hell can we do that when we all know there's probably no solution?"

I lifted a palm. "We'll make a list of questions we have about everything, and then we'll try to answer each one logically. That's a good starting point to figuring out a way through this shit. All right?"

I wasn't sure if my suggestion would actually help matters, but I figured it would bring some much-needed order to the situation and momentarily distract the others from the terror they felt. The last thing we needed right now was to give in to the crushing fear and hopelessness.

"Well... I have an answer to the question of how this is possible," Carey said, lifting her hand like we were in a classroom discussion.

"How?" Brooke asked.

Carey raised her voice several octaves as the howling wind picked up again. "It was the drugs. They transported us to the island while we were all unconscious."

"I was just thinking the same thing," I said, dipping my chin in a brief nod. "We assumed they put us to bed at 4 Sutherland Drive because we didn't have enough information to even consider that we might be somewhere else. But now we know better."

"We don't even know if we were only unconscious for one night," Carey added. "For all we know, it was longer. We might've lost a whole day and a half to those drugs."

Jasmine rubbed her arms as she shivered. "Can we talk about this inside? It's freezing."

"Good idea." I turned on my heel and headed for the spiral staircase. The others marched after me in silence.

"So, they moved us when we were knocked out from the spiked drinks, and they set up the foyer downstairs to look like the one at Sutherland Drive," Zach said once we were all settled back in my room. "That means they wanted us to think we were in the same mansion that we went to at the start."

"But *why?*" Jasmine turned her wide eyes to him. "Why the hell would they do that?"

"To mess with us," Brooke murmured. "It's all to mess with us."

"Agreed." I nodded. "Earlier this morning, we all had hope that we could be tracked here by the cops. The Game Master only wanted us to have that hope so he could rip it away from us. It's all part of his game."

"Exactly," Carey said. "No one is looking for us here. They'll track our phones to 4 Sutherland Drive, and they'll find nothing but an empty house."

We all remained silent for a moment as we contemplated her words. Then I stood up and clapped my hands together to snap everyone's attention back to me. "Let's do what I said before. We'll make a list of our questions. See if anyone has any solutions."

"Okay. First question. If we aren't at Sutherland Drive, where the fuck are we?" Rhys asked, cocking his head. "Anyone have any idea?"

Everyone bleakly shook their heads, including me. The Northern Californian coast was dotted with hundreds of tiny islands. Hell, the whole West Coast was like that. We could be fucking *anywhere*.

"Actually, forget that." Rhys shook his head. "I have an idea."

"What?"

"We have access to this tower thing now. As in, we can get *outside*. So it doesn't matter exactly where we are, because we can escape either way."

Zach raised a brow. "How?"

"We can take the sheets off our beds and tie them together to make a sort of rope. Then we can tie it to something in the tower and use the rope to abseil down."

April frowned. "That sounds really dangerous. You saw those rocks right at the base of the tower, right?"

"We can make it as safe as possible," Rhys replied. "We can add knots all the way along the rope, like steps to put our feet on as we climb down. That way we can stagger the journey down instead of just sliding all the way to the bottom and burning the shit out of our hands from the friction."

"What's the point of climbing down?" Carey asked.

"Escaping this prison, obviously," Rhys said, flashing her an incredulous look. "Is that not enough of a point for you?"

Her eyes narrowed. "There's no point if we don't have a plan for what to do once we're down there," she said frostily. "I also think you're wrong about it not mattering where we are. It *does* matter, because we have no idea where the nearest land is. It could be a hundred miles away, for all we know. So what are we supposed to do? Swim away and just hope there's something nearby?"

"No shit." Kiara sniffed. "Even if we magically found a boat somewhere, we don't know which direction the mainland is in. We could be rowing for days or weeks in the totally wrong direction, with no food or water."

Rhys's shoulders sagged. "Yeah. That's true. I guess I got ahead of myself," he muttered. He looked down and sighed deeply, rubbing at his temples. "Fuck. Sorry. I was just trying to think of a way out."

"It's fine," I said. "This is exactly what we need to do. Keep thinking, talking, and trying. Like a team. We'll figure something out eventually."

"Drop the fucking act, Maverick," Hudson said, rolling his eyes. "We all know the truth. There's no way out of this place."

"How do you know that for sure?" April said sharply. "Do you know something we don't?"

Hudson scowled at her. "No. It's just fucking obvious to

anyone with half a brain. There's no way out. Maverick's only trying to keep us calm with his bullshit 'let's figure it out' act so we don't freak out and kill each other." He paused and turned his sneering gaze back to me. "You know I'm right, deep down. We're all fucked. Totally *fucked*."

"Wait." Carey sat up straight. Her face had brightened considerably. "Maybe we're not."

"What do you mean?"

"I mean... I think I know where we are, and it's not that far away." Carey turned to Courteney. "This morning, you said this place looks familiar. That you have a déjà vu sort of feeling whenever you look around. I think I know why."

"Hurry up and spit it out, dumbass," Jasmine said, rolling her eyes. "We're all waiting."

Carey's lips tightened. "I have to explain it first," she said. "I think Courteney felt that way because this place *is* familiar. Think about it. The layout of this hall. The size of the rooms. The shape of the windows. Even the layout of the bathrooms. What does it remind you of?"

"Babylon," April said, brows knitting. "It's the same as the dorms."

"Exactly." Carey nodded fervently. "I think we're in Icarus Hall."

Courteney's eyes widened. "Oh my god, *yes*! That's why it feels so familiar! It's the exact same building design as the other Babylon buildings!"

"But they've been updated and modernized over the years, so it's not obvious right away," April said, looking around the room. "That's why we didn't notice until now."

"Yup."

I nodded, one hand slowly rubbing my jaw. "That would explain the island thing."

"Exactly. And it also means we aren't all that far from home,"

Carey said. "I mean, how far away is the island from the mainland?"

April's forehead wrinkled. "About three miles, I think. Maybe four?"

"Hold on." Rhys lifted a hand. "If we're at Icarus Hall, shouldn't we be able to see the mainland from the top of the tower? Because I'm pretty sure the horizon distance is around three or four miles to the naked eye."

"Not necessarily. You can only see Icarus Hall and the island from the Babylon dorms on very clear days, and even then, it's just a tiny speck on the horizon," Brooke said. "It goes both ways, and the weather today is awful. The mainland is probably shrouded in mist right now, so it's not visible on the horizon. It just looks like clouds and nothing else."

Rhys's lips twisted in contemplation as he drummed his fingertips against his left knee. "Shit. You guys might be right. We could be at Icarus Hall," he finally said, turning to glance at Carey. "Nice catch, Crim."

"Drop the shitty nicknames, man," I said, narrowing my eyes. "Now is really not the time."

"Someone's got a crush," Kiara said under her breath so that only Jasmine and I could hear.

I glared at her. I didn't have a crush on Carey. Firstly, this wasn't the seventh grade. Secondly, the fact that I didn't think this was the time nor the place for shitty attitudes didn't necessarily mean I wanted to fuck Carey. I just wanted some peace and harmony in this hellhole while we were trying to bang out an escape plan.

Oh, fuck, who was I kidding?

It was obvious that I found Carey attractive. Everyone did. She was objectively beautiful. I'd screw her brains out if I had the opportunity. None of that meant I had feelings for her though, like Kiara was implying. Attraction was just a physical thing. It didn't mean anything more.

"Three miles is a pretty long way to swim. Especially when it's this cold," Zach said. "Four would be even worse."

"Yeah, there's no way any of us are making that distance. Not in this weather." April replied, shaking her head. "If it was warmer and the water wasn't so rough, it would probably be okay for someone strong and fit. But right now, anyone who tries to swim away from here could be risking their life."

Hudson snorted. "Fuck that. I'm not dying of hypothermia for you guys."

"No one asked you to, dumbass," Jasmine snapped. "In fact, no one asked you for anything."

I lifted a palm. "Guys. We need to stay calm. No arguments."

Carey was the first to reply, and my eyes shot to meet hers as she spoke. "He's right. I know some of us really don't like each other, but we're all in this together, so we need to work as a team and try to put aside our differences for now." She dropped her gaze from my face and went on. "As difficult as that might be."

Jasmine pouted. "Whatever. I actually might have an idea," she said. "Icarus Hall was last used in the 60s, right?"

April nodded. "I think so."

"They used boats to get back and forth from the mainland, so they might have left some behind," Jasmine went on. "They'd be super old, but we could still try to use one."

Tate finally piped up from his spot by the window. "We should use Rhys's sheet rope idea to go outside and look for them."

"Are you serious?" April's face twisted with incredulity. "Look, props to you for the idea, Jasmine, but this whole nightmare shitshow has clearly been planned by someone for a very long time. Don't you think part of that plan would involve them removing any boats that happen to be lying around outside?"

Kiara's upper lip curled. "You don't need to be such a bitch about it."

April let out an exasperated sigh and threw up her hands. "I'm just trying to be realistic. I'm not trying to be a bitch to anyone."

"You're right," Jasmine muttered. "There are no boats anywhere. It was a stupid idea."

"Maybe not," Carey cut in. "I mean, how did the Game Master transport us here? Or himself?"

Brooke's brows shot up. "Good point. There must be at least *one* boat here," she said. "It would obviously be hidden somewhere, but still, it has to be on the island somewhere, right?"

An invisible bubble of hope seemed to float through the room, brightening everyone's faces. Unfortunately, someone had to burst it.

"You guys could be right. But boats aren't the only transport option, and while we were up in that tower, I saw a spot on the ground where a helicopter could land. They could've used that instead," Zach said. "Also, if more than one person is involved in this scheme—which seems really likely—then they could've dropped us and the Game Master off in a boat and then gone back to shore. That way there's no boat left here for us to find."

Shit. He was right.

April piggybacked off his point. "Even if there *is* a boat somewhere, there's no way they would've left it lying around outside for us to find," she said. "I mean, think about it. That window shutter being left open was no accident. It was fine this morning, and then it was suddenly cracked open. The Game Master obviously did it just to mess with us. He wanted us to crack it open all the way. He *wanted* us to know we're on an island, so we'd all feel totally hopeless."

The bleak expressions returned to everyone's faces as they realized Zach and April had made some good points. This place was very likely an inescapable prison, and I was running out of ideas on how to keep everyone's hopes up. How could I, when there probably wasn't any fucking hope for us at all?

A series of pings went through the room, alerting us to our phones. With a sinking feeling in my stomach, I checked the latest message from our captor.

Dinner is served in the drawing room. Please eat as much as you can handle, because you'll need your energy. Game two will begin in one hour.

CAREY

Dinner was a subdued affair, which was the least surprising thing ever, considering how we were staring down the barrel of yet another deadly game. No one made conversation, and I also noticed a lot of people purposefully avoiding each other's eyes. Paranoia was building in all of us, and it finally boiled over fifteen minutes before the game was due to start.

"You know what, guys? I've been thinking about this all day," Kiara suddenly said, putting her fork down with a clatter. She didn't wait for any of us to respond before she continued, head swiveled to stare right at Rhys. "Where did you go before?"

Rhys stared back at her. "Huh?"

"This morning, while we were hanging out in Mav's room. We were all in there for ages, just chatting or whatever. But *you*... you weren't. You insisted on going off alone to 'explore'," she said, lifting her hands to put the word in air quotes.

"And?"

"Well, like April said earlier, the window shutter was closed in the morning. Then, after you wandered off alone, it was suddenly open. You're also the one who just so happened to discover that it was open." Kiara paused and arched an eyebrow.

"Coincidence? Or are you the one who opened it to mess with us?"

Rhys narrowed his eyes. "Are you seriously implying that I'm the Game Master?"

"You have to admit, it *is* kinda weird, man," Tate said.

Rhys turned his fierce gaze to him. "Are you fucking serious? Your last theory about the Game Master got Evan *killed*. Now you're jumping in on the conspiracy theories all over again?"

Tate bristled. "I'm just saying, Kiara has a point. Where did you go earlier?"

"I told you. I went to explore."

"Did you find anything?" Courteney chimed in from across the table.

"Yes, I actually did." Rhys cocked his head in her direction. "I found every single camera and mic in the hall and foyer, just like I said I would. So now I know exactly how much surveillance we're under in this place. And let me tell you... it's a lot. The Game Master is always watching and listening. So you should probably be careful about what you say."

"Is that a threat?" Zach asked, leaning forward.

Rhys rolled his eyes. "Of course you're immediately jumping to defend her, given your pathetic little crush," he said, voice dripping with condescension. "We can all tell, by the way, in case you actually thought you were hiding it well."

Zach's nostrils flared. "I'm just asking a question based on what you said, because it sounded like a threat."

"It was just a comment."

"Oh, *sure*."

Maverick finally spoke up from the head of the table. "Guys, seriously. We agreed to stop arguing. We need to—"

"Work as a team, blah, blah, blah," Rhys cut in. "I know, Mav. We've all heard this bullshit out of your mouth a hundred times today, and I think most of us are sick of it."

"For once, I actually agree with you," Tate said. "I don't want to be in a team with any of you, and I'm sick of pretending I don't suspect everyone in this fucking room."

Brooke leaned forward, brows drawn into a quizzical expression. "I thought we all decided my theory was right. That the Game Master isn't really one of us. He just said that to make us all fight."

"No." Tate shook his head. "*You* decided that. I never said I agreed. In fact, only a few people said they agree. Everyone else just stayed silent. So I'm willing to bet most of us secretly have a suspect when it comes to the Game Master's identity. I'm also willing to bet most of us think it's someone in this room. Just like they said in the video."

That comment was like a lit match thrown in a powder keg. Almost everyone at the table began to snipe at each other, throwing out wild accusations while simultaneously defending themselves.

I was one of the few who remained silent, figuring it was better to keep my head down and draw as little attention to myself as possible. After all, I was one of the first people to be accused earlier, and I didn't want or need any more of that bullshit flung at me. April, Brooke, and Zach joined in with some of the arguments, but they all stayed true to their word and kept our earlier discussion about Rhys to themselves.

Maverick abruptly stood and slammed his hand on the table. "Calm the fuck down! The game is about to start!"

The room fell silent, and every pair of eyes flew to the closest speaker. Maverick was right—just ten seconds later, the speaker crackled to life. "Players, please proceed to Gaming Room 2."

The fear and tension in the room was palpable now. We marched outside and headed down the open east wing hall to find the door marked 'Gaming Room 2'. Maverick pushed it open, and once we were all inside, it automatically closed and locked with a soft hiss.

"That's weird," Rhys muttered. "It's a different sort of door than the last one."

"Who cares about the fucking door?" Tate said, looking around the room with wide eyes. "What the hell is this shit supposed to be?"

The space was adorned with shiny streamers and colorful balloons. A table stood in the middle, covered with a princess-themed tablecloth, and a tiered cake with pink icing and flickering striped candles sat in the center. Toys and board games were scattered on the floor around the crimson velveteen chairs that haphazardly surrounded the table. It gave the impression of an abandoned children's birthday party, silent and empty despite the joyful decorations and lit candles.

"This is creepy as hell," Kiara muttered.

"There's a birthday card over here," April said, looking down at the table. "Should we open it?"

"Might as well." Maverick peered around. "I don't see instructions anywhere, and the Game Master hasn't made any announcements."

April opened the card and held it up to show everyone the words printed inside. CUT THE CAKE.

"I'll do the honors, I guess," Maverick muttered. He blew out the candles and reached for the large silver knife that sat on the platter beside the cake. When he brought it down on the top tier of the cake, he let out an irritated grunt. "It won't go all the way through," he said. "There's something inside."

Zach stepped forward to help, yanking off the candles and peeling off thick pink layers of icing. "Uhh... this is weird," he said. "There's a box with a key inside."

He finished cleaning off the icing with a colorful napkin, and we all crowded around to inspect the transparent box. It had a lock on one side and appeared to be made of regular glass, but when Maverick picked it up and smashed it on the table, it didn't crack.

"It must be laminated glass," Rhys said, leaning in to get a closer look. "Made to be unbreakable."

Maverick squinted at the silver lock on the right side. "Looks like a combination lock," he said. "Like our lockers at school."

Rhys frowned. "So that's how we get in to grab the key, I guess. But how do we get the code?"

"No idea. And what's the key for?" April asked, looking around the room.

"The door, maybe? I'm not sure."

"Guys?" Tate piped up from under the table. "I found something."

He emerged with a triumphant expression on his face and a black laptop computer in his hands. "It was inside a compartment under the table," he said, setting the laptop down. "We must need it for something."

A speaker crackled at the front of the room. "Congratulations, players. You've found all the playing pieces for Truth or Die," said the robotic voice in its usual monotone. "It's like Truth or Dare with a fun little twist."

"Really? Truth or Die?" Kiara said, wrinkling her nose. "How cheap."

April snorted. "No shit."

"The game will begin as soon as the rules have been explained," the robotic voice droned on.

"Here we fucking go," Hudson muttered, crossing his arms over his chest. "Wonder what bullshit we're getting this time?"

"The key in the box will unlock the door. You can only open the box if you have the twelve-digit code, which you'll find on the laptop by responding to a series of questions. Each question must be answered correctly in order to receive the corresponding number. In this case, the correct answer is always the truth, so keep that in mind as you play."

"So all we have to do is unlock the door?" Rhys asked, tipping his head. "That's it?"

"Shh," Jasmine said, elbowing him in the ribs. "I don't think it's over."

The voice from the speaker continued. "When the game begins, the room will slowly fill with odorless, colorless gas dispensed from vents in the ceiling. The gas is fast-acting and extremely toxic to the nervous system, and the door has been sealed, making the room airtight. If you do not unlock the door and escape in thirty minutes, every single one of you will succumb to the gas and die."

"All of us?" Kiara said in a strangled voice, eyes bulging. "We can *all* die here?"

"Not the Game Master," Jasmine replied, casting a dark look over the group. "I bet he or she has some sort of escape maneuver hidden up their sleeve."

"Or maybe Brooke was right, and none of us are the Game Master," Maverick said.

"Sure," Jasmine muttered, suspicion-filled eyes coming to rest on me.

Once more, the speaker crackled to life. "Open the laptop to begin the game. Failure to comply will activate auto-mode in five minutes, releasing all the gas into the room at once," it said. "Have fun playing! And remember... if you lie, you die."

"See?" Rhys said, brows lifting. "I told you the door was different this time."

"For fuck's sake, man. Now isn't the time for your smartass bullshit," Maverick snapped. As he spoke, he opened the laptop lid and gestured for everyone to take a seat at the table. "If one of us fucks up, we all die, so we have to work together," he went on, eyes flashing with annoyance. "Just like I've been saying all fucking day."

Everyone grudgingly nodded.

"Carey, it looks like the first question is for you," Maverick said, eyes lingering on me. "What were the exact charges you were facing before you received the Babylon Prep scholarship?"

"Seriously?" Kiara said snidely. "We already know what she did. She crashed her car into your car, Mav. Big fucking whoop."

I lowered my gaze to the table, hands twisting in my lap. My cheeks felt like they were on fire. "There's a bit more to it than that," I muttered.

"Well, go on, then." Jasmine waved a hand. "We don't have all day, in case you hadn't realized."

I sighed and listed off the charges for Maverick to type in. "Driving under the influence, reckless driving, and grand theft auto."

"Wait, *what?*" Kiara's brows shot up. "You stole a car while you were drunk?"

"I wasn't drunk. I had drugs in my system," I muttered. I didn't bother explaining all the details. We didn't have time, and she wouldn't believe me anyway.

Her eyes narrowed. "That's even worse."

"That's quite the list of charges you have there, Carey. You could have gone to prison," Jasmine cut in, eyes gleaming. "And here I was thinking you were just a negligent driver."

"The charges were dropped in the end," I said, cheeks flaming hot.

"Still... you're a real criminal, and the person who brought us here is a criminal mastermind," she said. "You know what they say, right? Birds of a feather..."

"No shit." Tate leaned back, arms folding. "You just shot right back up to number one on my suspect list, Carey."

"I'm not the Game Master."

"But you could be helping him."

"Guys, we don't have time for this," Maverick said in an icy tone. "We have to move on to the next question."

I noticed he was looking over at me with the same old expression of disdain he used to reserve for me at school. A mix of anger, annoyance, and confusion bubbled up inside me.

Fuck it.

As soon as we got out of this room alive, I was going to confront him so I could find out once and for all why he had such a problem with me. I was tired of not knowing what I'd supposedly done to deserve so much hate—surely it wasn't really over a car?—and if I ended up dying in Icarus Hall at some stage over the next few days, I'd at least like to know the truth before it happened.

He finally dropped his gaze back to the laptop and pressed enter. "Carey told the truth," he announced. "Our first number is 5."

"Should I make a note of the numbers in my phone?" April asked, looking around the table worriedly. "I don't think my memory is good enough to remember all twelve digits by myself."

"No need. It's saved at the bottom of the screen," Maverick said. "The next question is for Evan, but he's dead, so it's allowing me to skip it. The code is now 52."

"Who's next?"

"Hold on. What was the question? And the answer?" Kiara asked, leaning forward.

Maverick briefly hesitated. "How long have you been making masturbation videos and selling them online?" he read off the screen. "The answer was one year."

"Oh my god, seriously?" Jasmine's eyes widened like saucers. "Evan was really doing that?"

"It makes sense," Hudson piped up. "I heard his parents cut him off a while back over some argument. So I guess he had to pay for himself ever since then."

"Guys." April snapped her fingers. "Did you forget we're on a time limit here?"

"Next question is for Tate. What's your secret hobby?" Maverick said, eyes shooting to the other side of the table.

Tate sighed. "I don't really have any hobbies apart from watching TV, so I'm gonna go ahead and guess the Game Master wants me to admit my little extracurricular activity to everyone," he said. "I deal drugs. So fucking what? It's hardly a secret."

"I didn't know about it," Courteney said in a small voice.

"I'll type in 'drug dealing' and see what comes up," Maverick said, fingertips flying over the keyboard. He pressed enter and nodded. "Yup, it says it's true. We have our third number. Next question is for Jasmine."

Jasmine shifted nervously in her seat. "What is it?"

"Who are you sleeping with?"

Jasmine averted her eyes and rubbed her forehead. "Is there another skip option?"

"No, because you're not dead," Maverick snapped. "Just answer the question. Unless you want us all to die."

She sighed. "Mr. Callahan," she muttered. "I've been sleeping with him."

"The history teacher?" Brooke said, eyes like saucers.

"Yes." Jasmine was still refusing to meet anyone's eyes. "It's not a big deal. He's only twenty-three. Let's just go to the next question, okay?"

"Uh... it *is* a big deal. Firstly, he's married, and secondly, he's in a position of power over you as your teacher. That's why it's fucking *illegal*," Zach said.

"I can't believe you didn't tell me about this," Kiara added with an injured sniff. "I thought we were best friends."

Maverick lifted a hand. "Jasmine's right. We need to move on to the next question. We can discuss everything else later if we want to. The next one's—" He abruptly stopped midsentence, and his jaw set like granite. "The next one's for me."

"What is it?" Hudson asked, thin mouth curving into a smirk.

Maverick remained silent.

"Let me read it." Rhys stood, leaned over the table, and snatched the laptop from him. "Maverick, whose fault is it that your brother died two years ago?"

A flush was creeping up Maverick's neck, betraying the turmoil inside as he struggled to maintain his composure.

"Answer the question," Rhys said. "Now."

"Fine." Maverick rearranged his features, attempting to affect a neutral expression, but his gaze remained haunted. "It was my fault. Write that."

Rhys tapped in four letters. M-I-N-E. "It's true," he said, glancing upward. "We have our fifth number."

I stared at Maverick, eyes widening. Before now, I didn't have the faintest clue that he had a brother, let alone that he'd apparently caused his death. A dark curiosity gnawed at me, craving more of the story, but his stoic, unwavering expression told me that he had no intention of divulging any of the details. Especially not to me.

His eyes flicked over to me again. As our gazes met, his lips contorted into a scowl, but beneath the veneer of anger, I could sense a profound melancholy. Whatever happened to his brother had clearly messed him up.

Embarrassed to have been caught staring, I quickly dropped my gaze from Maverick's face to the laptop screen, which I could see from my seat now that Rhys had it. The next question was for April.

I looked over at her as Rhys read it out. "April, where did you go on winter break two years ago?"

"Chamonix, right?" Brooke said, forehead crinkling.

April shook her head and hugged her arms around herself.

"But... that's what you told us," Brooke said.

"If you weren't skiing in France, what were you doing?" Rhys asked. "C'mon, April. Everyone has to answer. You know that."

April finally spoke up. "I was at a place called Elmwood. It's an in-patient eating disorder treatment center. I, um..." She trailed off and rubbed her chin, looking down at the table. "I used to have a problem. Bulimia."

Brooke's eyes filled with sympathy. "April," she said softly, reaching over to touch her hand. "You don't need to feel ashamed about that. You could have told us."

"But I understand why you didn't," Zach added.

I nodded to show my agreement with the others. "I'm really sorry you went through that. I hope you're feeling better now."

"Yeah." Her lips tightened. "Mostly. Some days are difficult. Especially when I'm stressed."

"Well, we're all fucking stressed right now, because we're twenty minutes away from being gassed to death," Tate said, rolling his eyes upward. "Put the answer in, Rhys. She said Elmwood."

Rhys nodded. "Done," he said, pressing enter. "It's true, so we have our sixth digit. And to be precise, we have eighteen minutes and twenty-six seconds left."

Jasmine gasped. "It's already been over eleven minutes since we started?"

"Yup. So let's try to speed things up. Brooke, your turn. What did you do on November 3rd last year?"

Brooke's cheeks instantly flushed, and she lowered her gaze to the table. "I cheated on an exam," she said, voice barely above a murmur.

Confusion flickered in Zach's eyes. "*What*? You're practically a genius! Why would you cheat?"

She lifted her chin to meet his gaze. "I was under a lot of stress, okay? I had a lot going on. Like, a *lot*. Also, my parents are always on my back about staying at the very top of my best classes. I was starting to have trouble keeping up."

I patted her arm. "I understand. It can be really hard."

"Save the sympathy discussions for later, please," Rhys said in a venomous tone, shooting me a filthy look. "Okay, the laptop accepted the words 'cheated on exam', so Courteney, you're up. Who is your uncle?"

It was Courteney's turn to look ashamed. She sighed and

scrubbed a hand across her face before replying. "Robert Paulaner."

Tate's eyes widened. "The serial killer who did all that fucked-up shit to high school kids?"

"Yes," Courteney muttered. "He's on my mom's side, and she changed her name when she married my dad, so no one has ever associated us with him."

"So you're related to a serial murderer who targets high school kids,"

Kiara said, pointedly tapping her chin. "Hmm. Sound familiar to anyone here?"

Courteney replied through gritted teeth. "I'm not the Game Master. And before you say it, I'm not one of his little helpers either."

"If you say so." Kiara sneered and flipped her hair over her shoulder. "Good luck convincing everyone later."

"Stop bitching, Kiara. It's your turn," Rhys said. A triumphant grin spread over his face. "Ah, this'll be good. How many followers have you bought across all your social media accounts?"

Kiara's brows shot up. "What the… I… I didn't buy any," she spluttered. She cleared her throat and straightened her shoulders, quickly regaining her composure. "I don't need to buy followers!"

"Just answer the question," Rhys said, affecting a bored expression.

"I did! The answer is zero!"

"Okay." He shrugged and typed her answer in. A dialog box instantly popped up with the word 'LIE' in big red letters. "Shit. One minute just got shaved off our time."

"I guess the Game Master forgot to mention that particular rule," Zach said.

"Nah, he didn't forget. I bet he wanted us to discover it on our own, just like this, to make everyone freak out," Tate replied.

"Oh my god, who cares?" April said. "Kiara, answer the question! Truthfully this time!"

Kiara sighed and put her face in her hands, elbows resting in front of her. She mumbled something inaudible to my side of the table.

"What did she say?" Rhys asked, looking at Jasmine, who was sitting right next to Kiara.

"She's bought 750,000 followers."

Kiara finally looked up again. "You guys just don't get it!" she said hotly. "When you're in my line of work, you need constant growth and engagement, or else everything falls off and you become totally irrelevant!"

"Wow." Rhys smirked as he typed the answer. "Irrelevant, you say. Sounds truly terrible."

"Shut up," Kiara hissed. "At least I'm not secretly poor like you."

"Wait, what?" Tate cut in, cocking his head.

Kiara leaned back and smiled. "That's right, Rhys—I already know *your* secret. Your dad sold me my latest car two months ago. He looks *exactly* like you. That's how I found out."

Rhys ignored her comments and looked over at Zach. "Your turn, man. Who did you cheat on your girlfriend with last year?"

Zach shifted in his seat, one hand rubbing the back of his neck. He wouldn't meet April's eyes, even though she was staring right at him.

"You cheated on Abby?" she said, eyes saucer wide.

"I... it was a mistake," Zach mumbled. "It only happened once."

I could practically see April's heart breaking right in front of me. "But... why?" she asked, blinking rapidly as she tried to stop herself from crying. "How could you do that to Abby? *How?*"

"I'm sorry. I swear, it was only one time, and it was a mistake. It never happened again."

"Oh my god." April stood and shook a finger at Zach. "This is why we got so close after she died, isn't it? And also why you helped me start the drug awareness campaign in her name. I always thought it was because you loved her so much that you saw me as a family member, and you wanted to stay close because of that. But it was all out of guilt, wasn't it?"

"No!" Zach looked stricken. "You're one of my best friends, April."

"Oh, so you *don't* feel guilty?"

"Of course I do! I just didn't tell you because I didn't want to make things even worse for you!"

Rhys lifted a hand. "Guys, we've been over this. Just answer the question, and we can have the big discussion later, okay?"

April whirled around, eyes flashing. "No! We still have thirteen minutes left on the clock, and we're almost done. You can give me at least one minute for this!"

She spun back around to glare at Zach. "So you didn't tell me for my sake? You seriously expect me to believe that?"

"I knew how you'd react, and I didn't want to lose our friendship." He slowly shook his head, one hand dabbing at his eyes. "I regretted it so much, and being friends with you helped so much with the pain after Abby died. I couldn't lose you too."

"Fuck you," April seethed. "How dare you?"

"April, please," Brooke said, rising to her feet. She lay a hand on April's shoulder. "I understand that you're hurt by this, but we really need to keep going. That clock is ticking down fast."

April slowly turned to face her. "Why aren't you more surprised by this?" she asked in a low voice.

Brooke bit her bottom lip and looked down at the floor.

"Oh my god." April's eyes narrowed. "You knew, didn't you?"

"No. I... I suspected. That's all."

"And you didn't tell me?"

"I didn't want to cause drama. Then, after Abby passed, I saw no reason to make things worse by dredging up stuff from the past. So, yeah... I never told you. I'm sorry."

Maverick stood and slammed his hand down on the table.

"Enough! Answer the question, Zach. Who was the girl you cheated with?"

Zach sighed and raked a hand through his hair, mumbling something unintelligible.

"It was me." Courteney put her hand up. "He's not lying when he says it was only one time. It really was. We were going home from our study group, and we—"

"*You?*" April cut her off, eyes widening with incredulity. "Oh my god. Of course it was! You two have been all over each other ever since we got to this place!"

"That's not true."

"It is. You know, I actually thought it was cute at first. I was glad that Zach was finally able to move on and have feelings for someone else. I thought he deserved it." April's lips twisted into a sneer. "But the whole time..."

She trailed off, and Courteney began to cry. "I swear, it only happened once," she said in a choked voice. "Nothing since then. We both felt too guilty."

"Oh, *sure*."

"Next question is for Hudson," Rhys said, raising his voice to drown out Courteney's sniffling. He gave a sidewards glance to April. "Sorry, but you only asked for a minute, and I actually gave you two for that little outburst. Clock's ticking."

Hudson rolled his eyes. "Shoot."

"How many girls have you sexually violated or attempted to violate?" Rhys asked. I noticed he'd lowered his voice again, ostensibly trying to defend his best friend by ensuring half the room wouldn't hear the question.

Hudson's eyes widened. "What the fuck?"

"He asked how many girls you've tried to force yourself on," Maverick said, loud enough for everyone to hear over Courteney's cries, which had turned from sniffles into plaintive sobs. "Answer the question."

"None." Hudson shrugged. "I don't know why that's even a question for me."

"Bullshit," Maverick said, eyes narrowing. "One of those girls is in the room with us right now. I won't say who to protect her identity. But I know it happened."

My brows rose. I never actually told Maverick what happened between me and Hudson after he rescued me that day in the hallway. He must have guessed based on the interaction he witnessed before he stepped in.

Or... perhaps he knew because he was the Game Master, meaning he already knew the answer to every single secret in this game.

Hudson shot me a sideways glance and smirked. Clearly, he knew hardly anyone in the room would believe me if I told them what he'd done to me.

"I didn't do shit," he said, turning back to face Maverick. "I have no idea what you're talking about."

"You're a fucking liar."

"Rhys, put zero in the answer box. Then everyone will see."

"Don't!" Brooke shouted. "We'll lose a minute!"

"But that could really be the answer," Kiara said. "Like, it could be a trick question. Right?"

Rhys entered 'o' in the answer box, and a familiar red popup appeared. "Shit," he muttered. "We just lost *two* minutes."

"So it's not just one minute we lose for every wrong answer. It doubles every time you put in a wrong answer," Tate said, eyes widening.

"Maybe it's the word 'zero' rather than the number," Rhys murmured, fingers flying over the keyboard.

"Don't!" I shouted, trying to snatch the laptop from him. He was too fast, and he pressed enter before I could get hold of it. The red dialog box popped up again, informing us that we'd lost four minutes this time.

"We're down to six minutes now," I said, shooting a helpless look at Maverick.

He stood and wrenched the laptop out of Rhys's grip. "You can't be trusted with this," he said. "Hudson, answer the fucking question, or we'll all die."

"I... I'm starting to feel a little lightheaded," Courteney mumbled.

"That's because the room is filling with gas, and we just got a massive new hit of it, thanks to Rhys losing us six whole minutes of time," Maverick said.

Hudson looked down at the table. His hands were splayed out in front of him. "I didn't do anything," he muttered.

"Answer now or we'll all die!"

"Fine!" Hudson threw up his hands. "Four. Happy now?"

Maverick rapidly typed in the number and let out a heavy sigh of relief. "That's correct. Just one more person now. Rhys."

Kiara let out a theatrical groan of satisfaction. "Oh, thank *God*. We already know his secret. He's been pretending to be rich." She paused, stood, and did a little mock bow. "You're welcome, everyone!"

"That's not the question." Maverick looked over at Rhys. "Who's your secret lover?"

Rhys's face instantly paled. Clearly, he hadn't expected the Game Master to know this particular secret. "I... how did he..."

"Just answer," Jasmine snapped. "I had to admit I was sleeping with a teacher. Surely yours is no worse."

Rhys was silent for several seconds. Then he jumped to his feet and ran to the door. "Let me out!" he shouted, pounding on it with his fists. "Let me the fuck out!"

"There's no way out unless you answer the question," I called out.

Rhys kept smashing on the door, but nothing happened. Maverick strode over, grabbed him by the shoulders, and dragged him back to the table. "This isn't the 1950s. No one cares if you're gay. You can just say it."

"I'm not gay," Rhys muttered.

"For fuck's sake, why can't you just tell us who you've been sleeping with?" Jasmine asked sharply. "I mean, our lives literally depend on it, or did you forget that?"

Rhys fell silent again.

"Is it some sort of creepy age gap thing? Much older woman? Or a young girl?" Kiara asked, nose wrinkling.

Rhys glared at her. "No! I'm not a fucking pedo!"

"Answer the question, man," Maverick said. He glanced at the laptop screen. "We're down to three and a half minutes."

"I... I can't. Really."

Maverick looked over at Hudson. He was sitting with his head down and shoulders hunched, presumably trying to make himself as small as possible to avoid attention after his shocking admission.

"Hudson, you're his best friend," Maverick said. "Who's he fucking?"

Hudson lifted his chin. "I don't know," he mumbled.

"Fucking say it."

"I swear, I really don't know the answer to this one!" Hudson said. "We don't really talk about shit like that. A few party hookups, maybe, but none of them are embarrassing."

Rhys was still silent. Hudson turned to face him. "C'mon, dude. Just tell us. It can't be that bad."

Courteney's head was starting to loll. I was beginning to feel weak as well, and it was getting difficult to focus.

Maverick leaned closer to Rhys. "Answer the question *now*. Or would you honestly rather die and take the rest of us with you?"

Rhys looked at the table. "Elena," he said in a ragged whisper.

Kiara and Jasmine's mouths dropped open in perfect O shapes.

"Your *sister?*" Hudson said, eyes bulging. "Are you fucking serious?"

"Half-sister," Rhys muttered.

"That's still a biological relation!" Jasmine said, face contorting with disgust. "What the fuck is wrong with you?"

Maverick typed the name in and let out a heavy sigh of relief. "We have the final number. Can someone work on the box as I call out the numbers?"

"We have to hurry," Brooke cut in, nervously glancing at the laptop. "We're down to one minute and seven seconds!"

Zach fiddled with the combination lock as Maverick recited the twelve-digit code. "5-2-9-5-7-8-2-6-4-1-3-8."

The lock fell away, and Zach quickly snatched the key out of the box and raced over to the door. We all followed him, clamoring behind him as his shaky hands inserted the key into the lock.

"Got it!" he said, twisting the handle to wrench the door open. "Run!"

We spilled out of the room and collapsed in the hallway outside, just in time to hear the automated message from the laptop we'd left behind.

"Time's up."

CAREY

The group trudged up the hall in silence. Some of us were undoubtedly too ashamed to speak after the brutally shocking revelations during the game, and others—like myself—were probably reflecting on the incredibly narrow escape.

"Anyone hungry?" Tate piped up, gesturing toward the drawing room. The door was still open, and the table was laden with half-eaten platters of food from our earlier dinner.

"Actually... yeah." Zach stepped forward. "I'm fucking starving."

"Me too, even though I had a big dinner," Kiara said. "Maybe it's an adrenaline thing?"

We all headed inside and took our usual seats. No one spoke the words out loud, but it was clear that none of us wanted to be alone right now.

I poured myself a soda and loaded up a plate with cheesy potato bake. The second game had gone so fast that the food was still warm. As I took my first bite, something occurred to me.

I finished chewing and stuck my hand up to get everyone's attention. "I just thought of something. About the games."

Jasmine rolled her eyes. "What now?"

"In both of the games we've had so far, there's been a way for all of us to survive as long as we follow the rules and work together," I said. "Maybe all the games are going to be like that. If they are, we just need to strategize and work as a team, like Maverick said earlier. Then none of us have to die, and we can all get out of here."

"Good point." Zach nodded slowly. "In the Game Master's video this morning, he said that if we win, we get to go free. He didn't say there can only be one winner. That means survival is definitely an option for all of us. We just need to be careful."

"Well, if everything the Game Master said in that video is actually true, then that means he or she is one of us," Tate said, eyes lingering on me. "I know we ran out of time to talk about it earlier because we've been so busy with other shit, but I want to finish that discussion. Right fucking now."

A message suddenly came through on our phones, cutting the conversation short.

Congratulations on clearing Game Two! There are no more games scheduled for today, so you can unwind this evening in the drawing room or in your bedrooms. Curfew is at 10pm, and doors must remain closed thereafter. Anyone caught outside their bedroom after curfew will be subject to consequences.

"Tate's right. We need to discuss this again," Maverick said, forehead creasing as he looked down at his phone. "Who the *fuck* is the Game Master?"

Jasmine cocked a brow. "I know a few of you decided that it isn't one of us, but I think it is, and I think it's Carey."

"You have got to be fucking kidding me," I muttered, shaking my head.

She shook a finger in my direction. "Think about it, guys. She had the easiest question in the last game. I mean, we already knew she was a dirty criminal, so her truth was hardly a shocking revelation, was it?" she said. "It's almost as if she designed the game to be utterly humiliating to everyone except herself."

"That's bullshit." April's eyes narrowed. "Obviously, the Game Master didn't have as much time to dig up serious dirt on her because she's the new girl at school. Or maybe she genuinely has nothing to hide."

"Exactly," Zach said. "Also, she wasn't the only one with an easy question. Tate's was easy too. Nearly everyone knows he's the biggest supplier on campus."

April looked at him, nodding enthusiastically. I knew she was still furious at him over the cheating admission, but she was clearly willing to work with him in my defense. "Courteney's secret wasn't too bad either," she said. "I mean, it's kind of embarrassing, but at the end of the day, who really cares if her uncle is a serial killer? It's not like *she* had anything to do with his crimes."

"Actually, there are serial killer genes that run in families. I saw something about it on TV once," Hudson replied. "So Courteney's question could've been a clue about her involvement in all this shit."

Jasmine's eyes rolled upward again. "Oh, you saw it on TV? I guess it must be true, then."

Kiara snickered. "Also, if Courteney was the Game Master, why the hell would she put a question in the game that makes her look guilty?" she asked.

"No shit. You're so fucking dumb, Hudson," Jasmine added. "Although, how much brainpower can we really expect from a dirty fucking sex predator?"

Hudson opened his mouth to snap back at her, but April lifted a hand and clicked her fingers to shush him. "Back to your earlier comment, Jasmine," she said, eyes fixed on her from across the table. "How could Carey possibly know any of our secrets in order to create that Truth or Die game? She's only been at school for a month, and judging by the secrets that were revealed, the Game Master has been digging up shit on all of us for years."

"Maybe she isn't really new," Tate chimed in. "Maybe she's been watching all of us for years now. Stalking us."

Maverick snorted. "Oh, fuck off, man. That's not possible."

"Okay, okay." Kiara rapped on the table. "I have an idea that might help us determine which one of us is the Game Master, if it's actually one of us."

"Yeah?"

"Let's go around the table, one by one, and figure out who had the most and least enemies *before* we entered the mansion. If someone had a problem with every single person in this room, then they're the most likely suspect, because the Game Master clearly hates us all." Kiara turned her catlike gaze to me. "Carey, seeing as you seem to have the largest number of targets on your back, you can go first. Who are you friends with here, and who do you have a problem with?"

I took a deep breath before answering. "Well, you already know I'm friends with April, Brooke, and Zach. I didn't know Courteney or Evan before I got here, so I never had a problem with them. And the rest of you..." I hesitated, eyes lingering on Maverick. "The rest of you have clearly had a problem with me since I started at Babylon. You haven't exactly hidden it."

"You forgot Maverick as a friend," Hudson muttered.

I frowned at him. "Huh?"

He raised his voice. "You and Maverick aren't enemies. You're always staring at each other. It's obvious you want to fuck each other's brains out."

My cheeks instantly flushed hot. "That's not true."

"Then why are you always looking at each other?"

"We aren't," I said hotly, gritting my teeth. "I look at him the same amount as anyone else around me."

Maverick jumped in. "Look, we share a dorm, so we're used to seeing each other a lot," he said, rubbing his jaw. "Maybe it's a familiarity thing. Totally unconscious behavior. We don't even notice we're doing it."

"Uh-huh." Hudson smirked. "Keep telling yourself that."

I stared down at my plate, mind whirling as I wondered if Hudson's little theory could possibly be correct. Could Maverick actually want me, and the reason he was always so nasty to me was because he didn't want to show it?

Hell no. I wasn't going to let myself become one of those delusional 'he's only mean to you because he likes you!' people. That was total bullshit. Guys who were mean to girls were assholes, plain and simple.

Still, the mere thought of Maverick possibly wanting me—even just a sliver—made me far more nervous about confronting him alone later. I was still going to do it, though. I needed to know why he hated me so much.

"Okay, Carey, we'll take your word about the Maverick thing and say you have five friends and six enemies here." Kiara abruptly turned her attention to April. "Your turn."

After we were all done, it was determined that Hudson and I had an equal number of haters before we arrived at the mansion. Everyone else had fewer enemies, meaning there wasn't a single person who had an issue with everyone in here.

"So it can't be one of us," Rhys said, speaking up for the first time since his shocking admission during the last game. "Like Kiara said, the Game Master clearly has a reason to hate all of us, and no one in this room fits that profile."

"Hold on." Tate sat up straight. "What if it's Evan? He could've faked his own death, and now he's watching us through all those cameras."

"God, Tate, are you really that fucking stupid?" Jasmine snapped. "We all saw him die. No one can fake something like that."

"Yeah. We've already established that the deaths here are *real*," Maverick said. "Also, Evan didn't have a problem with anyone here, as far as I know. So why would he be the Game Master?"

"Wait." I lifted a palm. "Kiara's idea was a good one, but it relied on all of us being totally honest about whether or not we have a problem with certain people in here."

Understanding dawned on Brooke's face. "She's right," she said. "What if one of us has a secret reason to hate everyone in here? It's not like they'd ever admit it. Not if they were the Game Master. And how would we ever know they were hiding this stuff? It's not like we can see inside everyone's minds and force them to tell the truth."

"Shit." Kiara's shoulders sagged. "We're back to square one, then."

"Yeah. Looks like it."

April scrubbed a hand over her face before flashing a meaningful look at me, Brooke, Courteney, and Zach in turn. "Should we?" she muttered.

"Tell them about the Rhys thing, you mean?" Zach asked, forehead wrinkling. She nodded, and he nodded too. "Yeah. I think it's time."

"What are you guys whispering about over there?" Jasmine said sharply.

"Something we talked about earlier," April said, leaning forward. "We didn't want to say anything earlier, just in case, but I think we should come clean now. We were discussing Rhys."

"As a suspect, you mean?"

April's lips tightened. "Yup."

Tate grinned. "Ah, yes, let's throw the sister-fucker under the bus. Makes sense."

"Shut up, Tate." Brooke glared at him. "This is serious."

"Okay, I'll bite. Why do you think it's Rhys?" Kiara asked, tilting her chin.

April haltingly ran through our earlier discussion about Rhys's capacity for lying, high intelligence, and aptitude for engineering.

"Whoever designed these games clearly knows a thing or two about engineering," Brooke added. "So... yeah. That's our theory."

Rhys sighed and put his head in his hands. "I get it," he mumbled. "Makes sense, really."

"Is that an admission of guilt?" Jasmine asked.

He lifted his chin and looked over at her. "No. I'm just saying, I can see how it makes me look suspicious when it's all put together like that. But it's not me. I don't know how to prove it, but I swear, it's *not*."

"Wow. Really? That's your only defense?"

Rhys slowly shook his head. "Actually, no. There's one thing I can say in my defense," he said. "A high schooler who has an interest in a future engineering career isn't necessarily an engineering genius. Do you guys really think I can plan and build this sort of shit by myself? Especially when I have no money, as Kiara and April have so kindly pointed out to everyone."

"You might be able to pull it off if you received financial help," Brooke said, eyes lingering on Hudson. "From a good friend, perhaps."

"Let's put it to a vote," Kiara said. "Who here thinks Rhys is most likely to be the Game Master?"

Seven hands went up, including my own. Only Rhys, Hudson, Jasmine, and Tate kept their hands down.

"What about you guys?" Kiara asked, eyeing the four of them. "Who do you think it is?"

All of them pointed in my direction. "Carey," they said in unison.

"Oh, great, we're still on that bullshit," Zach said sarcastically.

Maverick rose to his feet. "Obviously we can't come to an agreement right now, because there's not enough evidence," he said in an authoritative tone. "So, for now, I think we should go back to our rooms and go to bed. We've had a long day, and we don't know what sort of shit we're in for tomorrow."

"Good idea." April stood too. "We need to rest."

We filed out of the drawing room and headed upstairs to our respective rooms. I made a beeline for the shower, longing to wash away the perspiration that had clung to my skin all day. Despite the mansion's cool interior, the persistent stress and fear of being here had made me sweat like crazy.

When I was finished, I slid into a pair of clean pajamas that the Game Master had left for me in the drawer. Then I glanced at my phone to check the time. Only 8:22. That gave me plenty of time to confront Maverick.

I took several deep breaths, finally working up the nerve to do it. Then I left my room and headed to the top of the hall. Maverick's light was on, so I rapped on the door.

No answer.

I knocked again. "Maverick? Are you in there?"

I figured he might not have heard me, so I tried the door and found it unlocked. I slowly opened it. I understood how rude it was to enter someone's space uninvited, but I still wanted to do it anyway, given how long it had taken me to work up the nerve to come down here.

Maverick wasn't on the bed or in the chair at the desk. He wasn't sitting on the nook beneath the window, either. My eyes slid over to the bathroom door, and I heard a masculine voice faintly saying my name. He must have heard me at the door after all.

As I stepped closer to the bathroom, I realized Maverick was in the shower. I must have imagined hearing him say my name, because he wasn't speaking at all. He was grunting and panting and so clearly... *oh, God*. I shouldn't be here. I c*ouldn't* be here.

I retreated, quietly closing the door behind me. The image of Maverick touching himself in the shower was burned into my mind, and my cheeks were aflame with embarrassment.

I hurried back to my room, heart pounding, desperate to put some distance between myself and the awkward encounter. Despite my better judgment, a rush of conflicting emotions were stirring inside me at the thought of Maverick's wet body, hard cock, and pumping hand.

Closing my door with a soft click, I leaned against it, grappling with the unsettling truth I could no longer deny.

Whether I liked it or not... I had feelings for him.

CAREY

Morale was low at breakfast the next morning. Everyone at the table seemed to be suspicious of everyone else in the room, and hardly anyone was in the mood for talking, including me. I kept looking around instead, silently studying each face and wondering which one could belong to the Game Master.

I thought Rhys and Hudson still looked good for it, but I wasn't certain. Anyone else in the room could be guilty too. Or maybe Brooke was right at the beginning, and the Game Master really *was* an outsider who lied to us in order to sow discord. I had no way of knowing, and it was driving me crazy.

Speaking of crazy... there was one face I was studiously avoiding. *Maverick.*

Last night's revelation about my ridiculous crush on him embarrassed the hell out of me, and I kept worrying that he'd see the feelings written all over my face if we locked eyes. Thankfully, he was at the opposite end of the table, so there was only a slim chance of that happening.

Hardly any of us were sitting in our assigned seats, and we'd once again splintered into distinct groups. Courteney had moved away from her spot near Zach, due to the awkwardness between her and April, and she was now hanging out with Maverick, Jasmine, and Kiara at the top end of the table. Hudson, Rhys, and Tate were still in their nasty trio in the middle, and my own friend group had the far end.

It was awkward as hell for me and Brooke, who were right in the middle of April and Zach's newfound drama. Zach kept trying to make conversation, and April would occasionally look over at him with sparkling eyes and an open mouth like she was just about to respond. Then she'd suddenly seem to remember what he did to her sister, and her mouth would clamp shut as a stony expression returned to her face.

One of the speakers crackled on the wall. "Players, please make your way to Gaming Room 3."

In glum silence, we trudged out of the drawing room and headed down the hall to find that another wing of the house had opened.

"This must've been the dining hall," Courteney said, staring at the double-wide entrance. "It's in the right spot, and the entryway looks exactly the same."

"I think you're right," April said, doing a slow spin to assess the space beyond the doors. "Same place, but it's been renovated."

I looked around, wondering what fresh hell was in store for us in this room. The walls around us had been painted with colorful murals depicting a playground, and there were also several painted arrows on the floor pointing toward a walled-off area with an arched entryway. A wooden sign hung over the entryway, informing us that a maze lay beyond it.

Once we were all inside, the doors slammed shut behind us, and a clicking sound followed, indicating that we were locked in until the game was over.

"Welcome, players. Today, we're playing my version of Tag," a robotic voice said from a speaker on the left wall. "Please make your way over to the table on the right. There, you will find the game rules along with the playing pieces. Follow the instructions, or there will be dire consequences."

The underlying message was clear: play or die.

We headed over to the table to find eleven strange items laid out in neat rows. They looked like thick silver collars with hinge openings at the back and black strings hanging from the front. A small light bulb was attached to the end of each string.

"Are these for us to wear?" Jasmine said, gingerly poking at one.

"Yup." Maverick nodded, eyes scanning the rule sheet. "I'll read this out loud, okay?"

Everyone nodded their assent, and Maverick began. "Each player must equip one of the collars and press the small button on the right to turn it on. When activated, the light on the end of the string will turn green. After that, the game timer will begin. Players can either enter the maze or hang back in the playground area, and the aim is to tag other players by tugging on their strings to turn their lights red. A buzzer will sound whenever someone is tagged, in order to alert everyone else, and those whose lights are turned red will face their demise once the timer runs down to zero. You can tag and kill as many players as you want, or you can choose to tag none at all. However, at least *one* person's light must be red by the end of the game, and the collars must always remain on. If every light is still green when the timer runs out, you will all die. You have twenty minutes to complete the game."

The horrifying truth dawned on all of us at the same time.

"Carey was wrong yesterday," Kiara said, slowly shaking her head. "There's no way for all of us to survive this game, no matter how strategic we are. At least one of us has to die."

"Yup." Maverick set his jaw. "That's the rule."

"No fucking way." Zach fervently shook his head. "There must be *some* way we can all survive."

"I think so too," Brooke said. "There must be something obvious that we're all missing."

April shook her head. "I don't think so," she said, voice quavering. "The rules are pretty clear. One light must be red by the end."

"So then we just take someone's collar off and turn it red."

"No. It clearly says the collars must remain on us at all times," Maverick said. "There's no way around it. Someone has to die."

"How does the collar kill us?" Kiara asked, wide eyes filled with dread. "Will our heads explode?"

Rhys frowned as he examined one of the collars. "I don't see any kind of incendiary device on this," he said. "I'm guessing there's some sort of mechanism inside that slowly tightens it and chokes the person to death."

"Oh my god. I think I'm going to be sick," Jasmine said, leaning against the edge of the table. "Being choked to death is one of my worst nightmares."

Hudon smirked. "I thought most girls were into choking these days."

"Are you fucking serious right now?" April snapped, eyes narrowing. "You think *now* is the time for a dirty sex joke?"

"Who says I'm joking?"

"Hudson, unless you have something constructive to say, shut the fuck up," Maverick said, face twisting into a scowl.

Tate stuck his hand up. "I have something constructive to say," he said in a strangely flat tone. "Someone has to die, and I think it has to be Carey. Last one in, first one out."

I shrank back, mouth going dry.

"*What?*" April's eyes bulged, and she grabbed my arm. "No!"

"Yes." Tate's eyes glittered maliciously as he looked around the group. "If we have to pick someone, it makes sense for it to be her."

"Sorry, but I agree," Kiara said. "Most of us barely know Carey. So obviously we pick her."

"Stop talking about her like she's not in the room!" Zach snapped. "She's right here, and she's a fucking person! Treat her like one!"

"Okay. Fine." Tate's gaze fell on my face. "Carey, we're choosing you to die. Got it?"

"No, you're not!" April shouted, stepping in front of me. "Stay the fuck away from her!"

He shrugged. "I can tag you too if you want to get in my way," he said. "But either way, I'm tagging Carey. She's the one who really needs to go."

"You're not going to get me," I said in a low voice, shaking my head. "Not if I get you first."

"Oh, sure. You'll *totally* tag me first with those short, skinny little arms of yours," he replied, voice dripping with sarcasm.

"Yeah, sorry, Carey, but you don't stand a chance," Jasmine added, arching a brow. "Guess it's time to say goodbye, huh?"

"Jesus, can you all shut the fuck up?" Maverick said, slamming a hand on the table. "Let's just put the collars on, start the game, and see what happens. Okay?"

I swallowed hard, rooted to the spot in terror. April put her collar on with trembling hands, and then she helped affix mine to my neck. "Don't worry," she whispered as it clicked shut. "We'll defend you. Someone else will be gone by the end of the game."

"Can everyone activate their collars now?" Rhys called out. "I want to get this over and done with."

We all pressed our buttons with shaky hands. My light turned on, green like the others, and at the exact same time, an enormous red digital timer on the ceiling switched on and started counting down from 20:00.

"Run, Carey!" April screamed, shoving me in the back. "Hide in the maze!"

Adrenaline flooded my veins, and I sprinted away. Just before I entered the maze, I turned my head over my shoulder to see April clawing at the back of Tate's sweater to hold him back from going after me. Zach and Brooke were standing by, watching helplessly, and the other six players were heading for the maze.

I whirled back around, ran inside, and took the first left. Seconds later, I heard footsteps pounding on the ground somewhere to my right. I breathed a short sigh of relief, grateful that no one had picked the same path as me.

There was a sudden scuffling of footsteps behind me, and someone grabbed my sweater and yanked me backward. My heart sank. I wasn't alone on my path after all.

My attacker spun me around, and I came face to face with Rhys.

"Look," he said in a low voice. "I'm going to give you a chance, because I know exactly how you feel right now. Everyone is gunning for me too thanks to that little theory you and your friends put forward yesterday. So I'm going to let you hide now, and I'm going to try and hide too. But if I don't hear that buzzer before the last five minutes of the game, I'll find you and pull your string just so I know at least one person is red. Got it?"

I nodded silently, heart pounding. Rhys stared at me for a second longer. Then he turned on his heel and ran off in the opposite direction. I spun back around and kept heading down my original path.

I spent the next several minutes slipping down new paths, peeking around corners, and skidding to rapid stops so I could turn tail when I heard someone coming. There were a lot of shadowy nooks and cracks built into the painted walls, which allowed me to save myself from multiple close calls.

"I saw her come this way!" Jasmine called out to Kiara as they dashed past the hidden nook that I'd wedged myself into mere seconds ago. "Shit, where did she go?"

"That way!" Kiara said. "I can hear something over there!"

Their footsteps faded into the distance. I took a deep breath and stepped out onto the path again. So far, I'd had seven near-misses, and the timer on the ceiling was down to six minutes. If I kept making my way through the maze and hiding in the nooks, I could save myself for the rest of the game. Rhys had promised to tag me if no one else was tagged, but that plan hinged entirely on his ability to find me. If I was careful, that wouldn't happen, and I would survive against all odds.

Someone had to die, though. That grim reality kept gnawing at me, whipping up a strange combination of fear and guilt deep inside. Obviously, I didn't want to be caught and tagged, but if I wasn't, someone else would be tagged by the end of the game to avoid the outcome of everyone dying. I knew that wasn't my fault, but still... I couldn't help but feel partially responsible for whoever ended up losing their life today.

I spied a large black crack on the wall ahead, and I hurried over to it, assuming it was another nook to hide in. Unfortunately, it was just a huge streak of black paint.

"Shit," I muttered, whirling around to assess my options. I could go back the way I came, or I could choose between the left or right.

I picked the left again. That direction had saved my life many times, so I figured it made sense.

I sprinted several yards, only to find myself at a dead end. I whirled back around and skidded to a heart-rending stop as I spotted Tate striding toward me.

"Gotcha," he said, thin lips stretched into a smirk. "You can't hide forever."

Panic flooded me. "Please," I said, lifting my palms. "Don't do this."

He advanced, one slow step at a time. "There's only three minutes left, and I'm not dying in this fucking place," he snarled, eyes narrowed on the green light dangling over my chest. "It has to be you."

"Wait!" I lifted a trembling hand. "Just wait! Please!"

He glanced at the timer on the ceiling. "I'm a generous guy, so I'll give you a minute or two for your last words. But then

I'm yanking that string, and there's nothing you can do to stop me."

"Just listen to me," I said, voice cracking with fear. "It doesn't make sense for you to tag me."

Tate's brows lifted, and he folded his arms. "Oh, yeah? Why?"

"You've been trying to convince everyone that I'm the Game Master since yesterday morning, so you obviously really believe it's me. Right?"

"So what?"

I cleared my throat and raised my chin. "If I *am* the Game Master, and you pull this string, my light won't turn red, because obviously I'll have some sort of failsafe built in to protect me. Then every player's light will still be green at the end of the game, and that means everyone dies. Except me, obviously. Do you really want to risk that happening?"

Tate smirked. "Nice try, but I've been thinking about this shit for the last fifteen minutes, and here's what I've realized," he said, slowly rubbing his chin. "If you're *not* the Game Master, you'll die after I tag you. If you *are,* you'll want to keep hiding your identity while so many of us are still alive, because you can't fight off ten people at once. So you would never admit that your collar malfunctioned because you're the Game Master. Instead, I think some sort of automated announcement would play, telling us there was a technical issue and therefore the game is forfeited as it couldn't be completed, despite you clearly losing by getting tagged *on camera* while the footage is supposedly being live streamed to the Game Master." He paused and pointed to one of the many surveillance cameras overhead. "None of us would die then. We'd be allowed to move on to the next game, and everyone would see it as a lucky escape. But you know what, Carey?"

"What?"

He took another step closer. "If that actually happens, I'll know you really are the Game Master, and I'll tell everyone else. Then it's ten against one. I really like those odds."

"Tate, please…"

"Think about it." A malicious grin spread over his face. "If you're not the Game Master, you'll die. But if you are, your identity will be revealed, and we can take you down. Win-win, the way I see it."

"Don't do this to me. *Please,*" I said, eyes stinging with tears.

"If it's not you, it has to be someone else. You're the best option we have." He glanced upward. "Time's up."

"Please!" I screamed. "No!"

Tate lunged at me, arms outstretched. In a futile attempt to dodge him, I wound up slipping and falling flat on my ass with a painful thud. At the same time, footsteps pounded on the path ahead. Maverick appeared right behind Tate, and one hand shot out over his shoulder to tug on his string.

A shrill buzzer sounded, and Tate's light turned red. At the same time, a raucous cheer resounded through the maze. "Someone finally got her!" Hudson shouted distantly. "We're all good!"

Tate's jaw dropped as he looked down at his newly red light. Then he slowly turned to face Maverick. "What the fuck, man?" he spat out. "We agreed it would be her!"

Maverick stared down at him with a stony expression. "I didn't agree."

Tate lunged forward, presumably to tug on his string as a parting revenge shot. Maverick anticipated it, and he quickly knocked Tate's hand away and shoved him backward.

Nine seconds later, the timer ticked down to zero.

Tate was shaking like a leaf now, hands frantically clutching at his neck. "Get it off me," he said. "Please! Stop it!"

The collar was slowly tightening, just like Rhys predicted, and Tate's face and neck were turning crimson. "Stop it," he croaked, eyes bulging. "Help me!"

Maverick stepped forward and yanked me to my feet. "Come on," he said tersely. "We don't need to see this shit."

He led me down the path, one arm hooked around my shoulder. Neither of us looked back.

When we finally reached the maze entrance and stepped out, we were greeted by a sea of stunned faces.

"Oh my god," Jasmine said. "She's alive?"

"What the fuck?" Hudson roared, charging toward me. "You fucking *bitch*!"

Maverick held up a palm and stepped partway in front of me. "It wasn't her. It was me," he said. "I killed Tate."

Hudson stopped dead in his tracks, face contorted with slack-jawed shock. Then he backed down and trudged over to Rhys, jaw clenched and hands balled at his sides. As much as he despised Maverick, he clearly knew he was below him in the pecking order here.

April ran over and threw her arms around me. "I'm so sorry," she said, voice cracking with emotion. "I stopped Tate for as long as I could, but he kept threatening—"

I cut her off. "Don't apologize. You gave me the head start I needed, and it worked. I'm alive!"

Brooke and Zach came over and hugged me too, whispering their relief that I'd survived. Neither of them would meet my eyes when I drew back, and I knew exactly why.

At the start of the game, both stood back and watched as April wrestled with Tate, risking her own life to save mine. They weren't willing to do the same, and now they were ashamed of themselves.

I understood their choice, though. Our friendship didn't automatically obligate them to risk their lives for me. Also, deep down, I knew that things were probably going to deteriorate into an 'every man for himself' situation at some point during these twisted games. That wasn't Brooke or Zach's fault.

Only the Game Master was to blame.

An announcement from the nearest speaker informed us that the rest of the day was free for us to do whatever we wanted. No one wanted to do much, though, and no one seemed interested in talking either. Morale had never been lower. Despite Tate's general unpopularity in this crowd, his death was a stark reminder that these games and their consequences were real.

Lunch was eaten in fraught silence. At one o'clock, a text message ordered us to our bedrooms for five hours so the drawing room could be cleaned and prepared for dinner. We were warned of dire consequences if we disobeyed and went out in the hall during these five hours, and no one wanted to risk finding out what those consequences were.

Dinner was served at six. Afterwards, people either went back to their rooms to read or hung back in the drawing room to talk in huddled groups. I stayed for a while to hang out with April, Brooke, and Zach, but the mood was tense and awkward, and we all decided to leave just after eight.

I returned to my room to shower and read in bed. I left my door open so I could see and hear what was going on outside, and by nine, the last group members who were still out—Rhys and Hudson—were trudging back to their respective rooms.

I got up to close and lock my door, but when I reached it, I hesitated, hand hovering over the handle. Then I took a deep breath and headed for Maverick's room for the second night in a row.

This time, he answered when I knocked. He was shirtless, skin glistening with tiny droplets of water. I gulped, trying to push aside the mental image of him in the shower. That was the last thing I needed to be thinking about right now.

"What do you need, Carey?" he asked brusquely, staring down at me.

"I need to know why you did it," I said, boldly matching his gaze.

"Why I did what?"

"Why you saved me in the game today."

He was silent for a moment. When he finally replied, his voice was low. "You know why."

"No. I actually don't know at all." I folded my arms. "You hate me. You've always made that *very* clear."

"You're right," he said softly. He was staring right at my lips. "I hate you."

"So why did you save me from Tate today?" I demanded, eyes narrowing. "It's not the first time you've helped me, either."

Maverick rubbed his jaw and looked away. "I already answered your question."

"No, you just gave me some bullshit about already knowing why, and I'm telling you, I don't know why! So tell me. Now!"

He returned his steely gaze to me. "Fine," he growled, chest heaving. "I'll fucking tell you why, Carey."

With that, he enveloped my face in his hands, drawing me close before he crushed his lips to mine.

CAREY

Maverick snaked his arm around my waist and pushed me right up against the door, his lips never lifting from mine, his hands all over me. I kissed him back just as hard and fast, pouring out every ounce of frustration, irritation, and loathing into each clash of our lips.

His hand tangled in my hair, pulling me even closer, as if there wasn't enough room to contain the heat between us. The outside world faded to oblivion, and I no longer cared about the twisted games beyond these walls or the threat of death looming over our heads. All that mattered now was the press of Maverick's body against mine and the way his touch sent shivers down my spine, making me ache for more.

When his fingertips started moving lower, delving into the waistband of my pants, I didn't stop him. I kept kissing him, raking my hands through his hair as moans spilled from my lips and into his mouth.

He finally pulled back, just enough to catch his breath, and his eyes locked with mine. The dark intensity in his gaze said more than his words ever could, and I knew this was the beginning of something that neither of us could stop.

He ushered me toward the bed, hand sliding beneath my panties to skim my center. "You're wet," he muttered, breathing heavily against my neck. I could feel his heart pounding, echoing the rapid rhythm of mine.

"Yes," I said breathlessly, clinging to him. "Please…"

I trailed off, not entirely sure what I was asking for with that last whispered word. Maverick seemed to know anyway, expertly rubbing the tight bundle of nerves between my legs until I felt like I was melting.

"More," I murmured, lips ghosting over his ear. "I need more."

Our clothes vanished in a flurry of hands, leaving a trail of black and gray fabric on the floor beside the bed. We fell onto the mattress, and I rolled onto my back and sat up on my elbows, watching Maverick devour my naked body with his gaze. The expression on his face made me weak, radiating pure lust and need.

I snaked a hand down between my legs to slowly rub my pussy, as if daring him to come and take it. He let out a low groan. "Fuck…"

With that, he was on me, wrapping a fist around his hard cock and angling it to drag the head over my clit. I held my breath, willing him to do more. Once again, it was like he read my mind, because he dragged his cock lower, wetting himself with my desire. Down, and then up to stroke my clit, and then back down. Over and over, winding me up tighter and tighter.

I let out a low, breathy moan and bit my bottom lip, legs trembling with anticipation. It felt so wrong and dirty to be doing this with the guy who'd tried his best to wreck my life over the last several weeks, but the wrongness of it only stoked my need higher.

Maverick moved his cock back down to my entrance, and I tensed as he pressed inside. He was much bigger than I'd experienced before. "It's okay," he murmured as the burn from the sudden intrusion made me cry out. "You trust me?"

"Yes," I said breathlessly, winding my arms around him.

He slid out slowly before pushing back in. He did it over and over, each shift stretching me a little more until it started to feel incredible. "Oh my god," I panted, fingernails digging into his back. "More. *More*."

Maverick's movements picked up, cock hitting some spot inside me that had my eyes rolling back in my head. At the same time, his hand slipped between us to rub my clit in fast circles until the pressure inside me was too much to handle. I arched into his chest and clung to him even tighter as I came undone on his cock, moaning loudly.

"Fuck," he muttered in a shaky voice, his movements picking up. "I can feel you coming."

"Oh, god," I cried out as I spasmed around his cock once more. "Mav..."

He let out a low growl as he pumped faster, my body quivering beneath his. His breaths came faster and faster until he was panting and grunting, and then he pulled out to come on my stomach, cock twitching against the soft skin there.

He pressed a tender yet fierce kiss to my forehead before pulling away to grab a wad of tissues from the bedside table. I stayed motionless, dazedly watching the rippling muscles of his body as he gently cleaned my abdomen.

When he was done, he tossed the tissues on the table and collapsed next to me, still breathing heavily. I stared up at the ceiling with wide eyes, not knowing what to say or do.

"That was, uhh... unexpected," I finally murmured.

"No shit," came Maverick's muttered response.

"I always thought you—" I faltered midsentence and began again. "You hate me. You've hated me ever since we met."

He didn't respond.

"Are you ever going to tell me why?" I went on. "Or are you just going to keep hating me?"

"Carey..."

"No, seriously." I propped myself up on one elbow and looked at him. "I've been driving myself crazy for weeks wondering about this. Why do you hate me so much? Is it really just because I crashed into your car?"

Maverick averted his eyes and rubbed the side of his face. "I don't think this is the right time for this discussion."

"Sorry, but I think you owe me an answer," I said hotly, sitting up straighter. "You've tormented me for weeks over a fucking car, and I—"

He cut me off. "It wasn't just a fucking car!" he snapped.

My eyes widened, and I drew back. "What do you mean?"

"Long story," he muttered.

"Well, we've got a while until curfew, so I'm more than happy to listen to every word," I replied. "You know I'm right. I deserve an answer."

"Fine." He sighed heavily and sat up straight, eyes still not meeting mine. "You remember my question in the Truth or Die game?"

"About your brother?" I asked, brows knitting.

"Yeah. Julian."

"You said it was your fault he died."

His jaw tightened. "It was."

"What do you mean?"

Maverick was silent for a long moment before he began to explain.

"He was going through some shit for a really long time," he said. "Mental stuff, I mean. He was really down, and nothing seemed to help. I couldn't do anything, even though I tried. We all tried."

I nodded slowly and stayed quiet, giving him time to formulate his next words.

"One day he suddenly seemed fine again. He was in a good mood, acting all happy and friendly to everyone. It lasted a few days, so I thought he was back to his old self and everything was fine," he said. "Then one day he came and asked me if I knew the code to my parents' safe. He said he wanted to borrow a piece from Mom's jewelry collection to lend to a girl he was taking to prom. Something about it matching her dress. So I told him the code. I saw it ages ago when Mom was typing it in. But he didn't really want a piece of jewelry."

My stomach lurched. "What did he take?"

"My dad's gun was stored in the safe as well," Maverick replied. "He used it to..."

His voice turned hoarse as he trailed off, and he turned his head so I could no longer see his face.

"That's how he died?" I asked, softening my voice.

"Yeah. Turns out, when someone has severe depression and suddenly starts acting happy again, it's not a good sign. It can mean they've totally given up and accepted the fact that they're going to end it." Maverick swallowed thickly and went on. "Apparently it's pretty common with suicides."

I reached over and squeezed his hand. "God, Mav, I'm so sorry. But you couldn't have known. You were only fifteen or sixteen when it happened, right?"

"Yeah. But I think I was old enough to know better," he said gruffly. He was gripping the edge of the blanket so hard that his knuckles had turned white. "If he really wanted to borrow a fucking necklace, why wouldn't he just ask our parents for the safe code? I should've known there was a reason he was being so weird about it."

"Maverick, come on. It wasn't your fault."

"Well... I've always felt like it was."

"I get it. But it's not. I promise you that," I said softly. "And listen, if you ever want to talk more about it... I'll be here for you, okay? I might not know all the right things to say, but talking can still help."

"You don't have to say stuff like that," he said in a clipped tone. "It's not like we're friends."

"I'm not just saying it. I mean it," I replied. "Sometimes it's easier to talk about your feelings to someone who's basically a stranger instead of close friends and family. So the offer is there. You can talk, and I'll listen. Whenever you want."

"Thanks," he muttered.

He went silent for another long moment. I waited for him to talk again, not wanting to interrupt his grief-stricken thought process.

"Anyway... to answer your original question, my car actually used to be Julian's. He loved that thing," he finally said. "When he was gone, I started using it because it felt like a way to be close to him again. You know what I mean?"

I nodded. "Yes."

"Whenever I drove it, I felt okay for a while. Like I could just pretend he was right there in the passenger seat, or at home waiting for me to bring it back to him. That probably sounds fucking stupid, but—"

I lifted my hand and cut him off. "It doesn't sound stupid at all. Believe me."

Maverick finally looked at me. His gaze had hardened. "When you crashed into it, the whole thing got written off. Permanently fucked. And I know this might make me sound like an unhinged freak, but when it happened, it actually felt like I was losing Julian all over again."

"I get it. And I'm so sorry," I said, voice barely above a whisper. My stomach was twisting into knots. "You really don't sound unhinged at all. It makes total sense. That car must've felt like your last real connection to your brother."

He nodded curtly. "Yeah, it did. And then some drugged-up dumbass car thief took it away forever."

"I'm so sorry. Really. I wish I could take that whole night back," I said, eyes filling with tears.

"You can't." Maverick let out a heavy sigh and scrubbed a hand over his face. "You just can't."

I dabbed at my cheeks and sniffed back another wave of tears. "I know."

He glanced at me again. "I've tried not to hate you, you know? I've tried to tell myself you had no idea what you took from me. That it was just a car. But I can't get there. I look at you and I want you, because you're so fucking beautiful, but then I remember who you are and what you did and I just..." He trailed off and shook his head. "It drives me fucking crazy, Carey. *You* drive me fucking crazy."

"Maverick..." I squeezed my eyes shut, still trying to stem the flow of tears. "I'm not trying to excuse what I did that night. What I took from you. But can you just let me say something about it?"

"Sure," he muttered.

I opened my eyes and dabbed at them with my sleeve. "I was at a party that night. It was the first time I ever met Hudson."

Maverick cast a curious side-eyed glance at me. "Hudson Calloway?"

"Yes." I paused and swallowed hard. "I was actually sober that night, but he drugged me and tried to... well, I'm sure you can guess."

He was silent for a long moment. Then he swallowed thickly and looked at me again. "He hurt you?" he said in a low voice.

"No. But he tried."

Maverick's hands clenched into fists. "I knew it. I fucking *knew* it from the way you looked at him," he said. "I could tell something happened between you two. Something fucking bad."

"Yeah." I wiped my cheeks again and went on. "Anyway, I managed to escape from him, and that's when I stole the car. I was just trying to get the hell away from that place, but I really should've—"

Maverick bluntly cut me off. "Carey, stop."

"Sorry," I muttered. "I know it doesn't change what I took from you."

"I didn't mean it like that," he said. He hesitated, rubbing his jaw, before going on. "I just meant… stop blaming yourself."

My eyes widened. "What?"

"I had no idea something like that happened to you that night. I always thought you were some strung-out idiot on a joyride. I had no idea you were drugged and attacked," he said, head slowly shaking. "That changes everything. I mean… *shit*."

"I still fucked up. I stole a car and drove it even though I knew I was too messed up to drive."

"No. *I* fucked up." Maverick put a hand on my shoulder. "If I knew the truth about all this shit from the start, I would've seen everything differently. I know it. I'm sorry."

"You really don't need to apologize."

"No, I really do." He pulled his hand away. "Fuck. *Fuck*. I've been a total asshole to you."

"Well, I won't deny that," I said softly. "But I guess it's water under the bridge now."

"I should've talked to you. I should've asked for your side of things."

I looked down at my lap, picking at a fingernail. "Yeah, maybe. But you were hurt really badly. So I get it. You didn't want to talk to me when you saw me at Babylon. You just wanted to hurt me back."

"I'm an asshole."

"No. Hudson is the real asshole in this situation," I said, shaking my head. "I didn't need that Truth or Die game to know he's a predator. I have firsthand experience with it."

Maverick's jaw twitched. "I'll kill him," he muttered. "I'll fucking kill him."

I stared at him as he spoke, forehead creasing. Before we were plunged into these nightmarish games, I would've taken that statement from him as a figure of speech. Something to express his intense rage toward Hudson for the things he did to me and all those other girls. But now I knew there was a very real chance that he'd actually kill Hudson. After all, he'd thrown Tate right under the bus to protect me... and that was when he still despised me.

I fell silent, not quite knowing what to say.

Maverick leaned over and put a hand on my shoulder again. "I'm so sorry," he said. "Honestly, Carey. If I knew the whole story, I never would've blamed you for what happened. I'd be upset about the car, sure, but I would've understood."

I lifted my chin and met his intense gaze. "I'm sorry too. About Julian."

"Thanks," he muttered. He hesitated for a few seconds before speaking up again. "I was totally wrong about you."

"I guess we were both wrong about each other."

"I wish I could make it up to you." He rubbed his chin, slowly shaking his head. "The things I've said and done... I've been such a piece of shit."

"Maverick." I raised a brow, head slightly tilting. "You *killed* a guy because he was trying to kill me. I'd say that's a pretty decent start at making things up to me, wouldn't you?"

He let out a short, mirthless bark of laughter. "Jesus, we're really in a fucked-up place, aren't we?" he said. "We've only been here for two days and things have already devolved into this shit."

"Yeah." I pursed my lips and shook my head. "It's crazy. People are literally dying and we're just sitting here talking about it like it's normal."

"No shit," Maverick replied. "And you're right—this stuff already feels normal to me. I don't even feel bad for what I did to Tate. I just saw him getting ready to kill you and I knew I had to stop him. That was all I could think. I didn't even hesitate."

"I forgot to thank you," I said softly. "You saved my life."

"You didn't forget. You thanked me earlier."

I raised a brow. "No, I came to your door and yelled at you about it."

"Eh." He shrugged. "You acknowledged that I saved you. I think that counts."

"If you say so," I said, a ghost of a smile playing on my lips. "But... thanks. Seriously. There was no way I could've defended myself against Tate. If I'd even *tried* to reach out to grab his string, he would've instantly lashed out and gotten mine first. The bigger person would win nine times out of ten in a game like that."

A grim look appeared on Maverick's face. "Yeah. It was a nasty game. Whoever the Game Master is, he or she is a total fucking psychopath."

I was about to reply when our phones pinged. It was as if Maverick saying 'Game Master' out loud had summoned his presence into our space, like a damn demon.

"Sorry, players," I read aloud, heart pounding. "I tricked you when I said there were no more games today. It wasn't a total bald-faced lie, for technical reasons that you'll understand in a second, but I'm sure you still feel a little miffed. Oops! Anyway, please get dressed and meet in the drawing room at 11:30. The next game begins at midnight."

CAREY

At eleven-thirty, all ten remaining players were gathered in the drawing room.

Maverick and I had agreed to come separately, partly because of the ten o'clock curfew, and also figuring we might raise suspicions if we suddenly arrived together arm-in-arm after despising each other for so long. However, he hadn't let me leave his room without a lingering, passionate kiss first. Ever since, my entire body had been enveloped in a comforting warmth. It was almost enough to drown out the fear of what our next game might entail… but not quite.

Nothing could trump that terror.

April smothered a yawn and spoke up. "I'm glad those phones are automatically set to loud, because I was already asleep when the game was announced," she said. "Imagine if I slept through it. I could die for failing to take part."

"I guess that's why the phones are set up like that," Brooke said, absentmindedly rubbing her nose. "I only got half an hour of sleep. I feel totally fucked."

"I didn't get any at all. This place is too fucking stressful for me to fall asleep before midnight." Zach glanced at me. "How about you, Carey? Manage to get any shuteye?"

A hot flush instantly went up my neck and face. I was sure everyone would see the redness in my cheeks and sense what I'd spent half the night doing, but they stared at me blankly instead, awaiting my answer.

I shook my head. "No sleep. Same as Zach."

I felt bad for lying to my friends, but I knew that Maverick and I were right earlier—if we revealed our sudden lust and affection for each other to anyone here, they might begin to suspect that something else was up with the two of us. They'd probably never believe we made up so fast, given our previous bad blood, and then they'd start to wonder if we were secretly together all along and totally faking the hatred.

From there, they'd wonder what else we'd been hiding and lying about, and then it was only a short step until wild accusations were thrown at us about our potential association with the Game Master.

A familiar robotic voice rang out from a nearby speaker. "Thank you for arriving so promptly, players. Please exit the drawing room and head into the foyer. Arrows will guide you from there to Gaming Room 4."

As if drawn by a magnet, my eyes locked with Maverick's from across the room. He dipped his chin in the briefest of nods, a ghost of a smile playing on his lips. That small expression, coupled with the intensity of his gaze, told me that he'd do his best to protect me tonight, no matter what happened in the upcoming game.

The ten of us exited the room and marched toward the foyer. All the lights in the space were off, and a series of purple glow-in-the-dark arrows marked out a path through a newly opened hallway on the left.

The narrow hall led to a steep set of concrete stairs that

descended downward. The air on the lower level was cooler, and I had to rub my arms to stop myself from shivering.

"I didn't even know Babylon had a basement level," Jasmine grumbled, rubbing her arms as well. "It's fucking freezing."

"All the buildings at school have basement levels. That's where the cleaning equipment and maintenance stuff is kept," Rhys replied from up ahead. "So it makes sense that Icarus Hall had one built in too."

"How do you know that?" Kiara asked in a sharp tone.

"I'd love to know the answer to that too," Jasmine said. "I mean, why would you need to know everything about the exact layout of all the Babylon buildings unless you planned this whole thing?"

Rhys sighed. "I occasionally help the janitors after nightly curfew for some extra money. The school doesn't know about it, obviously, but the cleaners are glad for the help, and it's tax-free for me because it's cash. So *that's* how I know about it. Not because I'm the Game Master and set all this shit up for you guys."

Jasmine scoffed. "Wow. You really *are* poor."

"Shut the fuck up," April snapped. "I actually think it's admirable that Rhys manages to work on top of studying, unlike your lazy ass."

Jasmine turned and glared at her. "Yeah? How much work do *you* do, April? Or do Mommy and Daddy pay for everything?"

April's lips tightened. "I'm fortunate, but at least I'm willing to admit it," she said. "It wouldn't kill you to acknowledge that you're lucky too, instead of tearing people down for having less than you."

"Okay, Little Miss Social Justice Warrior." Jasmine turned back to face the front. "Jesus, how far does this basement level go? We've been walking for ages."

Zach lifted a shaky finger. "It ends down there, where the arrows stop."

"Is that a door?" I squinted into the darkness ahead. "I can't tell. It's too dark."

Rhys ran up ahead to see what lay at the end of the frigid passage. "Yup, it's a door," he called back to the rest of us. He rapped on it, producing a clanging sound. "Seems like reinforced steel."

"Can you open it?"

"With some help, yeah. Maverick, Zach, Hudson... get up here."

"April can help too! She loves working," Jasmine cut in.

"Oh my god, Jasmine, *shut up,*" Zach snapped. "How many of these fucked up games do we have to go through together to make you stop shitting on everyone?"

Weirdly enough, I was no longer angry at Jasmine for her constant snide remarks. Instead, I pitied her. She was obviously trying to cope with the stress and dread of being in a place like this, and the only way she knew how to deal with that stress was to take it out on everyone around her. It didn't excuse her behavior, but it at least made it easier for me to ignore it.

The boys got the thick metal door open with a few strained pushes, and we stepped inside. A series of lights instantly went on overhead, and the door closed behind us with a heavy thud.

The first thing in the room that caught my attention was the vast expanse of water stretching out before us. It shimmered under the lights, its surface reflecting the room's surroundings like a mirror. A series of thick wooden beams jutted over the edge like makeshift piers. Each beam led off into a maze of smaller beams, crisscrossing in every direction like a chaotic web, creating a daunting obstacle course that stood between us and the other side of the pool. Along the edge of the other side were twelve wooden targets standing on slightly elevated platforms. Two were marked with red crosses.

"I'm guessing those two were for Tate and Evan if they

survived this far," Maverick said, pointing to the red crosses. I murmured my agreement alongside the others.

"Guys, look over here," Brooke called out. She was standing by a large table near the door. "Our names are on these shapes."

We turned and examined the large wooden blocks on the table. As Brooke said, each one was labeled with a name. Each was also a different shape.

"Here, Carey. Yours is a star," Zach said, picking up the closest one. "April, you're a heart. Rhys, you're a triangle."

He kept handing out the blocks until we all had one in hand.

"I'm guessing these have something to do with those targets on the other side of the water," April said, frowning over at the enormous pool. "Each one has a shape right on the bullseye."

I squinted to see better. She was right. Each target had a different shape carved into the center.

"So, like... do we just walk across and stick our blocks in the correct target?" Kiara asked, brows knitting.

The objective seemed simple enough—make it across the water from one of the starting beams to a platform with a corresponding puzzle piece. However, the reality was far more complex. There were no straight or clear paths from any starting point to any of the platforms, meaning each step required careful strategy and calculation. I also had an awful sinking feeling in my stomach that told me we were all missing something. Something the Game Master was about to smugly inform us of at any second.

Just as I suspected, the same old artificial voice boomed out of a speaker just a moment later. "Welcome to the fourth game, everyone! This one is called '*Never Have I Ever Drowned*'."

There was a lengthy pause for dramatic effect, and a resounding groan went through the group.

"Really?" April muttered, rolling her eyes. "This is so fucking stupid."

"No shit." Jasmine snickered. "All we have to do is cross a pool and fit some shapes in a hole like we're in kindergarten. Like... *seriously?*"

"I have a feeling there's something else coming," I said, heart thudding. "Something really bad."

The speaker crackled to life again. "As you've probably already realized, the objective of the game is for each of you to make it over the water to the target that matches your personal puzzle piece. Once you arrive at the target, you must put your piece in the matching bullseye to register your presence. All puzzle pieces in play must be registered at their corresponding targets for the game to be cleared. Simple enough, yes?"

There was another dramatic pause before the voice went on.

"However, the water will begin to rise soon. Not only will it make the wooden beams slippery and therefore hard to walk on, it will also eventually fill the whole room. Now that the door has been shut and sealed, the room is watertight. That means every single one of you will drown unless you complete the game within the specified time limit, which will unlock the door. Oh, and another thing—the water will be electrified until it reaches the very top of the pool, so don't fall in unless you have a death wish."

"Well, that's fucked up," Jasmine muttered.

"If one of you *does* fall in," the voice went on. "Their puzzle piece is eliminated from play and no longer counts toward the end, giving the rest of you a chance to continue and survive. The mechanism for this is simple. When someone falls in, sensors in the water detect the sudden weight change, and a notification is automatically sent to everyone's phones. At least one player must open the notification and select the dead player to eliminate them from the game."

"Wow, how generous of you to give us all a chance to survive," Zach muttered, voice dripping with sarcasm.

The artificial voice piped up again. "Oh, and one more thing to make this game even more fun for you—your time limit is ten minutes, and it begins right now. Good luck!"

A large digital clock switched on across the room, displaying the time in minutes, seconds, and milliseconds.

"What the fuck?" Jasmine screeched. "Ten minutes for all of us to get across? That's nothing!"

"Stop complaining and figure it out!" Brooke said, hurrying forward. "I can see a way across to my platform, so I'll go first. One at a time is probably safest anyway."

I had a feeling Brooke's newfound bravery stemmed from her guilt over the Tag game, because I'd noticed she was still having trouble meeting my eyes, even though I didn't begrudge her for not helping me.

As she stepped onto a beam somewhere in the middle, the rest of us hung back, warily watching. She made it across to her target in one minute and thirty-eight seconds, jammed her puzzle piece in the bullseye, and turned to us with a thumbs-up. "See? Easy!" she called out. "But you need to hurry!"

She was right. We were already down to eight minutes, and there were still nine of us on the wrong side. Going one at a time simply wasn't an option, even if it was safer.

Maverick briskly clapped his hands to snap everyone's attention to him. "Okay, here's what we're going to do," he said. "It's going to be easier to see the correct paths from here on the edge, rather than when we're out on the water. So Zach, April, and I will hang back and direct Kiara, Rhys, and Carey over to their platforms. Then we'll do Courteney, Hudson, and Jasmine. Once they're across, we'll come over ourselves. April, Zach... that okay with you?"

Both of them nodded. "It's a good idea," April said. "Three at a time on the water isn't too crowded, and it means we'll all get across with time to spare."

"Hopefully," Zach added.

Maverick cast his intense gaze across the rest of the group. "Everyone understand what's happening?"

We all nodded and hurried to the edge. Maverick directed me

to begin from the farthest beam on the left and go forward until I reached a T-junction. With a deep breath, I took a tentative step, feeling the unstable wooden surface sway beneath my weight. One wrong move could send me plunging into the water below, so I had to concentrate on keeping my balance while simultaneously listening for Maverick's shouted instructions.

"Right, then immediately left!" he called out. "Good! Now right again, and follow that one until I say stop!"

Under his direction, I made it over to my target in a mere forty-three seconds. Kiara made it to her platform under Zach's direction just a few seconds after me. Rhys was still somewhere in the middle, nervously looking down at the water before each faltering step.

"Stop looking at the water!" April said. "Just concentrate on the beams, okay? Now go left!"

"No, go right!" Hudson shouted at the same time.

Rhys took one step forward and then doubled back, foot hovering between the two different beams in question. "What did you say?" he asked, turning his head over his shoulder.

"Left!" April shouted. "Hurry!"

At the same time, Hudson called out again. "It's the right one, dumbass!"

The conflicting instructions made Rhys hesitate again. It was all the time needed for disaster to strike. With his foot hovering between the two different beams, his whole body began to teeter. He slipped a second later, and with a heart-wrenching splash, he disappeared beneath the water.

My jaw dropped as a shockwave of horror smashed through me. "No!"

Panic erupted in the rest of the group, their screams mingling with the crackling of electricity in the water. The sense of calm and order that Maverick had forged moments ago devolved into chaos in the blink of an eye, with furious accusations flying like sparks.

"You sabotaged him, you psycho freak!" April screamed, hands balling into fists at her side.

"No, you were wrong! He was supposed to go left!" Hudson shot back.

"That's what she fucking *said!*" Kiara yelled over the water. "You were the one telling him to go right!"

Amidst the turmoil, Maverick's voice rang out again. "Listen!" he said. "We can argue later. Right now, we need to rally and focus on getting through this. We either work together or die together!"

The shouting instantly died down as his words sank in. We'd already wasted so much time screaming and panicking over Rhys's demise that we were only six minutes away from failing the game and drowning together as the room eventually flooded.

"Carey, deal with the text thing!" Maverick shouted across the water. "Courteney, I'll direct you. Zach, do Hudson. April, do Jasmine. Focus and try to stay calm. We can do this, guys."

With a shaky hand, I pulled my phone out of my pocket. As expected, there was a message on the screen with a series of prompts below it. *Weight change detected. Eliminate a player?*

I tapped on Rhys's profile picture with a heavy heart. As much as I'd disliked the guy at first—he was besties with Hudson, for God's sake—I'd developed the tiniest soft spot for him after he helped me during the Tag game. He didn't have to do it, but he did anyway.

Jasmine made it to her platform in a mere thirty-seven seconds under April's direction. Courteney arrived at her target ten seconds later, and Hudson followed twenty seconds later.

"Okay, final three!" Maverick shouted. "We've still got four and a half minutes left, so we'll go one at a time to be safe. April, you go first."

April stepped out onto the closest beam. Maverick and Zach directed her over, and she made it onto her platform in forty-seven seconds. Zach went next under Maverick's direction, and he stepped onto his platform with two minutes left on the clock.

Maverick was up last. He looked at me across the water and dipped his chin in the briefest of nods. Then he made his way to the starting beam on the far right of the pool and stared out at the wooden labyrinth, eyes narrowing as he silently plotted his path.

As I watched him take his first precarious step, my heart pounded in my chest, each beat echoing the palpable tension that hung in the air. The water had risen higher, its surface lapping at the bottom of the beams. Rhys's fall had also splashed a lot of water onto the exact beams that Maverick needed to walk across, making them slick and treacherous.

My stomach churned as he stepped onto another wet beam. He moved with a cautious yet resolute pace, determination etched on his handsome face. With every new beam he stepped onto, my breath hitched in my throat, a silent plea lingering on my lips. *Please be okay. Please be okay. Please, please, please...*

The water surged upward again, splashing the beams with relentless fury. Maverick faltered, and my heart clenched with a vise-like grip, a surge of fear coursing through my veins. I desperately wanted to cry out and beg him to maintain his composure, but I knew any sound from me—or anyone else—could mentally throw him off and cause him to fall. We'd all seen it happen to Rhys when April and Hudson were arguing over his path. I couldn't bear to see it happen to Maverick too.

He righted himself on the beam, set his jaw, and narrowed his eyes on a fork in the path ahead. He chose the beam branching toward the left. Then, in another heartbeat, he was finally all the way across the water, leaping onto his platform with a satisfied grunt.

Relief flooded me like a tidal wave, washing away the fear that had gripped me only seconds before.

"Twenty seconds to spare!" Zach called out. "Good job, man!"

Maverick grinned and slotted his hexagonal block into the target in front of him, and a loud beep echoed through the room, followed by an automated message on the speaker. "Game cleared."

We all turned and stared at each other with wide eyes, wondering what to do next. Another beep echoed throughout the space, and the speaker went on again.

"Congratulations to those of you who succeeded in the game," the voice said. "I hope it wasn't too *shocking* for you. The water is no longer rising or electrified, so you can go back across without concern. You'll find the door is now unlocked, so you can head upstairs and go back to bed. Sleep well!"

Brooke stooped by the edge and peered down at the dark water. "What if this is just part of the game?" she asked.

April stared at her, forehead creasing. "What do you mean?"

"I mean, what if it's not really over? What if we try to go back across, thinking it's totally okay if we slip and fall in, and the water is actually still electrified?"

Hudson knelt by the edge and stuck his hand in the water. "It's fine. See?" he said tersely. "Now can we get the fuck out of here?"

One by one, we made our way back over to the other side. The simple knowledge that the water was no longer electrified somehow made it seem ten times easier to traverse the beams, even though most of them were wet. Only one person slipped—Zach—and he managed to right himself before he fell in the pool.

Once we were out of the gaming room and back in the dim basement passage, the group splintered. I hung back with April, Brooke, and Zach, while Jasmine and Kiara whispered to each other a few feet ahead. Hudson trudged alone ahead of them, and Maverick and Courteney were also walking solo.

"So our theory about Rhys was totally wrong," Zach muttered, nudging Brooke. "Obviously he's not the Game Master."

I nodded. "I was starting to think he was innocent anyway. He helped me in the Tag game."

"Really?" Brooke looked over at me, eyes filled with a haunted mixture of guilt, regret, and sadness. "God, Carey, I'm so sorry. I totally froze, and—"

I lifted a palm and cut her off. "It's fine. No need to explain or apologize. I get it."

"For what it's worth, I'm sorry too," Zach said. "I froze too. But it's no excuse. I should've helped you."

"Really, guys. It's okay. Let's talk about something else." I raised a brow. "For example—Hudson. You guys all saw what happened in there, right?"

April's eyes widened. "Yes! He totally sabotaged Rhys! I mean, I definitely told him to go left, didn't I?"

"Yes. Hudson said right, and I checked afterwards. You were correct. Rhys should've gone left. It was the easiest path."

"But Rhys was Hudson's best friend. His *only* friend here, really. Why would he sabotage him like that?"

I hugged my arms around myself as I felt goosebumps cropping up beneath my sweater. "Revenge."

"For what?"

"The Truth or Die thing. The Game Master had to learn the information about all the girls Hudson has attacked from somewhere, right? Rhys is the most likely source, because they were best friends, so he'd probably know everything that's going on in his life. At least that's what I'd assume."

"Yeah, maybe Rhys got drunk at a party and spilled the whole nasty story to someone," Brooke said, nodding slowly. "Hudson must've realized he was the source, and he's been stewing on it ever since the game."

"Yep. So I bet he killed him partly out of revenge, and partly to tie up loose ends in case he survives this place," I said. "I mean, if Rhys is dead, he can't spill that info to anyone else, can he?"

"That means we're all in danger from his sabotage," April said. "Because we *all* know what he did to those girls now. So if he's getting rid of loose ends... that means every single one of us."

"Shit," Zach muttered. "You're right."

I stopped dead in my tracks. "Hold on," I said, grabbing April's sleeve to stop her too. "I just realized something."

The others turned and peered at me. "What?"

"If we're right about this, then that means Hudson can't possibly be the Game Master."

"Oh, shit. Good point," Brooke said, eyes widening.

"What do you mean?" Zach asked.

I lifted a brow. "If Hudson was angry at Rhys for spilling his dark secrets to the Game Master, then he can't possibly be the Game Master himself."

"I'm still not following." Zach yawned and rubbed his eyes. "Sorry, I'm half-asleep."

Brooke let out an impatient sigh. "If Hudson was the Game Master, then that would mean he wrote those Truth or Die questions himself, including the one about his own dark secret. That means the information wouldn't have come from Rhys. So he would've had no reason to be mad at Rhys or want revenge on him."

"Oh." Comprehension finally dawned on Zach's tired face. "Shit. You're right. He's *not* the Game Master."

"Well... I guess he could be," April said. "He could've had some other reason to get rid of Rhys in that last game, right?"

"Maybe." Zach frowned. "Also, he was the first one to test the water a minute ago. Almost like he knew for sure that it was no longer electrified. Only the Game Master would know for sure."

"Honestly, I think he was just showing off. Proving how brave and masculine he is," Brooke said. "I agree with Carey's first theory. Hudson isn't the Game Master. I mean, he was *so mad* about his secret being exposed during Truth or Die."

I nodded slowly. "Either way, we need to watch out for him. Like April said, he might sabotage all of us to save his own skin and reputation."

"Agreed."

April chewed the inside of her cheek as her brows knitted in a frown. "So, if we think Hudson isn't the Game Master, then who is?" she asked. "Who's the most likely candidate?"

The four of us turned and cast our gazes toward the others in the passage.

"If it's out of Courteney, Maverick, Kiara, and Jasmine, I think we can safely knock Courteney out of the running," Brooke said. "She's pretty nice, and I can't think of any reason for her to do something like this."

Zach lowered his gaze to the floor and shifted his feet, looking decidedly uncomfortable.

April let out an exasperated sigh. "For fuck's sake, Zach. Just say what you're thinking. I won't leap at you and tear your throat out," she said, folding her arms. "I *am* still mad that you cheated on my sister, but I think we can put that aside for now, considering our current situation."

Zach took a deep breath and looked up again. "I was just going to say, obviously I know Courteney pretty well, given that I... well, you know." He paused and nervously coughed, pointedly avoiding April's narrowed eyes. "Anyway, I just don't think she could pull off something like this. She's not smart enough."

I raised a brow. "I thought you told me she was the top student in one of her classes. Geography, or something like that."

"Well, I mean, she isn't stupid. She does have that one good class. But for everything else, she's just... average."

"I agree," Brooke replied. "She was my lab partner in chem last year, and I had to help her with everything. I'm still not sure what she was even doing in the class, to be honest."

"So it's down to Maverick, Jasmine, or Kiara." April frowned again. "Or one of us."

Brooke let out a sardonic laugh. "Yeah, it's totally me," she said, lifting her palms. "You finally figured it out."

"Very funny," Zach said, rolling his eyes. "Seriously, which of those three is the most likely?"

"Maverick," Brooke said.

I raised a brow. "Care to elaborate?"

"He's a guy," she said. "Men are *way* more likely to commit violent crimes. I think they're more likely to be psychopaths too. So it tracks that the Game Master is male."

"Okay, fair point, but I don't think we should blame Maverick and let the girls off the hook based on that alone," I said. "Women can still be psychopaths."

"True," April said, nodding slowly. "My money's actually on Kiara."

"Why?"

"Well, we've all been assuming that the Game Master brought us here as part of a revenge scheme, right? But none of us can figure out what we supposedly did to deserve it."

I nodded. "Uh-huh."

"We could be totally wrong about revenge being the motive. I mean, remember what Tate said the other day?" she said. "About Kiara's influencer stuff. I know she bought a ton of followers at the start to kick off her career, but she's super famous now. Fame can be addictive. People like that always want more likes, more followers... more attention."

"Yeah, that makes sense," I said. "She could've set this whole thing up so that she ends up as one of the only survivors. Or even the only survivor. Then she'd get a ton of attention and build her career even more, because she'd be the most famous influencer in the world after surviving something like this."

"Also, remember her birthday party last year?" Zach chimed in.

April's eyes widened. "Yes! Oh my god, I totally forgot about that."

"What happened at the party?" I asked.

"She invited the entire grade to a gigantic escape room," Brooke explained. "It was really fun. But now it's kind of suspicious."

"No shit. She's obviously into that sort of stuff, and this place is basically a giant escape room," April said. "So yeah... she's my number one pick right now."

"Me too," Zach said. "Jasmine is a total bitch, but I don't think that's enough of a motive to make her the Game Master."

"So we're pretty much agreed, then?" Brooke said. "We need to keep a really close eye on Hudson and Kiara. Hudson because he's sabotaging everyone, and Kiara because she's the most likely suspect for the Game Master."

"Hold on." April frowned. "I just thought of something else. Even if Kiara didn't bring us here for revenge, and it's just an attention-grabbing scheme... why *us*?"

"Good point," I murmured. "She'd know from the start that we're all going to die here if she intends on being the only survivor. So why pick *us* over anyone else from school? What did we do to deserve it?"

"Maybe she just went through a class list and picked eleven people at random," Brooke suggested. "A psychopath wouldn't care who got picked, because they don't feel remorse, so there wouldn't need to be any real reason behind it."

"Yeah, I guess that's possible."

"No, it's not random enough," April declared, shaking her head. "Like, what are the odds that the four of us are here together? When there's over two hundred students in our grade alone."

"I might have an idea that explains it," Zach said. "What if the people Kiara brought here were just the only people in school that she could find bad or embarrassing information on? For the Truth or Die game."

"Huh?" Brooke's forehead wrinkled. "Why would that matter?"

"Well, that game was clearly designed to make everyone dislike and distrust each other for however long we're trapped here, presumably to add an extra layer of drama to the rest of the games over the next few days. It also makes for a juicy story when

Kiara's telling the media all the sordid details afterwards. So it makes sense that she'd want people with the worst possible secrets, right?"

"Okay, yeah, that makes a lot of sense," April replied, slowly nodding. "Also, it means that she'd have no problem letting us know that she bought followers in the Truth or Die game, because I bet none of us are supposed to survive at all, like Carey said a minute ago. That means we won't be able to reveal her secret to the outside world when it's all over. Her version of the story will be the only narrative."

"Uhh... hold on. I just realized we've blown right past a major point," I said, heart thudding in my chest. "If Kiara *is* the Game Master, and she doesn't intend for any of us to survive this thing, then that means some of the games have to be rigged against us. I mean, we were told at the start that we can survive to the very end if we play the games properly. But that's just not possible if she wants to be the only survivor, is it?"

"So it doesn't even matter how well we play the games," April said. Her shoulders had begun to quiver. "We're all going to die here."

MAVERICK

I trudged upstairs, occasionally glancing behind me to check out the others. Hudson was walking alone, face set in a stony expression, and Jasmine and Kiara were lingering a little farther back, whispering to each other as they walked. Courteney was several feet behind them, hands stuck in her pockets and face etched with a gloomy expression.

As for Carey and her friends, the four of them had hung back in the passage downstairs to huddle together for a discussion. I wanted to stay back and join them, but I knew I wasn't welcome. Not while Carey and I were pretending there was nothing going on between us.

I cast another look over my shoulder, eyes narrowing as they fell on Jasmine and Kiara again. What the hell were they whispering about, and why had they frozen me out all of a sudden? Did they simply want some girl time together, or did they suspect something about me and Carey?

Or worse.... were they somehow linked to these crazy games, and I simply hadn't noticed their suspicious behavior until now? Had either of them said or done anything strange recently?

Dropped any information that could point to one of them being the Game Master?

I rubbed my temples, straining to recall every interaction I'd had with either of the girls over the last few days. I came up blank, and the myriad questions on my mind remained unanswered.

Fuck. It was so hard to think right now.

Part of it was due to the constant dread that stemmed from being in this place. The rest was because of Carey. I knew I should be thinking of ways to unmask the Game Master and escape this fucking hellhole, but no matter how hard I tried, my mind always floated right back to her. Her face, her body, her kisses. Her moans. That look on her face when she came... *Jesus.* I needed more. Needed her so fucking badly.

I went to my bedroom and hung out by the door until I heard Carey and her friends return to the hall and enter their respective rooms. I waited a few minutes to be safe. Then I quietly stepped out and made my way to Carey's room.

She answered on my third tap. "Hey," she said, eyes widening. "Shouldn't you be in your room?"

I raised a brow. "Not happy to see me?"

"Of course I am." Her cheeks were rapidly turning pink. "I just meant... the curfew. I don't want you to g—"

I smirked and pressed a finger to her lips. "I know. I was kidding. But I don't think the curfew matters tonight. Not after the Game Master broke it by dragging us all out at midnight for that fucked up game."

"Yeah, I guess that makes sense," Carey replied. Her shoulders sagged, and she slowly shook her head. "God, I still can't believe three of us are gone now."

"Yeah, it's crazy. Almost doesn't feel real." I dipped my chin toward the room behind her. "You gonna invite me in?"

"Oh, right. Sorry." She stepped aside. "Did anyone see you come down here?"

"Nope. I was careful."

"Good," she said. A wry smile played on her lips as she perched on the end of the bed. "The last thing we need is everyone thinking we're working together as co-Game Masters, even though we both know we're not."

I grinned as I sat next to her. "You said that so easily."

"Said what?"

"That we both know we're not the Game Masters," I said. I reached for her hand and squeezed it tightly. "What you're really saying is that you totally trust me."

"Yeah, I guess I do," she said softly. Her cheeks had turned a deeper shade of pink. "Maybe that makes me the biggest idiot on the planet, after everything that's happened between us, but... it's true. I really trust you."

"You won't regret it." I squeezed her hand again. "And for the record, I trust you too. I'm gonna do everything I can to figure out who's behind this shit and keep you safe."

"I know." She leaned over and planted a soft kiss on my cheek. "Thank you."

"Speaking of figuring this shit out, I have a new theory about the Game Master," I said.

"I have one to tell you too. But you can go first," she replied, tilting her head.

"Well, I've been wondering if there's more than one Game Master. I'm also wondering if it's Jasmine and Kiara working together."

Carey frowned. "Really? Both of them?"

"Yeah. I keep seeing them whispering to each other, and they totally iced me out tonight. It made me wonder if they're up to something." I rubbed my chin and shook my head. "I don't know. Maybe I'm imagining shit. Maybe they just wanted some girl time, or whatever."

"I don't think it's your imagination. April, Brooke, Zach, and I were actually talking about Kiara earlier," Carey said. "She's our main suspect right now."

"Why?"

She briefly ran me through the theory that her group had devised about Kiara's possible involvement in the nightmarish games; an attention-grabbing scheme she could've cooked up with a ruthless social media team to cement her status as the world's most famous influencer.

"We didn't suspect Jasmine," she said, shaking her head. "But I guess it's possible that Kiara's been getting help from her."

"Maybe she's planning to betray her at some point, so she can be the only survivor like you guys figured. You know... two can keep a secret if one of them is dead."

"Yeah, maybe." Carey scratched the back of her neck. "Anyway, I know we have no proof about any of this, but I still think it's the best theory we've managed to come up with so far. It explains why we're all here without it being a revenge scheme."

"True. It's fucked up, though. If she really wants all of us to die, I mean."

"Yeah. It's horrible." A sudden jolt shook Carey's body, and she rubbed her forearms, inhaling deeply. "Brooke and April are terrified of dying here. Zach is too. He doesn't want to admit it, because he's trying to act all brave and masculine, but I can tell."

"Honestly, I'm scared too," I admitted, rubbing her shoulder. "I'm scared something will happen to you. Something I can't protect you from."

"Me too," she murmured. She took another deep breath. "I keep thinking I'm going to lose you even though I only just found you."

"We can stop it." I paused and rubbed my forehead, jaw clenching hard. "We just need to find some proof that we're right about Kiara and Jasmine. If they're really behind all this shit, the rest of us can easily overpower the two of them."

"And then what?" she asked. "We tie them up and keep them as hostages until their minions are forced to release us?"

"I don't know." I rubbed my head again, brows dipping in a frown. "I haven't thought it all the way through yet. But speaking of minions, the Game Master definitely has outside help, right?"

"I'd say so, yeah."

"It's just way too much for one or two people to set all this shit up," I continued. "Also, someone is out there watching the games on the cameras, monitoring everything else that happens, making the announcements, and sending the texts. It can't be someone in the player group, because we'd see them doing it."

"Exactly. Whoever planned this whole scheme must be getting a lot of help, and that means they have access to a ton of money and manpower. That's something Kiara and Jasmine both have, given their backgrounds." Carey tilted her head slightly to the side. "But how can we find the proof we need to catch them out? It's not like we can search their bedrooms without them noticing."

"There could be evidence in other places. I think we should take advantage of the lack of curfew tonight. Go and explore."

Carey's nose wrinkled. "But we already tried exploring the other day, and we didn't find anything, unless you count all the mics and cameras Rhys found."

"I know, but other hallways have been unsealed now, remember? So there's a lot more for us to look at."

Her brows shot up. "True. I didn't even think of that."

"There's something else too," I said, sitting up straighter. "There's always been rumors floating around Babylon about secret passages somewhere on campus, and those buildings are all the same as Icarus Hall. Catch my drift?"

"You think there's secret passages here?"

I nodded. "I think there could be. The Game Master is getting around this place without the rest of us seeing or hearing anything, right?" I said. "That makes me think there could be passages or tunnels behind the walls or under the floors. Maybe even both. If I'm right, and we can actually find one of these hidden passage entrances, we might be able to find the main control room and get all the proof we need."

Carey shrugged, lips pressing into a flat line. "I don't know. Maybe they're just moving around the mansion when we're stuck in our bedrooms. That would explain the curfew."

"Maybe. But I think they're getting around at other times too, when we're all awake. That's how the drawing room keeps getting filled with freshly cooked food at breakfast, lunch, and dinner." I hesitated, raising my brows. "Also, the drawing room door is always locked between meals. But if the food is only getting restocked while we're stuck in our rooms, why would they even bother keeping that door closed and locked?"

"Just in case someone happens to break the curfew. They don't want to be seen going in and out of the room."

"But they know everyone's too scared to break the curfew, because they made it clear we'd be punished for that. So it's not like any of us are going to wander down to the drawing room at four in the morning and catch them bringing in coffee and croissants."

"True."

"Also, how exactly is that door getting unlocked and opened three times a day to let us in for meals? It's not magic, and we can see there's no automated locking mechanism on it, so it can't be controlled from elsewhere in the building," I went on. "I think someone is getting in there through another hidden doorway and serving up the food before they unlock the main door from the inside. If they were unlocking it from the outside, we'd probably hear their footsteps down in the foyer, right? When we're awake, that is."

"True. I've never heard a peep from the foyer." Carey's brows knitted. "But back to your earlier point... why bother closing the door and locking it between meals if they're not actually afraid of us seeing them going in and out?"

"I think they keep it closed between meals to make sure we don't spend too much time poking around in there," I replied. "Because if we did, we might find the passage entrance. If it actually exists, that is."

Carey frowned and looked over at the wall, lips twisting.

"Look, I know this secret passage shit probably sounds crazy," I said. "But I really think there could be something here."

"I don't think it's crazy. I think you might be right," Carey finally said, looking back at me. "I never really thought about any of this stuff before, but it *is* pretty weird. So I guess there could be an access point to a network of passages in that room. One that allows the Game Master and their minions to restock the drawing room, unlock the door without us seeing or hearing them, and creep around the rest of the building to set everything up."

"Yup. That's exactly what I think."

Carey's eyes narrowed with concentration. "You know, this also means that there might be hidden access points in other parts of the house."

"Ones we can try to find now that some of the halls have opened up," I said, nodding. "They didn't re-seal any of those entryways, so we could go down there and look right now."

Carey's shoulders sagged. "Maybe they didn't seal them back up because there's nothing there for us to find. Nothing but more locked doors."

"It's worth looking, though. Right?"

She nodded, face brightening a bit. "Yeah. Anything that gives us a snowball's chance in hell of getting out of this crazy place."

She was clearly trying to sound nonchalant, but I could tell from the slight hitch in her voice that she was secretly terrified of dying here.

"Carey." My voice softened, and I rubbed her arm. "I meant it when I said I'm going to do everything I can to keep you safe. Nothing's going to happen to you."

"But what if something happens to *you?*" Her eyes suddenly brimmed with tears. "I meant what I said earlier too. I only just found you. I can't lose you now."

I wrapped her in my arms and held her close to my chest, one hand rubbing her hair. "Not gonna happen. I promise."

"How can you promise that when we have no idea what's coming next?" she asked in a ragged murmur.

I didn't know how to answer that question, so I stayed silent and stroked her hair until her breaths started to come slower and deeper.

She suddenly pulled back and wiped her face. "Sorry. I'm totally freaking out," she muttered.

She was obviously embarrassed about the raw vulnerability she'd just shown me, but I didn't think it was anything to be ashamed of. I liked it. *Loved* it. I wanted her to keep opening up to me, tell me every feeling and thought on her mind.

"Don't apologize." I took her hand and softly stroked her palm with my thumb. "You can say anything you want to me. Anytime."

"Thanks." She sniffed and sat up straight. "Let's go and explore. Yeah?"

"Yeah." I smiled. "Let's go."

We headed downstairs and meticulously checked every inch of the first hallway that the Game Master had unsealed. Gaming rooms 1 and 2 were still unlocked, but every other door in the hall was locked. After unfruitfully examining the two rooms, I rapped on all the wooden panels lining the hallway to check for any echoes that could suggest a hollow spot. Unfortunately, I came up empty every time. Carey busied herself looking behind the paintings hanging on the walls above the paneling, but she didn't find any hidden openings either.

"Should we try the old dining hall now?" she said, giving me a doleful look. "There's nothing here."

"Yeah. The dining hall is a good idea. We should've gone there first."

"Yeah, we really should've," Carey said. "I totally forgot about all those alcoves in the maze until now. Some of them were in the outer walls, so they could be connected to passages, right?"

Unfortunately, that theory didn't pan out either. We were about to head down to the basement-level passage to check there instead when our phones vibrated in our pockets. With my heart pounding, I pulled mine out and scanned the screen. It was a message from the Game Master.

Maverick Reinhart, you are out of bounds during sleeping hours. Consequences will follow. Please return to your room promptly or face further consequences.

"Shit." I jerked my head up to look at Carey and tilted my screen to face her. "You got this too?"

Her eyes were wide and fearful. "Yeah. I guess the curfew *was* still in effect."

"It's my fault. I assumed it wasn't and I convin—"

"Maverick, it's fine," she said hurriedly. "We both made the decision to risk leaving our rooms. Let's just head back now so we don't make things even worse."

We hurried up the stairs, and I walked Carey to her door and quickly kissed her goodnight. Just as I turned on my heel to leave, my phone vibrated again.

With a sinking feeling in my stomach, I opened the message, expecting another threat from the Game Master. Instead, it was a set of files including two photos and a video. I could see at the very top of the message that the same files had been sent to every other person in the player group as well.

Everyone except Carey.

"What is it?" she asked, eyes widening again.

I reluctantly turned my screen to face her. "Judging by the mugshots, I'm guessing it's something to do with the night you were arrested."

She groaned and rubbed the side of her head. "Shit. That video. I think I know what it is."

"What?"

"It's probably the CCTV from the station when the cops brought me in. I was fucked up from the drugs, so I was screaming like a maniac and trying to fight them." She paused and let out a sigh. "It doesn't exactly make me look... stable."

"Wasn't that stuff supposed to be erased when your charges were dropped?"

Carey shrugged gloomily. "I'm not sure. But either way, the Game Master got their dirty hands on it, so I guess this is my so-called consequence. Everyone in the group is going to see that video of me acting totally unhinged."

"So what? Everyone already knows you were arrested that night."

"Yeah, but they didn't *see* it, did they?" she replied, shaking her head. "Once they see me acting like that, they'll probably trust me a hell of a lot less than they did before. That could lower my chances of surviving the next few games, because the others might be less willing to work with me. Know what I mean?"

"Yeah, I get it." I gave her shoulder a reassuring pat. "But I don't think that'll happen."

"I think it could. But it's okay." She pasted on a brave half-smile. "At least the consequence wasn't death, huh?"

"That's true."

"I wonder what yours is going to be. I didn't get any—" Carey stopped abruptly as her phone vibrated. She looked down at her screen for a painfully long moment, brows dipping in a frown. Then her eyes widened, and her next words emerged in a choked murmur. "Oh my god."

CAREY

"What is it?" Maverick frowned and craned his neck, trying to catch a glimpse of my screen.

I jerked my hand away and took a step back. "I, um... it's a long story. I'll have to tell you tomorrow," I said, averting my eyes from his penetrating gaze. My throat was closing up, making my voice come out in a croak. "I mean, uh... we should probably get inside our rooms before it's too late, because the Game Master said there'd be further consequences if we don't return promptly."

"Sure," he replied, nodding curtly. "We can talk later."

He didn't question why I'd refused to show him my phone screen, and I didn't question *why* he didn't question me, even though I knew he had to be desperately curious about whatever had caused such an intense visceral reaction in me.

I muttered a quick goodnight before stepping inside my room and locking the door behind me, heart pounding and hands trembling. Then I sat on my bed and turned my phone back on to get a closer look at the message I'd just received.

It was a patient profile from the school psychologist's office at Babylon. My eyes instantly fell on the highlighted part at the bottom, as the Game Master surely intended.

Diagnostic Impression: *Based on the assessment findings and clinical observations, there is very strong evidence to suggest that Maverick Reinhart meets the criteria for Antisocial Personality Disorder (ASPD) as outlined in the DSM-5.*

I'd listened to enough true crime podcasts to know exactly what ASPD was—it was a personality disorder that many people informally referred to as sociopathy or psychopathy.

That meant Maverick was a diagnosed sociopath.

I reread the highlighted sentence for the third time, and then I started reading from the beginning of the document, heart jackhammering in my chest.

Patient Assessment Report

Patient Information:
Name: Maverick Jonathan Reinhart
Date of birth: September 19, 2006
Date of first assessment: March 26, 2022

Referral information: *Maverick was initially referred for grief counselling after the death of his older brother. However, I continued our sessions due to concerns regarding his interpersonal relationships and patterns of behavior, including manipulation and disregard for social norms.*

Background information: *Maverick presented as a charming and articulate individual. He described a pattern of unstable relationships and a tendency to exploit others for personal gain. He denied feelings of remorse or guilt regarding these actions.*

Clinical observations: *During my sessions with Maverick, he displayed superficial charm and glibness of speech. He appeared to lack empathy and showed a clear disregard for the feelings and rights of others.*

He demonstrated a tendency to manipulate others to achieve his goals without any regard for the consequences of his actions.

Diagnostic Impression: *Based on the assessment findings and clinical observations, there is very strong evidence to suggest that Maverick Reinhart meets the criteria for Antisocial Personality Disorder (ASPD) as outlined in the DSM-5.*

Criteria Met:
*1) Failure to conform with social norms with respect to lawful behaviors.
2) Deceitfulness, as indicated by patient disclosures and my own observations of conflicting narratives.
3) Reckless disregard for the safety of self or others.
4) Irritability and aggressiveness, as indicated by disclosures of repeated physical fights and assaults.
5) Consistent irresponsibility.
6) Lack of remorse, as indicated by disclosures of being indifferent to or rationalizing having hurt or mistreated others.*

Recommendations: *Given the severity of Maverick's symptoms and their impact on his life (as well as the lives of others around him), it is recommended that he receive ongoing psychotherapy aimed at addressing his maladaptive behaviors and developing prosocial coping strategies. Close monitoring and potential involvement of authorities may be warranted to ensure the safety of others and prevent further harm.*

Beneath the patient profile was an audio file. With one shaky finger, I pressed play. At first, nothing happened, but then there was a short beep followed by what sounded like a voicemail.

'Dr. Prentiss, it's Dr. Paul Barry from Babylon Preparatory Academy. I'm not sure if you recall, but we actually spoke a few years ago when I referred a student to you for psychotherapy. I have another patient for referral right now, but I... well, I probably shouldn't be saying this on an answering machine. Probably shouldn't be speaking about it at all, really.

It's very unprofessional of me. But let me just say... I've never encountered a patient like this particular young man. I think you'll find him to be a very interesting and challenging case, if you decide to take him on. That's all I can say for the time being, for obvious reasons. Please call back at your earliest convenience so we can discuss this further.'

I dropped the phone and slumped against the bedhead, mind whirling. After everything I'd just seen and heard, I felt incredibly stupid for blindly trusting Maverick. He'd charmed me so easily and even made me start falling for him, despite our rocky past, but that was just what sociopaths did, wasn't it? They manipulated and tricked people into trusting them for their own personal gain.

But what did Maverick have to gain from me? Was it just sex? Or was it some sort of sick game he played with girls he hated?

No. Some deep-down part of me couldn't stop thinking that it was all fake. Surely Maverick wasn't really a sociopath. Surely he wasn't capable of lying and tricking me to such an extent. It was just too hard to believe.

The document and audio file could've been fabricated by the Game Master to make me—and every other player here—distrust Maverick, which could then impact his ability to survive future games. After all, that was exactly what the Game Master wanted: to sow discord amongst all the players.

Yes, that had to be it. The patient profile *had* to be fake, and I was being a total bitch by not trusting Maverick and practically fleeing from him in the hall five minutes ago. I should've swallowed the fear that struck me when I saw my phone and talked to him so he could have a chance to explain.

I picked up my phone to send him a message, but when I turned the screen on, I saw that he'd already messaged me.

Hey, Carey. I didn't argue with you out in the hall when you wanted to leave because I think I know what the Game Master sent you, and I knew it would scare the shit out of

you. It was a psychological assessment, right? That's why you freaked out so much?

Anyway, I didn't want to scare you even more by forcing you to talk to me about it in person, so I let you go without any drama. But if it's okay with you, I'd like to explain. Please give me that chance. I know I probably don't deserve much of a chance after all the shit I've done to you over the last couple of months, but I'm hoping you can give it to me anyway.

I sat up straight, heart pounding even faster. "Oh my god," I whispered, staring into space with wide eyes.

The patient profile *wasn't* fake. How else would Maverick immediately know exactly what was sent to me? He knew that patient file was out there in the world, and he knew it would make him look bad, so it was the first thing that came to his mind when he saw the shocked expression on my face a few minutes ago.

I tentatively tapped out a reply. **Okay. Explain.**

He replied instantly. **Can you call me? Pretty sure these phones allow that. It's a long story so texting it all will be hard.**

I took a deep breath and clicked the green telephone icon next to his name in the message folder.

He answered on the first ring. "Hey. Thanks for agreeing to talk about this," he said. "I know you're probably really scared right now. You might even be thinking I'm the Game Master. I totally get it."

I swallowed hard. "Is it true? Did the school psychologist really diagnose you as a sociopath?"

"Yeah, he did. But it's all bullshit. Really. I know that sounds like a total lie, but if we were in the outside world right now, I could prove it so fucking easily."

"How?"

He cleared his throat. "Well, firstly, I could show you that the current Babylon Prep psychologist is a woman named Dr. Chao. She was hired after Dr. Barry was fired in disgrace, which is all on record somewhere. I could also show you the assessment done by a psychiatrist named Dr. Prentiss. She totally debunked Dr. Barry's claims about me."

"So... he made it up?" I asked, frowning. "Or was he just really bad at his job?"

"He made it up."

That was a little hard to believe. I sighed and rubbed my forehead. "Why would a psychologist fabricate a diagnosis about a student?"

"Well, I started seeing him after Julian died," Maverick said. "I was totally fucked up over it, which you already know about."

"Yeah, it says you were referred for grief counselling."

"That's right. I was falling behind in my classes because I couldn't concentrate, so my teachers recommended it. I went in for a few sessions, and it actually helped a little bit. Dr. Barry was pretty good at his job."

"So what happened to make him accuse you of the personality disorder?"

Maverick let out a heavy sigh. "I was in his office for a session one day, and he was called out of the room by the receptionist. Some sort of issue with the patient record system on her computer, from what I remember," he said. "Dr. Barry excused himself and said he'd be back in a couple of minutes. I decided to check a baseball score while I waited, but that part of campus is a total dead zone for my phone network. Anyway, I know this was a dumb thing to do, but it was just a game score, so I thought, fuck it, I'll just quickly look it up on Dr. Barry's computer. It was sitting right there on his desk, and I was pretty sure he hadn't locked it when he left the room."

"Did you find something on it?" I asked, eyes widening. That certainly seemed to be where this story was going.

"Yeah. Something fucked up."

"What was it?" I asked, stomach churning with anticipation.

"When I opened up a browser, I saw that he had other tabs open already. Most of them were just normal things that I wouldn't think twice about, but one had a weird name. I was curious, so I clicked on it, and… uhh…well, I don't want to go into too much detail, but it made it very clear that Dr. Barry was into young girls. Not babies and very young children, but still… young. Like thirteen or fourteen, maybe."

"Oh my god." My stomach lurched. "That's disgusting."

"No shit," Maverick replied. "All I could think about when I found it was how many young girls he was counselling every day at school. It made me feel fucking sick."

I frowned. "So… he had that sort of stuff on his computer and left it unlocked around people? That seems stupid."

"Yeah. Really stupid, huh? But I think he figured he'd only be out of the room for a minute. I think he also figured I wasn't a rude asshole who'd jump straight on his computer. But I guess I am a rude asshole, and honestly, I'm fucking glad I am, because as soon as I saw that shit on his screen, I knew I had to get him off campus. I mean, like I said a second ago, this guy was working with young girls every day. I figured he could've been fantasizing about them, which is bad enough, or maybe even grooming some of them."

"That's really sick."

"Yeah, it is. So, I stormed out of the office and told everyone in the waiting room to stop wasting their time and get the fuck out. Then I told Dr. Barry I was reporting him to the principal and cops. That turned out to be a mistake."

"Telling him, you mean?"

"Yeah. He immediately panicked and went into self-preservation mode. He wiped everything incriminating off his computer and browser history, and then he made up a bunch of fake session notes claiming that I said and did stuff that never happened. He backdated them to make it seem like he'd written them in previous weeks, and he also called a work associate that day after hours, knowing she wouldn't be available, just so he could leave a voicemail that implied there was something seriously wrong with me. That way, when the cops finally started to investigate the case, they could interview that associate and get her to show them this voicemail that was supposedly about me."

"Was that Dr. Prentiss?"

"Yup. Anyway, Dr. Barry was trying to cover his tracks by making me seem like someone who'd make up shit just to hurt people, including him," Maverick went on. "But it didn't work. A digital forensics team went through his stuff and realized I was telling the truth. Turns out you can't really wipe a computer, even if you try really hard."

"Yeah, I've heard that."

"They were also able to check the creation dates and times on his session notes, and every single one about me was created the day I stormed out of his office. They also found his *real* session notes about me, which he'd tried to delete."

"And they were about your brother?"

"Yup. Anyone who read them could see I was just a grieving guy. Not a psychopath."

"So what happened to Dr. Barry?" I asked.

"He's in prison. Turns out he *was* grooming a couple of girls on campus. His patients, who he was supposed to be helping. They admitted it to the police when they interviewed everyone he was treating."

"God." My stomach was still churning, and a sickly taste had filled my mouth. "That's horrible. Those poor girls."

"Yeah, it was fucked up. But he's gone now." Maverick fell silent for a moment. Then he cleared his throat and spoke up again. "Carey... do you believe me? Because I can't prove any of this to you until we get the hell out of this place. Until then, it's just my word against the so-called evidence that the Game Master sent you."

I chewed on the inside of my cheek as I considered his words. As wild as his story sounded, I didn't find it completely implausible or unbelievable. On top of that, Maverick had helped and supported me throughout these awful games, and he'd helped the others too. He'd never done anything that could be seen as sabotage, and he didn't seem to have any motive to hurt me or anyone else either.

Also, the way he kissed me... he couldn't fake the feelings in that. No one could.

"I think I..." I trailed off, words dying in my throat. Then I began again. "Yes. I believe you."

There was a sharp intake of breath on the other end of the line. "Really?"

"Yes. I'm so sorry I ran off before. I was just so shocked, and I really—"

Maverick cut me off. "You don't have to explain or apologize. I would've been freaked out if I were in your shoes."

"Well, I still feel like an asshole," I murmured.

"Don't. You really shouldn't." His voice had turned slightly gruff. "I'm just glad you believe me. I don't deserve it after all the shit I've done to you."

I smiled faintly, even though he couldn't see me. "We decided that was all in the past, remember?"

"That's true. But I'm always going to regret what I did to you," Maverick replied. "And I'm always going to do everything I can to make it up to you."

The tiny smile on my face stretched a little wider. "I know."

"I'm going to get you out of here, Carey," he went on. "I promise. Even if it kills me, I'm getting you out."

CAREY

After breakfast the following morning, we were summoned to our fifth game. The gaming room was located in the same hallway where the first two games took place.

The room was dimly lit with flickering lights casting a hazy glow over the space. Posters of bands and bikini-clad women adorned the wood-paneled walls, and four rectangular tables stood in the center, laden with red Solo cups in pyramid formations and ping pong balls. Rock music pulsed from a stereo in the corner, bass thumping so loudly that the floor vibrated beneath our feet.

"I'm guessing this is meant to look like a high school party," Brooke shouted over the music.

"Looks more like a drug dealer's basement," Jasmine replied, upper lip curling with disdain.

The music died down, and the Game Master addressed us from a speaker on the far wall. "Welcome to the party, everyone!" the tinny voice said. "I'm going to let you have a ton of fun with an awesome game of Beer Pong!"

"For fuck's sake," Zach muttered, head shaking. "Just tell us the twist, asshole."

"You'll play in pairs that I'll announce in a moment. Obviously, there are nine of you, meaning one lucky player is exempt from today's game. I used a lottery system to determine that the lucky one is... Brooke!"

Brooke's shoulders slumped, and she let out a long sigh of relief. Hudson and Jasmine narrowed their eyes at her, obviously pissed about the exemption.

"Here are the rules. In your pairs, you play one round against each other. As with regular Beer Pong, the objective is to throw ping pong balls into your opponent's cups. However, if you sink one, your opponent doesn't need to drink from the cup immediately. Instead, they must move the cup to the side of the table and continue the game. At the end, whoever sank the most balls is declared the winner. The loser must then select one of their ten cups to drink from." The Game Master paused to let out a creepy hollow laugh. "Now, here's the catch I bet you're all waiting for. Several of the cups have poison mixed into the beer. You have no way of knowing which ones, so the losers must choose wisely, or else they'll die. If you draw, *both* players will have to select a cup to drink from, so keep that in mind. I'll give you a few minutes to let that sink in, and then I'll announce the pairings. Ciao for now!"

We all stared at each other with wide eyes.

"Oh my god," April said. "This isn't fair! We can't strategize because it's based on pure luck!"

"But we could all survive," Brooke said. "If all the losers just happen to pick cups without poison, we'll be fine."

"We? Who's *we*?" Jasmine said in a high-pitched tone. "You don't even have to play! Which, by the way, is totally suspicious. Kinda makes it look like you arranged all of this for your own convenience, doesn't it?"

Brooke rolled her eyes. "Oh my god, *really*? We're still accusing each other of being the Game Master?"

"Um, yes? Of course we are." Jasmine sneered. "You're sus as hell, Brooke."

"If anyone, it's Maverick," Courteney interjected. "You all got that text about him being a psychopath, right?"

I instantly opened my mouth to defend Maverick, but then I caught his eye. He slowly shook his head, intense gaze conveying a silent message. *Don't.*

"I don't think he'd let us all know about a sociopathy diagnosis if he's actually the Game Master," Zach said smoothly, lifting a palm. "It's just the same old shit. The real Game Master is trying to turn us all against each other."

"I agree," Brooke replied. "Also, that file said 2022, and the school psychologist was fired for being a pedophile that same year, so I don't know if anything he said about his patients is accurate. I mean, someone like that isn't exactly trustworthy, are they?"

"Just because the psych was a pedo doesn't mean he was bad at his job," Hudson said, glaring at Maverick.

"Oh, of course *you're* defending pedos now," Brooke shot back. "What else would we expect from a predator?"

The Game Master's robotic voice suddenly piped up again. "Okay, everyone! Here's the pairings. April versus Zach at table one, Jasmine versus Kiara at table two, Hudson versus Courteney at table three, and Carey versus Maverick at table four. Good luck!"

My eyes shot straight back to Maverick. He dipped his chin in a curt nod and stepped over to me. "Let's go," he said, gesturing toward the table at the end.

"Maverick," I whispered. "I don't want to pl—"

He put an index finger against his lips to signal for me to be quiet. Then he took another step closer. "We have to play each other," he muttered. "Let's just get it over and done with, okay?"

I swallowed hard and nodded, knowing he was right. If we refused to play the game, we'd die. The Game Master had made that very clear on our first day here. Also, we couldn't agree to draw with each other by sinking zero balls each, because then we'd *both* risk death by poisoning.

I stepped over to the other side of our table and picked up a ball, heart sinking as I looked over at Maverick's Solo cups. I wasn't bad at aiming, but I wasn't particularly good, either, and my hands were shaking like crazy. I'd probably lose this game.

Honestly, part of me *wanted* to lose. I didn't want to die, but I didn't want to lose Maverick, either. All I could really hope for was that whichever of us ended up losing just so happened to pick a cup without poison. As April said earlier, it all came down to luck.

"You can go first," Maverick said, eyeing me from across the table.

I nodded and took a deep breath before narrowing my gaze on his top cup. Then I sent the ball over with a flick of the wrist. It bounced off the edge of the cup and landed on the floor.

"Close," Maverick said, giving me an encouraging smile. He picked up a ball, threw it, and missed my top cup by half an inch. As the ball fell to the floor, he shrugged. "First round jitters, huh?"

"I guess so." I smiled tightly and picked up another ball. With another flick of the wrist, I sent it sailing toward his top cup. This time, it went straight in.

"Perfect." Maverick grinned. "My turn."

He tossed another ball. This time, it missed by several inches.

"Maverick," I hissed. "You aren't even trying."

"I don't need to. You got one in. That makes you the winner, as long as I don't get any in at all."

"That's not fair," I said, heart pounding. "On you, I mean."

He shrugged again. "I told you I wouldn't let anything happen to you."

I snapped my head to the right to see if any of the others had heard him say that. Fortunately, they were all too focused on their own games to be paying attention to our table.

"Please give yourself a chance," I said, turning my attention back to Maverick. "I want this to be a fair game for both of us. It's the right thing to do, and you know it."

His eyes locked right on mine, and he smiled. "Just take your next turn, Carey."

With a heavy sigh, I tossed another ball at his side of the table, purposely missing by an inch. "Your turn."

"I know you did that on purpose, but it doesn't matter," he said, lifting a brow. "As long as I keep missing, you'll still win."

"You're a real asshole sometimes, you know that?" I muttered.

He grinned. "If it keeps you safe, then I'm willing to be an asshole for as long as it takes."

The game went exactly as he planned after that, with me winning 1-0.

I watched with bated breath as Maverick carefully removed his cups from the pyramid formation and placed them in a line. I had no idea how many of them were poisoned, but if I had to guess, I'd say half. The Game Master wasn't nice enough to give us ten-to-one odds.

"Hm." He grunted and pointed toward the cup on the left end; the one I'd sunk my ball in. "This one seems lucky, huh?"

"Maverick..." My voice caught in my throat as I watched him toss back the beer.

Once he'd swallowed the last drop, he wiped his mouth and slowly tilted his head. Then he grinned. "Pretty sure that was just a regular beer."

"Some poisons can be tasteless," I said, heart still jackhammering in my chest.

"Carey, I'm fine. Really." He motioned toward the other tables. "Let's watch and hope everyone else is just as lucky as me. Okay?"

I nodded and turned to look. Because Maverick and I hadn't played 'properly' like the others, who were taking their time during each round to make the best shots they possibly could, we'd finished very early.

As I watched, Brooke came up to me and squeezed my arm. "I'm so glad you're okay," she said. "I feel really bad that I didn't have to play. It's not fair on the rest of you."

I shook my head. "It's not your fault. Everything in this game is down to luck, including the exempt player."

"Well, I'm not so sure about that. That it's all luck."

"What do you mean?" I asked, brows puckering.

Brooke lowered her voice. "I know I could be way off-base, so please don't get mad at me, but... um... is there something going on with you and Maverick?"

My heart began to pound all over again. "Why would you ask that?"

"I was watching you guys play, and he didn't seem to be trying. Like, *at all*. Almost like he wanted to lose. But that would mean he was giving you the victory, and that means..."

She trailed off, letting the implication hang silently in the air.

"He didn't lose on purpose," I said. "He's just really bad at Beer Pong. I'm bad too. I only sank one ball."

I felt awful for lying to my friend, but I truly believed it was for the best while we were stuck in this godforsaken place. The last thing any of us needed was the added drama of even more wild suspicions and accusations being flung all over the place, and I knew the revelation of my unexpected relationship with Maverick would result in exactly that, even amongst my own friends.

"It's not just that." Brooke hesitated for a few seconds, thumb rubbing at her chin. "That text the Game Master sent about you last night. I know you said it was a consequence for being out after the curfew, but..."

I picked up where she trailed off. "The Game Master sent a text about Maverick too. The sociopath one."

"Yeah. So... were you two breaking the curfew together last night?"

I figured a half-truth was better than an outright lie in this case. "Sort of," I said, dipping my chin in a brief nod. "It's like I said at breakfast. I thought the curfew wasn't in effect because of the late-night game, so I decided to explore. Maverick had the same idea, and I bumped into him out in the hall. We had a quick chat about what we were doing—he was exploring too—but then we got the texts from the Game Master telling us to get back to our rooms. I didn't mention seeing him when I told you guys about it at breakfast because it was such a quick, non-eventful thing. I was more worried everyone would judge me about that horrible video."

"Oh, right. So you two aren't…"

"No." Guilt churned my stomach as the lie slipped off my tongue. "I'm not hooking up with him, or anything like that."

Brooke's face brightened, and her shoulders relaxed. "Oh, thank *god*. For a minute I was actually worried you and that asshole were—" She stopped abruptly and shuddered. "Ugh, never mind. We don't need that mental image. Anyway, it's lucky for you that he sucks so much at Beer Pong."

"Yeah." Guilt was still twisting my stomach into knots. "I'm really lucky."

We turned our attention to the ongoing games. Zach won against April 5-3 a few minutes later, and April immediately looked over at Brooke and me with pure panic flashing in her eyes. "I can't pick," she said, voice choked with emotion. "Pick for me. Please."

"April…" Brooke shook her head. "We can't do that."

"Why?"

"If we pick a poisoned cup, it'll be our fault that you're gone. We'd never forgive ourselves. It has to be your choice."

April sighed forlornly and looked down at the table. "You're right."

"Maybe go for the very top or bottom-edge ones," Zach suggested. "The Game Master probably thinks most people will go for the middle ones, so they're more likely to be poisoned."

"Maybe, yeah." April blew out a deep breath and picked the top cup. "Well, here goes nothing."

She lifted the cup in a sarcastic toast. Then she knocked the beer back in a few gulps and wiped her lips with her sleeve. I watched with wide eyes, silently begging for her to be okay.

"How do you feel?" Brooke asked.

"Fine." April smiled faintly. "I think it was normal beer."

Courteney lost to Hudson a moment later, and we all watched as she selected a cup and drank the contents. Thankfully, she was fine too.

"We're down to the last game, and everyone's still alive," Brooke said. "Maybe we're all going to be okay."

"Don't jinx it, you idiot," Kiara called out. "If I die, it's totally your fault."

"You aren't going to die, babe," Jasmine said before tossing a ball toward her cups.

She sank it, and Kiara groaned. "How are you so much better than me?"

"It's only 3-2. I'm not *that* good," Jasmine replied.

Kiara missed the rest of her shots, and we all crowded around the table as her eyes darted between the cups in front of her. She twisted her lips for a few seconds. Then she snatched up a cup from the middle of the line, lifted her chin, and tossed it back.

"She sure picked that fast," Brooke muttered. "Almost as if she knew exactly which cups were safe."

April nodded slowly. "Yeah, it was a bit—"

Her voice was cut off by a series of choking sounds from Kiara's mouth. "Oh my god," she rasped, clutching at her throat. "It... it's burning. I..."

She fell to her knees, unable to get any more words out. Jasmine screamed and dashed over to her. "Throw it up!" she shrieked, smacking her on the back. "Get it out!"

It was too late. The poison was fast-acting, and within a minute or two, Kiara's lips had turned blue. She lurched several times, gasping for breath, and then she collapsed all the way to the floor, white foam spilling from her open mouth.

"No!" Jasmine screamed, crouching to shake Kiara's shoulders. "Wake up!"

She repeated this process for several minutes, shrieking and violently shaking her friend. Nothing happened. Kiara's body remained limp, her eyes glassy and unseeing.

"Jasmine..." Maverick gently pulled her away. "I think she's gone. I'm sorry."

Jasmine struggled against him for a moment, screeching and shouting, but then her eyes fell on Kiara's lifeless body, and she sank to the ground and burst into tears. "It's my fault," she choked out between sobs. "I should've let her win."

Courteney joined Maverick in trying to comfort her. I turned to my friends, lips compressed in a thin line. Their expressions told me they were thinking the exact same thing as me.

"We were wrong about Kiara," I muttered.

"Yup," Brooke said, nodding grimly. "Dead wrong."

"Wait." Zach lifted a trembling hand. "What if she faked it?"

"Faked it?" April said, brows shooting up. "How the hell could she do that?"

"Maybe all her cups contained sedatives so she could feign death. That way she could trick us into thinking she isn't the mastermind behind all this shit."

"Zach..." Brooke shook her head. "Look at her. She's not just unconscious from a sedative. She's *dead*."

Zach glanced over at Kiara's limp form and winced. Then he turned back to face us, head shaking. "I just... I really thought it was her behind all this shit," he muttered. "Now I have no fucking clue what to think. I feel like I'm going crazy."

"Me too," I said, rubbing my forehead. "This is exactly what the Game Master wants. For us to lose our minds before we die."

Before anyone could reply, the speaker on the wall crackled back to life. "The fifth game is now over. This room will be closing in five minutes for cleaning and maintenance," the voice said. "Please proceed to Gaming Room 6 down the hall. The next game begins in ten minutes."

"What?" Courteney shrieked. "We have to go straight into another game?"

"This is fucking bullshit!" Hudson added, glaring up at the nearest surveillance camera. "We need a break!"

Courteney started sucking down deep breaths, which rapidly turned into full-on hyperventilation. "I... I can't," she choked out between ragged breaths. "I can't do this. No more. No... more. I can't."

Zach raced over to comfort her as she sank to her knees, sobbing her heart out. April watched the interaction with her lips pressed into a thin line. "Can't blame her for having a total meltdown," she muttered. "I'm not sure how much longer I can do this shit either. I don't think I've slept more than two hours in the last three days."

"Me neither." Brooke sighed and rubbed her forehead. "How the fuck are we supposed to concentrate on playing these bullshit games when we can barely function from lack of sleep?"

"That beer we just drank didn't help either," April said, slowly shaking her head. "But what are we supposed to do? Petition the Game Master for a player's union that gives us some sort of rights?"

I snorted at her sarcastic jibe. "I wish."

Once Zach and Maverick had managed to coax Courteney and Jasmine into slightly calmer states, we reluctantly traipsed out of the room and headed farther down the passage to the next gaming room. The door was unlocked, but it slammed shut behind us and automatically locked as soon as we were all present.

As I peered around the cold, dimly lit room, shivers cascaded down my spine. The space was cloaked with shadows, and the air was heavy with the scent of musty old books and a faint odor of decay. In the center lay a giant chessboard, its checkered pattern stretching across most of the floor.

All the playing pieces were present, looming like sentinels from seemingly random squares all over the board. They were carved from weathered stone and looked to weigh several hundred pounds, if not more. I hoped we didn't have to move them as part of the game, because there was no way in hell most of us could manage that.

"I'm guessing there are landmines under some of the squares," Hudson speculated, stroking the stubble on his chin. "If we step on the wrong ones, we get—"

"Shut the fuck up, Hudson," Brooke hissed, cutting him off. "Courteney is already scared enough, and Jasmine is barely functioning after what happened to Kiara. So just save it, okay?"

He rolled his eyes and opened his mouth to reply, but at that exact moment, a nearby speaker made a loud clicking sound, and the Game Master's robotic voice echoed through the room.

"Welcome to Chess Club, everyone!" the voice said. "Don't worry if you've never played chess before. This game is only loosely based on the real thing. You'll find your player details and instructions on the wall to your right. There's no time limit on this game, so make sure you think carefully about every move. Good luck!"

Maverick stepped over to the wall and peered at a weathered-looking piece of paper that had been taped to the exposed brick. "We've all been given certain chess pieces to play as," he said, looking back at the rest of us over his shoulder. "Courteney and Hudson are rooks, April, Zach, and I are knights, Brooke and Jasmine are bishops, and Carey is a queen."

"No pawns or a king?" Brooke asked, tipping her head.

"Nope. I'm guessing there would've been more pieces available if we had more players," Maverick replied in a low voice. "But they're dead."

"So how does the game work?" April asked, rubbing her forehead. Her eyes were ringed with dark circles, and she looked as if she were going to fall asleep at any second.

"We've all been assigned an empty square to start on," Maverick said, eyes back on the paper. "April is B1, Courteney is A3, Zach is E3, Carey is C3, Jasmine is D2, Brooke is F3, Hudson is H1, and I'm G3. Everyone got theirs?"

There was a collective murmur of assent, and Maverick continued.

"The goal is for all of us to make it to the other side of the board. Once you're on the last row, you can step off the board entirely, and you cannot return after that. We all get one turn each, and they must be taken one at a time. We can't make any moves that cause us to collide with another player or any of the stone pieces that are already on the board. We also have to follow the rules of our particular playing piece. So for the rooks, that means you can move horizontally or vertically. Knights move in L shapes—two squares in one direction, either horizontally or vertically, and then one square perpendicular to that. Bishops move diagonally, and the queen can move vertically, diagonally, or horizontally."

"So Carey can just move wherever the fuck she wants?" Hudson spat, eyes narrowing. "How the fuck is that fair?"

"It's not. But these games are never fair," Jasmine said in a ragged voice, wiping her red-rimmed eyes. "I mean, Brooke was given a free pass to skip the last game while the rest of us had to risk drinking poison."

Maverick raised his voice and continued. "I'm not done, guys. There's another rule. If anyone accidentally steps on a square that's outside the range of their movement, they lose."

"You mean they *die*," Courteney muttered.

"Yeah, presumably," he replied in a grim tone. "So we all have to be very careful. For example, the bishops among us need to be sure to only move diagonally. If you accidentally move straight, you're gone."

"Can you repeat the rules for each piece?" April asked. "I haven't played chess in years and I'm tired as hell, so my brain isn't exactly going at full steam."

Maverick rattled off the rules again. "Everyone memorized theirs?" he asked, glancing around the group. There was a collective nod, and he went on. "I think we can all survive this one easily enough, as long as we're slow, careful, and help each other out. Once we're all on the board in our assigned spots, we need to take a lot of time to strategize our exact moves. Some of us will probably have to wait for others to take their turns so that certain players will be out of the way. But we won't know exactly what things will look like until we're all there. So let's go."

We trudged over to the board in silence. The tension in the room was palpable. Despite the supposed simplicity of the game, we were all exhausted, meaning it was easier than usual for any of us to make a mistake. One silly slipup or miscalculated move was all it would take for another life to be lost.

Once we were all standing on our assigned spots, Maverick snapped his fingers. "Okay, the game is supposed to start once we're all in place, so I guess that's right now. I think Carey should go first, because she can move any way she wants, and she's currently in the way of a few other players. So if we get her off the board, that makes things easier for the rest of us."

The group murmured their agreement. I took a deep breath and slowly began my journey across the board. My heart raced the whole time, and my breaths came in shallow, halting bursts. I knew I couldn't die from stepping on an incorrect empty square like the other players, because of my queen status, but I was still terrified of tripping and falling or accidentally putting the edge of my foot on a square that had a stone piece on it.

My last move was two diagonal steps to avoid several pieces that stood to the left and in front of me. I stepped onto D8 and released the breath I'd been holding. "That's it, right?" I called out to the others. "I can step off the board now?"

"Yup," Maverick called back. "You're done. Now you can help us plot out courses for the rest of us."

I stepped off the board and turned to face it, slowly scanning each square, player, and stone piece. "Brooke, you're a bishop, right?"

"Yes," she replied, eyes wide and fearful.

"If you move two steps diagonally to your left, then one diagonally to the right, one to the left, and one more to the right, you can get to F8 without hitting any players or stones. Then you'll be out of the way for the others to start their turns."

Brooke nodded slowly, eyes tracing the path over the board. "Two left, one right, one left, one right. All diagonal."

"You've got it." I smiled encouragingly. "Just go slowly."

She made it across safely. Maverick ordered Zach to take his turn next, getting him off the board so that Jasmine would have an easier time moving afterwards. Once she'd reached the last row, she stepped off the board and crumpled into a heap on the floor, covering her face with her hands as sobs racked her body.

"Sorry about Kiara," I murmured, crouching to lay a hand on her shoulder. "I know she was your best friend. I can't even imagine how terrible you must feel right now."

"Fuck off, Carey," she spluttered through her hands. "I don't need sympathy from *you*."

My lips thinned. "Got it," I said, rising to my feet so I could return my focus to the board. The others were still analyzing potential paths for the remaining players.

"April, I think I see a way across for you, now that Jasmine's off the board," Brooke called out.

"I think I see it too," she replied, pointing directly ahead. "If I go to A3 and then B3, I can then go to D3 and D4. From there, uhh... I can go to D6 and C6. Then... C8 to D8. Right?"

Brooke frowned as she calculated the path from the other side. Then she nodded. "That all sounds right. Ready?"

"No." April glumly shook her head and stifled a yawn. "Honestly, I feel like I'm about to faint. I really need you guys to help me as I go."

"We will," I said. "We'll call out the exact directions for you as you go. Okay? The first move is this: two steps forward and one right."

She nodded and took a tentative step. "Two forward, one right," she said, wearily rubbing her forehead. "Two forward, one right."

"That's it. You've got this," Maverick called out.

She made it to B3 and covered her mouth to stifle another yawn. "It was D4 next, right?"

Maverick nodded. "That's right. So two steps to your right, then one step forward. Okay?"

April blinked rapidly. Then she nodded and started moving. "Two steps right, one step forward," she said as she went. "Two steps right, two steps forward."

"No!" I screamed as she lifted her left foot to take an extra step onto D5. "*One* step forward!"

It was too late. Her foot had already come down on the wrong square. She stared across the board blankly, and then her eyes filled with horror as the gut-wrenching realization dawned on her. "Oh my god. I thought—"

She didn't get a chance to finish her sentence. A deafening crack split the air, followed by a sharp gasp from April. She staggered backward, clutching at the right side of her abdomen. Blood was seeping through her fingers, staining her pale gray sweatshirt crimson.

"April!" I screamed, dashing forward. If I could just get to her in time, apply enough pressure to the wound, she could survive this.

Zach grabbed me by the shoulder and yanked me backward a split-second before my feet touched the edge of the board. "You can't!" he said. "Once we're off the board, we can't return. Remember?"

He was right. If I'd actually taken that final step back onto the board, I'd be in the exact same boat as April right now.

As I looked on in horror, time seemed to slow to a crawl. April staggered backward again, almost bumping into Courteney, who was frozen in terror on her starting square. Then she lurched forward and fell to her knees, eyes filling with naked fear as they met mine.

"April!" I choked out, desperation and helplessness surging through me. "Stay with us! Please!"

Another sharp, agonized gasp escaped her lips, and she collapsed to the ground, blood pooling around her side.

I fell to my knees and let out a strangled cry, tears flooding my face. Everything seemed to blur as my mind struggled to process what had just happened. April couldn't be dead. She was just here a few seconds ago. She couldn't really be gone.

Brooke fell to her knees beside me, clinging to my shoulder. She tried to say something, but only a broken sob ended up spilling out.

"What the hell just happened?" Jasmine said from somewhere behind us. "Did she get shot?"

"Yes," Zach replied, voice thick with emotion. "There's either a sniper somewhere behind the wall, or some sort of automated sniping system. I don't know. But that was definitely a gunshot."

"Could she..." Jasmine paused and cleared her throat. "Could she survive that? Like, maybe she's just injured, and we can somehow get her off the board?"

Zach stood stock-still, staring at all the blood seeping across the black and white squares. "Courteney," he said in a hollow voice. "Is she... is she gone?"

Courteney looked down at April's motionless form and nodded listlessly. "I don't think she's breathing."

"Maverick, Hudson... what can you guys see?" Zach asked. His pitch had risen, adding a frantic air to his question. Clearly, he was hoping for a miracle. I was hoping, too. Praying, begging, clinging to the fragile thread of hope that Jasmine was right and April was only injured.

Maverick looked over at April's limp body. "I think Courteney's right," he said. "It looks like she's not breathing."

"She looks dead to me," Hudson bluntly added.

In that moment, the room seemed to fall silent. Brooke's sobs faded away along with my own, and all I could focus on was April's long blonde hair splayed out around her pale face.

That hair was the first thing I ever noticed about her when she waved me over to her desk in English class and took me under her wing. Beautiful and light, just like her soul. She was the first person at Babylon to show me any kindness, and she'd quickly become the best friend I ever made. Now that beautiful soul had been ripped away in a sick, twisted game, and the grief of it was threatening to consume me whole.

It was so cruel. So heartless. So unfair.

Anger suddenly boiled up beneath my sorrow, directed not only at the game that had stolen April from me, but at the senseless randomness of it all. What had she done to deserve this? What had *any* of us done to deserve it?

I didn't see or hear the rest of the game. I was too devastated, too blinded with heartache and guilt. I kept replaying April's final moments over and over in my mind, wishing I'd noticed her mistake a split-second earlier. If I had, I could've called out to her sooner, just before her foot came down on D5, and the whole thing could've been a narrow miss.

"Hey, Carey." Maverick's voice drifted into my ear, soft and soothing. "It's over. Courteney, Hudson, and I made it across."

I snapped out of my reverie and looked up at him. "Oh," was all I managed to get out.

"We have to leave."

I shook my head and returned my gaze to April's blonde head. "No," I whispered. "I want to stay here. With April."

"You can't. I'm sorry. The Game Master just announced that

the room is closing in five minutes. We're supposed to go to the drawing room for lunch now. Not that any of us feel like eating."

"Oh," I murmured again. I didn't know what else to say. Which words existed that could possibly convey the scale of the misery inside me?

"Let me help you up." Maverick hooked an arm under my shoulder and pulled me to my feet. At the same time, he used his other arm to help Brooke up. "Zach, do you want to help Brooke walk? I'll help Carey."

"Sure." Zach slung an arm around Brooke's trembling shoulder. His other arm went around Courteney.

Jasmine walked alone, arms wrapped around herself. Behind her, Hudson trudged with his hands in his pockets, eyes cast to the floor.

Maverick leaned down and murmured in my ear. "Ready?"

"No," I said listlessly. "I really don't want to leave April here."

"I get it." His voice had turned husky. "I'm so sorry, baby. I wish I could've stopped it."

"Me too." My voice cracked. "I should've told her to stop sooner."

"Hey." Maverick cradled my chin in one hand, forcing me to look up at his face. "It wasn't your fault. You can't let yourself get into that guilt spiral. Take it from a guy who's been there." He hesitated and went on. "I was there right up until the other night with you. You really helped me, just by talking to me and listening to me. That's so rare, you know? Having someone really listen to you instead of just waiting for their turn to speak. Someone who isn't being paid to do it."

"I guess."

"It's true. Now let me help you the way you've helped me."

I sniffed back a fresh set of tears. "I don't know if I can ever get over this," I said, voice scarcely above a whisper.

"You don't have to get over it. You just have to get through it." Maverick's jaw clenched, and his eyes turned steely. "And you will.

I promised you before. I'm going to keep you safe. You'll make it out of here."

Part of me wanted to believe him, but another morbid part of me was slowly beginning to realize the dark truth. I desperately wanted to make it out of this hellish place, along with all the others, but it seemed increasingly likely that April's fearful prediction from yesterday was correct.

We were all going to die here.

CAREY

The next day arrived with a chill in the air, anticipation and sorrow hanging like a shroud over our group. I couldn't bring myself to eat or speak to anyone at breakfast. I just stared at April's chair, wishing she would walk in and sit down.

"Y'know, if one more of us dies, we're officially down to half our original number," Hudson said through a mouthful of buttered toast, addressing no one in particular. He swallowed and went on. "Crazy, huh?"

"What's really crazy is you thinking it's a good idea to bring that up over breakfast, asshole," Jasmine said, narrowing her puffy red eyes. "Honestly, I hope *you're* the next one to go. None of us will have to mourn then."

As much as I couldn't stand Jasmine's bitchiness most of the time, I had to admit, I got a twisted little thrill from her burning Hudson like that.

He sneered. "You know, you should be careful what you say. You never know when you might need my help."

"Oh, like the way you helped Rhys?" Maverick cut in, cocking his head. "I think we'll all pass on that offer."

Hudson turned his stony face to Maverick. "Y'know, I'm just

about done with your bullshit, man. You think you run this fucking joint. Always ordering us around and speaking for everyone. But look how this shit's turned out under your so-called leadership. Five of us are dead in the space of four days, and we're still no closer to figuring out who this fucking Game Master is. So maybe it's time we go in another direction. Without you. By force, if necessary."

"Ah. More threats. Love it." Maverick's lips curled in a mirthless smile. "I guess we'll just have to see how things play out, won't we?"

"Yeah," Hudson said, nodding slowly. "I guess we will."

Their clash was interrupted by a text from the Game Master.

Morning, everyone! Today's game was my favorite to design, so I'm really looking forward to watching you participate. Please make your way to Gaming Room 7 in ten minutes. The entrance is on the far side of Gaming Room 6.

My throat ached with despair as the seven of us headed down the hall to the room where we were forced to watch April die eighteen hours ago. Her body had been removed and most of the blood had been mopped up, but there were still a few dark red smears on the chessboard that the Game Master's cleaner had missed. My stomach lurched at the sight, and I abruptly turned my head away, unable to bear it.

"Shit, I didn't even notice this yesterday," Zach said from the far end of the chessboard. He was peering into a dark, cavernous entryway beyond a wooden door that was swinging ever-so-slightly on its hinges, as if the Game Master had entered mere seconds ago.

"Me neither," Jasmine replied, hugging her arms around herself. "I guess we were all too focused on the game. Plus there's hardly any light in here."

"How about you stop yapping and get the fuck in there?" Hudson snapped. "The Game Master said it starts in ten minutes, and that was ages ago."

I hated Hudson, but he was right. We had to enter the next gaming room before it was too late.

The dark passage beyond the door led into a small, dim room, with only a few black and red candles casting feeble pools of light across the space from a low wooden table. Another door stood on the left side of the room, slightly ajar. More darkness lay beyond it.

Seven black and silver collars were laid out in a row beside the flickering candles. They looked like the collars from the Tag game, minus the string. Each one also had a small red button on the front.

The Game Master's ominous voice rang out over the nearest speaker. "Welcome to Seven Minutes in Hell, players! Please take the next few minutes to equip your collars."

Dread coiled in my stomach as I unhinged one of the collars, placed it around my neck, and closed it at the back. I helped Courteney with hers, because her hands were shaking so much, and then I turned my attention to Maverick. He was watching me from the other side of the room. When his intense gaze met mine, he dipped his chin in a tiny nod, instantly conveying his unspoken words. *You'll get through this. I'll make sure of it.*

The Game Master piped up again. "This game might seem easy at first, because it doesn't require any strategy or logic. In fact, it doesn't even require the slightest bit of intelligence. I suppose it's more of an experience than a game, really, and it requires one thing only: resilience. You'll enter the playing space via the door on the left when the timer starts, and then you'll make your way through to the end. As there are seven of you, I'm giving you forty-nine minutes to do this. You'll be faced with horrors at every turn, along with your worst fears. All you have to do is keep going until you reach the end. If things get too scary for you to handle, you can tap out by pressing the red button. Have fun, and good luck!"

The message ended with a loud beep, presumably to announce

the beginning of the countdown timer. Maverick headed over to the door and pushed it open, revealing the yawning darkness ahead. "Let's go," he said. "This game should be fine as long as we all keep our heads."

A familiar twisting sensation appeared in my stomach as we slowly stepped into a narrow passage. The walls were rough stone, damp with condensation. Dim torches flickered sporadically along the corridor, casting long shadows that danced ominously across the uneven floor.

"What the fuck is this place?" Jasmine muttered as we tentatively made our way along the twisting path. "Is this really meant to be scary?"

"I guess it's kind of spooky," Brooke replied, peering up at one of the flaming torches. "It looks like a tunnel from a horror movie."

As we wandered deeper into the passage, the air grew thick with the metallic tang of blood and the sickly-sweet stench of decay. Strange symbols and sigils were etched into the stone, conjuring up mental images of cackling witches and secret society rituals lost to time and obscurity.

We came across an alcove carved into the wall, containing a gruesome tableau. A bloated corpse with blistered pink skin hung from a chain, head hanging downward.

"Fuck, this almost looks real," Hudson said, reaching forward to lift the chin and expose the face. He leapt back with horror when he realized his mistake. "Oh, shit!"

It was Rhys's body.

I clamped my hand over my mouth and looked away, stomach roiling with horror. Courteney lurched forward and vomited on the floor, filling the narrow passage with the acrid scent of half-digested toast and eggs.

"Let's keep going," Maverick said, turning away. "Just try not to look at any of the stuff, okay?"

The passage twisted and turned, leading us deeper into the

darkness. Shadows danced and writhed along the walls, as if they were alive and watching our movements with malevolent intent.

We entered a new room a few minutes later. It was like a twisted nightmare come to life. Animal skulls littered the floor, black eye sockets staring accusingly into the abyss, and the walls were spattered with blood. But the true horror lay above us, on a glass ceiling illuminated by a flickering fluorescent light.

Evan's face, frozen in eternal shock, stared down at us. His body had been stripped and splayed on top of the glass, surrounded by a thick layer of dirt, dead leaves, and stones. Some blood had leaked from the top of his head onto his face, making it look like he was crying bloody tears.

Jasmine and Courteney screamed and staggered backward at the sight.

"Don't look," Maverick commanded. "Just keep your eyes on the path ahead."

We left the room and pressed on, making our way through room after room of fresh horrors. Pits filled with writhing snakes, floors crawling with insects, walls covered in screens that showed horrifying videos of torture and suffering. Each space seemed to outdo the last in its grotesque display of horror; a relentless onslaught on our senses.

All we could do was keep going and try not to look, as Maverick told us earlier.

I stepped into another dim, twisting passage, heart pounding and breath held tight. Whispered curses and screams echoed through the space, along with the voices of our fallen friends, begging for help. It truly felt like we'd stepped down into Hell itself.

"Please!" Kiara shouted from somewhere on our right. "Save me!"

"It's burning!" Rhys's disembodied voice chimed in. "Help me!"

"Get me out of here! It hurts so much!" April cried from the left.

A painful lump appeared in my throat as her words registered in my mind. Earlier, I'd wanted nothing more than to hear her voice again, but not like this.

"It's not real," Maverick said from up ahead, hands clenching at his sides. "It's deep-fake tech. You can take a video that someone's put online and use the program to simulate their voice to say anything you want."

I opened my mouth to reply, but a scream tore from my throat instead. Kiara's corpse had just dropped into the passage directly in front of me, swinging from a knotted brown rope.

"Is *that* real enough for you?" the Game Master boomed from a nearby speaker. The question was followed by hollow laughter that sent a chill down my spine.

Maverick turned, grabbed my hand, and pulled me around the swinging body. Jasmine was in tears, and Brooke's face had turned a deathly shade of white. Even Hudson looked disturbed.

"C'mon," Zach muttered, taking Courteney's trembling hand. "Let's go."

"No." Courteney refused to budge. "I can't see or hear any more of this shit. I need a break. Please."

"We're on a time limit, Court," Zach said. "Otherwise we'd all say yes to a break, believe me."

"Please." Her voice had dropped to a broken whisper. "If I see one more body..."

"You won't. I'll cover your eyes if you want. Okay?"

"Yeah, we can guide you," Maverick added. "But we've already been down here for at least thirty minutes, and we have no idea how many more rooms we have to go through until we reach the end. So we have to keep going."

Courteney grudgingly nodded and stepped forward, waving Zach's hands away from her face with an indecipherable mutter.

The next room was lit by candlelight, casting eerie shadows

that danced over peeling wallpaper adorned with faded floral patterns. The awful sounds from the previous passage had faded away, leaving us in an ominous silence that made me shiver with anticipation. But it was the dolls that truly sent a chill down my spine. They lined every surface, porcelain faces frozen in grotesque smiles and lifeless eyes staring vacantly ahead. Some sat on chairs or shelves, limbs twisted at unnatural angles, while others lay scattered on the floor. The flickering light and shadows from the candles made it seem as if some were moving, hands reaching out to grasp at our ankles.

"Oh, fuck," Hudson croaked, one hand pressed to his chest. "I hate dolls."

"Oh my god, *this* is what scares you?" Jasmine said, planting her hands on her hips. "*Dolls?*"

"Fuck you. I'm getting out of here." He sucked in a deep breath and fled into the passage leading out of the room.

"I guess this room was designed to scare him," Brooke said, glancing around. "It's not that bad unless you have a doll phobia."

"Yeah. Except..." Zach pointed a shaky finger at a large doll on a rocking chair in the corner. "What's that?"

The doll's right arm had been removed and replaced with what appeared to be a bare human forearm, sewn onto the dress with rough black stitching.

Courteney keeled over and vomited again. Jasmine stepped closer, upper lip curling with disgust. "It's either April or Tate's arm," she muttered. "I don't know, though. It's too bloated to properly tell."

Acid rose in my throat as horror ricocheted through me.

"I think it's Tate," Zach said softly, taking a step closer. "April had her nails painted pink."

"We need to keep moving. We're running out of time," Maverick said. "So let's—"

He was cut off by a masculine shout from the passage ahead. "Fuck! Help!"

We dashed out of the room and headed toward Hudson's voice. He was standing in a large space surrounded by screens playing black and white videos of ghosts and zombies. At first, I thought that was what had scared him, but then I saw the huge black spiders crawling all over the floor and walls. Some were dropping from webs above us, dangling right above our heads, and one had just landed on Hudson's shoulder.

"Get this shit off me!" he shouted.

Zach stepped forward and brushed it off, sending it skittering away. "Coward," he muttered. He turned back to return to Courteney's side, and his eyes widened. "Oh, shit. Court!"

Courteney had dropped to the floor behind us and curled into a ball. "I can't do this. Can't do this," she said between short, sharp gasps. "Get me out of here. I'm going to die. I'm going to die."

"Oh my god, I forgot she has a full-on arachnophobia thing," Jasmine said, hands on her hips. "Remember that camp we went on in sixth grade? She freaked the fuck out then too. Honestly, I don't get it. They're basically just big bugs."

"Not helpful, Jasmine," Zach said sharply as he crouched by Courteney's side. He brushed several spiders away and rubbed her back. "Hey, it's okay. I don't think they're venomous. Try to breathe deeply."

She did as he said, sucking down several deep breaths. "I hate this," she croaked. "I hate it so much. I can't handle it anymore. Really. I can't."

"Just a few more minutes, okay? We should almost be at the end by now."

Courteney took another deep breath and nodded. Then she finally opened her eyes. At that exact second, an enormous spider dropped down from directly above her head, landing right on her face. She let out a gut-wrenching scream and clutched at her throat.

"No!" Zach shouted, trying to tear her hand away. But it was too late. The tap-out button on her collar had begun to flash.

My heart sank as the collar immediately began to tighten around her neck. It didn't slowly choke her, though, like Tate's collar in the Tag game. There must have been a thin wire embedded in the material that was released when the button was pressed, because blood started seeping around the edges of the collar within a matter of seconds.

"Why the fuck did she press the button?" Jasmine shrieked. "They're just spiders!"

Courteney writhed on the floor, clutching at her bleeding throat. "I... I didn't," she choked out. "Didn't even touch it. I swear, I didn't..."

She was unable to get any more words out. Her head lolled backward, hitting the floor with a thud, and her eyes fluttered shut.

"No!" Zach roared, tearing at the collar as blood spilled over his hands. "*No!*"

"Player three eliminated," the Game Master's voice boomed out over Zach's anguished cries. "Remaining time: eight minutes and forty-seven seconds."

"Oh my god." Brooke's hand flew to her mouth. "I can't believe she actually tapped out."

I narrowed my eyes. "She said she didn't."

"She must've accidentally pressed the button when she grabbed her throat," Maverick said. "Fuck, what a horrible way to go."

I kept staring at Courteney's lifeless body as Zach sobbed over her. The metallic scent of her blood was lingering in the air, making nausea rise in my throat. "She said she didn't touch the button," I said in a low voice, head slowly shaking. "Accidentally or not."

"Maybe she just didn't realize she touched it," Maverick replied.

"Yeah. Maybe," I muttered. "Or maybe I was right the other day."

Brooke's gaze snapped to mine. "About some of the games being rigged against us?"

"Yeah. Maybe we only play so the Game Master can watch us suffer. Not because there's actually any chance of survival."

"We can't think like that," Maverick said gruffly. "We have to believe there's a way out of this place."

He stepped past several skittering spiders and knelt to place a hand on Zach's shoulder. "Sorry, man. We have to go. Only eight minutes left."

Zach refused to move, so Maverick hauled him to his feet and dragged him away from Courteney's body. He shouted and struggled the whole way, but I didn't intervene. It was for the best.

The next room was a cramped space with red lighting, like a photographer's dark room. The floor was littered with bullets, and a black rifle sat in a glass display case on one of the walls. The walls were lined with photos of April. Some were taken from a distance, showing her lifeless body splayed on the enormous chessboard, while others were closeups of her abdomen, gray sweatshirt lifted to reveal a gaping gunshot wound. As awful as the wound was to look at, the worst photo was a closeup of her face, pale with blue lips and dried blood that had trickled down from one corner of her mouth.

"You were all too late. You could've helped me. It's your fault I'm gone," her voice said over a tinny speaker. "All your fault. All your fault. All your fault."

I set my jaw and clamped my hands over my ears to drown out the awful chant. Maverick squeezed my shoulder. "Remember, it's not real. Just deep-fake bullshit," he murmured. "It wasn't your fault she died."

I swallowed the hard lump in my throat and nodded. "Let's get out of here," I said, voice quavering as I spotted April's torn, bloodied sweatshirt crumpled on the floor beside another array of bullets.

The final few rooms were similar to the first ones—shadowy spaces filled with bones, skulls, teeth, and blood, accompanied by creepy whispers and the occasional bloodcurdling scream.

I steeled my jaw and tried my best to ignore the gore around me, along with the sharp pains in my chest that had appeared after seeing all the awful reminders of Evan, Tate, Rhys, Kiara, and April's demises. Finally, we reached a door with the words 'THE END' daubed on it in dark red paint.

"Congratulations!" the Game Master's voice boomed out. "You made it with four minutes to spare, and only one of you lost your head, so to speak."

"Fuck you!" Zach screamed, shaking his fist at the speaker. "I'll fucking kill you!"

"Please proceed to the drawing room for morning tea. There are no more games until tomorrow, so you can relax for the rest of the day. The arrows on the floor beyond this door will guide you back to the main hall," the Game Master droned on. "Thanks for playing!"

"I'm so fucking sick of hearing that shit," Jasmine muttered as we stepped through the exit. "As if we're *choosing* to play."

For once, I agreed with her.

We headed back to the drawing room in somber silence. Courteney's death was weighing heavily on our shoulders. Half of the original players were dead now, and the rest of us had no idea what lay in store for us beyond more games, more torment, and more terror.

We had to do something to figure out the truth behind this place, but how? Maverick and I had already tried to explore every available space the other night, and we hadn't turned up a single clue about the Game Master's identity, let alone any possible means of escape.

I lost myself in my thoughts as I sat in the drawing room,

reflecting on my time in this awful place. The games. The messages. The perpetual fear. The seeming lack of motive. By the time my tea had gone cold, I'd realized that something was bothering me about the Seven Minutes in Hell game. However, I couldn't quite put my finger on it. It seemed to be gnawing at the very edges of my brain, and every time I tried to grasp the thought, it slipped away.

"Does anyone else think there was something weird about that last game?" I asked, looking up at the others.

"Like what?" Jasmine asked, wrinkling her nose.

"I don't know. I just keep getting this weird feeling about it. Like... something wasn't right."

"It's because it wasn't really a game," Zach said in a ragged murmur. "It was an *experience*, like the Game Master said at the start."

I frowned. He was right, but that wasn't the thing that was bothering me. If I could just figure out what it was, then this annoying itch in my brain would go away.

Once the Game Master announced via text that the drawing room was closing for cleaning, I spent several hours talking to Maverick, Brooke, Zach, and surprisingly, Jasmine. We sat in Maverick's room and shared every thought we had over our situation and every suspicion we'd ever had over the Game Master's identity, but in the end, we all turned out to be in the exact same boat. Utterly clueless and no closer to a solution.

"Wait." Jasmine suddenly sat up straight, gaze flicking between me and Maverick. "You said you guys explored a bit the other night, when you broke the curfew. Because of your secret passage theory."

"Yeah, but we didn't find anything."

"You said the drawing room was locked. Have either of you tried searching it since then? Like, when we have breakfast or whatever?"

My eyes widened, and I looked at Maverick. "I forgot all about the drawing room."

"Me too," he said, head shaking. "And we were right fucking there today. Twice. Not to mention yesterday. *Fuck*."

"Well, if this secret passage theory has any weight to it, there'll be an entry in there, just like you guys suspected," Jasmine said, lowering her voice like she was afraid the Game Master was listening. "We can look once it opens up for dinner."

By the time the drawing room finally reopened at six, we were all buzzing with excitement. Unfortunately, our search turned up nothing. The large oil paintings weren't concealing any extra doorways, and none of the wooden panels on the walls sounded hollow. Our last attempt was a search under the carpet, in case there was a small trapdoor with a ladder that led to the room below, but the floorboards were all uniform with no hint of a hatch.

"Well, there goes that theory," Jasmine said, shoulders glumly slumping. Her eyes flitted over to the nearest surveillance camera. "And now the Game Master totally knows we were looking, too."

"So what?" Zach clenched his jaw. "What the fuck does he expect? For us all to give up and not even try to find a way out?"

I lifted a hand and cut in. "He would've seen me searching for a secret door the other night when I broke the curfew. Maverick, too. I don't think he cares, because he's so arrogant that he assumes we'll never find anything."

"Right." Jasmine looked around the group. "Does anyone else suddenly have any bright ideas on how to escape?"

"Well... there's that rope and boat idea someone had a few days ago," Brooke said. "But we already figured that there's no way the Game Master would leave a boat lying around outside."

Jasmine threw her hands up. "Great. We're all screwed," she said. "I'm going to shower and go to bed. Might as well enjoy the hot water and comfy mattress while I still can, right?"

She stomped out of the drawing room. Brooke and Zach

decided to follow her, and Hudson left as soon as he finished his last bite of dinner.

Maverick reached over to squeeze my hand. "Want to stay? Or should we go to bed?"

Suddenly all I could think about was his strong arms, warm skin, and big hands. That was exactly what I needed to distract me from my grief and terror right now. I might not be able to escape this place, but I could escape the pain, even if it was just for an hour or two.

"Bed," I declared. "But I don't want to sleep."

We made it to my room in record time. "Are you sure you want this right now?" Maverick asked, one hand stroking my back as I locked the door.

I didn't answer. I just turned and kissed him roughly. He growled deep in his throat and kissed me back, his lips just as hungry as mine. Then he pulled back, took my hand, and pulled me across the room.

We pulled our clothes off as we headed toward the bed, not caring if anything got ripped or torn. Desire rocketed through me as we tumbled downward and landed on the soft mattress, lips and hands wildly exploring each other's mouths and bodies.

Maverick pushed me onto my back, grabbed my thighs, and yanked them apart. He slid down the bed, tongue tracing a teasing path down my left thigh as he went. I could feel the heat radiating from him, and it made me crave him even more. When his mouth finally reached my center, I gripped the sheets on either side of me and lifted my hips, moaning as he licked and sucked at my clit. It felt like every nerve ending in my body was on fire, and I couldn't get enough.

"Omigod," I moaned, writhing beneath him as he continued his assault on my senses. It was exactly what I needed right now; the perfect mind-numbing distraction from a reality that had never looked darker. "Yes!"

Maverick slid a finger inside me, curling it upward as his

tongue worked its magic on my clit. I was already teetering on the edge of a climax, but just as the pressure was about to explode from within me, he pulled away, leaving me gasping. I lifted my head and looked down at him, eyes silently begging for more.

He positioned himself above me, the tip of his hard length pressing against my entrance, and I gasped as he pushed inside me, stretching and filling me completely. When he began to move, I wrapped my legs around his waist, urging him deeper. He groaned in response, movements quickly becoming faster and more aggressive.

My muscles tightened as tension built inside me. I could feel myself drawing closer and closer to the edge, every inch of me straining and quivering.

"Come for me," Maverick muttered in my ear, roughly gripping my hips as he thrust into me. "I need to feel you come on my cock."

His words sent me over the edge, and I cried out as my body shook and convulsed beneath him. He let out a low groan, his own climax following soon after mine.

For a long time, we just lay there, bodies entwined and hearts racing. I didn't want to move. Didn't want to speak. Didn't even want to think about anything beyond this bed. I knew as soon as I did, the grief would flood back, and I'd be sobbing and screaming all over again.

Maverick seemed to understand all of this, because he didn't try to make me talk about yesterday, or anything else. Instead, he stayed quiet, gently stroking my hair and occasionally leaning in to kiss my forehead.

We stayed like that for hours, wrapped up in each other's arms. At 9:45, Maverick finally sat up and stretched. "It's nearly curfew," he said. "Should I stay with you?"

"I think we all have to be in our own rooms after curfew," I said, softly stroking his back. "Otherwise I'd say yes."

He stared down at me, eyes filled with concern. "Should I just risk it? I don't want you to be alone right now."

I bit my bottom lip and considered it before shaking my head. "I don't know what the next consequence will be. The first was just a text with information that made you look bad. But the next one…"

I trailed off, leaving the dark implication hanging in the air. Maverick groaned. "Yeah. You're right. I should go," he said. "I wouldn't be much help to you if I was dead, would I?"

I winced. "Don't even say that. Please."

"Sorry." He leaned down and kissed my forehead. "I'll see you in the morning, okay?"

Once he was gone, I switched off my light and lay in the darkness, heart pounding. Maverick's company had distracted me for a while, but now my brain was working overtime, going haywire with a thousand different thoughts.

My mind kept returning to the last game. What was it that was nagging at me so much? I must have seen *something* that aroused my suspicions in there, or else I wouldn't keep coming back to it again and again.

I let out a frustrated sigh and tried to replay the entire experience in my mind's eye. There was the dark tunnel, the creepy sigils painted everywhere, the snakes and insects, the flashing lights and terrifying sounds, the blood, the gore, the bodies… *wait.*

I sat bolt upright, heart jackhammering in my chest.

I knew exactly what was wrong.

CAREY

It wasn't something I saw earlier. It was something I *didn't* see. Something that should've been there but was missing instead. That was why I couldn't put my finger on it for so long.

As we were making our way through the twisted labyrinth during the Seven Minutes in Hell game, we saw Rhys's corpse chained in an alcove, Evan splayed over a glass ceiling above us, Kiara hanging from a rope, and Tate's dismembered arm sewn on a doll.

We never saw April's body.

We saw the gun that killed her, multiple photos of her corpse and the wound that caused her demise, and the bloodied sweater she was wearing when she was shot. But never a body. Not even a part of the body, like we saw in Tate's case.

I leaned back, sucking down a deep breath. *No.* I was just being paranoid, surely. This place had finally succeeded in driving me mad. After all, why would April fake her own death? Why would she be the Game Master? Why would she do *any* of this?

God. I was a horrible bitch for even considering this shit for a second. April was my friend. I should be loyal. Should be grieving her death.

But even as the guilt poured in, the suspicions kept coming just as strongly.

The Game Master told us from the start that he or she was one of us. Kiara was our strongest suspect for a while, but I knew she was truly dead. We all saw her die right in front of us, and then we saw her corpse dangling from that rope in the dark passage this morning. Judging by the appearance and the stench emanating from it, it was really her. Not some sort of Hollywood-designed fake corpse.

As for Evan, Tate, and Rhys, they couldn't possibly have faked their deaths either, given how they occurred. But April... she died from a gunshot wound that theoretically could've been faked.

I had a rough idea of how they did it in movies—some sort of red ink pack would be affixed to the person beneath their shirt, and when the prop gun went off, they'd press a hidden button to release the ink, splattering their clothes with realistic-looking 'blood'. That could've happened in this case. It would also explain why someone as smart as April made such a silly mistake during the game. At the time, I put it down to her exhaustion and stress, but now I wasn't so sure.

On top of that, none of us were allowed near April to check her pulse and confirm her death. The remaining players on the chessboard couldn't move to any wrong squares for fear of dying, and those of us who'd already made it across weren't allowed to return to the board. The closest person was Courteney, but she was still a few squares away, meaning she might not be able to tell for sure if April was breathing or not. April could've lain there motionless, taking only short, shallow breaths as infrequently as possible so the players on the board wouldn't notice that she was still alive.

As for the rest of us—we saw and thus believed exactly what was presented to us. We saw someone get shot, we saw them stagger and fall, and we saw them lying still on the floor with blood pooling around them. Of course we all assumed that person was dead. Especially when none of us had any reason whatsoever to suspect that person of being the Game Master.

The questions kept flooding in, making my stomach churn with confusion and fear. If April was really the Game Master, what made her decide to bring us all here? Why fake her death halfway through the games? How the hell did she even design this place and pull this thing off?

My mind drifted back to a conversation between Kiara and April on our very first day here. *'Your family are literally military contractors. You totally could've built something like this,'* Kiara had said.

'Oh, sure,' April retorted. *'I just called my parents, along with the US Army and the Pentagon, and asked if they'd help me set something up to deal with some kids at school who are being mean to my friend. That all sounds totally reasonable and realistic.'*

She made it sound so ridiculous at the time, but was it really *that* outrageous to consider? The Garrick family was uber-wealthy. Beyond billionaire status, if you combined the net worth of every family member. That sort of money bought a ton of influence, power, and most importantly in this case… silence.

A place like this could've been designed and built in a hush-hush way, as long as the right people were contacted and bribed. April's family probably could've acquired Icarus Hall on the downlow too, given her father's close ties to Babylon Prep.

Still, none of this answered my biggest question. *Why?*

All this time, I'd wanted so badly to believe that someone like Hudson, Rhys, Kiara, or Jasmine was the one behind these games. Or even a total outsider. Never, ever my good friend. But now my gut was telling me there was something to this theory, even though I had no clue about possible motives.

I glanced at the time on my phone. 9:51. Still nine minutes until the curfew. If April's room was unlocked, I could quickly check in there for any clues she might've inadvertently left behind. If I didn't find anything, I could return first thing in the morning with Maverick and carry out a longer search.

I quietly left my room, tiptoed down to the end of the hall, and tried April's door handle. It was unlocked, as it should be, given that she supposedly never returned after the Chess Club game. Guilt instantly flooded back in, and I took a deep breath and stepped inside, wondering if I was a total monster for doing this.

The room was laid out similarly to my own—stacked bookshelf and desk on one side, closet, oil paintings on the wall, and a queen-sized bed. I hastily went through the books on the shelf before attempting to pull on the shelf itself, in case the furniture was concealing a secret doorway. No dice. After that, I checked under the bed for any hidden trapdoors. I even checked the bathroom.

Again, there was nothing.

With a sigh, I slumped on the end of April's bed, face flushing hot with shame. I was either a total bitch for suspecting an innocent person—my closest friend, no less—or I was right but still a total idiot for thinking April would leave any obvious clues lying around her room. What did I expect her to do if she was truly the Game Master? Leave a book on the shelf titled '*Killing Your Friends 101*'? Or a journal on the desk with daily entries detailing her joy at how things were progressing in the games?

My eyes fell on the oil painting on the opposite wall. I stared at it for a full thirty seconds, wondering why my senses were suddenly tingling. Then it hit me. The painting on the corresponding wall in my bedroom was less than half the size of this one. The painting in Maverick's room was the exact same as mine, and from what I recalled of Brooke and Zach's rooms, their paintings were also quite small. So why was April's so massive? Was it just a coincidence, or could there be something behind it?

I leapt up and grabbed the gilt edge of the frame from the left side. It didn't budge. I tried the right side, and it creaked open to reveal a large hole in the wall.

"Holy shit," I said breathlessly. I was right. April had been hiding something after all.

The hole was too dark to get a proper look inside it, so I used the light from my phone to illuminate it. I expected to see a stash of food or tech gear, but instead, I saw a tight space with a wooden ladder heading upward.

Curiosity overwhelmed me, outweighing my fear. I took a deep breath and slowly began to ascend, being careful not to make a sound. When I reached the open hole at the top of the ladder, I poked my head out just an inch or two to see what lay on the new level. It was a large room with three single beds, a couch, several cluttered tables, and a large desk at the far end with a computer and multiple screens.

The lamps and overhead lights in the room were off, but the faint, blue-tinged light from the computer screens illuminated the space enough for me to spot a familiar blonde head resting on a pillow on the closest bed.

April was alive.

Disbelief coursed through my veins like icy tendrils, momentarily freezing me in place. How the hell could she do this? How could she be capable of such unspeakable horrors? It didn't make any sense. She was the last person I ever would've suspected of being the Game Master.

I had to believe it, though. The truth was literally laid out right in front of me.

I drew in a shaky breath and started descending as quietly as possible. There was no way I could confront April alone. That was far too dangerous. I had to wake up Maverick and the others so we could figure out our next move together.

When I was halfway down the ladder, a click sounded above

me, and my eyes shot up to meet April's cold gaze. She was crouching over the hole in the floor with a pistol pointed right at my face.

"God, Carey," she said, slowly shaking her head. "I really wish you hadn't come here."

CAREY

"I wasn't actually asleep," April went on, waving the pistol at me. I flinched, and she went on. "I was watching you go through my room on the monitor, and I was hoping you wouldn't find anything. But... you did. So now you're going to have to come back up here. Okay?"

I swallowed hard and nodded, eyes fixed on the gun barrel. "Okay," I whispered.

I slowly climbed back up, heart pounding. When I reached the top, April grabbed me under my left arm with her free hand and hauled me out of the hole. "Take a seat," she said, waving the pistol toward the couch.

"Okay," I repeated, unsure of what else I could say without incurring her wrath. This wasn't the April I knew and loved. The version I knew didn't carry guns and point them in people's faces. She was sweet, kind, and witty.

This version of her was a total wildcard.

"What gave me away?" she asked, staring down at me. There was such venom in her eyes that I was afraid she was going to reach into my chest and rip my heart out with her bare hands.

"The last game," I said. "All the bodies were there except yours."

"Dammit." She let out a heavy sigh of frustration, as if she'd simply missed an important phone call instead of being caught out for a diabolical murder plan. "I told Mom and Dad that could be a problem, but they thought it would be fine."

"So you're here with your parents?"

"Yes, of course. Do you really think I could've pulled off this whole thing without any help?" she replied. "C'mon, Carey. Use your brain."

"I just..." I faltered and started again. "I don't get it. None of this makes any sense."

"It does if you know exactly why I wanted to kill everyone here," she said. She paused and cocked her head. "Well, almost everyone."

I stared up at her, still unable to believe it was truly *her* all along. So many memories of our friendship were flashing before my eyes, each one now tainted with the sickening realization that I'd been best friends with a monster. How many times had I confided in her, unaware that I was confiding to the very person who'd ripped apart so many lives? How many times had she hugged me and reassured me while plotting to kill me?

"Are you going to tell me why?" I asked, finally realizing it was my cue to speak.

April fixed me with a steely expression. "I told you to use your brain, Carey. If I was going to murder a bunch of people from our school, what would be the most likely motive behind it?"

"I honestly have no idea."

"You do." She tapped the side of her head with her free hand. "C'mon. It's in there somewhere."

My mind raced through every conversation that April and I had ever had. Every story we'd shared, every moment of laugher, and every tear shed together flooded my thoughts in a chaotic whirlwind. Amidst the memories, one story burned brighter than the others.

"Abby," I said in a hollow voice. "This is about her, isn't it?"

"Ding, ding, ding. We have a winner."

"But... I don't understand what anyone here has to do with what happened to her. I thought she died from an accidental overdose."

April nodded. "She did. But this isn't about her death. It's about her *life*. Every single thing that led up to the moment of that overdose," she said. "I mean, people don't just start taking drugs out of nowhere, do they?"

"I guess not," I said softly.

"You want to know what everyone here did to contribute? Let's see." April frowned and lifted a finger. "We'll go with Jasmine first. You know what that bitch is like, right?"

"Yes."

"She had a target on Abby from the second she met her, because she was so pretty. She spread some of the nastiest rumors I've ever heard about her. Seriously fucked up stuff. For *years*. A lot of people believed the shit, seeing as Jasmine is the big Queen Bee on campus." She sighed and shook her head. "Abby was scared to go to school some days because of all the gossip about her. You know what it's like to feel that way, don't you?"

"Yes. It's awful," I murmured.

"A lot of people jumped on the bandwagon of treating her like shit after the rumors first started. Some were worse than others. Like Evan, for instance. He used to follow her every single day and tell her how fat and ugly he thought she was." April's nostrils flared. "Remember in the Truth or Die game, when I said I was at an eating disorder treatment center over winter break two years ago?"

"Yes."

"It wasn't really me. It was Abby. All those shitty comments from Evan affected her so much that she started throwing up her dinner every night. One day, I even caught her Googling where she could find a tapeworm to infect herself with, just so she could be skinnier."

I winced. "That's horrible."

"Yeah. And things got even worse for her after her friend Ava's sweet sixteenth party. Hudson was there, and you know what he does to girls he wants."

My eyes widened. "He attacked her?"

April nodded, lips pressed in a grim line. "She wasn't as fortunate as you after he drugged her. She didn't wake up and escape. We tried to report it to the police, but Rhys helped him cover it up. He lied to the cops and said he was with Hudson all night. They believed him."

"I know what that's like too," I murmured, hands twisting on my lap.

"It destroyed her. That was when she started taking stuff to try and escape the pain. Tate was her dealer. Pills, speed. Coke sometimes."

"I'm guessing she also found out about Zach and Courteney at some point?"

"Yeah. That's why they were brought here." April paused and gritted her teeth. "Cheating assholes. They broke her heart."

"What about Brooke? I thought she was one of your best friends."

She nodded. "She was. But she has a nasty little secret. You know how she's the top student in chemistry?"

"Uh-huh."

"She really does love that subject. A little too much, in fact. She's the one who cooks everything up for Tate to sell."

Shock rippled through me. "Seriously?"

"Yeah. Apparently, his old supplier ended up in prison. He needed someone new, so he approached Brooke and offered her a fifty-fifty split if she became his cook. Her parents are super stingy, even though they're rich as hell, so she was glad to have the extra cash," she said. "Tate gets the necessary ingredients, and Brooke borrows equipment from the labs at school to do it. The teachers don't even notice. After all, no one would ever suspect sweet, innocent little Brooke of doing something like that."

I nodded slowly. "So if she didn't agree to it, Tate wouldn't have had anything to sell anymore, and Abby would still be alive. That's how you see it?"

"Exactly." April waved her free hand around the room. "Everyone here either directly contributed to the development of her drug habit or allowed it to continue in some way. That's what eventually led to her death. So as far as I'm concerned, it's their fault. My parents agree."

"What about Kiara?"

April's nose wrinkled. "I almost forgot about that bitch. She was blackmailing Abby, which was actively making her life even worse. She saw her buying from Evan one day and told her that she had to write all her essays from that moment on, or else she'd tell someone. She also made her steal English tests from Dad's office. I guess that gave her more time to focus on her stupid influencer shit instead of studying," she said. "She's also besties with Jasmine, so she helped spread those horrible rumors about Abby."

"And Maverick?"

She sighed and pinched the bridge of her nose. "I could see how depressed Abby was, even after she finished the treatment at Elmwood. She was too ashamed to tell our parents how she felt, because she thought they were judging her after the bulimia thing, even though they totally weren't. So I convinced her to talk to the school psychologist. Then, on the day of her first appointment, she was sitting in the waiting room, and Maverick came storming out of the psych's office and told her to get the fuck out."

"But that was—"

April cut me off. "I know what you're going to say. He was just trying to help everyone in that room by getting them away from

Dr. Barry, because he was a fucking creep," she said. "But he scared the shit out of Abby, and it put her off seeing someone ever again. She literally refused point blank every time I recommended a new psych for her to visit."

"So you would've preferred it if Maverick said nothing and let her see Dr. Barry?" I asked, face twisting in an incredulous expression. "So she could potentially become his next victim?"

She scoffed. "Oh, please. Abby was too old for Dr. Barry. He liked them a few years younger."

"That's really sick, April," I replied in a low voice, stomach roiling.

"Maybe so. But I was thinking pragmatically," she said. "Dr. Barry might've been a fucking creep, but he was good at his job. He could've helped Abby. Maverick stole that chance from her."

I slowly shook my head, wondering if she realized how truly insane she sounded right now. Then again, I wasn't sure what I expected. A person who'd pull off this sort of scheme obviously wasn't mentally stable.

"What about me?" I said, tipping my head. "What did I do to your sister? I didn't even know her."

"You didn't do anything, Carey." April smiled sweetly. "When my parents and I decided to punish everyone who contributed to Abby's death, we realized we'd need someone like you. Someone who had nothing to do with Abby at all. That way, when the investigators combed through possible motives for the killings, they'd rule out revenge. Revenge over Abby, that is."

I swallowed thickly, eyeing the gun. "So you're going to kill me now?"

"Of course not. You've totally derailed everything with your snooping, so we'll have to come up with something to explain why you've disappeared to the rest of the group. But we were never going to kill you. The plan was always for you to survive."

"Why?" I asked, frowning. "And *how?*"

"We had measures in place to protect you in every game. If

there was ever a situation where it seemed like you might be about to die, we would've flipped a switch to shut off the power. Then the game would be canceled due to the blackout, and you'd be fine," she explained. "In some games, it was even easier than that. For example, your assigned table during the Beer Pong game didn't have a single poisoned cup. You were always safe. Same as me."

"Okay," I said in a skeptical tone, eyes narrowing. "But why keep me alive at all?"

"Because we realized that we needed someone to be the sole survivor. You'd tell the police exactly what happened, thinking that all of us were dead, including me, because obviously you weren't supposed to realize that I faked my death. That way, with everyone thinking I'm stone-cold dead, I would never be a suspect, and neither would my parents," she said. "They'd suspect you of something at first, given your shady background and the fact that you were the only survivor, but then you'd go free due to lack of evidence. They'd probably wind up thinking that some random psycho set the whole thing up for a sick thrill."

"And then?"

"I'd remain in hiding for a while, and April Garrick would officially be dead. Eventually, my parents would tell everyone they were moving away because they couldn't stand to remain at Babylon after losing both of their daughters there. Too many reminders. So they'd move down to South America, where we have our own private island. I'd move with them and assume a new identity. Those are easy enough to buy. Then I could either stay there forever, or I could return to the States once I'd aged a bit and changed my appearance enough to get away with it."

I rubbed my forehead and sighed. "So this is why you befriended me on my first day at school," I muttered. "Here I was thinking you were just a nice person."

"We actually chose you a long time before that day." April

arched a brow. "Who do you think came up with the idea for the Babylon Foundation Justice Project?"

"That was *you*?"

"My parents, actually. We knew we'd need a random new student for this scheme, for all the reasons I just outlined, and we also knew the person would need to have... well, a *colorful* background, if you catch my drift."

"Why?"

"It's like I said a minute ago. The police would initially focus their attention on our little pawn with the shady history before eventually ruling the case unsolved. Basically, we had to do anything we possibly could to keep their attention away from my family," she said. "So, we came up with the idea of plucking some no-hoper kid from the wrong side of the tracks and giving them a chance at Babylon. Funnily enough, a lot of the parents at school *loved* the idea and immediately wanted to get involved with the project. It makes them feel good to think they're helping the less fortunate, you know? Even if it means there's a literal criminal being educated alongside their kids. Typical bleeding-heart attitude."

"So all that talk about how you care so much about the less fortunate... it was all bullshit," I said. "You're just as willing to exploit and destroy a poor person as someone like Jasmine. But hey, at least she's honest about being an entitled bitch."

April shrugged. "No one's perfect, I guess," she said. "Actually, that's not true. *You* were perfect. For our plan, that is. The right age, the right area, the right murky past. We made a few calls, gave some money to the right people, and voila—your charges disappeared, and you were free to start at Babylon as our little pawn."

"Great. Thanks a lot."

"I know you're being facetious, but you really should be grateful to us," she said, face hardening. "Not only are you getting a free education at the best school in the world, you'll also be super famous after this. The only survivor of the world's creepiest mass murder. Everyone will love your story. You could write a bestselling book about it. Maybe even get your own Netflix special."

"Again, thanks. It really means a lot," I said, voice dripping with sarcasm.

"You're welcome," she said, matching my tone.

I frowned and cocked my head. "Why not punish Abby's friends? Didn't they notice what was going on with her and fail to help her in the end?"

"Yes, but they didn't really do anything wrong. They tried to help her with her issues just as much as I did," April replied. "Half the stuff I knew about Abby's life came from them. Like Evan's bullying, for example. Abby never actually told me about it. I found out about it from Ava. Same with the Kiara blackmail stuff. Her friend Liana told me about that."

"Right."

"Her friends were sitting on a virtual treasure trove of information," she went on. "You remember how I said Abby had that idea about starting her own version of Gossip Girl?"

"Yeah."

"She wanted to do it because she thought it would give her enough power to stop the bullying. So she and her friends started gathering secrets. Of course, it never ended up going anywhere, but those secrets still existed, and her friends were more than happy to share them with me after Abby died."

"Ah. So that's how you knew everything for the Truth or Die game."

April smiled thinly. "Yup. It's also how I knew everything in general about who was most responsible for Abby's overdose. Like Brooke, for example. She didn't tell me she was cooking drugs, even though she was supposed to be my best friend. I had to find out from Abby's friends."

I gestured around the room. "What about all of this? How did you get it built?" I asked. "Some of the games required some serious engineering. Not to mention all the surveillance equipment around the place."

"My family has a lot of contacts. Comes with the territory of being military contractors."

"I figured that much, but how did you do it without anyone finding out?" I asked. "Aren't you worried someone will come forward eventually?"

"Nope." April's eyes glittered triumphantly. "The right amount of money can buy almost anyone's silence. As for those who can't be bought... well, everyone has secrets they don't want to come to light. So blackmail is always an option. You tell our secret, and we tell yours. Tit for tat."

"Right." I glanced around the room. "Where are your parents now?"

"Downstairs putting the finishing touches on the gaming room for tomorrow. It's a simple one, but it should be fun to watch."

I motioned toward the desk. "Is that where you guys keep track of everything?"

"Yes. All the cameras and mics are linked up to that computer. Mom and Dad were taking turns watching and listening while the other slept, but now that I'm supposedly dead, I can help out too."

I lifted my chin and looked into her cold eyes. "What happens now?"

"Now that you know the truth, you mean?"

"Yes. I can't be the sole survivor now, because I can tell the cops the truth about you."

She nodded. "Yeah, that's definitely a problem. If we stick to the plan of keeping you alive, we'll need to set things up so that it looks like *you* orchestrated the whole thing. That way no one will believe you when you point the finger at me and my parents," she said. "It's going to be a lot of work, but I think we can pull it off. After all, you have a sordid criminal past, don't you?"

"How can you possibly pin this shit on *me?*" I asked. "Criminal past or not, there's no way they'll think I could've pulled off something like this."

April tapped her chin with one finger. "Hmm. Off the top of my head, I guess we can say your motive was that you were tired of being bullied by the rich kids at Babylon. As for the means to do it... we can set up a fake financial trail to make it look like you had a rich sponsor. Someone you later killed in order to cover your tracks. Maybe Maverick."

My blood ran cold. "No."

"Why? He's actually the perfect fall guy. I know you've been sleeping with him, as much as you've tried to cover it up. I guess you didn't realize the bedrooms have cameras and mics in them, like everywhere else in the building," she said. "By the way, so much for us being friends, huh? You wouldn't even tell me what's going on in your love life. That's so shitty of you."

"I... it only happened a few days ago."

April rolled her eyes. "Whatever. We'll make it seem like he used his family money and connections to help you set this up. His parents are friends with my parents, so they'd probably know our family purchased this island and the old school building last year to turn it into a nature reserve for sea birds. So he knew it would be empty for a while and therefore usable for this diabolical plan of yours. Then, at the last minute, you betrayed him and killed him."

"No one will ever believe that."

Her forehead wrinkled. "Won't they? You and Maverick have been sharing a dorm for weeks at school. Plenty of time for you to fall in love and hatch a crazy plan together," she said. "Anyway, I feel like I've been talking forever. Are we done with question time?"

"No," I said, glaring at her. "I want to know something else."

"What is it?"

"Why risk so much by setting this up and making everyone play these games?" I asked. "Wouldn't it be easier for you and your parents to hire a hitman?"

April let out a brittle laugh. "Isn't it obvious?" she said. "We want them to suffer before they die. Mentally as well as physically. A hitman can't provide that."

"Right. I guess that makes sense to an unhinged maniac," I said in a hollow voice. "You know that's what you are, right?"

"Whatever, Carey. It doesn't matter in the end," she said. "Anyway, now that I've got you here, I'll have to come up with a reason to explain to the group why you've suddenly disappeared from the games. Any suggestions?"

"Nope."

She hesitated and scratched her head. "I guess we'll just say that you broke the rules by leaving your room after curfew yet again, and you paid the ultimate price. They'll all believe that," she said. She took a couple of steps closer. "And for now..."

With that, she twisted the gun in her hand and smashed it into the side of my head.

MAVERICK

The alarm on my phone blared, signaling that it was six o'clock. After a quick shower, I dressed and headed directly to Carey's room.

She didn't answer when I knocked. Figuring she was in the bathroom and unable to hear me, I tried the handle and found it unlocked. *Weird.* I could've sworn I heard her lock the door after I left last night.

I stepped inside and peered around. "Carey?"

The room was empty. So was the bathroom. She must've hopped out of bed and gone straight to the drawing room for breakfast while I was getting ready a few minutes ago. That made sense, seeing as we were still trying to hide our relationship from the others.

I headed down the stairs to find a full breakfast spread awaiting the group on the drawing room table. I only counted five place settings. Heart hammering, I hurried back upstairs and pounded on Brooke's door. She opened it a couple of minutes later, eyes heavy-lidded with exhaustion. "What's going on?"

"Is Carey with you?" I asked, peering over her shoulder.

"No. Why?"

I didn't bother answering. Instead, I headed down to Zach's room. Carey wasn't there either, and I knew there was no way she was hanging out with Jasmine.

"Oh, shit," I muttered, stomach flipping as something occurred to me. Hudson could've finally decided to make good on his threat to hurt Carey.

I broke into a run and headed to the other end of the hall. Hudson's room was locked, and he didn't answer for several minutes, even though I was hammering on the door the entire time.

"Jesus, man," he said when he finally opened the door a crack. "What the fuck is your problem?"

"Where's Carey?"

He sneered. "How the fuck would I know where your little girlfriend is?"

I shoved his door all the way open, pushing him aside. "Carey! Are you okay?"

"She's not in here, dumbass," Hudson said. "Why would she be?"

I whirled around, jaw clenched with fury. "You know exactly why."

Before he could respond, our phones chimed loudly. I ignored mine, still glowering at Hudson. He grabbed his phone off the bedside table and lowered his smarmy gaze to the screen. "Shit," he muttered. "I guess this explains where she went."

With my heart suddenly racing again, I pulled my phone out and opened the latest text from the Game Master.

Good morning, everyone! I must inform you all that Carey has been eliminated from the games. She broke the curfew yet again, and now she has paid the ultimate price. As for the rest of you, breakfast is served. Please eat quickly, because your next game starts in forty-five minutes.

My blood ran cold as I re-read the message, unable to believe my eyes. "No," I muttered. "It's not possible."

"It is," Hudson said. "Check the attachments."

The message was accompanied by a short video and a photo. The video was surveillance footage from the hall showing Carey leaving her room and heading down to the far end of the hall. The accompanying photo was a closeup of her face, eyes closed and blood caked on one side of her forehead.

I staggered backward, reeling from the shock to my system as if it were a physical blow. Then I slumped on the side of Hudson's bed and put my head in my hands, breaths coming in harsh, shallow wheezes.

I promised Carey I'd protect her; vowed to shield her with every fiber of my being. But I didn't. I failed, and now the weight of that failure was pressing down on me, suffocating me with guilt and regret.

"Get up," Hudson said in a clipped tone. "You saw what the Game Master said. New game soon."

I should've known he wouldn't give two fucks about what he'd just seen. He was probably glad Carey was out of the way.

In a numb haze, I stepped out of his room and headed to the drawing room to meet the others. Brooke and Zach looked as shocked and horrified as I felt. Even Jasmine seemed unhappy.

"I can't believe he just took her in the middle of the night," she said, head shaking with incredulity. "I didn't even hear anything."

"Me neither," Zach said. His eyes were filled with tears, and his words came out in a choked murmur.

Brooke couldn't speak at all. She was slumped on one of the chairs, staring into space.

"I really don't want to play the next game," Jasmine said, slumping down next to her. "What's the point? We're all going to die here anyway."

Zach turned his watery gaze to me, presumably expecting me to jump in with one of my usual remarks about how we had to keep trying, just in case the Game Master had been honest about letting the 'winners' go in the end. But I couldn't do it. Couldn't bring myself to give a shit. I'd lost Carey, and now I didn't give a shit if I lost everything else too.

Brooke finally spoke up. "Maybe Carey's not really dead," she murmured, twisting her hands in her lap.

Jasmine sighed. "Come on, Brooke. We all saw the photo."

"All we saw was her face with a bit of blood on it. It doesn't mean she's dead."

"Why would the Game Master lie about that?"

"I don't know. Maybe it's part of the next game?" Brooke said, sitting up straighter. "I mean, everything in this place is designed to break us, mentally as well as physically, so it wouldn't surprise me if a fake death was in his repertoire of nasty tricks."

Zach's face brightened slightly. "Yeah. Maybe it's a time-limited thing where we have to save her before it's too late."

"You guys are being totally delusional," Jasmine muttered, gingerly picking up a muffin. "Carey is obviously dead."

Hope flickered to life inside me, despite Jasmine's pessimism. Perhaps Brooke and Zach were right. After all, we directly saw the others die. But not Carey. Unless her body was right in front of me, I didn't have to believe she was really gone.

I clung to that fragile thread of hope until we arrived in Gaming Room 8 half an hour later. Carey wasn't there waiting for us to rescue her. In fact, there was nothing in the room except a glass bottle and a gun.

"Welcome to Spin the Bottle, players," the Game Master boomed from the nearest speaker. "As usual, we've got a bit of a twist on the usual game. In this version, the person the bottle lands on doesn't have to kiss someone. Instead, they must pick up the revolver in the center, put it to their head, and pull the trigger. This revolver has a twenty-round capacity, but only one bullet has been loaded into it. If the person survives, it's not necessarily their turn to spin. The turn goes to whoever was next in the circle. That way, you all get an equal number of spins until someone dies, upon which the game is over. Hudson will spin first. Have fun!"

Zach sighed heavily. "Great. Another game that comes down to pure luck."

"See?" Jasmine said, shrugging helplessly. "The Game Master wants us all dead."

"Not all of us," Hudson said, eyes laser-focused on me. "Only one of us."

I folded my arms. "Why don't you just say what you fucking mean, Hudson?"

"Fine." He turned to look at the others. "There's something you should all know. Maverick has been sneaking around with Carey. At least he *was,* until the Game Master smacked her down. So if one of us is going to die here, it might as well be the snake who's been lying and hiding shit from the rest of us."

"Even if that's true, this game still comes down to luck," Jasmine said, giving him a withering look.

"It *is* true. The Game Master texted me the other day and told me to keep a close eye on him, so I've been doing exactly that. And guess what? I've seen him sneaking out of Carey's room at night, even though he's always pretended to hate her."

Brooke's eyes widened, gaze shooting between me and Hudson. "Is that really true?" she asked.

"Yeah. It's true," I muttered. There was no point denying it anymore. "Carey and I are together. But we hid it for a good reason."

"See? I told you so," Hudson said. "Do we really need a dirty fucking liar in our ranks? Also, it's not just luck in this game. There's a strategy here. If you hold the bottle and flick your wrist the right way, you can almost guarantee it'll land on the person of your choosing. I can show you."

Brooke kept staring at him. "Okay. Show me," she said flatly.

I looked over at her. "Are you fucking serious?"

"Yeah, I am. C'mon, Hudson. Show me."

"Me too," Zach said. "You're right, man. We should eliminate the snakes from our ranks."

Jasmine nodded. "Hard agree."

I pinched the bridge of my nose and sighed heavily. "Guys, this is exactly what the Game Master has always wanted—for us to start turning on each other," I said. "But if you kill me now, I won't be able to help you find Carey if she's really still out there somewhere."

"She's not. She's dead, dumbass," Hudson said with a sneer. The others ignored me and watched him as he sat cross-legged on the floor.

"This is how you do it," he went on, grabbing the bottle an inch above the base. "You hold it right here and line the top up at the person *next* to the person you want it to land on. Then you flick it like this..." He paused and demonstrated the move. "And there you go. It almost always works."

"You know I can do that too, right?" I said. "I can make it land on you during every single one of my turns."

"I know. But it's four against one," Hudson said, smirking. "I like those odds."

Jasmine smiled thinly. "Me too. Let's begin."

I grudgingly joined them in the circle, knowing I didn't have a choice but to play. Hudson's smirk remained in place as he grabbed the bottle, and it landed right on me after his spin.

I clenched my jaw and picked up the revolver. I wasn't afraid, because I was certain the Game Master wouldn't load the bullet into the first chamber. After all, killing the very first person to pull the trigger would destroy his chance to obtain some sick pleasure from watching the rest of us squirm.

With a deep breath, I pulled the trigger, hoping I was right. It made a faint clicking sound, but nothing else happened.

"My turn," Jasmine announced from her spot next to Hudson. She lined up the top of the bottle with Brooke's feet, clenched her hand over the base, and flicked her wrist. It spun around quickly before stopping with the top end aimed directly at Hudson. "You were right! The trick works!"

Hudson's smirk faded. "Wait... what are you doing?"

Jasmine smiled sweetly. "It's like you said. We should eliminate the snakes from our ranks. And you're the only snake here, Hudson."

"Exactly," Zach muttered.

"But he... he's been lying to everyone!" Hudson spluttered, jabbing a finger in my direction.

Zach shrugged. "Honestly, I don't give a shit. I've never been a huge fan of Maverick, and he knows that, but he made it pretty clear to me this morning that he actually cares about Carey. Not only that, he's helped us through every game."

"But *you've* sabotaged people," Brooke added. "Your own best friend. We all saw it."

"Pick up the gun, Hudson," Jasmine said in an icy tone. "Now. Or else we'll do it for you."

Nostrils flaring, he did as she said and pulled the trigger. Once again, nothing happened.

It was my turn next, followed by Zach and Brooke. We all made the bottle land on Hudson, and he survived each round.

"My turn," he muttered, glaring daggers at me as he snatched up the bottle.

When it landed on me again, I took a deep breath, picked up the revolver, and pressed it against my right temple. I closed my eyes and pulled the trigger.

"Thank god," Jasmine murmured when nothing happened.

We went around the circle once more, targeting Hudson every single time. When it finally came to Brooke's second turn, she glared at him and spun the bottle to land on him yet again. "Your odds are getting worse, asshole," she hissed across the circle.

He rolled his eyes. "If I survive this, it'll be Maverick next. And who knows? Maybe that's where the bullet is."

"Maybe. Maybe not." She fixed him with a steely gaze. "Why don't you pull the trigger and find out?"

He lifted the revolver and pressed the barrel to his temple. When he pulled the trigger, a deafening crack echoed through the room.

The once sinister smirk on Hudson's face twisted into a split-second of shock before he crumpled to the ground, lifeless and still. The metallic scent of his blood hung in the air, mingling with the acrid scent of gunpowder.

"Well, I guess we all saw that one coming," Jasmine said. "Can't say I'll lose any sleep over it."

"Me neither," Zach muttered through gritted teeth.

Brooke stared at Hudson's crumpled body. "This place has turned us all into heartless monsters," she said, shaking her head. "And I don't even care. It's the weirdest feeling."

"You aren't a monster," I said stiffly. "We're just doing whatever it takes to survive."

"Game over," the Game Master finally announced. "Congratulations to the survivors. The remainder of the day will be free for you while I prepare for tomorrow's games. Lunch and dinner will be served at the usual times. Thanks for playing!"

I stood and looked down at Hudson's lifeless body, face impassive. Like the others, I couldn't even muster up a sliver of guilt or regret over his death. "Let's get the fuck out of here," I said, jabbing a thumb toward the door.

As we left the room and trudged down the hall, Zach looked at each of us in turn, eyes misty. "Do you guys still think Carey might be alive somewhere?"

Brooke sighed. "I really hope so," she said. She turned to me. "Maverick? What do you think?"

"I really hope so too," I said gruffly. "I promised I'd get her out of here."

We settled into a grim silence as we headed upstairs. I returned to my room and slumped on my bed, mind reeling with unanswered questions about Carey's disappearance.

What was she doing out of her room after the curfew? Where was she going? I knew she wasn't coming to see me, because the surveillance video showed her heading to the very end of the hall. Only April and Courteney's rooms were down there, and they were both dead, so she wasn't going to see them either.

What else was down that end of the hall that could've tempted her out of her room in the middle of the night? Was she going to climb out of the window again, like we all did on our first day here?

No. That didn't make any sense. There was simply no point in doing it, which meant she was either headed for April's room or Courteney's room. But that brought me back to the previous point—both of those girls were dead. So why go to their bedrooms?

I ruminated on it for the next couple of hours, and my mind kept coming back to one thing: Carey must've realized something about either April or Courteney. But what was it? What could either of the dead girls possibly have hidden that would be important enough to make Carey venture out alone in the night?

My thoughts eventually drifted back to something Carey said yesterday. *'Does anyone else think there was something weird about that last game? I just keep getting this weird feeling about it. Like... something wasn't right.'*

I was getting closer now. I could feel it building inside me; the same realization that must've struck Carey last night. Something so shocking that she couldn't wait until the morning to share it. Something that could possibly be hidden in one of the end rooms. But whatever it was, it continued to evade me.

As I mulled it over, it slowly occurred to me that I could just be completely delusional. This train of thought could be my heartbroken brain providing a distraction during one of my darkest moments; a coping mechanism to help me process the fact that Carey really died last night. I didn't know exactly *how* it happened, so instead of being able to deal with that, I had to turn to *why*.

"No," I muttered to myself, curling my hands at my sides until my nails dug into my palms. I had to believe there was a chance Carey was alive. Had to believe the Game Master was just messing with us, like Brooke suggested earlier.

My mind drifted back to that exact conversation, replaying her words. I found comfort in them, knowing she held the same hope that I did.

'All we saw was her face with a bit of blood on it. It doesn't mean she's dead,' she'd insisted.

'Why would the Game Master lie about that?' Jasmine had replied, ever the naysayer.

'I don't know. Maybe it's part of the next game?' Brooke said next. *'I mean, everything in this place is designed to break us, mentally as well as physically, so it wouldn't surprise me if a fake death was in his repertoire of nasty tricks.'*

I sat up straight, eyes widening. *Fake death.* Those two words were buzzing in my brain now, heightening all my senses. There had to be a reason for that.

Perhaps that was what Carey got too close to last night. It could be why she left her room in the night and headed to the end of the hall. She suspected that either April or Courtney had faked their death.

I cast my mind back to Courteney's death. There was absolutely no way she could've faked it. I saw that wire cutting into her throat as the collar tightened around her. Saw the blood spilling and the light fading from her eyes.

But April...

"Holy fuck." I drew in a harsh, guttural breath as the possibilities cascaded through my mind. "No way. No fucking *way*."

But the more I thought about it, the more it made sense. That was what Carey picked up on during yesterday's game. April's body was absent, while all the others were present in some form. April was also the only one whose death could possibly be faked.

But why? The question burned in my mind, begging for elucidation.

I honestly had no idea why she would do something like this. What had any of us done to her to incur such a terrible wrath? Especially Carey. She only met April at the start of the school term a couple of months ago. So what the hell did she do to get dragged into this shitshow?

I leaned back against the headboard, mind whirling. If April was really the Game Master, did it even matter what her motive was right now?

Nope.

All that mattered in the end was keeping Carey safe and getting her home, just like I promised. That meant saving her from April if she was truly still alive... and the more I thought about it, the more convinced I became that she *was* still out there.

After all, whatever April's motive was, she'd probably want some sort of fall guy to pin this shit on once the authorities finally tracked us down and found all the dead bodies. That was the most reasonable explanation I could think of for why she'd dragged Carey into this, and it meant Carey was definitely still alive.

A small part of my brain told me I was crazy; grasping at straws and making connections that didn't really exist. A bigger part of me told me I was really onto something. I just needed some sort of proof so the others wouldn't think I'd totally lost my shit.

I snatched up my phone and opened my text thread with the Game Master. It only contained texts from them, but on the first day here, they'd clearly stated that we could communicate both ways if we wanted to.

I shot off a quick message. *Hey. Are you there?*

The Game Master responded instantly. **Of course. How can I assist you, Maverick?**

Me: *I want some exercise. Feeling really cooped up. Are we allowed to walk/run through the old gaming rooms, or do I have to stick to the hall and stairs?*

Game Master: **You can return to the previous gaming rooms if you want. They are all unlocked. The only one I wouldn't suggest is Gaming Room 7, because there might still be a few loose snakes and spiders in there. Other than that, you have free rein. But if you're hoping to find a way to escape, you'll be sorely disappointed. Those rooms are totally sealed from the outside.**

Me: *I know. Just need to stretch my legs.*

I got up and feigned interest in doing some pre-workout stretches in the hallway outside my room, knowing my every move was being monitored on the extensive array of surveillance equipment in this joint. Then I jogged down the hall, headed downstairs, and did a few laps of the first gaming room.

After enough time had passed to make it seem like I was genuinely interested in exercising, I headed into the sixth gaming room, where April had supposedly died. I pretended to cough while I licked my left index finger. Then I jogged onto the chessboard, headed to a spot where some bloody smears remained, and quickly crouched down, pretending I needed to tighten the shoelace on my right sneaker.

While I did that, I quickly swiped my hand along the floor next to my shoe, gathering up some of the blood with my wet finger. Then I rose to my feet and jogged out of the room.

I did a few more laps of the hall and entered another couple of gaming rooms for good measure. After leaving the last one, I stopped and bent slightly forward, pretending to catch my breath. While I did that, I stuck my finger in my mouth and sucked off the so-called blood. It was sickly-sweet with a vague caramel flavor.

Fucking *corn syrup*.

April wasn't shot on that chessboard. She was never shot at all. She was the Game Master.

MAVERICK

Possessive fury lit in me, filling me with combustible rage. April had to be stopped. Forever. It was one thing for her to hurt me. But not Carey. Not my sweet, brilliant, beautiful girl.

I sprinted back upstairs and knocked on Brooke, Jasmine, and Zach's doors. "Come to the drawing room," I told each of them in turn. "I've got an idea for something to pass the time."

I couldn't announce my discovery out loud. Not with all the mics listening in on every conversation. I'd briefly considered using my bathroom, but I had no way of knowing for sure that it was a safe place to talk. Knowing the level of surveillance in this place, I was willing to bet there were cameras and mics in every single nook and cranny. Even the fucking toilets.

I'd also considered writing everything down for the others to silently read, but then I realized that was out of the question too. I had no idea of the zooming capabilities of the surveillance cameras, and I couldn't risk April seeing what I'd written.

I couldn't even whisper to the others, because then April—and whoever was helping her—would see it happening, and then she might start wondering if we were onto her. I couldn't let that happen. Instead, I had to pretend I knew nothing. Keep April thinking her identity as the Game Master was still shrouded in secrecy. That way she'd never see us coming when we finally figured out how to take her down.

Five minutes later, Brooke, Zach, and Jasmine were staring at me expectantly across the drawing room table. "So, uhh... this idea," Zach finally said. "What is it?"

"I want to play a game."

"Okay, Jigsaw." Jasmine's nose wrinkled. "You *are* joking, right?"

"Nope. Think about it. We need something to take our minds off everything, and all we've done for the last few days is play games that can kill us. So I think it might help if we play a game that we know for sure is totally safe. A game of our own."

Brooke and Zach exchanged pointed glances. Jasmine kept staring at me like I was totally off my rocker. "I'm done with games at this point," she said. "Aren't we all?"

"No," I insisted. "Come on. It'll cheer us up, I swear. A game of Telephone, like we used to do when we were kids."

Jasmine rolled her eyes. "Fine. If it'll make you feel better."

Brooke and Zach nodded reluctantly, and we all moved onto the carpet and sat in a row. I leaned close to Brooke and whispered in her ear. "Don't react. Don't look surprised," I said. "I'm 99% sure that April faked her death, but we can't let her know that we know just yet. I also think she's keeping Carey alive to be the fall guy for this shit."

Brooke nodded slowly as my words sank in. Her face was expressionless, but her eyes were flashing like crazy. She stayed silent for a moment, and then she swallowed audibly and leaned over to Zach. He listened carefully before whispering to Jasmine.

At first, I was worried that Jasmine would mess things up, given the look of pure shock on her face, but then she affected an innocent expression and slowly shook her head. "Um... a giant raccoon went to a pride parade with my cousin and wore an orange jumpsuit. Is that right?"

I let out a brittle laugh. "Not even close. Let's try again."

"Okay." She lifted one shoulder in a casual shrug. "This is actually kind of fun."

I whispered to Brooke again. "We can't openly talk about it because of the mics everywhere. We can't even write it down because April could be looking on the cameras."

She passed it down the line. When it reached Jasmine, she invented some bullshit line about cows in a field. Then she cocked her head. "My turn now."

Her words eventually got back to me through Brooke. "If you're right, what are we going to do about it?" she wanted to know.

I passed another message down the line. "I don't know yet. All I know is that we need to figure out a way to explore April's room without making her suspicious. I'm pretty sure Carey was in there before she disappeared."

Brooke's hand shot up. "Can I have a turn?" she asked.

"Of course."

The four of us went on like that for the next twenty minutes, awkwardly and tediously discussing the new development through the guise of multiple Telephone games.

Finally, Jasmine sat up straight and stretched her arms. "Okay, I'm getting bored with this game now," she declared. "I have another idea for a group activity to keep us occupied."

I stared at her, hoping to God that she actually had some sort of plan. "What is it?" I asked in a clipped tone.

"You guys will probably think this is totally lame, but..." She trailed off, biting her bottom lip. "Well, as much as I couldn't stand most of the people in this place, I guess everything that happened here brought us closer together. Do you know what I mean?"

"Um... yeah, I guess so," Zach muttered.

"So I was thinking, seeing as we're down to the final four, maybe it would be nice to create some sort of memorial thing on the table," Jasmine went on. "We could grab something from everyone's bedrooms. Something that reminds us of them. Then we could put it all on the table and say a few words about each person."

My brows rose as she spoke. It was actually a decent plan to get into April's room and hunt around without her thinking we were up to anything shady. "That's a nice idea," I said, nodding slowly.

Jasmine swiped a finger under her right eye, like she was mopping up a tear. "Thanks. I honestly thought you guys would think it was stupid."

"It's not stupid. We've all lost people we care about here," Zach said softly. "I know none of us had any personal items here, but the bedrooms are stacked with books. So we could look in each room for a book that reminds us of certain people, right?"

"Yeah, I really like that idea," Brooke said, nodding fervently. "We could also look for some other things. Like with Kiara, for example. She had such beautiful hair. So for her, we could use the comb from her bathroom."

"That sounds perfect," Jasmine said, dabbing at her cheek with her sleeve. "Kiara would've loved that idea."

I rose to my feet. "Brooke, you can take Carey and Evan's rooms. I'll take April and Tate's rooms. Zach, you take Courteney and Rhys. And Jasmine, you can do Kiara. I think we can leave Hudson out of this, right?"

"For sure." Jasmine gave me a tight smile. "Let's go."

I went to Tate's room first and took my time looking around, pretending I deeply cared about finding an item that reminded me of him. I wound up selecting a copy of Fear and Loathing in Las Vegas from the bookshelf. It seemed like something a guy like him might've enjoyed.

With the book in hand, I headed to April's room and hunted around, looking for some sort of clue while pretending to ponder what she might've liked. At one point, I purposely dropped Tate's book on the floor so I could peer under her bed in search of any concealed trapdoors, but there was nothing there.

Mind whirling, I went to the shelf and started picking through the books, trying to figure out my next move. There didn't appear to be anything unusual in this room, but Carey certainly seemed to think there was something worth looking for last night. I just had to figure out what it was and find it.

Jasmine stepped into the room a moment later. "Hey. I got the comb from Kiara's bathroom," she said, voice thick with emotion. "Did you find anything for April yet?"

I shook my head. "None of these books really make me think of her."

Jasmine sniffed and stepped closer. Then she burst into tears and threw her arms around me. "I miss Kiara so much," she said, nestling into the crook between my neck and shoulder.

"I know," I muttered.

She tilted her face ever-so-slightly until her lips were near my left ear. "Keep looking," she whispered. "There *has* to be something in here. I can literally feel it in my bones. You're right about everything."

I broke away from the hug a moment later. "I'll keep hunting around," I said, scratching the side of my head. "Maybe there'll be something in the bathroom that really screams 'April'."

"It's okay. You have a lot of time to think about it. No more games today, remember?" Jasmine said. "Anyway, I'll go and start setting up the memorial table."

She gave me a watery smile and stepped outside. I swept my gaze around the room once more, wondering if this was all a giant waste of time.

Even if it *was*, I still had to find something in here for the memorial table, just so April wouldn't get suspicious about our true motive for going through her room.

I frowned and twisted my lips, wondering what sort of stuff she might like. I honestly didn't know her very well, even though we'd attended school together for twelve years. We ran in different crowds, so we never really spoke or interacted much beyond the occasional shared classes.

I knew she liked English class, because her dad taught the subject, and I knew she was good at math. I also remembered that she liked our art classes all the way back in elementary school. Maybe there was a book about writing on the shelf, or something about famous painters and sculptors.

Wait...

The word 'art' had shaken something loose inside my head. My eyes snapped to the large oil painting on the opposite wall, and a frisson of curiosity surged through me. When Carey and I explored everywhere the other night, we'd spent a lot of time checking behind paintings for any hidden doors or alcoves where the Game Master could be hiding something.

I couldn't check now without making April realize I was onto her, if she happened to be watching me on the surveillance system, but something told me that giant painting was probably covering a lot more than old wallpaper. If it was some sort of entryway to the secret passage system I'd always suspected of existing behind these walls, then that would explain what Carey was searching for when she came in here. It would also explain how April managed to sneak around at night without any of us seeing or hearing her out in the hall.

The more I thought about it, the more certain I became that some sort of door lay behind the painting. I could practically feel the truth of it pumping through my veins.

I went back to the bookshelf and inspected it, heart pounding. Then I grabbed a random novel and strode back to the drawing room. "Here," I said, tossing down the books on the table. "Fear and Loathing in Las Vegas for Tate, and Catcher in the Rye for April."

"Good choice." Brooke smiled. "April won an award for an essay about that book in ninth grade."

"Cool. Now that we're all here, should we huddle up and say a few words about everyone?" I asked.

Zach, Brooke, and Jasmine nodded enthusiastically and joined me in a tight group hug. "Stay awake tonight," I whispered to them. "Leave your bedrooms at three o'clock and meet me in April's room. I think there's a door behind the painting there."

Now there were only two things left for me to do. Wait for the middle of the night... and hope to God I was right.

CAREY

"Dinnertime!" April called out in a sing-song voice, appearing next to me with a bowl of food.

I fixed her with a stony stare, trying to ignore the throbbing pain in the side of my head. "How am I supposed to eat?" I asked. "I'm tied to a fucking chair."

Her eyes skated over the bindings around my legs and arms. "I'll have to feed you. But that's okay," she said breezily. "I made this stew, by the way. Took a French cooking class last summer break."

"So you've been the one catering for us all along?" I said, skeptically eyeing the steaming bowl.

"No, we all took turns preparing the meals," she said, gesturing toward her mother and father. They were sitting by the computer on the other side of the control room, deep in conversation. "It was really rough sometimes, you know. I had to wake up at four A.M. most days to help get breakfast ready."

"Wow, yeah, that sounds really rough," I said, voice dripping with sarcasm. "Too bad I can't relate. Things have been a total cakewalk for me in this place."

April sniffed. "I know you're being sarcastic, but things really *have* been easier for you here. Like I said earlier, you were never in any real danger."

"But I didn't know that when I was going through it, did I?" I said, still glowering at her. "And what about the others? They've always been in danger. You're planning to kill all of them!"

"They deserve it," she said, voice silky-smooth. "You know that."

I sighed and lowered my eyes to my lap. In the several hours since I woke up tied to this chair, I'd tried to reason with April and her parents multiple times, but there was really no point. They were all obsessed with the idea that Abby's death wasn't truly accidental, but a form of murder instead. They genuinely believed that anyone who had ever negatively impacted her life had helped to kill her and thus deserved a death sentence in return.

"Chin up and open wide." April held out a spoon in front of me, filled with deliciously scented chicken stew. "Let me know how it tastes."

I accepted the spoonful and chewed slowly. "It's good," I muttered after swallowing.

"Awesome," she said, beaming. "I've been experimenting with the herbs a lot, and I think I finally got the right ratio of thyme to rosemary."

I frowned as something occurred to me. "How did you get all the meals into the drawing room without any of us seeing?" I asked. "We thought there was a secret door in there somewhere, like the one I found in your room, but there was nothing."

"Are you sure about that?" April asked, lifting a brow. "I watched you through the cameras, and I saw you guys checking everywhere on the walls and floor. But you forgot one angle."

She jabbed a finger upward, and understanding finally dawned on me. "The entryway was in the ceiling?"

"Yup. This control room isn't the only space we have on the third level," she said. "We installed a kitchen in the room next door, and we put a trapdoor in the floor that looks exactly like one of the big wooden ceiling panels in the drawing room below. So we'd send one person down with a rope ladder, and then we'd slowly lower the food down to them on trays to set out on the table. Easy."

It didn't sound particularly easy at all, but I wasn't about to start an argument with her over such an inane subject.

"So what's happening with the plan to set me up as the fall girl?" I asked, glancing over at her parents again. "Are the three of you finally starting to realize it won't work?"

"It will. You keep forgetting about all the connections we have. We've already started with the paper trail to make it seem like Maverick was funding you." April lifted the spoon again. "Open up."

I chewed fast and swallowed. "Tell me one more thing. Was I right about the games being rigged?"

"Sort of. Some of them weren't, but others were. Like the one that got Courteney, for example. She didn't push that button on her collar. We triggered it remotely."

I frowned. "Why would you set things up that way?" I asked. "Why not make all the games real?"

"Because we didn't have endless game ideas," she replied, dipping the spoon back in the bowl. "And we needed to make sure that everyone was dead by the end of the twelfth game. Everyone except you, that is."

"So the next few games will all be rigged, then?" I asked, stomach churning at the thought of anything happening to Maverick and the others. "Seeing as there's still so many people left."

"Yes. By the way, tomorrow's game is going to be *so* fun." April slid another spoonful of stew into my mouth. "Remember the snake pit from the Seven Minutes in Hell game?"

"Mm-hm," I mumbled through the mouthful.

"We've repurposed the snakes for our own version of Snakes

and Ladders. It's going to be so fun to watch." She cocked her head. "It's Zach's turn to die tomorrow. We figured we've made him suffer enough by making him watch his little girlfriend die right in front of him, so it's his time to go."

"What about Maverick?" I asked in a hollow voice. "When is it his turn to die?"

She sighed. "Well, we actually hoped it would happen earlier today. We had a game of Spin the Bottle crossed with Russian roulette, and we assumed everyone would turn on Mav after some secret prompting we gave to Hudson. But they ended up turning on Hudson instead. In hindsight, that's not too surprising, because Hudson was a colossal piece of shit, but it *is* annoying. It was a quick and easy death, and we had something really terrible planned for him in the twelfth game. Now it'll have to happen to Maverick instead."

"Please don't do it," I said, tears springing to my eyes. I knew there was no point begging, but I had to do it anyway. I couldn't just stay silent while they plotted to murder my boyfriend. "*Please.* It's not too late to change the plan. You can let us all go free, and in return, I promise I'll never say a single word to the cops. I swear, April. I won't."

April rolled her eyes. "Oh, sure. That old chestnut," she said. She jabbed the spoon toward me again. "Shut up and eat."

With that, the conversation was over. April fed me the rest of my dinner in silence, face remaining impassive as she watched the tears roll down my cheeks.

Her mother Ruth approached us a few minutes later to ask if I needed to use the bathroom. When I nodded, the two of them untied me and led me into the bathroom next door. "Don't bother screaming," April said as she watched me step into the toilet cubicle. "Every single room up here is soundproofed. Not just the control room."

I didn't bother responding. What was the point?

After I'd relieved myself, April and Ruth put me back in the chair in the control room and fastened the ropes around my legs and arms. "You should try to get some sleep, honey," Ruth said, offering me a ghost of a smile. "You look exhausted."

"I wonder why," I muttered.

"I need to sleep too," April said. She glanced over at her father. "Dad, it's our turn to rest. Mom will keep watch over Carey and the cameras."

Her father stood and headed over to one of the beds, smothering a yawn with one hand. I watched him through narrowed eyes, mind whirling. It was so weird and unsettling to see him like this, taking part in a series of revenge killings, when I was so used to seeing him at the front of our English class discussing literary conventions and analytical responses. Even though I recognized his tall frame and bespectacled face, it felt like I was looking at a different person entirely.

I bowed my head and closed my eyes, but I couldn't sleep. The chair was too uncomfortable, my mind was racing like mad, and my stomach wouldn't stop churning with despair at the thought of Maverick's impending demise. My heart broke for Zach and Brooke, too. Hell, even the idea of Jasmine's upcoming death made me feel like shit. She was a bitch, but she didn't deserve to die for it.

By three o'clock in the morning, I was still awake. Mr. Garrick had been snoring loudly for hours, and April was sleeping peacefully on the couch, where she'd decided to curl up for the evening. Her mother was sitting at the desk, reading a book and occasionally glancing up at the live surveillance feeds on the computer monitors to make sure no one was breaking the curfew.

I sighed and looked back down at the floor, tears welling in my eyes as I pictured Maverick lying dead in front of me, skin pale and eyes unseeing. I winced and tried to shut out the terrible mental images, but they kept on pouring in. Maverick's limbs twisted and broken. Maverick's blood spattered over every surface. Maverick's head removed from his body.

A slight movement on my left snapped me out of my morose reverie, and my eyes shot to the screens on the desk. I couldn't see much from where I was sitting, but I could make out a few shapes here and there, and I was certain something had just moved on one of them.

Ruth didn't seem to have noticed, though. Her eyes were glued to her book. It seemed she was quite confident that nothing was going to happen at this time of night, which in turn made her slack at her duties.

I craned my neck and squinted at the screens as another flash of movement caught my attention. I still couldn't make out what it was, but I figured it had to be one or more of the four remaining players out in the hall. Nothing else could possibly show up on the monitors.

Ruth still wasn't paying attention to any of the screens, and I silently prayed for her eyes to remain fixed on the pages of her book. She must have felt my gaze on her, though, because she twisted in her seat to frown at me. "You're still awake?"

"I can't sleep," I said, heart thundering in my chest as I caught yet another flash of movement on one of the monitors. Something was happening on the floor below us, and I instinctively knew I had to keep Ruth distracted for as long as possible while it went on. "I really need to use the bathroom again. Any chance you could take me?"

She pursed her lips and stared at me for several seconds, presumably assessing my threat level. "Fine. Give me a minute," she finally said, turning to set her book down on the desk. She suddenly sat up straight, peering directly at the security feed. "Oh, shit."

Dammit. She'd spotted the other players on the screen.

"David!" she shrieked, jumping to her feet. "April! Wake up. Now!"

April sat up, rubbing her eyes. "What's wrong?"

"They're coming!" Ruth said, shaking a finger at the monitors. "They found the door in your room!"

"What the fuck?" April's eyes bulged, and she jumped up. "Dad, wake up!"

Her father sat up on one elbow, finally awoken from his deep slumber by all the panicked shouting. "What's happening?"

"They're coming up here! Right now!" Ruth shrieked. "Get the gun!"

He rolled over to fumble on a low table next to his bed. "Try to block them!" he called out as he picked up the pistol and flicked off the safety with a loud click.

April hurried over to the hole in the floor, but she was too late. Maverick and Brooke had already hauled themselves up and out, fury and ferocity burning in their eyes as they faced her.

"Stay back!" she shouted, scrambling backward. "We have a gun!"

Brooke screamed and tackled April, knocking her flat on her back with a loud thump. At the same time, Maverick lunged at Mr. Garrick, who was now pointing his pistol directly at the hole. The two of them collided with a forceful impact, crashing into a nearby table and sending papers flying.

"Careful, Maverick!" I shouted, heart in my throat as I watched his hand close around Mr. Garrick's wrist. "The safety's not on!"

As the fight went on, Zach hauled himself out of the hole and made a beeline for Ruth. He wrestled her to the ground, pinning her with his bodyweight and resisting her attempts at scratching and biting until he managed to drag her arms up over her head.

Jasmine emerged from the hole last. Her wide-eyed gaze briefly scanned the chaotic scenes unfolding in the room before landing on me. She hurried over. "I never thought I'd be so glad to see you!" she shouted over the commotion. Her eyes dropped to the ropes around my legs. "Is there a knife anywhere?"

"Try the desk!"

She ran over to the desk and quickly rummaged through the drawers. "Here!" she said triumphantly, rushing back over to me with a pair of scissors. "Even better!"

While she snipped at the ropes, rapidly freeing my limbs one by one, I watched Maverick and Mr. Garrick, who were still twisting and grappling in their desperate battle for control of the gun. Every time it wavered, barrel pointing in a different direction, I felt as if my heart was going to leap right out of my chest.

Maverick's jaw clenched with determination as he tried once more to wrench the gun from Mr. Garrick's grip. The barrel swiveled wildly, and then the two men twisted around so I could no longer see who had the upper hand.

A split-second later, a deafening gunshot shattered the air.

MAVERICK

The impact of the bullet in my upper arm barely caused any pain. I felt it happen, but it was a distant sensation, almost as if I were imagining it happening to someone else.

My adrenaline surged, and I lunged at Mr. Garrick and grabbed the end of the pistol, turning it upward so he couldn't shoot me again. He jerked backward, gaining a momentary advantage as I lost my grip, but I took the opportunity to lunge forward again, slamming my elbow into his ribs.

He buckled, and the gun slipped out of his hand. It clattered on the floorboards, spinning away from us. Carey dove for it.

"It's over!" I shouted, pushing Mr. Garrick against the same table we collided with earlier. "She'll shoot you if you don't stop!"

I was pretty certain that Carey had no idea how to use a gun, but Mr. Garrick didn't know that. He lifted his hands in a shaky surrender, eyes going blank.

"Get on your knees," Carey said, aiming the pistol right at him. She jerked her head toward Jasmine. "Bring me that rope."

Jasmine picked up two lengths of rope from the floor and hurried over to help me tie up Mr. Garrick. When he was secured, she darted around the room, searching for more ropes so we could properly restrain April and her mother.

While we waited, Carey kept a firm grip on the pistol, waving it back and forth between the two women to deter them from any attempts to hurt Zach and Brooke, who were keeping them pinned down.

A moment later, Carey's eyes briefly flitted over to me. "I can't believe you found me," she murmured.

"Of course I did," I replied, rubbing my left arm. "I always told you I'd get you out of here."

Her gaze dropped to my bloody sleeve, and her brows shot up. "Oh, shit, he got you! I thought he miss—"

"It's fine." I cut her off, smiling faintly. "Just a graze."

"No, we need to get help. It's bleeding a lot." She craned her neck and called out to Jasmine. "Look for a phone! Maverick's been shot in the arm!"

Jasmine abandoned the search for the rope and hurried over to the desk. "I think this is a satellite phone," she called out, holding up a large black phone that resembled a Walkie Talkie toy. "It should work even with all the cell signals blocked, right?"

"Yes. Hurry!"

She called 911 and blurted out our location and situation. When she was done, she headed over to us and gestured to me and Zach. "Take off your sweatshirts. I don't think there's any more rope in this room, and we need to tie up these two bitches."

April glared at her. "You really think we're going anywhere?" she asked in a hollow voice.

Jasmine's lips curled in a sneer. "Probably not. But after all the shit I've seen you pull this week, I'm not willing to risk it," she said. With that, she crouched down and slapped April across the face so loudly that the cracking sound echoed through the room. "That's for Kiara. And the only reason I'm not taking that gun from Carey and shooting you in the head instead is because I want to see you rot in jail for the rest of your life, you fucking bitch."

I pulled off my sweatshirt, grimacing as I slowly peeled the fabric over the injured part of my arm. I tossed it to Brooke and Jasmine, who used the long sleeves to restrain April's wrists behind her back. At the same time, Zach used his own sweatshirt to tie a stony-faced Ruth to the nearest table leg.

While they worked on that, Carey put the gun down and clamped her right hand around the wound on my arm to stem the flow of blood. "Oh my god," she muttered, eyes shimmering with tears. "This looks bad."

"It's fine. Just my arm. Besides, it was worth taking a bullet to stop these assholes from hurting you."

Tears were spilling down her cheeks now. "I really thought I was going to lose you," she said, voice barely above a whisper. "They were going to kill you."

"You aren't going to lose me. I'm right here. Worst thing that'll happen is a gnarly scar."

She inhaled deeply. "I just...well..." She trailed off and started again. "I know this'll sound crazy because we only just got together a few days ago, but with everything that's happened in here, it feels like it's been months. And I... well, I feel like I already..."

She seemed so nervous, tripping over her words and unable to say what she wanted. That anxiety wasn't necessary, though. I felt the exact same way as her. Only a few days had passed, but in that short period, we'd experienced more defining moments than some couples did in a year.

"I love you, Carey," I said gruffly, swiping away the tears from her cheeks.

Her eyes widened. "You do?"

"Yeah." I leaned in and kissed the tip of her nose. "Of course I do."

"I... I love you too," she murmured. "That's what I was trying to say."

"I know." I smiled, cradling her chin in one hand. "I know another way you can say it too."

With that, I shifted even closer to her, wrapped my arm around her waist, and crushed my lips to hers.

MAVERICK

Seven months later...

I clamped a hand over Carey's mouth. "We have to be quiet," I muttered.

She nodded, but a tiny moan escaped her lips anyway, mostly muffled by my fingers. I gripped her left hip with my other hand, then slid it down over her ass and between her thighs to feel the wetness there.

My cock was harder than granite, but footsteps were echoing in the hall outside, getting louder and louder by the second.

We shouldn't be here right now. Shouldn't be doing this.

"Fuck me," Carey urgently whispered through my hand, arching her back. Her hands were firmly planted on the desk in front of her. "Please."

Jesus. I couldn't resist for another second. I pressed my hand down tighter on her mouth so she couldn't make another sound. Then I adjusted my hold on her and slid inside her, grunting as her muscles clenched around me.

The footsteps in the hall grew louder still. I leaned forward and bit Carey's shoulder through her graduation gown, using the thick fabric to mask my harsh grunts as I began to move, thrusting in and out of her with powerful strokes.

I tensed and froze when a shadow appeared at the closed door. "Just a second, Sadie," Professor Giamatti called out. "I think I left my phone in here earlier."

"Shit," I said hoarsely, cock still buried to the hilt inside Carey.

We were so fucking busted.

Carey looked at me over her shoulder, expression still hungry for me. My hand dropped from her mouth and slid down to rub her clit, nice and hard. Just the way she liked it. If we were going to get caught fucking in a classroom, I could at least make her come first.

A key turned in the door, and it slowly started to open. Carey bit her bottom lip, but then her head lolled and her mouth dropped open in a low whimper.

"Oh, never mind!" Professor Giamatti said chirpily. "It's right here in my left pocket! I usually use the right, you see."

The door closed again, and the footsteps faded away. Fucking *finally*. I breathed a heavy sigh of relief and started moving again, fiercely pounding inside Carey as my finger worked her clit. Her orgasm hit a moment later, pussy squeezing my dick as she gasped and moaned. The sensation was enough to send me over the edge too, and I stopped inside her, groaning as I came.

We stayed like that for a minute, her ass pushed back against me with her hands splayed on the desk for support. I cupped her jaw and turned her head to face me again, leaning down to kiss her.

"That was fun," I said when I finally pulled away. "I've been wanting to defile this desk ever since Giamatti gave me a shitty mark back in eleventh grade."

Carey snorted with amusement, one hand reaching for the

tissue box on the side of the professor's desk. She passed one to me before taking care of herself, hitching up her gown and the skirt beneath it with her free hand.

"God," she murmured, still panting to catch her breath as she cleaned herself. "I can't believe we almost got caught."

"Well, fucking in a classroom is a dangerous game." I grinned and lobbed my tissue in the wastebasket. "Luckily we're used to much more dangerous games, huh?"

"No shit," she said, eyes flashing as she hiked her underwear back up. She straightened her shoulders and smoothed her gown. "Anyway... shall we?"

"Yup." I hitched one arm under hers and reached over to adjust her lopsided cap. "Let's go and graduate, baby."

We left the room and headed down the hall, arm in arm. When we stepped outside, we saw Jasmine, Zach, and Brooke standing by a fountain, faces harried.

"Oh my god!" Jasmine said when she spotted us. "We've been looking for you guys everywhere!"

"You know the ceremony starts in ten minutes, right?" Brooke added, wide-eyed gaze flicking between us.

"Yeah. It's fine." I grinned. "Plenty of time."

"Where *were* you?" Zach asked.

"Um..." Carey lowered her eyes and rubbed her chin. "Just walking through the halls. Reminiscing."

Zach's brows lifted. "Hm. Okay."

"I saw two people sitting in the chairs with your surname on them. Is it your parents?" Brooke asked.

"It must be," Carey replied. "They told me they'd come, but I wasn't sure they actually would."

"That's good. That they're finally trying with you, I mean."

"Yeah. All it took was me almost dying in a murder mansion last year," Carey replied, rolling her eyes. "But you're right. It's good."

I dropped my arm so I could squeeze her hand. Her parents

weren't the greatest people in the world, but ever since we escaped Icarus Hall last October, they'd started making a serious effort to improve their relationship. Her father had even managed to last seven straight months without getting arrested for whatever dumb shit he usually got up to back in Oakfield. As for her mother, who usually got through ten bottles of wine per week, the devastating realization that she'd almost lost her only child had shocked her into near-sobriety. She'd barely touched a drop of alcohol since all the shit went down, and she'd started calling Carey once a week to talk and catch up.

Baby steps, but it was better than nothing. Carey deserved it. Deserved a real family who loved and cared about her. And hey, even if her parents never managed to fix their shit and make up for all the years of neglect, she'd always have a family with me, because she wasn't just my girlfriend.

She was my whole world.

"So, um..." Jasmine looked down, briefly gnawing at her bottom lip. "Does this mean our little survivor's club is over and done with? Seeing as we're all heading off to different parts of the world?"

Zach patted her on the shoulder. "We can still do Zoom meetings, right?"

Jasmine's shoulders sagged with relief, and a rare smile lit her face. "Sure. That'd be great."

She'd changed a hell of a lot since the Garrick family imprisoned us and forced us into those fucked up games. She was no longer the school Queen Bee, ruling the girls of Babylon with an iron fist and venomous tongue. Instead, she'd mellowed out and thrown herself into her studies, raising her GPA to a level no one ever thought she could achieve. She'd also organized weekly meetings for the Final Five—as the media had annoyingly dubbed us after our rescue—so that she, Zach, Brooke, Carey, and I could talk things over and help each other out with the mental trauma we were left with after our time at Icarus Hall.

I knew she and Carey would never be best friends, given Jasmine's toxic treatment of her in the past, but everything our little group went through together had forged an unbreakable bond between us, so they treated each other with respect and even smiled and waved whenever they spotted each other on campus. Sometimes they even shared exam notes or texted each other funny stories they read online.

Zach glanced at his watch. "We should really get going now. We're down to eight minutes," he said.

He was doing okay, too. He'd lost a ton of weight from depression in the weeks after our rescue, but the weekly survivor's club meetings had really started to help him after a while. By spring break, the weight had come back, along with the color in his cheeks.

After graduation today, he was hopping on a plane to Singapore. An international university had offered him a place there, and he'd snapped it right up, telling the rest of us that he needed to be as far away from California as he could possibly get for the next few years. Maybe even forever. We all understood, and we were happy for him.

Brooke nodded, lips turning upward in a sad half-smile. "Yeah, I guess we should head off," she said, looking around the courtyard. "Never thought I'd miss this place, but I think I actually will."

Brooke's life had been hit the hardest in the aftermath of the now-infamous Garrick Games, because everything that had been revealed in our time at Icarus Hall had instantly become public knowledge when the media got wind of the case. From there, the Babylon staff found out about her past exam cheating, along with the drug-cooking operation she'd shared with Tate.

In any other case, she would've been charged by the cops and instantly expelled from school. However, the police decided not to file any charges over the drugs, figuring the suffering she'd endured at Icarus Hall was punishment enough. The school was much the same, allowing her to finish off the year with the stipulation that she could never be alone in any of the chemistry labs. On top of that, none of the teachers were allowed to write her recommendation letters for college, and the mark she received for the big exam she cheated on was changed to a zero, lowering her once-sky-high GPA.

It didn't matter too much in the end, though. Now that we were all household names because of the Garrick Games, colleges all over the country had been champing at the bit to convince us to pick them, leaving Brooke with multiple offers despite the lack of school support. She was going to be just fine.

Carey smiled at her. "I know exactly what you mean," she said. "I hated this place when I first started here. But now I really think I'm going to miss it. Weird, huh?"

The others nodded and murmured their agreement. I squeezed her hand again and leaned down to plant a kiss on her forehead. "Ready?"

She nodded, and the five of us headed over to the Babylon auditorium and made our way to our seats on the stage. Jasmine was the first of us to graduate, and we all cheered our lungs out as she walked across the stage to accept her diploma.

Carey was the last to go. As soon as they called her name, I let out a loud wolf-whistle, followed by a whooping cheer. Pride swelled in my chest as I watched her take her diploma. "That's my girl!" I shouted before whistling again.

She laughed as she stepped off the stage, shaking a finger in my direction. Breaking all the rules, I jumped up and sprinted over to her, engulfing her in a bear hug before lowering my face to hers for a fierce kiss.

"I love you," she murmured as she pulled away, eyes shimmering with tears.

"I love you too," I replied, throat clogging with emotion as I stared down at her.

I never knew I could be so fulfilled. So happy. Especially after everything that went down in those games last year. But that was what love did. It made everything better, even if the rest of the world was a total shit-show.

It was the one game Carey and I would never lose.

EPILOGUE

Carey

One year later...

April was right about one thing.

After all the shit she put me and the others through two years ago, I was now super-famous—even though that was the last thing I ever wanted—and a TV streaming network had just contacted me to tell me they were doing a special docuseries on everything that happened. 'Incident at Icarus Hall' was the working title, and they wanted me to fly to LA for several interviews if I was interested in taking part.

A publishing house had also contacted me last year to gauge my interest in writing a book about my experience. I'd accepted their offer, figuring I could really use the money. I'd worked with a professional ghostwriter and editor between college classes over the last eight months, and now Wicked Games was set to publish in a few more months.

As for April... she was exactly where she belonged now. Prison. She contacted me every so often, trying to get me to visit her, but I ignored the letters. I had no idea how she got my new address in Boston, but I wasn't surprised that she did. She had a brilliant mind. It was just a shame it had turned out so awfully dark and twisted.

Her parents had been sentenced to life without parole too, and the judge presiding over the case had made one thing abundantly clear during the trial: their stacks of money and influential connections weren't going to help them a single bit. The whole world was sick of watching rich people get away with heinous crimes, and the judge intended to make an example of them to dissuade other too-rich assholes from assuming they could get away with anything, just so long as they had enough power and money.

A sharp rapping sound snapped my attention to my door, and I smiled and hurried across the room. "Hey," I said as I threw the door open. "How was your last class?"

Maverick stepped inside and slid his arms around my waist. "It was okay. How's my favorite writer?"

I laughed softly. "I'm hardly a writer."

"You're about to publish a book."

"I know, but I had a ton of help," I said, lightly shrugging. "I feel like I can't really call myself a writer."

Maverick smiled. "I think you definitely can. But let's start again. How's my favorite computer science major?"

"Good." I grinned back at him. "How's my favorite finance major?"

"Also good," he said, leaning down to briefly peck my cheek. "My econ professor offered me a spot in his internship program next semester."

My eyes widened. "That's awesome! We totally need to celebrate!" I said, heart swelling with pride. "We could go and have dinner at that new Greek place on Trowbridge. I've heard it's really good."

"Yeah, let's do it. But I have a surprise for you first." Maverick's lips twisted into a wicked smirk, and he reached into his pocket.

"Uhh... what is that?" I asked, watching him pull out a black strip of fabric.

"A blindfold."

"Is this a sex thing?"

He laughed. "It could be. But no. It's for you to wear in the car so the surprise isn't spoiled."

"Well, don't keep me in suspense," I said, standing up on my tiptoes to kiss his nose. "Let's go."

Once we were in Maverick's car, he tied the blindfold at the back of my head and adjusted it until he was sure I couldn't sneak a single peek at my surroundings. We drove for around fifteen minutes—very slowly for most of it, because of the damn traffic—and then Maverick carefully led me over a street and up several flights of stairs. I heard a key turning in a lock, followed by the sound of a door swinging open. Then I was slowly led forward again.

"Here it is." Maverick untied the knot behind my head and pulled off the blindfold. "What do you think?"

I looked around with wide eyes, soaking it all in. We were standing in an open plan apartment with gleaming hardwood floors, marble countertops, stainless-steel appliances, and abstract art hanging on the walls. The whole place was bathed in light thanks to the massive floor-to-ceiling windows on one side, and I could see the Boston skyline with the Charles River catching the sunlight in the distance.

"Oh my god." I turned to Maverick, brows rising high on my forehead. "Did you buy this place?"

"No." He smiled. "I rented it, because I wasn't sure if you'd like it or not. But we don't need to live on campus anymore, now that our first year is done, so I figured it was about time we moved in together. What do you think?"

"I think it's amazing," I said breathlessly, taking another quick spin to assess the furnishings. "But there's no way I can afford half the rent on a place like this. My book advance is still pending, because the stupid bank keeps—"

Maverick cut me off by pressing his lips to mine in a soft kiss. "I already paid the rent for a whole year," he said when he pulled away. "My gift to you."

"But..." I stared up at him, eyes saucer wide. "That's too much for a gift. Way too much. And I don't want to mooch off you."

"I don't think you're a mooch at all," he said, sliding an arm around my waist. His free hand went to my face, thumb lightly stroking my jaw. "We already know we want to share each other's lives, and that means we're going to be sharing our finances at some point, along with everything else. So let's do it. Right now. Let's finally move in together."

I craned my neck to check out the view again. "It's a really beautiful place," I said. "I love it."

"So that's a yes?"

"Not yet." A mischievous smile curled up my lips. "I have a question first."

Maverick's eyes flickered with curiosity. "What is it?"

"Why did you say *finally*?" I asked. "We've already lived together, remember? Back at Babylon, when we had to share a dorm."

He laughed, head slowly shaking. "Oh, man. That was crazy. I can't believe the school actually allowed that shit."

"Me neither," I said, giggling lightly. "We were at each other's throats all the time."

"I know. I was so stupid back then. Such an asshole." He rubbed his jaw, still grinning. "Who would've ever thought we'd end up like this, huh? If they saw us back in the day."

"Probably no one," I said. "But anyway... *yes*. I really want to live with you again."

Maverick leaned down and kissed me, long and deep, arms tightly wrapped around me. "We can make some better memories this time," he murmured when he finally pulled away. "I promise."

"I promise too," I whispered back, smiling so hard my cheeks ached. "I love you."

"I love you too."

With that, he leaned in for another electrifying kiss, sending tingles racing up and down my spine. I closed my eyes and melted into his embrace, sighing with happiness.

The two of us had fallen in love so fast after we were flung together in those twisted games at Icarus Hall, and that love had lasted and grown with every moment, every challenge, every milestone.

From here, it would only grow more and more. He was mine and I was his, and we were going to spend the rest of our lives making unforgettable memories together.

THE END

∼

Turn the page for a free sample of Mine!

PROLOGUE
Sienna

April 12th, 2019

"Please!"

I jolted awake, eyes flying open. A distant sound had reached my ears. A faint shattering of glass, followed by a screamed word.

I strained to listen, senses sharpened by the eerie atmosphere in the lake house bedroom. It was engulfed in darkness, with the only source of illumination being the occasional flash of lightning. A storm had been raging all night, crashing thunder and howling wind matching the turmoil swirling inside my mind.

What was the word that startled me awake? Who screamed it? It was already slipping away, leaving only a vague recollection of its piercing tone.

I slowly sat up, grimacing as I leaned on one elbow. My head was throbbing from a mix of alcohol and exhaustion, but I tried my best to mentally slap myself out of the haze and make sense of the situation. Was it just a bad dream? Were the strange noises all in my head?

No.

There was a scream. I was sure of it. But it wasn't just that. Something felt off. Something I couldn't quite put my finger on in my foggy, still-tipsy state.

It finally hit me when I reached out to touch Paxton for comfort and wound up patting cold, unoccupied sheets instead. I'd spent most of the night flirting with the gorgeous star of the hockey team and fallen asleep tangled up in his embrace. Now he was nowhere to be seen.

Doubt and panic instantly swept through my mind. Did he leave because I didn't have sex with him tonight? Did he sneak out once I fell asleep and hook up with one of the other girls instead? I didn't think he was one of *those* guys, but it wouldn't be the first time one of the uber-popular hockey guys had screwed over a girl from our school. My best friend Tate warned me about that earlier today.

"Paxton?" I called out in a tentative tone, tilting my head toward the en-suite bathroom door. Maybe I was just inventing drama in my mind, and he was in there peeing or splashing water on his face. "Are you in the bathroom?"

No reply.

A low, muffled moan filtered through the opposite wall from the bedroom next door. My stomach twisted painfully as I registered the sound. Callie Ruiz had claimed the room in question earlier, and I was certain she'd gone to bed alone. Perhaps my paranoid theory about Paxton's bed-hopping wasn't so off-base after all.

With a sigh, I lay back down and closed my eyes, trying to ignore the ache in my heart. Despite my drowsy state, sleep eluded me.

Another scream pierced the air, jolting me upright again. The sound was instantly swallowed by a deafening crack of thunder, but I knew I heard it this time. It wasn't just my imagination playing tricks on me. It wasn't the result of a pleasurable midnight encounter, either. Something terrible was happening.

I sucked in a deep breath, dread and fear mingling in the pit of my stomach as I tried to piece together the possibilities. An intruder, perhaps. Someone who wanted to rob the place or assault one of the girls. Or maybe one of the boys drank too much and horribly injured himself while attempting a stupid dare to impress the others.

The sudden clunk of footsteps on the lake house stairs sent my pulse into overdrive. I clapped my hand over my mouth to stop myself from shrieking and hurriedly buried myself under the blankets as the door creaked open.

"Sienna."

I peeked out as a low voice muttered my name. A figure was standing by the bed. My eyes struggled to adjust in the gloominess, but I could just make out Paxton's silhouette. Relief washed over me. He was tall. Strong. Powerful. He could protect me.

"What's going on?" I asked. "I heard weird noises. Did someone break in?"

Lightning flashed, briefly illuminating the room. Paxton was drenched in blood, and a large knife was clenched in his white-knuckled right hand. The sight froze me in terror, throat constricting so much that I couldn't even conjure up a tiny squeak.

Paxton looked down at me, pressing a finger to his lips in a silent command. I stared at him with my mouth hanging open, shock and primal fear still stifling my voice.

The room flickered to life once more, brightened by another flash of lightning, and Paxton's blood-soaked form became clearer, cementing the reality of the nightmare before me.

A scream tore from my lungs as adrenaline poured through my veins, sending me scrambling across the bed. At the same time, Paxton leaned down and hissed something at me.

"*Run.*"

SIENNA

September 5th, 2022

Today was day 1236.

1236 days since what I referred to as The Incident occurred, and 1237 days since my last proper night of sleep. Nearly three and a half straight years of looking over my shoulder whenever I left the house, enduring stomach-twisting anxiety, and jerking awake drenched in sweat from the nightmares when I finally managed to get a few hours of rest.

It was no way to live, but somehow it was my life anyway.

"Hey." Tate looked at me, brows furrowed. "You okay?"

I bit my lip, hoping the maelstrom of emotions churning inside me wasn't showing on my face too much. I definitely wasn't okay, and I was only slightly closer to getting my shit together today than I was a year ago. But I damn well intended to try anyway. I was sick of languishing. Sick of feeling sorry for myself. Sick of making my friends and family feel sorry for me too.

Tate would know if I lied to him, though. So would Michaela, the third member of our trio; a friendship that had lasted since we were all seven years old.

"Honestly, I'm a little nervous," I admitted, glancing at the belltower to our left. It was the centerpiece of Worthington University, made of gray stone with a spire proudly stretching toward the heavens as its bells softly chimed in the wind. Carved gargoyles perched on the edges, their weathered stone faces seemingly judging everyone who passed.

"About what?" Tate asked, cocking his head.

"Just being here, I guess," I said, gesturing around us. I didn't want to tell the whole truth. Not even to my best friends. I was tired of looking and sounding unhinged to everyone around me.

Michaela hooked her arm in mine. "Don't worry. The campus seems massive at first, but once you get used to it, it's really easy to find your way around."

"Is that what you meant?" Tate asked. "You're worried about getting lost?"

"No, it's not just that." I twisted my lips, looking back at the belltower again. A cluster of students had gathered at the base, and they were loudly discussing their schedules for the upcoming semester. "I feel kind of weird starting so much later than everyone else."

He laughed. "Trust me, that's not an issue at all. There are lots of older students. A guy in one of my classes last semester was in his fifties."

"Exactly," Michaela chimed in. "Besides, you're *nineteen*! Practically an embryo. So you don't even count as an older student. You basically just took a gap year. Tons of people do that."

"I guess that's true." I forced a smile and shook my head. "Don't worry, I'm just being stupid. I'll be fine."

A girl walking in the opposite direction slowly passed us, eyes lingering on me. I swallowed hard and looked down. Maybe she was simply admiring my camel suede jacket... or maybe she recognized me.

Was I even recognizable on the streets these days? I'd changed a lot—dyed my hair, started wearing makeup, ditched my reading glasses for contacts. Still, if anyone looked closely, they could probably tell it was me. It mostly depended on how much they followed the Forrester case back in the day.

As if she'd read my mind, Michaela lightly touched my hip with her right elbow. "I forgot to say—I love the new hair color. It's perfect."

"Thanks." I patted the side of my head. "It looks way more natural now, right?"

"Yeah. But the highlights you had before still looked really nice," Tate replied, looking over at me with a faint smile. "It actually feels kinda weird seeing you as a brunette. I'm so used to the blonde."

Michaela raised a brow. "Get used to it. It's the new Sienna," she said, sweeping one arm out like she was announcing the new and improved version of a tech product.

Tate laughed and dipped his chin toward the left. "That's Whittaker Hall over there," he said. "You're on the fifth floor, right?"

"Yep. Dorm 512," I said, eyes skating over the majestic grey stone building. It matched the other stately buildings on campus with its ornate arched windows and ivy vines clinging to the walls.

"I'm on the fourth floor," Michaela said. "We're practically neighbors!"

When we finally reached Whittaker, we hauled my suitcase and bags up to the top floor, shoes clattering loudly on the marble stairs. As I fumbled in my pocket for my new dorm key, Michaela gave Tate a side-eyed look, lips twisting with amusement.

"Why do you two look like you're up to something?" I asked, brows scrunching together.

Tate grinned. "I know you absolutely hate surprises, but we had to do it anyway."

"Do what?"

He nodded toward the door. "You'll see."

I finally located my key and turned it in the lock, pulse racing with anticipation. Tate threw open the door for me, and Michaela squealed right in my ear. "Ta-da!"

A sparkly banner reading 'Welcome to Worthington!' stretched across one of the walls of the spacious dorm. Colorful streamers hung from the other walls and bathroom door, and an enormous cake adorned with my name in pink frosting sat on the desk by the window.

"Oh my god." I laughed softly and turned to my friends. "Thanks, guys. The cake looks awesome."

"We managed to convince one of the RAs to let us in this morning," Michaela explained, hurrying over to the desk. She produced a large knife from her coat pocket and raised a brow. "Want a piece now?"

"Sure! Thanks." I tilted my head. "Have you been carrying that knife around all day?"

"Guilty as charged. Thank god we didn't get pulled over and searched by cops on our way here," she said with a grin. "Imagine trying to explain that one."

She handed me a slice of cake—banana, my favorite—and cut herself and Tate a piece as well.

"Wait a sec." Tate lifted a hand, signaling for her to put his piece back down. "There's one more surprise."

"Oh?" I raised my brows. "What is it?"

He produced a plastic card from his pocket and held it out to me. "Fake ID," he said, eyes glimmering with mischief. "So we can hit all the bars. It has your real name and address, but it says you're three years older than you actually are."

"Half the places around here don't even card," Michaela added. "But it's always helpful to have a fake, just in case."

"Wow, thanks." I briefly scratched my ear and smiled. "It looks so real."

Tate frowned. He must've caught the split-second of uncertainty on my face when I first laid eyes on the card. "What's wrong?"

"Nothing." I shook my head. "It looks awesome."

Michaela glanced over at the fake driver's license and huffed. "Tate, you forgot!"

"Forgot what?" he asked, looking helpless.

Michaela snatched my new student ID off the welcome pack on my desk and dangled it in front of his face. "Remember?" she said. "She's Sienna McConville now. Not Sienna Holland."

Tate's face fell. "Shit. Sorry. I totally forgot you changed your last name."

"It's fine." I waved a hand. "No one's going to see this fake ID except for a few bouncers, so it really doesn't matter."

"True." He stooped to pick up my suitcase and dumped it on the bed. "All right. I'll get started on this one. You two can unpack the bags."

I raised a hand in protest. "You guys don't have to help me unpack. Seriously."

"The sooner you're done here, the sooner we can show you the best stuff in the dining hall," Michaela said. "Also, I'm *way* better at organizing things than you. I've watched every Marie Kondo episode ever made."

I smiled and laughed softly. "Fine. If you insist. But you guys have to let me pay for your food later, okay?"

"Deal." Tate's eyes lingered on my admission pack as he placed my laptop charger on the desk. "How's your class schedule looking?"

"Not bad. I managed to fit all my lectures into three days."

"Lucky you. You should try doing forensics." He grimaced. "I'm in back-to-back lab classes five days a week."

Michaela lifted a palm. "Um, if we're doing the whole Suffering Olympics thing, then you should award the gold medal to me. I'm doing a double degree."

"Yeah, in politics and international relations. So at least there's no lab work," Tate said.

"It's still hard!"

"I know. Just messing with you," he replied with a grin. He looked back over at me. "You know, I was really surprised when you told us you enrolled in journalism."

"Me too," Michaela said.

"Why?" I asked.

"Just... you know." She lowered her gaze to the bag she was yanking clothes out of and bit her bottom lip. "You weren't exactly treated fairly by any of those reporters back in the day."

"Exactly," Tate said, eyes narrowing. "They were total assholes to you."

"Well, that's actually what inspired me to do it," I said, reaching into my other big bag.

Michaela arched a brow. "So you know there's at least one reporter in the world who isn't a total vulture?"

"Yeah. I mean, I have other reasons too. I've always loved writing."

"True." She nodded slowly. "Plus you're great at it."

"Thanks. Also, my dad helped me get an internship at the Worthington Observer. So that should help," I said, pulling a pair of boots out of my bag.

"The college paper?" Michaela's brows shot up again. "That's awesome! Your dad is the best."

"It's really competitive," Tate added. "Hardly anyone gets an internship spot there."

"Oh." I frowned. "Damn. I hope I didn't steal it from someone else who was meant to have it."

Michaela snorted and flicked her blonde hair over her shoulder. "Don't worry. Your only competition would've been a bunch of other nepo babies, so you don't need to feel bad."

"Hey! Sienna's not a nepo baby!" Tate said.

I laughed. "It's fine. Like I said, my dad got the internship for me because he knows a bunch of people here. So technically, I *am* a sort of nepo baby, right?"

Michaela waved a hand. "Don't worry. Half the world runs on nepotism. Especially in DC. I think the three of us know that better than most," she said. She waltzed over to my closet and opened the door. "By the way, you're *so* lucky to have a single! I was in a double room for my freshman year, and my roommate had a parrot. That fucking thing squawked *constantly*. And there was nothing I could do, because she was allowed to have it for some reason."

"Yikes." I grimaced and turned to Tate. "Speaking of pets, how's your cat?"

"She's okay. Getting old, though. She has arthritis in her hips and hyperthyroidism."

"Poor thing." I looked back at Michaela. "That's what you have, right?"

"Arthritis?" she said, wrinkling her nose.

"No, the other one. The thyroid thing."

"I have hypothyroidism," she said, shaking her head. "It's different."

"Oh, that's right. How's that been for you?"

She shrugged. "I'm always cold and tired, but it isn't life-threatening. Mostly just a huge bummer." She paused and stared right at me, brows dipping in a slight frown. "Speaking of health stuff... are you completely done with New Zealand?"

I inwardly sighed. I knew this question was coming eventually.

After our high school graduation last year, Tate and Michaela —along with everyone else I knew from Forrester Academy—had either gone to college or found themselves jobs. I wasn't able to do the same. Spending my last two and a half years of school being hounded by the media and called a liar, attention whore, or crazy by every second person I encountered had really done a number on my head. All because I accused the wrong guy of committing one of the worst crimes of the century.

Supposedly, anyway.

By the time my senior year was over, I was a total wreck. Therapy hadn't helped at all, and I desperately needed a break from the world before I fell apart. My father knew that, so the day after graduation, he generously presented me with a one-way plane ticket to New Zealand along with a six-month admission to a holistic wellness retreat on the South Island.

At first I felt terribly guilty for needing the extended break from reality. It didn't make any sense. Why was I so much more traumatized than Tate and Michaela after everything that went down in 2019? They were survivors too—hell, Tate lost his *brother* that awful night—but they were both able to get on with their lives easily enough after a few months of counseling sessions. Something about my brain was different. I couldn't shake what happened. Couldn't stop obsessing over it.

The online and in-person abuse didn't help, either.

Once I settled in to Harmony Haven, I realized it was actually perfect for me. No one knew me. No one asked me anything, apart from the program counselors who only wanted to help. No one harassed me or called me a dirty liar or crazy bitch. I spent my days helping out on the retreat farm, which was hard but satisfying work, and attending holistic therapy sessions in the evenings.

No phones or computers were allowed in the lodgings, which was difficult at first but wound up being the best thing I'd ever done for my mental wellbeing. Once a week, I was allowed to make a call to a friend or family member or send a letter from the admin's office, so I was still able to keep in touch with people without ruining my progress.

Six months stretched into twelve. Before I knew it, fourteen months had passed, and I realized it was finally time to stop hiding from the world. I enrolled in Worthington, where both of my parents had gone to college—as well as my two best friends—and waited with bated breath to see whether or not I was accepted. As soon as the acceptance email arrived, I giddily hopped on the next plane and returned home.

Now, here I was. Ready to give the world a real shot.

"I'm not going back there," I said, lifting my chin. "I'm ready to be here with you guys. Just like we planned when we were kids."

Michaela gnawed at the inside of her cheek. "It's just... oh, never mind. It's super rude of me to ask," she said.

"No, what is it?"

"I ran into your dad a few months ago. He basically implied that Harmony Haven was actually..." She hesitated again and affected a more delicate tone. "Well, he called it a nuthouse."

I rolled my eyes. "Oh, don't worry, I know about that. Every time I called him from there, he asked '*How's the asylum?*' He thought it was hilarious."

Tate's nose wrinkled. "I know he paid for it all, which is cool, but honestly, he's kind of a dick sometimes."

"I know." I let out a sigh. "But like you said, at least he was generous enough to pay for it. That's more than what most people get, right?"

"So it was really just a wellness retreat like you said in all your letters?" Michaela cut in, eyes flashing with concern. "You didn't have a full-on breakdown or something? Because I was really worried when he said that stuff. I swear I'm not trying to be rude, by the way."

"No, I didn't have a full-on breakdown. But if I didn't go there, I think I *would've* had one," I said, casting my eyes to the floor. "I really needed to get away from the world for a while."

The wellness center actually had a section for inpatient treatment for people suffering from addictions, eating disorders, and other mental health conditions, but that was on the other side of the property. I was in the low-risk patient area, where people could simply go to clear their heads if they were having a rough time.

I looked up at Michaela again. "And don't worry," I added. "I don't think you're rude. It was hard for us to stay in touch properly when all I could do was write you letters. So you didn't really have any way of knowing everything that was going on."

She smiled and wrapped her arms around me. "We really missed you," she murmured, resting her chin on top of my head. "And we're so glad you're back."

"For sure," Tate said, stepping over to join the group hug.

"This is going to be so cool," Michaela said, worming out of the hug a moment later. "The three of us finally hanging out together, just like old times."

"Well, uhh…" It was Tate's turn to look nervous, though I couldn't imagine why. "Speaking of hanging out… I've got a season pass to the Worthington Blades, and I bought two extra tickets for tonight's exhibition game. I was hoping we could all go together. But I totally understand if you don't want to, Sienna. You know, considering…"

He trailed off, and I furrowed my brows. "Who are the Blades?"

"It's the hockey team here. They're one of the latest additions to the NCAA," he explained hurriedly. "Basically a feeder team to the NHL. They've only played one season so far, but they're awesome."

My chest tightened as a mix of dread, fear, and disappointment welled up inside it, pouring over my ribs like ice water. God, it was just a sport. Just a *game*. Why the hell did the mere mention of it still elicit such a raw physical reaction from me? It was so stupid. So childish. So weak.

I thought I was doing better than this. Apparently not.

"Oh." I cleared my throat and tried my best to keep a neutral expression on my face. "Right."

"Like I said, I totally understand if you don't feel up to it." Tate lifted his palms. "No stress. I really don't mind skipping tonight's game if you'd rather do something else."

Michaela snickered. "Since when do you *not* mind skipping a hockey game?"

"I told you, it's just an exhibition game tonight. As in a preseason thing," Tate replied, frowning at her. "Honestly, I don't mind. We'll just go and do something el—"

"No." I took a deep breath and cut him off. "I'll come to the game with you."

"Really?"

"Yeah." I lifted my chin and forced a smile. "I mean, hockey is literally your favorite thing in the whole world, right?"

Michaela snorted with amusement. "No shit," she said. She looked at Tate. "By the way, aren't tickets free for Worthington students?"

"Yeah, in the shitty upper section where you're far away from all the action," Tate said, rolling his eyes. "That's why I prefer to pay."

"Must be nice having all that trust fund money," Michaela said, elbowing him with a cheeky grin on her face.

"Oh, as if *your* family is broke," Tate shot back. "Didn't your dad get in trouble for accepting millions in dark money for his Super PAC a few years ago?"

As the two of them jokingly sparred, I kept an amiable smile pasted on my face so they wouldn't realize how much I was spiraling. This stuff wasn't their problem—it was all mine. I had to move on and stop being so damn weak-willed. Had to stop myself from falling apart when someone suggested something as simple as a local sports event.

The game started at seven, so the three of us ate at the dining hall before traipsing north across the campus.

"The new arena looks awesome," Tate said as we huddled together against the sudden cold wind blowing through the area. "Apparently it took five years to construct it all."

"So this new team has been planned for a while?" I asked, glancing at him.

"Yeah, there weren't any NCAA teams in DC before this. So it was in the works for a long time."

"I'm just trying to picture a giant new arena amongst all these old buildings," I said, making a sweeping gesture at the towering Gothic buildings surrounding us. "Doesn't it look out of place?"

"Nope. It's in the new section on the other side of 23rd Street. Where the old treasury building used to be."

I groaned. "You mean there's even more to explore?"

"Yup. Sorry. We really should've taken you there earlier."

It felt like we'd already wandered around Worthington for hours today. I had no idea there was another section of the campus on top of all that. It honestly blew my mind how they managed to pack so much into such a small pocket of Foggy Bottom.

Michaela shrugged one shoulder. "I doubt any of your classes will be in the new buildings," she said. "It's mostly for sciences over there."

"Including sports science, presumably?"

Tate nodded. "Yup. I have a friend studying physical therapy. He gets to do prac stuff with the Blades." He paused and pointed ahead of us. "There it is."

Even from across the street, the grandeur of the arena was impossible to ignore. It was huge and imposing, fashioned with sleek modern lines of glass and steel that embodied power and athleticism. Towering banners, emblazoned with the Blades' red, black, and white team colors and logo fluttered in the wind, signaling the arena's allegiance.

"Let's go." Tate grinned and motioned for us to cross the street after a car cruised past us. "Don't worry about the tickets. They're on my phone."

I tucked my hands in my jacket pocket and took a deep breath as we stepped through the entrance to join the hordes of fans making their way to their seats. Excited energy thrummed throughout the arena as upbeat music pounded through the speakers, and several groups of fans unfurled banners to hold up once the game started. Every so often, someone set off an air horn, which would always be followed by a rousing cheer.

We located our seats in the ticket-holder section—Tate was right, they were good spots in the lower rows close to the rink—and settled in. I looked around, taking in the bright lights, enthusiastic fans, and pumping music. This place was nowhere near as bad as I thought it would be. In fact, I felt totally fine. Even a little excited.

A crowd of people in black and orange attire sat on the other side of the ice, holding matching banners and tassels. "Is that the other team?" I asked, nudging Tate. "Their supporters, I mean."

"Yup. From Princeton." He cocked his head and gave me a side-eyed glance. "I should've asked earlier. How much do you actually know about hockey?"

"Well, you've talked about it almost every day since we were kids, so let's see…" I jokingly tapped the side of my head. "Somehow I've managed to retain zero information."

He let out an amused snort. "Really? None of my obsessive ranting and raving got through?"

"Sorry." I grinned. "You know I've never been sporty. I did try to listen, though! I swear."

"I know. Just like I've always listened to your nutty fan theories about Supernatural." He returned my smile and ruffled my hair. "Don't worry, it's easy to understand, so you can pick it up as they play. But I'll give you one tip to enjoy it better."

"Yeah?"

He dipped his chin toward the rink. "When it gets started, don't always follow the puck. A lot of the action takes place away from it."

"Uh… how so?"

He laughed and shook his head. "You'll see."

Michaela leaned over from the seat on my other side. "Hey, are you sure you're okay with this?" she asked in a low voice.

I nodded. "Yeah, I'll be fine."

Uncertainty flickered in her eyes, but she didn't say anything more on the matter.

The lights dimmed, and an announcer's voice boomed over the speakers to introduce the Princeton Tigers. The fans in their section whooped and cheered, jumping out of their seats to wave their flags and banners as the Tigers streamed onto the ice.

"And now, for the home crowd... let's welcome our team!" the announcer boomed. "The Worthington Blades!"

A door opened diagonally across from us. The Blades burst onto the ice, clad in black and white gear with red accents. They started doing loops on the rink, zooming around to tap on the plexiglass and raising their gloved hands in the air to acknowledge their fans. The crowd replied with shrieks and frantic waving, along with a few flashed boobs from some girls in nearby rows.

"Now we know why Tate loves these games so much," Michaela murmured to me, raising a brow.

I stifled a giggle and leaned forward to get a better look at the team as they circled the ice. One of them seemed to be getting more attention from the crowd than the rest of the team. More attention from the female members of the crowd, to be specific. Girls screamed and giddily jumped up and down as he passed. Some even pretended to faint when he tapped his stick on the boards near them.

I craned my neck, trying to catch a proper glimpse of him. He had his helmet tucked under one arm, but he was angled away from our section, so I couldn't see his face. Just dark floppy hair. I couldn't make out the name emblazoned on his jersey, either. Only the number was big enough to read from where I was sitting. Number eleven.

He lifted his right hand to wave up at the student section in the arena. Then he rapidly spun around on the ice—a cocky show-off move to impress the boob-flashing girls, no doubt—and zipped around to our section.

I finally caught a glimpse of his handsome face as he turned to bang on the plexiglass right in front of us. His ocean-blue eyes focused right on me for several seconds, piercing in their intensity. My heart instantly dropped into my stomach.

It was Paxton Cole.

My high school boyfriend... and the man who tried to kill me.

PAXTON

Pulsating music reverberated throughout the arena, and whoops and screams from the crowd echoed off the walls, fueling the fire within me as our team surged onto the ice and began our usual just-for-fun laps to greet the home crowd. It was only a pre-season game, but our loyal fans had shown up in full force anyway. Barely any seats were left empty.

My pulse synchronized with the beat of the music, intensifying the rush of adrenaline inside me as I skated around, waving and occasionally smacking my stick on the boards to show my appreciation. A girl with her face painted in team colors stood and lifted her red sweater to show off her tits as I passed. I grinned and turned to share a knowing look with Justin, my longtime best friend who also happened to be one of our team's best defensemen.

We both spun around and lifted our fists high in the air. The fans erupted in another chorus of cheers and applause. Spurred on by their unwavering enthusiasm, I did another full spin before sliding over to a section I hadn't paid much attention to yet. With a face-splitting grin, I tapped on the glass and waved.

Wait.

Was that...?

Time seemed to stand still as I did a double-take, staring at the brunette girl in the second row. *Fuck me.* She looked a lot like...

No. It couldn't be her. Sienna Holland wouldn't dare to show up here. Would she?

I looked closer. The girl's pretty face was frozen in an expression of disgust. Holy shit, it *was* her.

For the first time in my entire playing career, I felt the chill of the ice below my skates. Felt it all the way up to my chest, sinking its frozen claws between my ribs to grasp at my heart.

My lips tightened into a grimace, and I turned my face away and whipped around on the ice, smashing right into my friend Justin's bulky back.

"Hey, man. Tryin' to start something?" he said in a joking tone, grinning at me as he jammed his helmet over his unruly brown curls.

I turned my head over my shoulder to glance at the second row. Sienna was gone. Did I just imagine her being there? If so, why the fuck did I imagine her with a brown dye-job? The Sienna I knew always had tiny blonde streaks scattered throughout her hair.

I turned back to Justin, wondering if I should mention it to him. He knew Sienna too, once upon a time.

I quickly decided against it, not wanting to throw him off his game. It was bad enough that I'd already experienced what felt like an electrical shock mixed with a fucking heart attack when I saw that little bitch staring back at me from the paid ticket-holder's section. I didn't need to push that shit onto him too.

"Just keeping you on your toes," I said, forcing a grin as I shoved my helmet on.

Justin snorted. "As if I need it."

He wasn't wrong. He could check guys into the boards like he was simply swatting a mosquito.

A whistle blew somewhere behind me. The announcer called out Princeton's starting lineup, followed by ours. All the nonstarters left the ice, and the rest of us skated over to the center and put ourselves in formation.

I gripped my stick tightly as the referee spoke to us, wishing my mind wasn't still laser-focused on Sienna. I just couldn't shake it. Was it really her? If so, what the fuck was she doing at one of my games? Hadn't she wrecked my life enough the first time around?

Beyond that... wasn't she terrified of what I might do to her if I ever saw her again? I would be if I were her.

Echoes of her cries and screams played in my head over and over as I pictured her wide, petrified green eyes on mine. Her presence was clinging to me like a shadow. Even as the arena roared with excitement, I felt completely detached from it all, barely even registering the sound.

My mind was so far away from reality that I almost missed the puck drop. *Shit.* Adrenaline surged through my veins again, and I quickly took control and snapped it over to my left wing, Keegan Reddick. He sent it to our right wing, Todd Laurier, who deftly swept it back over to me as I zoomed down the ice. I took it and weaved around a defenseman before trying to send it back over to Keegan, who had moved into the perfect open spot near the crease. Unfortunately, my movements were sluggish and my timing was totally off, resulting in me turning over the puck.

"Fuck," I muttered to myself as the Tigers shot it back down the ice, taking it into their offensive zone.

This wasn't like me. I never played this badly. Not even when I was a kid.

My lungs burned from exertion as I trudged off the ice for the line change. A few of my teammates cast concerned glances my way, probably trying to decipher what was going on with me tonight. They were used to me dominating the ice, not fucking up every single play like a total amateur.

My next shift was no better. Doubts kept creeping in as the internal battle intensified, eroding my confidence. My passes lacked their usual precision. My reaction times were slower. It felt like I was skating through fucking molasses.

I tried to break off the mental shackles, but Sienna's face kept flashing in my head. Every time it happened, my hands or feet betrayed me, fumbling the puck or messing something else up as my usually-sharp instincts abandoned me.

When it was time for the next line change, I briefly glanced over at Sienna's empty seat. Searing anger flashed through me like lightning. This was her fault. Her showing up tonight had thrown me off my game entirely, turning me into a bumbling idiot.

But even as it occurred to me, I knew I was just making excuses. It was *my* fault. I should be better than this. Stronger. I shouldn't let this shit affect me so much.

After the first period was over, leaving the game tied at 0-0, I headed to the locker room, dropped my gloves, and sagged on a bench. Coach Mikkelsen headed over to me, rugged face painted with an expression of confusion and annoyance.

"You're off your game tonight, Cole," he said, icy blue eyes narrowing.

"I know." I rubbed my brow. "I'll get a handle on it."

He scoffed. "The way things have been going, I suspect you wouldn't even be able to handle a beach ball out there."

"Yeah," I muttered. "I'll pick it up."

"You better, or I might have to reconsider the starting lineup for the season. I've seen toddlers crawl across the ice faster than whatever the hell you've been doing out there."

My lips tightened into a grim slash, and I nodded curtly. I couldn't argue—he was right. I was playing like shit.

He wouldn't really knock me off the starting line, though. There was a good reason the Blades—along with a few other college teams— wanted to recruit me when they heard I was available, even after all the shit that went down in the spring of

2019. Before any of it happened, I was the number-one-ranked prospect for that year's NHL draft, destined to soar to the top. That renown was ripped away from me after the lake house killings, but I was building it back now, one game at a time.

The second period started. I tried my best to concentrate and channel my rage into the game, but my first shot slid wide. *Fuck.* I was still letting Sienna's little visit affect my performance. Letting her control my every movement with her haunting presence.

As I zipped down the ice again, one of the Tigers followed closely. Number forty-two. He suddenly zoomed forward to cut me off and shoved me right into the boards, sending a burst of pain down my left shoulder and arm.

"What the fuck?" My eyes narrowed on him as I waited for the referee to blow the whistle and announce the penalty.

"Chill, man. It was just an accident," the guy said with a shit-eating grin on his face that made it abundantly clear that it was actually fully intentional. He turned away and dipped his chin toward the ice before adding something under his breath. "Unlike that shit you did out in Michigan."

My anger surged. "What the fuck did you just say?"

"Nothing."

Nostrils flaring, I dropped my gloves and wrenched off my helmet. Forty-two did the same, smarmy smile growing wider. I could sense the crowd holding their collective breath around us, anticipation hanging thick in the air as they waited for us to go for each other's throats.

"You really wanna do this?" he asked, eyes locked on me with an unyielding intensity.

I matched his gaze with a determined glare. "Yeah. I really fucking do."

Before he had a chance to say anything else, I clocked him right in the jaw. He retaliated swiftly, launching a torrent of rapid punches aimed at my face. Undeterred, I smashed him right back, fueled by sheer rage.

The crowd went feral around us, screaming and chanting our names. The sound was punctuated by the dull thud of hockey sticks smacking against the boards as our teammates announced their approval of our fight.

The referees finally showed up to intervene, but their presence barely registered in the frenzy of the moment. Finally, after another linesman arrived, they were able to drag us away from each other. A five minute penalty was announced for both teams, and we were sent off to the box to wait it out.

As I sat down, I blew out a deep breath, wiping my sweat-soaked brow with the back of my hand. Coach Mikkelsen shot a pissed look in my direction, but I knew he wouldn't threaten to keep me off the ice for the rest of the game as punishment. No one actually gave a fuck about fights on the rink, as long as we didn't take it too far.

Hell, most of the people at this arena probably *expected* to see at least one throwdown tonight. It was just part of the entertainment, really. Guys dropping their mitts and going at each other always fired up the crowd, and sometimes the fans even cheered louder for punch-ups and scuffles than they did for points.

When the penalty was over, Coach ordered me back onto the ice. Just as I hopped over the edge, one of the refs called another penalty for the Tigers having too many men on the ice, leaving us with a two-minute power play.

Another surge of adrenaline hit me, and I gritted my teeth, determined to pick up my game and channel all of the anger I felt toward Sienna—and that motherfucker from Princeton—into my stick-handling.

My new resolve worked wonders. Thirty seconds into the play, I took the puck from Todd, weaved my way around the nearest defender, and corralled it with the hook of my blade before firing it into the open side of the net. Precise and targeted, like a fucking sniper. I was finally back on my game.

The goal ignited the crowd. I grinned and slid around to

the right, waving at the cheering fans, until I saw Coach's face. He was glaring at the opposing team's head coach, who was leaning close to one of the referees near the penalty box.

"What's going on?" I asked, sliding up to Justin.

"It's fucking stupid," he muttered, shaking his head. "Offside review."

"Wait, what?"

He jerked a thumb toward the Tigers coach. "He's challenging the goal. He claims Todd didn't have the puck completely over the line when Keegan went into the zone."

"Bullshit."

"They have to check now that it's been challenged. The puck might've *just* been on the line when his back foot came in. Not all the way over. It'll be marginal if the call is right, but still..." He trailed off and shrugged.

We waited at the edge of the ice, eyes narrowed as we watched the referee look down at a small screen in his hand, watching a slowed replay of the action preceding my goal. I tried to recall exactly what I saw Keegan doing when Todd took the puck across the line a couple of minutes ago, but the memory was fading fast. I was certain it wasn't offside, but only the review could tell us for sure.

The referee looked up from the screen, skated out onto the ice, and called out to the crowd. "After the coach's challenge for Princeton, the play has been determined to be offside!" he said, spreading his arms wide. "No goal!"

"You've gotta be fucking kidding me," I muttered, shaking my head. Could tonight's game get any worse?

The arena filled with a cacophony of jeers and boos from the Blades fans, and Coach Mikkelsen tightened his lips and clapped me on the shoulder. "It was a good goal. Not your fault this happened," he said. "Just keep going."

The rest of the second period was a blur. By the time the

buzzer sounded, the game was still tied at 0-0. Princeton were playing just as poorly as us tonight.

"Shit, I forgot to tell you," Justin said, jabbing me in the side. "You'll never guess who I saw tonight, just before the game started. Right over there."

I gritted my teeth as my gaze homed in once more on the seat previously occupied by Sienna. She was still gone. "Who?" I muttered.

Justin pointed to the exact spot I was staring at. "Tate Cavanagh and Michaela Langdon," he said. "They left before we started, though. Dunno why."

Tate and Michaela. They were Sienna's best friends back in high school, so any notion that I might have hallucinated her earlier was shattered now. She was really here tonight, and her friends must've followed her out after she decided to dip.

"Huh," I muttered, looking down at my skates. "I guess they go to Worthington too."

"Yeah, I guess so." Justin stood. "I need more water. See you in a sec, man."

I kept staring at the floor, losing myself in my thoughts as the intermission crawled by at a snail's pace. I still couldn't understand why Sienna Holland would deign to show her face in this arena. Surely she did it on purpose, knowing I was playing for the Blades now. It was hardly a secret—anyone who Googled my name could easily discover that the upcoming season would be my second with the Blades.

I steeled my jaw, glancing back over at the opposite side of the arena again. Sometimes the memories of 2019 almost crippled me with the hatred and fury that arose with them. It permeated everything, filling me up with stress and weighing me down until it felt like I might implode.

It was all because of Sienna. That bitch nearly snatched my entire future away from me... and now I had to wonder if she was back for more. In her eyes, I probably hadn't suffered enough the first time she fucked with me. No, I had to suffer more. Had to bleed the way she bled that night. Had to feel everything she felt.

I wouldn't let her do it. Wouldn't even give her the chance.

The third period finally began. I continued channeling my rage into my performance and scored two goals in a row, easily undressing the defenders and slipping the puck past the goalie like he wasn't even there.

The game finished 2-1, and our fans went wild, cheering and whooping to congratulate us. I should've been happy that I'd turned my shitty first-period performance around to save the game in the end, but all I felt was a red ember of rage burning deep in my body. The same rage I'd felt all night, ever since I saw Sienna's face behind that glass.

Justin trudged up behind me and clapped a hand on my back as we trudged off the ice. "Hey, you okay?"

I glanced at him. "Yeah. Why?"

He scratched the stubble on his jaw. "Honestly, you seemed a bit off in the first two periods. I was worried."

"Guess I'm just having an off day," I said.

I didn't have off days. Anyone who knew me knew that.

Doubt flickered in Justin's eyes, but he let it go. "All right, man. Keegan's having people over for an afterparty. You coming?"

"Yeah," I muttered, turning to look back at the ticket-holder's section one last time, as if Sienna might magically appear there again. "I'd kill for a drink right about now."

As I turned around again, a decision crystallized inside me, filling my heart with ice. I still had no idea what the hell Sienna Holland was doing here at Worthington, but I knew one thing for sure.

She wouldn't be around for much longer.

Like the small taste and want more? You can grab the full book on Amazon!

ABOUT THE AUTHOR

Kristin Buoni is the shared pen name of bestselling dark romance author Stella Hart and her romance-loving sister-in-law, K, who has always wanted to write something in her favorite genre (especially angsty high school bully romances with tinges of mystery and suspense!).

S and K both love to come up with fun ideas and gut-wrenching twists, so it was only a matter of time before they decided to team up and write books together. When they aren't plotting, reading, or writing, they're hanging out with their cats and bingeing their favorite TV shows.

Printed in Dunstable, United Kingdom